PELICAN BOOKS

THE BLACK AMERICAN WRITER

volume I: fiction

Christopher Bigsby is a lecturer in American Literature at the University of East Anglia. Bigsby received his M.A. in American Studies at Sheffield University and his Ph.D. at Nottingham. He studied for a year in this country at Kansas State University on a Fulbright Student Exchange grant, and he did part of his doctoral work while a fellow at the Salzburg American Studies Seminar in Austria. In the spring of 1968, he was a visiting professor at the University of Missouri, Kansas City, and he has recently compiled a book on his observations of the Kansas City riots in April, 1968.

Bigsby's earlier publications include, besides many articles, *Confrontation and Commitment: A Study of Contemporary American Drama 1959-1966* (1967) and *Edward Albee* (1968).

THE BLACK AMERICAN WRITER

volume I: fiction

edited by
C. W. E. BIGSBY
Lecturer in American Literature
University of East Anglia

PENGUIN BOOKS INC
BALTIMORE, MARYLAND

Penguin Books Inc
7110 Ambassador Road
Baltimore, Maryland 21207

First published by Everett / Edwards, Inc. 1969
Published in Pelican Books 1971

ISBN 0 14 021225 6

Printed in the United States of America by
Kingsport Press, Inc.

ACKNOWLEDGEMENTS

"Problems of a Negro Writer" by John A. Williams and Langston
Hughes, copyright 1963 Saturday Review, Inc. Reprinted by permission of the Saturday Review, Harold Ober Associates, Incorporated, and John A. Williams. "The Negro Writer: Pitfalls and
Compensations" was first published in *Phylon* and is reprinted by
permission. "The Negro in American Culture" is reprinted by
permission of Pacifica Radio (WBAI-FM), "Black Orpheus" is
reprinted from *The Massachusetts Review*, ©1965, The Massachusetts Review, Inc. "White Standards and Negro Writing" is reprinted by permission of *The New Republic* and Richard Gilman.
"Our Mutual Estate: The Literature of the American Negro" was
first published in the *Antioch Review* and is reprinted by permission. "Disturber of the Peace: James Baldwin" is reprinted by permission of Eve Auchincloss and Nancy Lynch. "The Black Arts
Movement" was first published in *The Drama Review*, Vol. 12, No
4, Summer, 1968, T. 40. c. Copyright 1968 *The Drama Review*.
Reprinted by permission of the publishers and author. All rights
reserved. "An Interview with Ralph Ellison" is reprinted from
The Tamarack Review. "Poetry in the 'Sixties" © Paul Breman.
All rights reserved. "Contemporary Negro Fiction," by Hoyt W.
Fuller, used by permission of the author, first published in 1965,
in *Southwest Review*.

for Warren French

Contents

THE
BLACK
AMERICAN
WRITER

volume I: fiction

General Introduction

This two-volume study of the black American writer makes no claim to be completely comprehensive, certain authors of considerable merit being omitted altogether. Its aim is rather to examine the achievement of some of the major talents to emerge from the black community, to analyse and assess the difficulties facing the black writer, and to examine the problems of criticism in a field so fraught with social, cultural and political prejudices.

In recent years the white critic has found himself increasingly under attack. His motives and qualifications for the assessment of black literature have been called in question. This study consists of essays by both black and white critics and the reader will thus be in a position to judge for himself. Considerable space is devoted to this issue, and many of the general essays and interviews attempt to come to terms not merely with the achievement of the black American writer but also with the critical dilemma in an era of committed literature.

The bulk of the essays in this study were specially commissioned and appear here for the first time in print. Where articles have appeared elsewhere these are works of special significance which have not previously been published in book form. Most important among these are the symposium on "The Negro in American Culture" which appears in volume I and Sartre's seminal essay on *négritude*, "Black Orpheus" which appears in volume II. In the former James Baldwin, Langston Hughes and Lorraine Hansberry confront Nat Hentoff and Alfred Kazin in a crucial debate on the nature of the black experience and the writer's response to it. In the latter, Sartre, writing some twenty years ago, examines the concept of *negritude* and offers some profoundly significant insights into the nature of black writing. As will be apparent from the essays which appear in both volumes, *negritude* is by no means regarded with that mixture of awe and respect which it was accorded only a few years ago. Indeed a sustained attack was launched on it in the summer of 1969 at the Pan-African Cultural Festival held in Algiers. Nevertheless, Sartre's insights have played an important part in the criticism of black writing and provide a useful example of the white critic at his best.

At present the function of black writing is the subject of heated and often irrational discussion. It is appropriate, therefore, that we should choose this moment to examine the substance of Negro literary achievement and the nature of those cultural assumptions which underlie contemporary literature. It is hoped that this two-volume study by writers and critics from Great Britain and the United States will contribute materially to this examination and provide a useful tool both for the student and the general reader.

The Critical Dilemma

The Black American Writer

by C. W. E. Bigsby

THE NEGRO PLAYWRIGHT and poet LeRoi Jones has characterised the quality of Negro writing as "impressive mediocrity" and although he has attacked white critics who have expressed a similar opinion his judgement is largely sound. The reasons for this are of course primarily historical. The middle class Negro writers were anything but innovators; neither, for the most part, were they prepared to meet head on the prejudices of the white society which largely constituted their audience. Their philosophy was summed up in the chilling words of Sutton Griggs, "The bird that would live must thrill the hunter with its song."[1] In terms of the twentieth century, ironically, the initial impetus for black literature even came in part from white writers; from Carl Van Vechten in the novel and from Ridgely Torrence and Emile Hapgood in drama, although this fact tends to be somewhat overstated. It was only really in poetry that the Negro writers of the so-called "Negro Renaissance" had anything genuinely original to offer. The Negro novel, despite competent works by James Weldon Johnson and Arna Bontemps, did not come of age until 1940 and even this was an imperfect début. If this seems a harsh judgment it is perhaps necessary as a corrective to that particular form of paternalism which evidences itself in a suspension of critical judgement.

The inferior quality of black writing until comparatively recent times is in part the result of white influence on black creativity but it can also be ascribed to the indecent eagerness with which the Negro writer has submitted himself to the dominating political and cultural philosophies of his day — whether it be the African stereotype of the 20s, the communist idylls of the 30s, or the post *Native Son* protest tradition of the 40s. The Negro writer has always been supremely conscious of his dual role as author and spokesman — most conscious, indeed, when he is striving to avoid that duality. As with any polemicist, however, there is a constant temptation to resort to the easy formula; hence the naïveté with which the Negro has seen himself as the noble savage, the red slogan, the social delinquent, the archetypal outsider or, more recently, the black revolutionary. Richard Wright's call for "Negro writers to stand shoulder to shoulder with Negro workers in mood and outlook"[2] or Langston Hughes's declaration that he was placing himself "on the solid ground of the daily working-class struggle"[3] scarcely differs from more recent calls for the black writer to direct his work towards the establishment of a purely ethnic culture. The fact that the real achievement of writers such as Richard Wright, Langston Hughes and even LeRoi Jones is built on precisely those works in which they fail to abide by their own strictures suggests that these formulas fail to realise the full potential of the black writer. Nevertheless the process whereby the romantic images of the 1920s have come to coalesce in the powerful myths of black national consciousness is central to an understanding of the development of black writing in the present century and explains in part some of the literary and critical dilemmas of the late 60s.

Frantz Fanon, doctor, psychiatrist, revolutionary and author of *The Wretched of the Earth,* recognised three stages in the development of the black writer: assimilation, ethnic discovery, and revolution. While it is not necessary to accept the implicit qualitative progression, his analysis can be readily applied in general terms to the situation of the black writer in America, from the assimilationist writers of the 19th century to the revolutionaries of the 60s.

Both Fanon and Jean-Paul Sartre take pains to underline the irony of black writers laying claim to the values of Western culture when they see those values subverted daily. Universal brotherhood, the significance of the individual, the prime importance of rationality, are all cast in doubt by racial intolerance, enforced conformity and expedient morality. The immediate effect of this dissonance between white Western values and the black experience is thus to detach the Negro writer from his former cultural matrix and to send him in search of new and specifically black values. This search leads naturally enough to the cult of *negritude*, that ethnic self-discovery which Fanon had established as his second stage.

Sartre sees *negritude* as a temporary phenomenon which will precede a Marxist union of the proletariat. While it involves a non-revolutionary subjectivism he is prepared to accept this as a stage in a developing political consciousness. Fanon, however, after an earlier change of heart, wished to short-circuit this process and thus denounced with equal virulence a slavish acceptance of Western values and "withdrawal into the twilight of past African culture," for "the only true culture is that of the Revolution."[4] This, of course, assumed that *negritude* is merely an exotic affectation — a romantic yearning for the past which is little more than a substitute for political analysis and practical action. This was true enough of the America of the 1920s, when it became simply another means of evading the immediate realities of the moment. But, as Sartre recognised, *negritude* also constituted a potentially powerful political weapon — a fact which has become still clearer in the 60s. There remains an element of that exoticism against which Fanon had inveighed, but now there is a sharp political edge to this movement which clearly marks it off from its earlier banality. *Negritude* is perhaps on the verge of being superceded by revolution.*

Certainly recent years have seen the emergence of apparently more radical writers in a way which suggests that we may indeed be on the verge of Fanon's third stage, a period in which "a great many men and women who up till then had never thought of producing literary work, now they find themselves in exceptional circumstances — in prison . . . on the eve of their execution — feel the need to speak . . . to compose the sentence which expresses the heart of the people and to become the mouthpiece of a new reality in action."[5] The work of Malcolm X, Claude Brown and Eldridge Cleaver seems to demonstrate the applicability of these

---

*There was of course a brief flirtation between black and white writers in the 30s when it seemed that the revolutionary stage might be imminent but this was a movement which subsumed ethnic awareness in the interests of international communism. As the cynicism of the Party became more apparent so this uncertain and largely unreal alliance began to crumble leaving a conviction that revolution would grow out of ethnic solidarity rather than inter-racial collaboration.

remarks to the American situation. The writer and the political activist become closely identified as the new ethnic literature establishes direct links with the social and political struggle. Some of these new writers seem to have adopted the stance outlined by Sekou Touré when he suggested that in order to take part in the revolution "it is not enough to write a revolutionary song; you must fashion the revolution with the people. And if you fashion it with the people, the songs will come by themselves."[6] Herein, perhaps, lies the distinction between Cleaver and a writer like LeRoi Jones; the former believing that culture is a product of social action and the latter, rather like Clifford Odets, seeing art as a spur to political involvement.

Fanon's rejection of ethnic culture was based fundamentally on his revolutionary optimism. He believed that it was merely a transitional stage because in the last resort it was dependent for its continued existence not only on the vigour and commitment of the black writer but also on the arrogant exclusiveness of white society. As the social and political situation changes so ethnic culture itself disintegrates. As he himself puts it, "To believe that it is possible to create a black culture is to forget that niggers are disappearing, just as those people who brought them into being are seeing the breakup of their economic and cultural supremacy." In terms of America this process is barely under way and the real debate is not so much between the revolutionaries and the ethnic writers as between the "cultural nationalists," who see the future as lying with an exclusively ethnic literature, and the "cultural integrationists" who lay claim to a broader tradition. Indeed, there is evidence to suggest that the concern with *negritude* is being superceded not by a union of the proletariat nor by a permanent ethnic culture but by a new sense of cultural universality (though not homogeneity).

Fanon's schematic account of black writing of necessity tends to over-simplify the situation. Distrust of Western culture has by no means been evidenced by all Negro writers, many of whom see the job of ethnic renewal as lying in individual fulfillment rather than racial separatism or political revolution. This in fact is the central point of conflict between writers like Ellison, Baldwin and Hansberry and others like LeRoi Jones, Ed Bullins and Eldridge Cleaver.

Negritude is in essence the invention of the exile. As the Nigerian writer, Wole Soyinka, has pointed out, "I don't think a tiger has to go around proclaiming his tigritude."[7] The native African feels little or no need to bolster up a self-image which for the most part is not threatened by an alien culture. In America that self-image has been eroded by slavery and the indignities of an unjust social system. In Sartre's words the black writer has his back up against the wall of authenticity. In his attempt to "reveal the black soul" he has frequently been drawn towards an African past which seems to have the virtue of conferring on him a distinctive identity, unaffected by the demeaning impact of his American experience. Yet, whatever the stance of the ardent black nationalist there remain only vestigial remnants of African culture. The slave owners were too successful in stamping out indigenous traditions for the contemporary writer to be able to draw on a genuine cultural heritage (outside of the world of music and, perhaps, religion). Thus the black writer intent on reviving a sense of identity which has its roots in a distant African past is trapped into creating rather than discovering a usable heritage and into manufacturing usable myths. This emphasis on *negritude* is an aspect of the Negro's declaration of independence. In the words of Aimé Césaire, "Blackness is not absence, but refusal."[8] The "Negro Renaissance" of the 20s, with its romantic emphasis on Africa and with its new assertiveness, marked a radical departure from the standards and values of the middle-class Negro writers of the past. The 'New Negro' refused to be simply grist to the assimilationist mill, grudgingly allowed access to Western culture as to public transport and public accommodation. Instead of being on the margin of an alien culture he now made his bid to be accepted as the heir to a separate culture with a distinctive history of its own, and the fact that most Negro writers had only an imperfect understanding of Africa and its traditions seemed hardly relevant to those carried away with the zeal of their own evangelism.

In terms of politics this movement manifested itself in the philosophy of the Garveyites, with their back-to-Africa policy and their morale-building plans for a Black Star shipping line and Black Cross nurses. However bizarre this may seem in retrospect, Garvey clearly touched an exposed nerve not only in the Negro community but also among white politicians, who were all too happy to see him deported in 1927. Thus his movement played an important part in the developing self-awareness of the Negro community. As LeRoi Jones has pointed out, "it was necessary first to crystallize national aspirations behind a Garvey. The Africans who first came here were replaced by Americans or people responding to Western stimuli and then Americans. In order for the Americans to find out that they had come from another place, were, hence, alien, the Garvey times had to come."[9] It is worth recalling, however, that Garvey, who assumed the title of Provisional President of Africa, had himself never been to Africa which remained for him a symbol of black destiny rather than a genuine reality. His prime importance was as a myth maker.

So far as the black writer was concerned *negritude* seems to have meant primarily African allusions, sentimentality, and an emphasis on the emotional at the expense of the intellectual. Nevertheless, beneath the exoticism could be heard a muted note of protest even in the exuberant 20s, although the extent to which this was a conscious protest must be in some doubt. In the first place the stress on emotionalism could itself be seen as an attack on the rationalism of America and even of Western society. The black writer in other words was announcing with Frantz Fanon, "I wade in the irrational."[10] Secondly, if Negro poets idealised Africa it was in direct contrast to their own country. It was an outcry against their present degradation and was based on the notion that the move from Africa to America was in essence a fall from grace. Reversing a favourite image, Africa and not America came to be seen as Eden. In the words of Countee Cullen's significantly named poem, "Heritage":[11]

> What is Africa to me:
> Copper sun or scarlet sea,
> Jungle star or jungle track,
> Strong bronzed men, or regal black
> Women from whose loins I sprang
> When the birds of Eden sang?
> *One three centuries from me removed*
> *From the scenes his father loved,*
> *Spicy grove, cinnamon tree.*
> *What is Africa to me?*

The same anguished yearning for some kind of roots in an African past is expressed five years later by Langston Hughes:[12]

So long,
So far away
Is Africa.
Not even memories alive
Save those that history books create,
Save those that songs
Beat back into the blood —
Beat out of blood with words sad-sung
In strange un-Negro tongue —
So long,
So far away
Is Africa.
Subdued and time-lost
Are the drums — and yet
Through some vast mist of race
There comes this song
I do not understand,
This song of atavistic land,
Of bitter yearnings lost
Without a place —
So long,
So far away
Is Africa's
Dark face.

In the abounding enthusiasm of the 20s there were few who challenged the kind of assumptions which lay behind Cullen's poem or who doubted the desirability of idealising the African past. Neither were there many who raised serious objection to the naïve primitivism which increasingly characterised the Negro writer's attitude toward Africa. Indeed, Aimé Césaire, who was responsible for defining the concept of *negritude* itself, saw the chief virture of the African as lying in the fact that he operated outside the sometimes savage course of history, announcing, "Hurray for those who never invented anything."

The African himself, particularly in more recent times, has not always been prepared to accept a myth which was so clearly designed for the expatriate, for the colonial living in the 'mother country', or for the slave long since sundered from his African past. As the African writer Ezekiel Mphahlele pointed out, after being denounced by an American Negro for his attack on *negritude* at a conference on African literature held in Dakar in 1963, "Who is so stupid as to deny the historical fact of *negritude* as both a protest and a positive assertion of African values? All this is valid. What I do not accept is the way in which too much of the poetry inspired by it romanticizes Africa — as a symbol of innocence, purity and artless primitiveness. I feel insulted when some people imply that Africa is not also a violent continent."[13] Yet, in a sense, this protest was no longer really relevant for the attitude which he attacks had already undergone a considerable change by the time of the Dakar conference.

By the 1940s the response to Africa had altered. In "Old Laughter," which appeared in Gwendolyn Brooks' Pulitzer Prize-winning volume, *Annie Allen*, in 1949, we find a much more sophisticated attitude toward modern Africa. She no longer feels bound by the elements of the myth, emphasizing instead the contrast between past simplicity and present corruption:[14]

> The men and women long ago
> In Africa, in Africa,
> Knew all there was of joy to know.
> In sunny Africa
> The spices flew from tree to tree.
> The spices trifled in the air
> That carelessly
> Fondled the twisted hair.
>
> The men and women richly sang
> In lands of gold and green and red.
> The bells of merriment richly rang.
>
> But richness is long dead,
> Old laughter chilled, old music done
> In bright, bewildered Africa.
>
> The bamboo and the cinnamon
> Are sad in Africa.

Even Langston Hughes who, as Mphahlele puts it, "once wrote a good deal of maudlin verse about being *black, black, black*, and joined the faddist movement of the 'rhythm boys' in the 'twenties and 'thirties who were crazy about jungle tomtoms" has since said that, "I was only an American Negro — who had loved the surface of Africa and the rhythms of Africa — but I was not African. I was Chicago and Kansas City and Broadway and Harlem."[15] Thus the exoticism of the 20s tended to go out of fashion, killed partly by the Depression and partly by a growing sophistication of outlook. *Negritude* no longer consisted merely of appeals to a primitive past. Now the writer began to stress the significant role which the Negro had played and was playing in modern society. In direct contrast to the pride which Césaire had professed in the Negro's non-involvement, Melvin Tolson, following the lead set by Marcus Garvey twenty years before, chanted the achievements of his race in a poem called "Dark Symphony" which he wrote in the early 40s.[16]

> The New Negro
> Breaks the icons of his detractors,
> Wipes out the conspiracy of silence,
> Speaks to his America:
>
> "My history-moulding ancestors
> Planted the first crops of wheat on these shores,
> Built ships to conquer the seven seas,
> Erected the Cotton Empire,
> Flung railroads across a hemisphere,
> Disemboweled the earth's iron and coal,
> Tunneled the mountains and bridged rivers,
> Harvested the grain and hewed forests,
> Sentineled the Thirteen Colonies,
> Unfurled Old Glory at the North Pole,
> Fought a hundred battles for the Republic."
>
> The New Negro:
> His giant hands fling murals upon high chambers,
> His drama teaches a world to laugh and weep,
> His voice thunders the Brotherhood of Labor,
> His science creates seven wonders,
> His Republic of Letters challenges the Negro-baiters.

For Tolson, pride in race could scarcely be derived purely from a talent for music and a happy mastery of the art of living for he was aware of just how close this stereotype was to that treasured by the 'Negro-baiters.' Thus, when he speaks of the "wizardry of our dusky rhythms" it is as an ironical preface to his pointed comment that:

> They who have shackled us
> Require of us a song

So the assumed connection between the experience of the African and that of the American Negro began to be challenged. In 1956, at the first International Congress of Black Writers and Artists, Richard Wright chose to deny the usefulness and indeed the reality of this African heritage. Ralph Ellison, who recalls being bewildered by the sentiment of Countee Cullen's "Heritage," has similarly confessed that "I have great difficulty — associating myself with Africa."[17] He even turned down a trip to Africa. Meanwhile Baldwin has admitted that "Whenever I was with an African, we would both be uneasy. . . . The terms of our life were so different, we almost needed a dictionary to talk."[18]

Africa no longer stood for simple primitivism. The hold of empire on the African continent was weakening and as countries began to acquire independence so the old attitudes themselves began to crumble before this insistent new reality. The American Negro could no longer see himself, in Alain Locke's words, as "the advance-guard of the African people in their contact with Twentieth Century civilization."[19] On the contrary, the roles had in many senses been reversed so that the African leaders, who had successfully challenged white power, became the new culture heroes and even the prototypes for the new revolutionaries. With the increasing vehemence of the civil rights campaign there came not merely a revival of pride in racial identity but also a new-found belief that men like Nkrumah, Castro, Guevara and Mao were more genuinely products of the twentieth century than those indigenous leaders who had felt such a sense of duty towards the Africans only two decades before, or the non-revolutionary leaders of the moment who based their claims on liberal humanitarianism. When Patrice Lumumba was murdered in the Congo it was not only the white world which watched in bewilderment the concern of many of America's Negroes as manifested in the demonstration at the United Nations. The attitude of the 'New Negro', as outlined by Locke, seemed suddenly scarcely distinguishable from the colonial arrogance of the imperialists themselves.

Yet, fundamentally, one suspects that this new vision of Africa is finally as suspect as that of the Negro Renaissance. Eldridge Cleaver, for example, sees not so much a real Africa as one which is useful as a symbol of rebellion and black achievement. As a consequence he is forced to turn his back on the ambiguity surrounding such figures as Sukarno, Nkrumah and even Mao. One thinks, similarly, of Elijah Muhommad's exotic distortions of the Muslim faith which eventually led Malcolm X to break away in an attempt to gain a clearer perception of the reality of African thought and spiritual beliefs.

This new appeal to Africa, therefore, is still something of a defensive gesture. It emerges from a profound distrust of the Negro's American experience, as if by appealing to a largely illusory and mythical Africa it would prove possible to ignore the debilitating truth of Negro history in America. But, as LeRoi Jones has pointed out, "The traditions of Africa" must surely "be utilised within the culture of the American Negro where they *actually* exist, and not because of a defensive rationalization about the *worth* of one's ancestors or any attempt to capitalize on the recent eminence of the 'new' African nations." As he goes on to point out, "The American Negro has a definable and legitimate historical tradition, no matter how painful, in America, but it is the only place the American Negro exists. . . . He is, as William Carlos Williams said, 'A pure product of America.' "[20] Thus the foundation both of identity and cultural independence rests on a willingness to accept the facts of one's history and racial origins rather than on a determination to embrace the chimeras of atavism.

Therefore, despite the romanticism of writers like Lorraine Hansberry, who retained to the end a somewhat naive vision of Africa, there has been a move away from the African-centered concept of *negritude* towards on the one hand a sense of universality and on the other a sense of black national consciousness, existing, as LeRoi Jones insists, "in the land the black captives had begun to identify as home."[21] This is not to say that Jones is calling for cultural assimilation. On the contrary, he is demanding the growth of an independent black American literature. The swing against integration as a civil rights strategy has thus been mirrored by a swing against cultural integration — the logic of the one being applied to the other. Where Stokely Carmichael opposes social integration on the grounds that it presumes the superiority of white values, the irrelevance of black experience and the destruction of black identity, he is in fact defining at the same time the basis of Jones's call for black art. To join the mainstream can no longer be considered a neutral act. Where Senghor had once spoken of being a "cultural mulatto" and DuBois of an inescapable "double consciousness" Jones denounces this as the "yoke of cultural compromise" and Harold Cruse as a "cultural imperialism" which has to be defeated. DuBois had once pointed out that "We are Americans, not only by birth and by citizenship but by our political ideals, our language, our religion" adding significantly, however, that "Further than that our Americanism does not go."[22] We have clearly reached a time now when for many Negroes Americanism does not even go that far. The Christian religion, rejected by the Black Muslims as the 'graveyard' of the Negro people, is increasingly associated with the passive acceptance of white brutality; American political ideals are challenged by revolutionaries for whom the American system represents merely injustice, oppression and distorted materialism; while even the language is subverted by a generation who, in LeRoi Jones's words, do not want to become "fluent in the jargon of power."

Thus, while granting the need to create a culture out of American experience Jones wants the Negro to create a separate black culture with its "own symbols" and its "own personal myths" which would owe nothing to Europe and little to America.* This wish owes its origin partly to the desire for positive self-definition and partly to the need to escape a black identity created by whites —even by those ostensibly embracing their cause. Kerouac, Mailer and even Sartre, for example, adopt an attitude towards the Negro which, their sincerity notwithstanding, smacks of paternalism. For Sartre he is "the great male of the earth, the world's sperm" characterised by a "great vegetable patience,"[23] while to Kerouac he represents "joy, kicks, darkness, music" and, occasionally, "the dusky knee of some mysterious sensual girl."[24] Mailer, whose tolerance for Negro assertion has been wearing a little thin of late,

---

*It is telling, however, that when Jones searches for an image of the Negro's situation he should turn naturally to Melville's Bartleby. Moreover for all the self-indulgent anti-white rhetoric of *Dutchman* and *The Slave* these two plays invite comparison not only with Albee but also with Strindberg and Brecht while his own early work, such as *The System of Dante's Hell*, owes a great deal to European models.

suggests that the black, "all exceptions admitted," subsists simply "for his Saturday night kicks."[25] While each of these writers recognise a privileged racial mystique, the role which they ascribe to the black world is a familiar one and the fact that LeRoi Jones has pledged his support to Kerouac says more for his own early involvement with the beats than for the validity of his views. The beats, accepting too readily the images of the Harlem Renaissance, saw in the Negro a kindred spirit. Since they themselves were alienated from commercial civilisation and chose to emphasize the emotional at the expense of the intellectual they eagerly embraced an ancient stereotype with which the Negro writer himself had earlier wrestled. Looking for one who rejoiced in emotion and physical sensation unrestricted by bourgeois standards of morality, much to Lorraine Hansberry's disgust they professed to find him in the Negro. In an era of political disaffiliation they espoused the disenfranchised. And yet behind this there is surely something of the attitude of those who went slumming in Harlem in the 20s. The envy which such writers professed for the Negro not only depended on a somewhat distorted conception of Negro life but also suggested a patronising sense of superiority, implied in the limitless possibilities of the questing white and the simple inflexibility of the black trapped in his quaint sensuality and scarcely aware of his own advantages. For the whites this image became a true reflection of Negro reality — a fact which Ralph Ellison satirises in the figure of Trueblood in *Invisible Man*. This man, who has had an incestuous relationship with his own daughter, is true not to the reality of black life but to the vicarious expectation of impotent whites.

It is in the face of such false images that some black writers have insisted on the need for ethnic literature. As the young writer Julius Lester has put it, "I'm an Afro-American. This implies that I'm an amalgam. It is my responsibility to reflect the Afro side of the hyphen. The other side has been too much reflected. Too, no one else can reflect the Afro side except Afro-Americans. Certainly not a cracker from Georgia writing *The Confessions of Nat Turner*."[26] It is this evangelistic attitude which leads LeRoi Jones, among others, to reject the achievement of virtually every Negro writer of any significance, be it Wright, Baldwin or Ellison, while Harold Cruse, who is equally committed to the idea of ethnic culture, helpfully adds Hansberry and Killens. We are perilously close, in other words, to the crusading atmosphere of the 30s when literature was judged according to its adherence to the party line. Now the dialectic is no longer Marxist but ethnic. Nevertheless we still hear the same strident demands for orthodoxy and the same intolerant rejection of all art which fails to conform to the cultural philosophy of the elite.

— This spirit pervades Cruse's recent book, *The Crisis of the Negro Intellectual*, in which he attacks Negro writers for concerning themselves with the white world, reserving his bitterest assault for Baldwin's *Giovanni's Room* and Hansberry's *The Sign in Sidney Brustein's Window*. Of this latter author he says, "to see today a Negro stage writer bending over backwards to glorify the Jewish image in the face of the rising tide of color, seeking new social status and new identification in world culture, is to witness a cultural phenomenon nothing short of a political sell-out."[27] For all the stringency of Cruse's analysis of the role of the Negro intellectual his racial imperatives lead him into extremely deep critical waters. For not only does he dismiss those authors with whose cultural philosophies he disagrees but he is forced into extreme positions in defence of ethnic literature — even going to extraordinary lengths to destroy the opposing traditions. Thus T. S. Eliot is rejected because he felt that "the cultural status of his ethnic group was wide open for invasion by other culturally impure ethnic groups, such as niggers, Jews, wops, Polacks and bohunks."[28] At the same time he feels obliged to make excessive claims for the importance of the ethnic tradition, commenting that "the cultural and artistic originality of the American nation is founded, historically, on the ingredients of a black aesthetic and artistic base."[29] Statements such as these, while underlining the crude manichean nature of Cruse's imagination, do, however, serve to demonstrate the passion of the debate between the 'cultural nationalists' and the 'cultural integrationists' who frequently attack one another with all the virulence of the Stalin-Trotsky factions. The critic of Negro writing is thus placed in a difficult position, assailed by the cultural separatists for treating black writers as part of the mainstream and by the integrationists for treating them as elements of a separate culture. In particular the passion which these competing ideologies inspire makes it virtually impossible to gain a clear impression from Negro critics. Yet, ironically, it is precisely at this moment that the rights of the white critic have been challenged and that black critics have been most brutal in their attacks on a white writer like William Styron.

The basis for the violent denunciation of *The Confessions of Nat Turner* is itself revealing. The novel is attacked primarily for being un-historical. It is alleged that Styron deliberately suppresses some facts and invents others and that by doing so he reveals an entrenched racism and a contempt for historical truth. But outside of the more obsessive naturalists few writers have laid claim to objective accuracy of this kind and if such objections are to be upheld we are liable to find ourselves in the ironical position of rejecting not merely Styron's *Nat Turner* and many other such works but also Arna Bontemps' novel of the Virginia slave revolt of 1800, *Black Thunder*. This, too, is guilty of very similar sins of omission and commission. Where Styron chooses to forget Nat Turner's black wife, making him instead into a bachelor who is alternately attracted and repelled by a white woman, Bontemps removes a black wife and replaces her with an "apricot-colored" mistress. Where Styron creates a character obsessed with the idea of raping white women and only restrained by the dominant will of his leader, Bontemps creates an exactly similar character in the person of Criddle, a black rebel who resists the temptation only because of his leader's injunction not to "touch no womens."

Much more revealing is the attack launched against Styron for suggesting that the Nat Turner rebellion was defeated with the aid of slaves who remained loyal to their masters. Obviously this has been seen as a conscious blow at black pride. Yet Bontemps makes precisely the same point in his novel where he admits that the rebellion is finally defeated by black treachery. But he does suppress one significant fact. The rebel leader, Gabriel, was actually betrayed by two Negroes; in the novel he gives himself up to save a fellow Negro from persecution. Bontemps' distortion of the truth on this point is more fundamental than any of Styron's changes yet basically details such as these are irrelevant to the power and achievement of either novel. What is interesting is the kind of selective criticism which will accept from a black author what it will not accept from a white man. *The Confessions of Nat Turner* has become a *cause célèbre*; *Black Thunder* escaped a similar vilification when it was first written and continues to do so today. We are left with the inescapable feeling that the black writers who have attacked William Styron are less concerned with the real nature of his craftsmanship and the extent of his achievement than they are with protecting their supposed hegemony of black experience.

A somewhat similar point could be made about some of LeRoi Jones's criticism. In an essay in *Home* he remarks that Richard Wright, James Baldwin and Ralph Ellison can only be thought of as "serious" writers so long as one has never read Herman Melville or James Joyce. The point is an important one. Yet pages later he attacks those for whom "Negro literature" is synonymous with the second rate "in much the same way all American Literature was thought of before Melville."[30] The inherent contradiction unfortunately lends itself to a racial interpretation. In the former remarks he, a Negro, is offering his assessment of the relative inferiority of modern Negro writers, while in the latter he is indicting white critics for saying the same thing.

According to Cruse the "criticism of Negro writing is mainly the Negro's responsibility"[31] — an attitude which is supported to some degree by Richard Gilman, the white former literary editor of the *New Republic*. Cruse is so violent in his demands that he comes close to seeing white criticism as an arm of political policy. To his mind, "The fear of black cultural assertion is so strong in the white Left that every precaution must be taken to influence even the most feeble rise of cultural self-evaluation among Negroes."[32] Unfortunately his own response to writers such as John O. Killens, Ossie Davis and Lorraine Hansberry is so coloured by his commitment to ethnic literature that one can scarcely place much confidence in the idea of exclusive cultural self-evaluation. So extreme is this in-fighting, in fact, that we find ourselves in the position of hearing Killens denouncing Ellison's *Invisible Man* as a "vicious distortion of Negro life" while himself being attacked by Cruse for much the same thing. Similarly Lorraine Hansberry attacks Richard Wright's *The Outsider* for forwarding the cause "of our oppressors" while herself falling victim to Cruse's invective. This critical cannibalism is conducted on such a superficial and non-literary level, moreover, that one would be justified in despairing of the present state of black literary criticism. Despite the obvious truth that a similarly cavalier approach has characterised such white critics as Norman Mailer, not to mention the Marxist critics of the 30s and the left-wing writers of the present day, the sheer virulence of the integrationist/nationalist debate amongst black writers and critics makes the present call for ethnic criticism ring a little hollow.

Richard Gilman says of Eldridge Cleaver that "his writing

remains in some profound sense not subject to correction a.
emendation or, most centrally, approval by those of us who are
not black."[33] He is careful to restrict his remarks to polemical
works by Cleaver, Malcolm X and Frantz Fanon yet even so his
claim is a little doubtful. The racial myth and the social dogma
have their part to play in the task of cultural reconstruction but
emerging, as they do, so directly from the American experience of
the Negro they can scarcely demand a totally alien aesthetic. Nor,
to be strictly accurate, do Cleaver's book or Malcolm X's (written
by Alex Haley) demand the suspension of critical faculties which
Gilman would seem to suggest. *Soul on Ice* consists of a series of
related essays, some of which are clearly directed at a black audience
but others of which are equally clearly directed at a white public.
The essays do indeed add a new dimension not merely to an
understanding of black consciousness but also to the essay form
as Cleaver manipulates the potent myths of racial identity. But
though he offers a unique vision he has not moved outside the
indeterminate boundaries of Western art but like any creative
artist he has moved the boundary stakes. Malcolm X's book is
less remarkable, being primarily of interest for the light which it
throws on the putative author himself who emerges as a *naïf* of
stunning integrity. Aesthetically, it differs little from Claude
Brown's *Manchild in the Promised Land.*

├─Gilman's argument follows that of Frantz Fanon fairly closely.
He accepts his strictures on the need for the black writer to reject
Western culture, although with less point than Fanon who was after
all writing for a society which had a more direct access to alternative
cultures. But Gilman, like Fanon, recognises that the revolutionary
writer has a specific role to play which may take his work outside
the bounds of conventional criticism. In any time of social or
political turmoil there will always emerge some ostensibly literary
works which, whatever their claims, are intended purely as political
vehicles and which are not susceptible of criticism — be it black
or white. One suspects, however, that such works tend at times to
inspire some critics with an unbecoming sense of modesty as they
invoke the mystique of blackness in preference to outright condemnation. But, as Mphahlele remarks the real question is perhaps
"Why should *la littérature engagée* be so spoiled as to want to be
judged by different standards from those that have been tested
by tradition? Why should it be afraid of being judged against the
social context that gives rise to it and run for cover behind the

black mask?"[34] While this begs too many questions for comfort it does stand as a useful challenge to the subordination of the aesthetic to the political.

Gilman suspends judgment for two main reasons. Firstly, he is afraid of applying irrelevant criteria. This motive is legitimate enough. The critic has always had to guard against outmoded standards, but this is not a problem which is specific to black writing, as critics of Joyce, Beckett and Ionesco have discovered, while capitulation is a poor substitute for adaptation. The white critic's duty is to accept that he is facing a relatively new manifestation in American writing — and this does remain American writing — but at the same time to refuse to be cowed by strident demands for critical withdrawal. Gilman's second reason is more dubious. He is wary of demonstrating cultural arrogance by presuming to judge Negro writing by reference to white values. But in these circumstances the line between arrogance and paternalism is not always as clear as one would like. Besides which the end product of this critical apartheid is to deny the worth of such inter-cultural studies as Arthur Waley's work on oriental culture, or Allen Watt's book on Zen or, indeed, Sartre's seminal essay on African poets, which is included in this study.

It is true, though, that whereas earlier Negro writers had written for predominantly white audiences we are now faced with black writers whose primary public is black. If this is not entirely true of either Cleaver or Malcolm X it is true of playwrights like LeRoi Jones (in his later work), Ed Bullins and Marvin X who do seem to confront the white critic with an apparently major problem. Accordingly, it may be worthwhile briefly examining the nature of this 'revolutionary' black theatre, aimed at the black masses, which ostensibly challenges the critical apparatus of the white critic. For this is a theatre which goes beyond the simple claims of *negritude* and yet while apparently bordering on the verge of Fanon's third stage remains totally committed to an ethnic creed.

It is true that Negro literature has in the past meant very little to the Negro masses. They have largely remained as untouched by black culture (with the exception of music) as they have been by middle-class oriented civil rights legislation. The Renaissance was the province of a relatively small group of intellectuals. It was largely disdained by the middle class because of its tasteless exuberance and its insensitive attraction for the unsophisticated; but it was equally meaningless for the tens of thousands of Negroes in the ghetto who had more immediate problems than those dealt with by Hughes, McKay and Toomer. The same was true of the 30s, despite anguished attempts to present the realities of black working-class life. It was not until the 60s that any really serious attempt was made to establish genuine contact with the masses and this, as always, was through the theatre — through the initially inter-racial but eventually black dominated Free Southern Theatre and through LeRoi Jones's Black Arts Theatre. Although this latter was itself in some ways a failure it did inspire a series of similar ventures in cities across the country. It is questionable as to how far these groups have really been successful for, as Arnold Wesker discovered in England, the working-class is not naturally drawn to the theatre which even in its revolutionary guise still seems a bourgeois form. Nevertheless, in venturing onto the streets, as LeRoi Jones did in Harlem, a certain degree of contact was established. The nature of this theatre is made clear by a manifesto published by Ed Bullins, author of *The Electronic Nigger*:

> STREET PLAYS (Black Revolutionary Agit-Prop)
> 1. Purpose: communicating to masses of Black people. Contact with Black crowds. Communication with diverse classes of people, the Black working class, or with special groups (e.g., winos, pool hall brothers, prostitutes, pimps, hypes, etc.) who would not ordinarily come or be drawn into the theatre. . . . Types of plays: short, sharp, incisive plays are best. Contemporary themes, satirical pieces on counter-revolutionary figures or enemies of the people. . . .[35]

LeRoi Jones explains his own attitude in similar terms. The revolutionary ethnic theatre is, he explains, "a political theatre, a weapon to help in the slaughter of those dim-witted fatbellied white guys who somehow believe that the rest of the world is here for them to slobber on."[36]

In a theatre which has for so long been dominated by Ibsen-esque naturalism or, at the most extreme, the mannered meta-physics of Albee, these new myth makers come as a startling innovation. Yet they obviously have their distant forbears in the European political theatre of the 20s and 30s and even in the more recent experiments of the Living Theatre. The images, the myths and the racial assumptions all derive from a specifically black experience but at the same time this does not invalidate white criticism. If this is indeed to be taken as the true product of that cultural nationalism before which the white critic is called upon to retreat with due deference then one might justifiably reject Cruse's suggestion that "without an ethnic theatre, the Negro playwright is hampered in his development."[37] But it would be a mistake simply to equate Jones's 'revolutionary' theatre, with its stress on racial melodrama, with ethnic drama, although at the present moment the Black Arts movement is the uncompromising staple of that drama. Rather, it is to be seen as the radical wing of the black theatre which, through organisations such as the Negro Ensemble Company, is also attempting to establish a less politically oriented drama. This latter group, however, is at present financed by the Ford Foundation and has a repertory which includes Peter Weiss as well as Lonne Elder and Ray McIver. Although it has demonstrated anew the potential of ethnic theatre its final direction must still be in some doubt.

The primary question now is whether the future of the black playwright lies in a totally black theatre, situated in the heart of the ghetto, or in the broader and admittedly more lucrative fields of the American theatre. In the early years it seems clear that an ethnic theatre, catering for an ethnic audience is vitally important both to writers and performers. Under these conditions, no longer limited by the social and cultural prejudices of white audiences and managements, they could feel free to try their hand at a whole range of material formerly denied them. Previous attempts at establishing ethnic theatre, however, have proved for the most part short-lived. Rose McClendon's Negro People's Theatre saw only one performance before the death of its founder brought about its collapse.* A similar fate met the Negro Playwrights' Company, which closed after its production of Theodore Ward's *The Big White Fog*. Langston Hughes's Harlem Suitcase Theatre lasted only a single year while the Rose McClendon Players survived a bare two years. By far the most successful attempt at founding a black theatre group was the American Negro Theatre (ANT), founded by Abram Hill, which flourished in the 40s. Significantly, this collapsed under the growing influence of those who saw their future lying in the American theatre at large rather than in the

---

*A similar case of misfortune occurred in January 1968 when the New Lafayette Theatre, founded only three months earlier, was burned down.

rarefied atmosphere of a racial drama group. The backwash from the collapse of the ANT is still distinguishable, particularly with the recent revival of the debate between the cultural nationalists and the cultural integrationists. Thus when actor-playwright Douglas Turner Ward, director of the Negro Ensemble, is quoted as saying that "there is no ideological reason for a black theatre"[38] he invites and receives a tart response from those passionately committed to ethnic literature. James Baldwin's denial that 'there is a Negro theatre in the United States, or that such a development would be especially worthwhile"[39] merely confirms them in their belief that he, along with Ossie Davis and Lorraine Hansberry, has sold out to the white world.

It seems evident that whatever the evangelistic arrogance of some spokesmen on either side there is room for both strands of Negro creativeness but there is also little doubt that in terms of literary achievement, as opposed to political utility, the revolutionary black theatre has as yet offered very little of real note. Whatever we make of LeRoi Jones's reminder that ethics and aesthetics are indissolubly linked we must still permit ourselves the distinction between a polemical gesture and an imaginative insight. All too often these plays are no more than gratuitous wish-fulfilment fantasies or politically significant rituals. The Negro theatre has come alive with the black arts movement but it has not come of age. The greatest achievements of black playwrights in recent years remain Ossie Davis's *Purlie Victorious,* LeRoi Jones's early plays, *Dutchman* and *The Slave* and, Cruse's excoriation notwithstanding, *The Sign in Sidney Brustein's Window.* On practical grounds one can hope that the new ethnic theatre will not precipitate a destructive rapprochement with Broadway of the type which undermined the ANT but at the same time the achievement of writers such as Hansberry and Davis demonstrates clearly enough that the Negro writer has already staked an important claim in the American theatre at large.

In "Black Orpheus" Sartre describes *Negritude* as "black men . . . addressing themselves to black men about black men."[40] As a definition this would certainly satisfy the cultural nationalists. However, Sartre goes on to stress what he sees as its universal significance, insisting that black writing is "actually a hymn by everyone for everyone" and that the white man "can gain access to this world of jet."[41] There is in fact evidence that the Negro writer has a growing realisation, shared by the Jewish writer, that his own experience is not merely relevant to that of society at large but that in a sense he has become an archetypal image of modern man in a complex industrialised community — alienated, uncertain of his identity, and adrift in a world which values the material above the human. In Richard Wright's words, "The Negro is America's metaphor"[42] or, as Robert Penn Warren remarked, broadening the terms of reference even further, he is "an image of man's fate."[43] This does not mean that the black writer is producing assimilationist works "which are universally human" because they are about white characters and white problems — a prospect which the cultural nationalists view with some alarm. The potency of the Negro's metaphorical role derives precisely from its ethnic specificity. At the same time as the Jewish writer, after an assimilationist period, is rediscovering the special significance of his Jewishness (Bellow with *The Victim*, Malamud with *The Fixer* and Arthur Miller with *After the Fall, Incident at Vichy* and *The Price*) the Negro writer has come to appreciate the relevance of his own experience to a nation searching for its own sense of identity and purpose. Thus he is no longer merely concerned with demonstrating that he is the product of white bigotry but rather that the iniquities of white society serve to exacerbate a situation which is essentially shared by oppressors and oppressed alike. In the words of Ellison's *Invisible Man*, "Who knows but that, on the lower frequencies, I speak for you?"[44] Even LeRoi Jones's racial rebel, in *The Slave*, is as meaningful on a larger scale as Melville's Bartleby or Camus' Rieux. To say this is not to suggest that the black writer is pandering to a fashionable universality but rather to acknowledge that in modern times and particularly since the Second World War the pariah has gained a painful relevance. These works are therefore not anguished cries for integration but dispassionate analyses of contemporary reality. If this is a reality to which white Americans respond this can scarcely be taken as reflecting on the racial integrity of the black writer.

Whatever the wishes of the racial dogmatists, therefore, it seems that, at least in the realm of the novel, the black writer can now be seen as an endemic part of American literature not because he is consciously aping middle-class white values but because his experience is in some essentials merely a more extreme version of white fears and neuroses. The primary difference lies in the fact that what to the white writer is a matter of intellectual enquiry to the black is an essential formula for day-to-day survival. Thus while many American writers have felt it necessary to question anew the principles on which the country was founded, balancing the American reality against the animating dream, the gap between truth and illusion confronts the black American throughout his life. So, too, when Baldwin says that "I'm part of a country which has yet to discover who and what it is"[45] he is recognising the relevance of his own situation to that seemingly endless American game of self-definition. From Cooper's hero, with his ever-changing identity, to the anonymous protagonist of *Invisible Man* these desperate attempts at self-realisation have been a staple of the American writer. But once again what to the white writer is simply a fashionable sense of anomie is a central fact of black experience. Nevertheless, despite these distinctions it is increasingly apparent that the modern Negro novelist is animated by basically the same aspects of contemporary life which move the white writer. In spite of Fanon and Cruse's rejection of those writers whose primary interest seems to lie in the developing consciousness of the individual rather than in ethnic solidarity or political activism, it is clear that this has been the fundamental subject not only of Baldwin and Ellison's work but also of LeRoi Jones's *Dutchman* and even Richard Wright's *Native Son*.

The task, as Cleaver has suggested, is indeed that of "rejuvenating and reclaiming the shattered psyches and culture of the black people."[46] But, as Ralph Ellison asserts in *Invisible Man*, this is not to be achieved by worshipping any of the gods which offer a ready-made identity and a simplistic description of human affairs. Identity depends not on the nature of one's polemical stance but on the essence of one's personal commitment to reality as expressed through concrete action. It is no accident that from Richard Wright's *Uncle Tom's Children* and *Native Son*, through Ellison's *Invisible Man*, and William Melvin Kelley's *A Different Drummer* the dominant philosophy of the Negro writer should have been an existential one. Moreover, in so far as the *bildungsroman* is by its very nature existential one might be excused for extending the line back to James Weldon Johnson's *The Autobiography of an Ex-Coloured Man*. Harold Cruse is clearly wrong when he calls Wright's *The Outsider* "just about the first Negro literary exploration of the existentialist theme"[47] but right in drawing our attention to a vital aspect of black writing. Thus the real problem facing the Negro, in the words of the lecture recalled by Ellison's 'invisible' hero, "was not actually one of creating the uncreated conscience of his race, but of creating the *uncreated features of his face*. Our task," he continued, "is that of making ourselves individuals," for "The conscience of a race is the gift of its individuals who see, evaluate, record. . . . We create the race by creating ourselves."[48] Even LeRoi Jones, who insists that in terms of the racial struggle "the only 'individuals' would be people who do not have to worry about the racial struggle," is forced to amend this to the simple aphorism that "Individuality is only gained by first realizing that it is not important in its most superficial states."[49] As the African writer, Ezekiel Mphahlele reminds us, "We must strive to visualize the whole man, not merely the things that are meant to flatter the Negro's ego."[50] To interpret the black man merely in terms of an exotic African tradition or a revolutionary dogma is clearly not to visualise the whole man. This is the central truth learned by both Ellison's invisible man and Richard Wright's tortured protagonist, Bigger Thomas.

It is ironical, therefore, that Eldridge Cleaver, otherwise an acute observer of the Negro writer, should see Wright's chief virtue as lying in his "profound political, economic, and social reference,"[51] for Wright at his best rejects an analysis which deals with man in such terms. In *The God That Failed* he has said that "It was not the economics of Communism, nor the great power of the trade unions . . . that claimed me," for "The Communists, I felt, had over-simplified the experience of those they sought to lead. In their efforts to recruit masses, they had missed the meaning of the lives of the masses, had conceived of people in too abstract a manner."[52] Wright's forte, then, whatever the nature of his earlier political alignment, does not lie in his ability to reflect "the intricate mechanisms of a social organisation"; but rather in his skill at expressing the anguish of that individual who sees no social organisation in which he can place his trust or by reference to which he can sustain his own sense of individuality. The same is essentially true of Ellison who, as a colleague of Wright's, had flirted with communism in the 30s, and, indeed, of James Baldwin. One wonders, therefore, why Cleaver should indict Baldwin for his so-called white values while praising Wright who, the violence of his commitment notwithstanding, looked forward with equal fervour to a time when such divisions would no longer have any relevance. Wright's 'outsider', in the novel of the same name, although a Negro, is essentially a product of modern civilisation rather than simply of racial discrimination. It is perhaps significant that the man who approximates Wright's own frame of mind most closely is in a fact a white district attorney.

Thus the black writer today, as we have seen, is placed in an unenviable position. As in any time of political and social upheaval he is required to stake out his position and declare his loyalties. As both an American and a Negro he is already confronted with a painful dilemma but this is heightened by the persistent and conflicting demands of the different literary factions. Urged on the one hand to become a voice for the 'black soul' or even to become a simple publicist for the masses and on the other to aspire to that sense of universality so admired by Western culture, it is scarcely any wonder that he chooses all too often to evade such conflicts by retreating to Europe* as Richard Wright and James Baldwin had before him.

James Baldwin, indeed, embodies these conflicts to such an extent that his career offers a useful paradigm of the anguish of the American Negro writer. In 1948 he left the United States with a one-way ticket to France, convinced that unless he escaped the pressures of American society he would be destroyed both as a writer and an individual. He wanted to evade literary classification as a 'Negro writer' and social classification as an inferior citizen. In Baldwin's mind the connection between art and society at that time lay primarily in the fact that art offered an apparent escape from otherwise destructive social circumstances. As for so many black writers before him it was the ticket to the middle class and to the international coterie of artists. Yet he had not been in France very long before he came to realise that he had carried the conflicts of his American experience with him and that his colour and his nationality were the twin axes against which he would perforce plot his literary graph. This realisation was crucial to his development as a writer. As Baldwin himself put it, it "is a personal day . . . a terrible day . . . the day he realises that . . . if he has been preparing himself for anything in Europe he has been preparing himself — for America."[53] Yet even so it took the impact of Little Rock to convince him that he had a role to play in correcting the injustices of American society.

---

*In the 1920s Claude McKay and Countee Cullen and in the 60s William Melvin Kelley, William Gardner Smith, Carlene Polite.

When the civil rights movement in America really began to get under way Baldwin felt a sense of guilt at his lack of involvement. Accordingly he was drawn back to the country he had vowed "never, never" to revisit and on assignment for *Look* magazine visited the South for the first time in his life. Here, at the age of thirty-three, he came to see himself as a spokesman. As he later explained, "I suppose the depth of my own involvement began then."⁵⁴ By 1959 he had reversed the opinion of his earlier years, when he had tried to avoid a conflict between his writing and his racial identity. Now, in a review of Langston Hughes's poetry, but with obvious relevance to his own circumstances, he said that "Hughes is an American Negro poet and has no choice but to be acutely aware of it," commenting, significantly, that "He is not the first American Negro to find the war between his social and artistic responsibilities all but irreconcilable."⁵⁵ Baldwin now began to feel this paradox more acutely in his own life. As a writer he felt obliged to step back in order to gain perspective and objectivity while as the victim of prejudice and discrimination he felt obliged to lend his particular strength to the battle. But this is scarcely a new problem nor one restricted to the Negro writer. Camus outlined the problem clearly enough when he pointed out that "the artist of today becomes unreal if he remains in his ivory tower, or sterilized if he spends his time galloping around the political arena." It is precisely this paradox which hounds not only the Negro writer but any creative talent which feels drawn towards commitment. Yet, as Camus went on to point out, "between the two lies the arduous way of true art." Indeed this "continual shuttling, this tension that gradually becomes increasingly dangerous, is the task of the artist of today."⁵⁶

Baldwin's new sense of commitment evidenced itself not only in the powerful polemic, *The Fire Next Time,* but also in a personal involvement in the civil rights movement. More recently, however, he has come to feel that literary achievement does not necessarily qualify him as a public spokesman, "I am not a Negro leader. . . . It is impossible to be a writer and a public spokesman, I am a writer."⁵⁷ While insisting that he will never be able to retire entirely from the political arena and while recognising that his art and his public role are aspects of the same commitment, he has increasingly withdrawn from the forefront of the movement. He has come to feel that "others can do better . . . because it is still terribly true that a writer is extremely rare."

The apparent precocity of this remark explains something of the bitterness with which LeRoi Jones and Harold Cruse regard Baldwin, while in choosing to write *Giovanni's Room,* which has no Negro characters, he obviously laid himself open to attack by those who feel that the proper study of the Negro is the Negro — despite the symbolic relevance of the alienated characters in that work. Where Julius Lester insists that "If the black artist does not commit his art to the liberation movement . . . he is not fulfilling his responsibility" because at "this point in history, the black artist has no other responsibility,"[58] Baldwin claims simply that he "can't make alignments on the basis of colour."[59] To his mind the truly urgent thing is not so much the incantation of the appropriate formulas and slogans as a genuine attempt to come to terms with the failure of individual and social values, which in the end transcends the immediacies of colour. As he has said, "Ultimately, it's a moral evasion of oneself, which really menaces . . . the very future of this country."[60]

The exoticism of *negritude* has thus given way in part to an assertive sense of racial pride and identity accompanied by revolutionary fervour and in part to a detached humanism which, however different in outlook, also relies on a racial self-confidence lacking in former years. The choice is presented in a stark form: LeRoi Jones versus James Baldwin; Harold Cruse versus Lorraine Hansberry. It is a conflict which is wasteful of creative energy and which, at its most extreme, menaces the integrity of black criticism but which, nonetheless, goes right to the heart of those dilemmas which confront the black American writer. Perhaps, as Camus suggested, from these tensions the paths of true art will open up, for it is already clear that the work of contemporary black writers can no longer be so easily dismissed as "impressive mediocrity."

[1]Quoted in Robert Bone, *The Negro Novel in America* (New Haven, 1965) , p. 17.
[2]Quoted in Seymour Gross and John Hardy eds., *Images of the Negro in American Literature* (Chicago, 1966) , p. 16.
[3]*Ibid.*
[4]Frantz Fanon, *The Wretched of the Earth* trans. Constance Farrington (Hamondsworth, 1967) , p. 11.
[5]*Ibid.*
[6]*Op. cit.,* p. 166.

[7]Quoted in Gerald Moore, *Seven African Writers* (London, 1966), p. XVI.

[8]Quoted in Gerald Moore and Ulli Beier, *Modern Poetry from Africa* (Harmondsworth, 1963), p. 16.

[9]LeRoi Jones, *Home: Social Essays* (New York, 1967) p. 244.

[10]Frantz Fanon, *Black Skin, White Masks,* trans. Charles Markmann (London, 1968), p. 123.

[11]Langston Hughes and Arna Bontemps eds, *The Poetry of the Negro* (New York, 1969), p. 121.

[12]*Op. Cit.,* pp. 102-103.

[13]Ezekiel Mphahlele, *African Writing Today* (Harmondsworth, 1967) p. 249.

[14]Gwendolyn Brooks, *Annie Allen* (New York, 1949) p. 45.

[15]Ezekiel Mphahlele, "The Cult of Negritude," *Encounter* (March, 1961) p. 51.

[16]*The Poetry of the Negro,* pp. 74-75.

[17]Quoted in Harold Isaacs, "Five Writers and their Ancestors," *Phylon* XXII (1960), p. 319.

[18]*Op. Cit.,* p. 324.

[19]Alain Locke, "The New Negro," in *Images of the Negro in America* ed. Darwin Turner and Jean Bright (Boston, 1966), p. 41.

[20]*Home: Social Essays,* p. 11.

[21]*Op. cit.,* p. 242.

[22]E. U. Essien-Udom, *Black Nationalism: The Rise of the Black Muslims in the U.S.A.* (Harmondsworth, 1966), p. 41.

[23]See Vol. 2, p. 27.

[24]Jack Kerouac, *On the Road,* (London, 1963), pp. 187-188.

[25]Norman Mailer, *Advertisements for Myself* (London, 1959), p. 244.

[26]Julius Lester, "The Arts and the Black Revolution," *Arts in Society* V, ii (Summer-fall, 1968), 229.

[27]Harold Cruse, *The Crisis of the Negro Intellectual,* (London, 1969), pp. 413-414.

[28]*Op. cit.,* p. 465.

[29]*Op. cit.,* 189.

[30]*Home: Social Essays,* p. 180.

[31]*The Crisis of the Negro Intellectual,* p. 182.

[32]*Op. cit.,* p. 187.

[33]See Vol. 2, p. 40.

[34]*African Writing Today,* p. 252.

[35]Ed Bullins, "A Short Statement on Street Theatre," *The Drama Review* XII, iv. 93.

[36]*Home: Social Essays,* p. 212.

[37]*The Crisis of the Negro Intellectual,* p. 37.

[38]Woodie King, Jr., "Black Theatre: Present Condition," *The Drama Review* XII, iv, 122.

[39]*The Crisis of the Negro Intellectual,* p. 521.

[40]See Vol. 2, p. 7.

[41]*Op. cit.* pp. 7-8.
[42]*Images of the Negro in American Literature*, p. vii.
[43]*Op. cit.*, p. 25.
[44]Ralph Ellison, *Invisible Man* (Harmondsworth, 1965), p. 469.
[45]James Baldwin and James Mossman, "Race, Hate, Sex, and Colour," *Encounter*, XXV (1965), p. 57.
[46]Eldridge Cleaver, *Soul on Ice* (London, 1969), p. 99.
[47]*The Crisis of the Negro Intellectual*, p. 276.
[48]*Invisible Man*, p. 286.
[49]*Home: Social Essays*, p. 118.
[50]*African Writing Today*, p. 251.
[51]*Soul on Ice*, p. 108.
[52]Arthur Koestler *et. al.*, *The God That Failed* (London, 1950), pp. 123, 125.
[53]"Five Writers and their Ancestors," p. 323.
[54]Fern Maria Eckman, *The Furious Passage of James Baldwin* (London, 1968), p. 149.
[55]Maurice Charney, "James Baldwin's Quarrel with Richard Wright," *American Quarterly*, XV, i (Spring, 1963), 65.
[56]Albert Camus, *Resistance, Rebellion, and Death* trans. Justin O'Brien (New York, 1960) p. 182.
[57]James Baldwin, "James Baldwin . . . in Conversation," *Arts in Society*, III (1967) 551.
[58]"The Arts and the Black Revolution," p. 229.
[59]*The Furious Passage of James Baldwin*, p. 181.
[60]James Baldwin *et. al.*, "The Negro in American Culture," *Cross-Currents*, XI, iii (1961), 223.

White Standards
and Negro Writing

by Richard Gilman

THERE IS A growing body of Negro writing which is not to be thought of simply as writing by Negroes. It is not something susceptible of being democratized and assimilated in the same way that writing by Jews has been. The movement there was, very roughly, from Jewish writing to Jewish-American writing to writing by authors "who happen to be Jews." But the new Negro writing I am talking about isn't the work of authors who *happen* to be Negro; it doesn't make up the kind of movement within a broader culture by which minorities, such as the Jews or the Southerners in our own society, contribute from their special cast of mind and imagination and their particular historical and psychic backgrounds something "universal," increments to the literary or intellectual traditions.

These Negro writers I am speaking of take their blackness not as a starting point for literature or thought and not as a marshaling ground for a position in the parade of national images and forms, but as absolute theme and necessity. They make philosophies and fantasias out of their color, use it as weapon and seat of judgment, as strategy and outcry, source of possible rebirth, data for a future existence and agency of revolutionary change. For such men and women, to write is an almost literal means of survival and attack, a means — more radically than we have known it — to *be,* and their writing owes more, consciously at least, to the embattled historical moment in which American Negroes find themselves than to what is ordinarily thought of as literary expression or the ongoing elaboration of ideas.

That universality is not among the incentives and preoccupations of this writing is something that makes for its particular, if sometimes provisional strength. A book like *The Autobiography of Malcolm X,* the type and highest achievement of the genre (if we have to call it that), forges its own special value and importance partly through its adamant specificity, its inapplicability as a model for many kinds of existence. Its way of looking at the world, its formulation of experience is not the potential possession — even by imaginative appropriation — of us all; hard, local, instransigent, alien, it remains in some sense unassimilable for those of us who aren't black. And that is why it has become, to an even greater degree than novels like *Native Son* and *Invisible Man,* the special pride and inspiriting book of so many American Negroes.

Malcolm's literacy, his capacity to write the book at all, were of course formed by what we have to call white traditions, but the book was not a contribution to those traditions, not another *Education of Henry Adams* or *Apologia Pro Vita Sua,* documents of the white, normative Western consciousness and spirit, which Negroes in America today have begun to repudiate in ways that are as yet clumsy, painful and confused. The point is that most Western intellectual autobiographies, apart from the writings of revolutionaries in whom the life was subordinate to the action in the world, have been luxury documents. Rising out of an already assured stock of consciousness of technical means, building on a civilization which had thrown up many precedents and models for the extension of the self into memorial and apologetic literature — writing which *takes for granted* the worth, dignity and substantial being of the individual, his right to talk about himself in public — such books could only have provided Malcolm with certain technical or organizational principles of procedure. As for spiritual models, could he have learned from *Up from Slavery,* that book which so many American Negroes so fiercely repudiate today as much for its having been written in the borrowed, deferential spirit of imitation of Western sagas of the self as for its explicit Uncle Tomism?

There was a central element of dishonesty in White liberal

reactions to Malcolm's book. It should have alarmed them far more radically than it did. But by praising Malcolm for his candor, his "power" or his "salutary indictment of our society," by making a literary compatriot of him, the White cultured community effectively blunted the really unsettling fact about his book: that it was not written for us. It was written for Negroes: it is not talking about the human condition (that Western idea which from the battle line looks like a luxury product) but about the condition of Negroes; it was not, moreover, anything less — although it was other things as well — than a myth for Negroes to live by now, as we have our myths of so many kinds.

The Negro doesn't feel the way whites do, nor does he think like whites — at the point, that is, when feelings and thought have moved beyond pure physical sensation or problems in mathematics. "Prick me and I bleed," Shylock rightly said, but the difference begins when the attitude to the blood is in question: Negro suffering is not of the same kind as ours. Under the great flawless arc of the Graeco-Roman and Judeo-Christian traditions we have implicitly believed that all men experience essentially the same things, that birth, love, pain, self, death are universals; they are in fact what we mean by universal values in literature and consciousness. But the Negro has found it almost impossible in America to experience the universal as such: this power, after all, is conferred upon the individual, or rather confirmed for him, by his membership in the community of men. Imagine how it must be to know that you have not the right to feel that your birth, your pain, your joy or your death are proper, natural elements of the human universe but, are, as it were, interlopers, unsanctioned realities, to be experienced on sufferance and without communal acknowledgement.

"We shall have our manhood. We shall have it or the earth will be leveled by our attempts to gain it." So writes Eldridge Cleaver in his book, *Soul on Ice,* a collection of letters, essays, reflections and reports from his life which go to make up a spiritual and intellectual autobiography that stands at the exact resonant center of the new Negro writing I have been referring to. Cleaver's book is in the tradition — that just formed current — of Malcolm X's, and the latter is its mentor in the fullest sense. Unsparing, unaccommodating, tough and lyrical by turns, foolish at times, unconvincing in many of its specific ideas but extraordinarily convincing in the energy and hard morale of its thinking, painful, aggressive and undaunted, *Soul on Ice* is a book for which we have to make room — but not on the shelves we have already built.

Cleaver was born in Arkansas in 1935, grew up in the Negro ghetto of Los Angeles and at eighteen was sent to prison for possessing marijuana. Since then he has spent most of his time in one or another California prison, being at present on parole from the institution at Soledad and living in the Bay Area where, the dust jacket quotes him as saying, he works as a "full-time revolutionary in the struggle for black liberation in America." He is a staff writer for *Ramparts*, minister of information for the Black Panther Party for Self-Defense, and at work on a book about "the future direction of the black liberation movement."

The year he first went to prison was the year of the Supreme Court decision overthrowing school segregation, and Cleaver holds the two events in firm, unambiguous relationship. The decision moved him into thought for the first time: "I began to form a concept of what it meant to be black in white America." As his intellect sought materials he turned to the great White revolutionaries — Marx, Tom Paine, Lenin, Bakunin, Nechayev (most of whom he must have read in periods outside prison) — and later to Negro writers like Richard Wright, W. E. B. Du Bois and of course, with enormous impact on him, Malcolm X. The last stages of his education seem to have been his reading of white writers like Mailer, Burroughs and Ginsberg, who put him in touch with certain energies and approaches which he badly needed to escape provincialism.

He started to write a few years ago, he says, "to save myself." For from being jailed for possessing pot he had passed to true criminal status. Agonized, furious, blind with vengefulness, he had embarked after completing his first sentence on a deliberate career as a rapist, first with Negro women as victims — "in the black ghetto where dark and vicious deeds appear not as aberrations or deviations from the norm, but as part of the sufficiency of the Evil of the day" — and then with whites. "I had gone astray — astray not so much from the white man's law as from being human, civilized. . . ."

This struggle, to be human and civilized without submitting oneself to the *whiteness* of those words, and above all without submitting to fear of the Law which embodies them, is at the heart of much passionate activity among Negroes in America today. It was Malcolm X's struggle: in that change of heart and mind he underwent before his death, and which was the immediate cause of his death, Malcolm worked himself free of racism, out of the trap of being merely opposed, of being, therefore, fixed in the reduced identity of the opponent. "I have, so to speak," Cleaver writes, "washed my hands in the blood of the martyr, Malcolm X, whose retreat from the precipice of madness created new room for others to turn about in, and I am now caught up in that tiny space, attempting a maneuver of my own."

That tiny space: from one perspective it is the space between absolute hatred and repudiation of all whites and Uncle Tomism, from another, wider one the murderously curtailed room anyone of us has to remain human and yet to *make something happen,* to change things. For Cleaver, the "maneuver" he carries out is an effort at grace, complexity and faithfulness. It is to *be* Negro, with no concessions, no adaptations to white expectations, but at the same time to hold back from excess; it is to be able to invent myths and intellectual schemes for holding Negro experience and providing for a Negro future, but at the same time to distinguish in the white-controlled present whatever has remained human and might recommend itself as ally.

Cleaver finds the ally among young whites, whose "prostrate souls and tumultuous consciences" are evidence to him of the great split in this country of which the racial war is only one, if major constituent. "There is in America today," he writes, "a generation of white youth that is truly worthy of a black man's respect," "a rare event" in our "foul history." They are a generation which has lost its heroes, and Cleaver has no hesitation in asserting that the new heroes are black or yellow or Latin, in any case never Anglo-Saxon: Mao, Castro, Ché Guevara, Martin Luther King, Ho Chi Minh, Stokely Carmichael, Malcolm. (In the several years since he wrote this, his list of heroes has been reduced by time's erosion of ideality — Nasser, Ben Bella and Kwame Nkrumahs have of course lost their revolutionary credentials — but the general truth holds up.)

Yet having made his acknowledgements to white revolutionary youth and distinguished, as it is crucial to do, the fact that the political conflict in this country is "deeper than race," Cleaver keeps going back to race as his theme and arena. As a self-described "ofay-watcher," he has his eye on a hundred manifestations of American ugliness or depravity or dishonesty, but he is not a social critic for *our* sake: his is a Negro perspective, sight issuing from the "furious psychic stance of the Negro today," and in its victories of understanding, its blindnesses and incompletions, its clean or inchoate energies, its internal motives and justifications, his writing remains in some profound sense not subject to correction or emendation or, most certainly, approval or rejection by those of us who are not black.

I know this is likely to be misunderstood. We have all considered the chief thing we should be working towards is that state of disinterestedness, of "higher" truth and independent valuation, that would allow us, white and black, to see each other's minds and bodies free of the distortions of race, to recognize each other's gifts and deficiencies as gifts and deficiencies, to be able to quarrel as the members of an (ideal) family do and not as embattled tribes. We want to be able to say without selfconsciousness or inverted snobbery that such and such a Negro is a bastard or a lousy writer.

But we are nowhere near that stage and in some ways we are moving farther from it as polarization increases. And my point has been that it would be better for all of us if we recognized that in the present phase of interracial existence in America moral and intellectual "truths" have not the same reality for Negroes and whites, and that even to write is, for many Negroes, a particular act within the fact of their Negritude, not the independent, universal, "luxury" work we at least partly and ideally conceive it to be.

Here is Cleaver on a social manifestation of what I am talking about:

> One thing that judges, policemen and administrators never seem to have understood, and for which they certainly do not make any allowances, is that Negro convicts, basically, rather than see themselves as criminals and perpetrators of misdeeds, look upon themselves as prisoners of war, the victims of a vicious, dog-eat-dog social system that is so heinous as to cancel out their own malefactions: in the jungle there is no right and wrong.

To turn from this to intellectual creation is to indicate how I myself, a "judge" who passes on writing, must take something into account. Cleaver's book devotes a great deal of space to his elaboration of a structure of thought, a legend, really, about the nature of sexuality in America today. Some of it is grand, old-fashioned Lawrentian and Maileresque myth-making:

> This is the eternal and unwavering motivation of the male
> and female hemispheres, of man and woman, to transcend
> the Primeval Mitosis and achieve supreme identity in the
> Apocalyptic fusion.

Some of it is a Marxist-oriented analysis which ends by creating
certain large controlling figures by which to account for experience.
These are the white man, the "Omnipotent Administrator," the
white woman, the "Ultrafeminine," the Negro man, the "Super-
masculine Menial," and the Negro woman, the "Subfeminine
Amazon." Sexually each has been forced into a role, as a result
of his or her position in the society, and this frozen typology is
what we have to battle against.

I find it unsatisfying intellectually, schematic and unsubtle
most of the time. I don't want to hear again that the white man
has been cut off from his body or that the Negro male has been
forced back into his, that the Negro penis is more alive or the
white woman's sexuality is artificial and contrived. Yet I don't
want to condemn it, and I am not sure I know how to acknowledge
it without seeming patronizing. For Cleaver has composed a myth
to try to account for certain realities, Negro realities more than
white ones: the fascination of Negro men with white standards of
female beauty, the painfulness of having one's sexuality imprisoned
within class or racial lines, the refusal of the society to credit Negroes with mind, the split between Negro men and women.

He knows what he is talking *from*, if not fully what he is
talking *about*, and it is not my right to compare his thinking
with other "classic" ways of grappling with sexual experience and
drama; it isn't my right to draw him into the Western academy
and subject his findings to the scrutiny of the tradition. A myth,
moreover, is not really analyzable and certainly not something
which one can call untrue.

But Cleaver gets me off the hook, I think, by providing me with
a very beautiful section to quote, a letter "To All Black Women,
From All Black Men," in which ideas are subordinated to intense
feeling and the myth's unassailable usefulness is there to see. In
it he addresses the Negro woman as "Queen-Mother-Daughter of
Africa, Sister of My Soul, Black Bride of My Passion, My Eternal
Love," and begs forgiveness for having abandoned her and allowed
her to lose her sense of womanness. The last lines of the letter,
and the book, make up an enormously impressive fusion of

Cleaver's various revolutionary strands, his assertion of a Negro reality, his hunger for sexual fullness and the reintegration of the self, his political critique and program and sense of a devastated society in need of resurrection:

> Black woman, without asking how, just say that we survived our forced march and travail through the Valley of Slavery, Suffering and Death — there, that Valley there beneath us hidden by that drifting mist. Ah, what sights and sounds and pain lie beneath that mist. And we had thought that our hard climb out of that cruel valley led to some cool, green and peaceful, sunlit place — but it's all jungle here, a wild and savage wilderness that's overrun with ruins.
>
> But put on your crown, my Queen, and we will build a New City on these ruins.

The passage is not addressed to me, and though I have called it beautiful and impressive and so on, that is out of the habit of the judge-critic, and I don't wish to continue in this strange and very contemporary form of injustice, that of sanctioning Negro thought from the standpoint of white criteria. I will go on judging and elucidating novels and plays and poetry by Negroes according to what general powers I possess, but the kind of *Negro writing* I have been talking about, the act of creation of the self in the face of that self's historic denial by our society, seems to me to be at this point beyond my right to intrude on.

The following was written in response to letters which Gilman received after the publication of "White Standards and Negro Writing."

THE MAIL ELICITED by my review several weeks ago of Eldridge Cleaver's *Soul on Ice* has been heavy enough for me to feel justified in going back to it. The letters were about evenly divided for and against, but the negative ones all made a criticism which I think it's important to deal with. The whole issue of Negro writing and white criticism is enormously significant, in its own right and for what it may tell us about some changing conditions of writing, thought and imagination.

I wrote that I knew I was likely to be misunderstood, for I was presenting a quite radical and potentially unsettling idea: that white critics have not the right to make judgments on a certain kind of Negro writing, which I was careful to distinguish from what might be called "writing by Negroes," in the same way that Southern or Jewish writing may be distinguished from writing by Southerners or Jews. In refusing to pass judgment on certain essays and personal statements by Cleaver, a former prisoner and current Black Power spokesman, I argued that his writing, like *The Autobiography of Malcolm X*, was not intended for me but was an act of creation and definition of the self on the part of a Negro who, as a measure of the wound and dissociation in our society, was estranged from me and other whites, had some new and different values and impulses and lived now across an abyss not bridgeable by simple good-will or by independent, "disinterested" intellectual criteria.

The misunderstanding on the part of my critics was, just as I had feared, almost complete, and took the form in nearly every case of the accusation that I had "subverted the very notion of criticism" itself. This phrase is from a letter by the sociologist Lewis Coser of Brandeis University, who went on to say that by the "standards" I had set up I "could not assess the writings say, of Jean Genet," since I am "presumably neither a thief nor a homosexual," and that I "could scarcely write about Doris Lessing's *The Golden Notebook*," since I "am not a woman and hence [don't] know what it means to menstruate."

The first thing I want to say to Dr. Coser, whom I will regard as my representative critic, is that, as he riskily assumed, I *am* a non-larcenous male heterosexual and as such am shut out in certain essential ways from Genet's universe of crime and homosexuality (as from his Frenchness, his status as a famous writer, his being 58 years old, and so on) and from Miss Lessing's life as a woman. We are all excluded from one another in ways like these, and criticism (of any kind) has never depended on our not being so. There are several crucial points to make in regard to all this, and I am grateful to Professor Coser for so handsomely setting up the opportunity for me to attempt them.

To begin with, both Genet and Miss Lessing are imaginative writers who produce *fictions,* however autobiographical these may appear, works of literary art whose governing impulses are aesthetic, not psychological or sociological or political. Like other writers, they may and do put to use what they know themselves to be — criminal or invert or woman — but this, if they are true artists, will emerge as data, constituent, ground or presence, never as "subject." When I enter the world of their fictions I encounter these psychological or social or biological materials, and it is precisely through the work's function as art that I am enabled to overcome much prior separation, to slip past, as though by a ruse, the barriers of exclusion that make up an existential fact.

But I have not overcome physical or ontological separation. For this world of fiction, Genet's, Miss Lessing's or any other writer's, is merely (miraculous understatement) a *possible* world, an artifice, a creation, not a report on an actual state of affairs, not the *truth,* and judgment therefore rests on how successfully the writer has established this possibility, what authority his vision has. I am put by this authority in the presence of the writer's imagination, and it is this movement, a matter of analogical process, by which I draw closer and escape exclusion, at the same time as I am left with no more knowledge in the cognitive sense than I had before.

If Genet's or Miss Lessing's writing works for me as literature, it isn't because I now know more about homosexuality or what it's like to be a woman. Actually, I now know less, in a strange, merciful sense. And this is because I have had my otherwise invincible structure of inevitably and inherently wrong ideas about homosexuality or womanness (inevitably wrong precisely because I am not these other persons and my ideas are a means of *warding off* their differences) replaced by the only form of knowledge that truly breaks down barriers, the knowledge of another person's imagination as it refashions the materials of the world in a work of art. This is what we really mean by communication, and when it is happening it hits against the stupid pride we have in our ostensible knowledge of the world, to which art is forever restoring the strangeness and unexpectedness that the habit of life is always destroying.

Judgment doesn't then, rest on how accurately the writer has described or "captured" (a favorite word of utility-minded and predatory critics) the milieu, or lineaments or significance of the particular condition; in some final and decisive sense literary works have nothing to do, *as literature*, with the particularities of their instigation, with the places where writers start. Thus Proust's fiction leaves homosexual love behind, Faulkner's leaves the South, Conrad's the sea, Joyce's Dublin and Hemingway's virility or honor — to reveal these scenes or subjects as pretexts. For what is being sought is a fiction, an increment to the known world, and a corrective to it.

Now Genet and Miss Lessing may indeed be evaluated by homosexuals or thieves or women, but the latter would not be functioning as literary critics (or even as proper readers) if they were to address themselves to the pretexts, to praise or damn, say, *The Miracle of the Rose* or *The Golden Notebook* on sexual or moral or feminist grounds. (It goes without saying that we have plenty of purported literary critics who do just this kind of thing, without even the justification — on that level — of claiming kinship with a writer in one or another condition of specific being.) And by the same token, deprivation of homosexual or female being is no disqualification when I come to judge, to respond to, Genet's or Miss Lessing's work any more than my not being French or English is, although being American may of course make me lose some nuances and subtleties.

But *not being a Negro is*, I argued in my Cleaver review, just such a disqualification when it is a matter of judging a kind of writing in which one's condition is not a pretext, not the raw material for art, but the very subject of the work, and when the work, furthermore, has been instituted as a reply, a counterstatement to those ideas of universal value which we (whites) of the West have for so long been propagating and into which, for all their radical inversions, Genet's writings easily fit.

Cleaver's book seemed to me to fall into that category of new objects, books written with obvious and inescapable debts to

Western literacy, to the prevailing and, for anyone in the West, only traditions of organizing thought and experience, but also with an almost wholly new morale and subversive intention — to propound new values and new myths for Negroes, in the face of white monopoly of values and myths. Such books are Malcolm X's autobiography and Frantz Fanon's *The Wretched of the Earth*.

Writing about the colonial world in his introduction to Fanon's book, Jean-Paul Sartre describes a change of consciousness and attitude on the part of black Africans which was the fore-runner of what has lately been happening here:

> A new generation came on the scene. . . . With unbelievable patience, its writers and poets tried to explain to us that our values and the true facts of their lives did not hang together, and that they could neither reject them completely nor assimilate them. By and large, what they were saying was this: 'You are making us into monstrosities; your humanism claims we are at one with the rest of humanity, but your racist methods set us apart'.

Fanon is even more explicit about the sundering that has taken place between white and black consciousness and ways of looking at the world:

> The colonialist bourgeoisie, in its narcissistic dialogue, expounded by the members of its universities, had in fact deeply implanted in the minds of the colonized intellectuals that the essential qualities remain eternal, in spite of all the blunders men may make: the essential qualities of the West, of course. The native intellectual accepted the cogency of these ideas, and deep down in his brain you could always find a vigilant sentinel ready to defend the Graeco-Roman pedestal. Now it so happens that during the struggle for liberation, at the moment that the native intellectual comes into touch again with his people, this artificial sentinel is turned into dust. All the Mediterranean values — the triumph of the human individual, of clarity and of beauty — become lifeless, colorless knicknacks. All those speeches seem like collections of dead words; those values which seemed to uplift the soul are revealed as

worthless, simply because they have nothing to do with the concrete conflict in which the people is engaged.

In my original essay I argued for a suspension of judgment — more specifically a moratorium on the public act of judgment — in the light of the phenomena Fanon was talking about. And Fanon, who wrote about societies which were literally colonial or had just recently been, so that the colonial mentality was still strong, is extraordinarily relevant. In far more than a metaphorical sense American Negroes are a "colonial" people (it is the coherence they find with their own experience that make Fanon's reflections on Africa so useful and inspiriting a book to the leader of the black revolution here), and we whites who subscribe to all those Mediterranean values which have become so nearly empty but which we continue to offer all underdogs as though they were immediately convertible into food or housing, or into automatic self-respect, we whites who go on making empty gestures are, vis-à-vis the Negroes, the ruling class, the imperialists.

This is why our vocabularies of rational discourse are so different now from Black Americans (when a subject people finds its voice at last, it has to be different from the masters'). This is why certain books by Negroes seem written in a new language and are not therefore for us, why the fact that they are not for us is so threatening to our historical belief in the universality of ideas and values. In all the letters I received from white readers there was evident an anxiety, which mostly expressed itself as anger, over the threat I had posed, or revealed, to tradition, to the ways in which judgments have always been made and so to the very principle of judgment, or criticism, as that which allows us to distinguish for the militant purposes of our culture among the multifarious phenomena that minds and imaginations are constantly throwing up. Beneath the statements about my abandonment of critical procedure, my surrender to . . . what? pressure? guilt? . . . there seemed to me to exist a strong and menaced belief in the powers of critical method, that analytic sword which the West has so actively brandished, for keeping us from chaos and disaster.

It is a faith I share. If I didn't share it, I wouldn't have taken the risk of seeming to support an anti-intellectual position in order to turn such powers as I possess to the analysis of a situation broader than the problems of style and statement in a particular book. But my belief in the power and necessity of criticism is tempered by my awareness of the constant danger of what Kierkegaard called the "deadlock" which can result from a persistence in the habits of reflection and criticism, which try to turn the world into manageable and categorical realities. The deadlock is reached when the critical mind insists so vehemently on the primacy of its activity that it ends by "transforming the capacity for action into a means of escape from action."

This is what I think is happening, and will go on happening to our deeper injury, as long as we refuse to recognize that we can no longer talk to Negroes, or Negroes to us, in the traditional humanistic ways. The old Mediterranean values — the belief in the sanctity of the individual soul, the importance of logical clarity, brotherhood, reason as arbiter, political order, community — are dead as *useful* frames of reference or pertinent guides to procedure; they are even making some of us sick with a sense of lacerating irony.

To look at each other now in this country, black and white, across a gulf of separate speeches, gestures, intentions, hopes, is more *reasonable* than to go on insisting that Negroes or any other group have got to be enrolled under the ancient Western humanist flags, so that progress can be guaranteed and chaos averted. Fanon writes:

> The natives' challenge to the colonial world is not a rational confrontation of points of view. It is not a treatise on the universal, but the untidy affirmation of an original idea propounded as an absolute.

When an idea is made into an absolute, we may see it is being fashioned into a myth. The new myths (of which Fanon's own books which among other things document and describe the process of myth-making, are themselves examples) may share in Western, white literary and intellectual procedures, but are not subject to being brought into the critical arena and there dispatched or pardoned. Such themes or myths as Black Power, Negro sexual superiority, white decadence, Negro eschatology, the white man as devil, the inheritance of the earth not by the meek but by the outraged, have no basis, in *the concrete reality* that faces us, for being analyzed, criticized, turned into abstract, sound or unsound theory. They are "untidy affirmations," and they are to be encountered by us, in all the mysterious and frightening ways this has to happen, without recourse to the mouldering Western arsenal of brilliant clarifying intellectual weapons from which we have always felt ourselves supplied.

The rejoinder may be made that what I have been saying adds up to something very near that kind of fanatically Marxist (or any other type of rigidly sectarian) approach to events by which truth is defined as that which serves the cause. But I am not asking us to subvert truth in this way. I am saying that I don't know what truth for Negroes is, that I don't wish any longer to presume to know, that I am willing to stand back and listen, *without comment*, to these new and self-justifying voices. And I am also saying that something has happened to our means of gaining access to human truth, of which the Black Revolution is only one sign and factor, that demands of us an unprecedented effort to get past the deadlock, in order for reflection and thought to become again a springboard for action and not an occlusion.

Our Mutual Estate: The Literature of the American Negro

by Theodore L. Gross

Grant me that I am human, that I hurt
That I can cry.
Not that I now ask alms, in shame gone hollow.
Nor cringe outside the loud and sumptuous gate.
Admit me to our mutual estate.

—*Gwendolyn Brooks*

"WHAT HAS CAST a shadow upon you?" Captain Delano asks Benito Cereno in Melville's story and the Spaniard, finally freed from the domination of his former slaves, feebly answers, "The Negro." In the years since the publication of *Benito Cereno* (1853), the shadow of the Negro has lengthened so as to touch the people of America in every aspect of their lives. Wherever Americans meet, the subject is race, and, one suspects, not only because of the unsettling practical problems aroused by the subject but because it threatens the very preconceptions that Americans have about their own morality. And insofar as the subject of race provokes questions of morality, it finds its clearest definition in the current literature concerning American Negroes and in the writing of American Negroes themselves. Unlike the insurgent slaves in Melville's story, Negroes are fluent, and their fluency, as translated into literature, has resulted in an extraordinary moral indictment of America.

Until recently, the literary image of the Negro was determined by white authors; and that image was largely comic. Writers rarely conceived of the Negro as a person and thus could not inform him with anything resembling a tragic sensibility: the mask of laughter was no different from the face of the man. So long as the Negro was not human, so long as his suffering was unexplored, the Negro did not threaten assumptions about his humanity; even writers like Twain and Faulkner could not escape the burden of inherited stereotypes. When the Negro himself began to write fiction and poetry, he did not challenge the images that had been created by white authors — for economic as well as social reasons. White editors would not have accepted his work if it had seriously modified that benevolent, condescending concept of the Negro that dominated nineteenth-century Southern literature. The Negro author turned to the forms of the slave narrative and autobiography, accepting *a priori* the myths and shibboleths of the white world and recording his achievement in traditional American terms. *Up From Slavery* (1900), *Finding a Way Out* (1920), *Out of the House of Bondage* (1914), *In Spite of Handicap* (1916), *Bursting Bonds* (1923) are typical titles of autobiographies by Negroes who take pride in their ability to adapt to the criteria of white Americans. Isolated autobiographies and works of social criticism — most notably Frederick Douglass' *My Bondage and My Freedom* (1855) and W. E. B. DuBois' *The Souls of Black Folk* (1903) — did censure racial injustice, but not until the Negro Awakening of the 1920s were the intrinsically original features of Negro literature clearly evident; and it was not until the work of Langston Hughes and Richard Wright that "the souls of black folk" became a significant subject of poetry and fiction.

Since Wright's death in 1960, Negro writing has flourished and Negro studies now may occupy a significant position in the curricula of major universities; the history of Negro cultural life in America is finally undergoing serious definition and revaluation. But before any sensible account can be given of so broad a subject, some remarks about the historical condition of Negro culture and the present state of Negro scholarship and creativity need to be made. The confusion that attends the political discussion of race is not absent when serious critics speak of Negro literature. Just as the morality of Americans is threatened by the very subject of Negro life in America so the aesthetic standards of critics are often confused — even morally confused — when these critics consider the literature of the American Negro.

Negro culture in America has never been seriously measured by reputable white scholars. Materials have not been widely available, for the scholars have not created a sympathetic audience that might demand the books of American Negroes. The entire field of black culture in America is parochial and chauvinistic and disorganized. Bibliographies are scarce, and those that do exist are unreliable; libraries contain only a few of the most popular books, and those libraries that have extensive collections are few in number; magazines about Negro culture cater to a Negro audience, with the attendant provinciality that arises when people praise one another; and those who work in this field, with rare exceptions, have not been professionally trained in our best universities. Before the appearance of the anthology *The Negro Caravan* in 1941, the Negro's contribution to American culture had not been presented in any formal sense, and it is significant that anyone interested in Negro literature written before 1940 must still use *The Negro Caravan* as a kind of source book. No volume of comparable magnitude and seriousness has been published in the past twenty-eight years.

Those scholars who have historically attempted to give order to the field of Negro studies — W. E. B. DuBois, James Weldon Johnson, Alain Locke, and Sterling Brown — have been Negro social leaders, and in their desire to preserve the artifacts of a cultural past they have often acted as benevolent censors of their creative contemporaries. DuBois, who was a scrupulous social scientist and was certainly aware of realistic literature, lamented that Negro writers of the 1920s only emphasized the underworld of black experience; Sterling Brown, one of the three editors of *The Negro Caravan*, suggested that "the drama of the workaday life, the struggles, the conflicts [were] missing in much of the Renaissance literature." Part of the intent of this criticism, however justified it might have been, was to make the Negro artist more conscious of his social responsibilities as well as an artist who should write simply in response to his own interior needs.

These social leaders were not successful in restraining Negro writers in the twenties and thirties, but it scarcely mattered — the writers, as they began to assume public importance, restrained themselves. The inevitable conflict between the scholar and the creative artist, between the cultural spokesman and the writer who asserts his independence, never achieved any great intensity in Negro culture. The Negro could not assume the role of the rebellious artist, for both he and the scholar sought to conserve their desire to root out the forces that intended to repress the development of their culture. They wrote, as John A. Davis has suggested, for a non-Negro market that was often the object of their protest. This union of scholar and artist seems like a rather unholy alliance in America, where the professional scholar and the professional writer have usually assumed antagonistic roles; but the Negro intellectual has not made the customary and invidious distinctions between scholarship and creativity. DuBois, Johnson, and Brown were poets, novelists, essayists, teachers, social leaders, and scholars: renaissance men in a time when the concept had ceased to have vitality.

Like many artists, Negro writers have tried to free themselves of social commitment, but the burden of creating a solid culture with which they could identify has restricted them. Langston Hughes, for example, began his career in the early twenties by announcing his liberation from all social strictures: "We younger Negro artists who create now intend to express our individual dark-skinned selves without fear or shame." But Hughes, after an extraordinarily varied career, became in his later years a kind of curator of Negro culture, editing and writing more than a dozen books on Negro life and art — on jazz and folklore, on Negro heroes, on the Negro in America and the West Indies and Africa, on the NAACP, on Negro poetry, and the Negro short story. Hughes was particularly responsive to the needs of his race, but a similar self-consciousness informs the activities and work of Richard Wright, Ralph Ellison, James Baldwin, and lesser authors. Wright turned into an unofficial ambassador for Negro affairs when he lived in Paris. Ellison has become increasingly affirmative in his recent interviews and essays, avoiding the bleaker aspects of Negro life and stressing diversity and optimism and idealism. Baldwin has grown to sympathize so greatly with the black power movement that the characters of his recent fiction are often caricatures of bitterness and love; and the tone of his essays and public proclamations has taken a stridency that he once censured in the work of Richard Wright.

The desire to preserve the finest aspects of Negro culture has led to a racial chauvinism that is understandable in political or social terms but that can have so insidious an influence on literary standards that the value of the culture itself can be distorted. This distortion is not only the responsibility of Negro scholars who have exaggerated the literary merits of various Negro writers; it is also the fault of those white critics who, writing from a liberal and at times sentimental point of view, see masterpieces where none exist at all. Much of this criticism is of little intrinsic significance, and one need not document its unimpressive record; but the dangers can be most clearly measured, the case put most forcefully, by noting the reactions of several sophisticated white critics to the work of an important Negro author, Richard Wright.

Robert Bone has written one of the basic modern studies of fiction by American Negroes, *The Negro Novel in America* (1958). Bone usually brings to his subject the thoroughness of a disciplined scholar, but in attempting to create a meaningful tradition of the Negro novel, he is occasionally not accurate — Jean Toomer's *Cane*, for example, is not "an important American novel" but a collection of stories and poems, and there is no reason to devote an impassioned section to it — and his criticism tends too often to be hyperbolic. Wright's *Native Son*, in Bone's view, is "a modern epic, consisting of action on the grand scale." Bone admits that "Book III, and therefore the novel [*Native Son*], suffers from a major structural flaw, flowing from the fact that Wright has failed to digest Communism artistically"; but he still offers an elaborate defense of the novel as a work of art, characterizing "the symbolic texture of *Native Son*" as "exceptionally rich" and ranking the book as "major," on a level with Toomer's *Cane*, Ellison's *Invisible Man*, and Baldwin's *Go Tell It on the Mountain*.

Constance Webb, who has recently published a biography of Richard Wright, unintentionally warns the reader of her critical standards by introducing Wright as "a genius, a skilled, dedicated, meticulous craftsman, an example of the very best that America can produce." She then proceeds to write a lengthy memoir in which she scarcely suggests the limitations of Wright as an author or a thinker. Having had access to Wright's materials, having had the co-operation of Wright's widow and many of Wright's friends, Miss Webb had the opportunity to create an important biography, but she mixes fact with nostalgia, and the result is a sympathetic account that resembles those affectionate nineteenth-century memoirs written by the author's loyal son or son-in-law, wife, or daughter, or niece.

Irving Howe, a critic who has exhibited catholicity of taste and has demanded high standards in judging French, Russian, English, and American literature, seems to modify those standards when he considers the work of Richard Wright. In an essay that deals with Wright, Baldwin, and Ellison — "Black Boys and Native Sons" — Howe stresses the truth of the Negro's experiences that one finds in *Native Son,* "the hatred, fear, and violence that have crippled and may yet destroy our culture." Howe is too intelligent a critic not to recognize the many weaknesses of *Native Son* as well as of Wright's other work, but his great sympathy for the Negro's social protest conditions the criteria of his criticism:

> And when we come to a writer like Richard Wright, who deals with the most degraded and inarticulate sector of the Negro world, the distinction between objective rendering and subjective immersion becomes still more difficult, perhaps even impossible. For a novelist who has lived through the searing experiences that Wright has there cannot be much possibility of approaching his subject with the 'mature' poise recommended by high-minded critics.

Perhaps so; but then Wright's "experiences" are not necessarily more "searing" than those of Kafka or Hemingway or a dozen other twentieth-century novelists whose " 'mature' poise" is in fact one of the distinguishing characteristics of their art. As Ralph Ellison, in an effective rebuttal to Howe's essay, points out: "How much, by the way, do we know of Sophocles' wounds?"

This is not the place for an extensive appraisal of Richard Wright's critics or of Wright's works, and I note these estimates only because they suggest the distortion of standards that so easily accompanies the criticism of Negro literature in America. Richard Wright is an interesting author and the story of his life, although crudely recorded in *Black Boy,* has undeniable authority and authenticity; but when judged by anything like the standards applied to other writers of his time, who deal with similar subjects, Wright is a mediocre novelist, and mediocre in a fundamental sense: he does not inform his experiences with a meaning deeper than their representational value. The liberal critic may give the facts of Wright's life significance beyond their mundane actuality, but it is important to remember that Wright does not do so. James Baldwin sensed the limitations of Wright's work in the criticism of *Native Son* that appears in "Everybody's Protest Novel" and "Many Thousands Gone," two of Baldwin's early essays, but the younger writer found the limitations to be those inherent in the protest novel itself, whereas the limitations are really those of Wright the novelist. Baldwin's final estimate of Wright, in the three essays that appear in *Nobody Knows My Name,* is some of the best criticism of Wright's work yet published, but Baldwin himself becomes so entangled in the personality of the author whose "work was an immense liberation and revelation for" him, that he surrenders his critical distance and writes a private commentary, at times almost a private meditation, upon Wright's character.

In these guarded approaches to a significant and influential Negro writer lies the great danger of the parochialism that has traditionally burdened the criticism of American literature. Anyone who has completed a doctoral dissertation in this country knows how easy it is to make his subsequent writing into one long footnote. Learned societies, specialized journals, newsletters, and the academic establishment in general encourage narrow research in which scholars are often jealous of their individual rights to an author or a subject. Now that Negro culture is ready for the graduate schools — for codification and documentation, for analysis and evaluation — the danger of parochialism looms large, whether it takes the form of excessive sympathy for an author or simply incompetent scholarly appraisal. Behind the assimilation of Negro writing into American literature at large broods a question that will recur and that lies at the center of all other questions that must be answered: "Who is qualified to understand, to interpret, and to judge Negro writing in America?"

"Not I," argues Richard Gilman in "White Standards and Negro Writing," an essay that appeared in *The New Republic* (March 9, 1968). Speaking of *The Autobiography of Malcolm X,* Gilman notes it

> was not written for us. It was written for Negroes: it is not talking about the human condition (that Western idea which from the battle line looks like a luxury product) but about the condition of Negroes; it was not, moreover, any-

thing less — although it was other things as well — than a myth for Negroes to live by now, as we have our myths of so many kinds.

Speaking of Eldridge Cleaver's *Soul on Ice,* another kind of autobiographical memoir by a Negro, Gilman claims that Cleaver

> is not a social critic for *our* sake: his is a Negro perspective, sight issuing from the 'furious psychic stance of the Negro today,' and in its victories of understanding, its blindnesses and incompletions, its clean or inchoate energies, its internal motives and justifications, his writing remains in some profound sense not subject to correction or emendation or, most centrally, approval or rejection by those of us who are not black. . . . I will go on judging and elucidating novels and plays and poetry by Negroes according to what general powers I possess, but the kind of *Negro writing* I have been talking about, the act of creation of the self in the face of that self's historic denial by our society, seems to me to be at this point beyond my right to intrude on.

This argument is worth considering, for it seems to offer persuasive reasons for the parochialism I have lamented. Every important American Negro writer, including Malcolm X and Eldridge Cleaver, has been intellectually shaped by a white western tradition. Across all that he has learned — the words, the techniques, the ways of looking at character — falls his own experience; and the friction of mind and fact creates the special tensions of Negro art — as indeed it creates the friction of all art. So long as he builds his experiences upon a white western intellectual tradition, the Negro author speaks to whites — intellectually; and he speaks to Negroes — intellectually and empirically.

"In the face of one's victim, one sees oneself," runs the famous line from Baldwin's "Fifth Avenue, Uptown"; and, we might add, in the literature of one's victim, one sees a singular dimension of one's character. If the word "sees" has anything to do with perception any more, it surely implies the ability to evaluate experiences that are not one's own. When a critic can say that an autobiography like Malcolm X's "is not talking about the human condition . . . but about the condition of Negroes," then he encourages parochial literary standards that are clearly dangerous — any author who speaks of the condition of Negroes is of course speaking of the human condition. When one maintains that the writing of an American Negro is not subject to "approval or rejection by those of us who are not black," one has come to a strange pass in the history of literary criticism. No one seems to question the human credentials of a twentieth-century urbanized American graduate when he evaluates some medieval tract in which the language is different, the country and time are strange, the religion of the author may be alien; if a leap of the imagination is possible for that student, then surely a similar student, with similar motivation, ought to be able to look at black people of his own time, speaking his own language, in his own country, and measure their literary achievement.

This argument needs to be put in the strongest possible terms, for if ever literature and literary criticism had relevance to one's life, it is now; if ever an aspect of American life could be better known through its literature, it is the life of the Negro. One can even say, as one rarely can these days, that literary criticism may help to change the spirit of our time. In these tense moments of American history, few people — black or white — are capable of speaking rationally about race; reactions toward the subject are usually radical, wild, or, to use the really accurate term, uneducated. Somehow, the mind must triumph, or all Americans will perish; somehow literature has to tell white Americans about lives they do not know and as a consequence make those lives less threatening, less distant, more humanly complex. The chaotic state of Negro studies, the absence of white scholars in the field of Negro culture, the inaccessibility of important materials all suggest how little is known of black people in this country. This would seem to be precisely the time when the writing of Negroes should not be judged only by Negroes.

The work that must be done in the study of Negro culture would make the subject of another and much longer essay. I can only offer some general observations and hint at directions that scholars might take.

There are, to begin with, certain obvious needs: a society for the study of Negro literature that will apprise interested scholars of the work accomplished in this growing field; a library of Negro classics, most of which are now unavailable, carefully edited by competent scholars; annotated bibliographies that will direct students to the proper sources.

Specific tasks immediately suggest themselves to anyone who has studied Negro culture: the editing of letters by authors like Richard Wright, Countee Cullen, and Claude McKay; the publication of memoirs by such writers as Claude McKay and Richard Wright; the editing of uncollected, superb stories by Rudolph Fisher, Jean Toomer, Eric Walrond, Ralph Ellison, and many others; reliable biographies of almost every Negro writer in American literature; critical appraisals of slave narratives, of the Negro Renaissance, of Negro literature in the 1930s, and of the expatriation of American Negroes.

These projects — and the list could easily be extended — should signify how little has thus far been accomplished in this field. Most libraries scarcely represent Negro literature to the general public; but there are great repositories of black culture in some key libraries throughout the country that have not yet been studied or widely publicized. Howard University, for example, has more than 30,000 items, including the valuable Springarn Collection. The Arthur Schomburg branch of the New York Public Library has more than 11,000 books, 3,000 manuscripts, and 2,000 prints as well as many folders containing primary materials that have not yet been published. Yale University houses the James Weldon Johnson Memorial Collection of Negro Arts and Letters, which contains a large number of items, left by Carl Van Vechten, that are indispensible to an understanding of the Negro Renaissance. Atlanta University, The Boston Public Library, Columbia University, Fisk University — these and other institutions have materials hardly touched by professional students of literature. When the primary sources of Negro literature are examined, evaluated, and recognized finally as one of the main currents of American thought, large aspects of our cultural history may well have to be rewritten. The study of Negro culture is at a moment historically comparable to the study of American literature in the 1920s: a vast and varied literature awaits the consideration of American scholars and ultimately of American readers. We need to give the writing of American Negroes the kind of professional attention it deserves and challenge many of the shibboleths and pieties of our cultural history.

We. Americans. Black and white. Perhaps by studying the documents of the past, scholars will help to influence the future. In our time, there has been an increasing demand for courses concerning Negro culture in America: in the colleges and the high schools, in states across the country. But in this scientific age, when scholarly organizations sponsor the definitive editions of American authors, major and minor, we do not even have available the original texts of Negro authors, not to speak of all the scholarly apparatus one would normally expect to find. The courses in colleges and high school await the books that will give definition to the development of Negro literature in America. One cannot teach without a text of some sort; and in a field so little known by even sophisticated scholars, the text assumes an importance that cannot be overestimated. The pressures to respond immediately to social necessity are indeed great, so great that we must guard against them and not manufacture books that are as ephemeral as the passions that provoke their publication. Already publishers are planning instant biographies and instant texts, ready for fast delivery in the next fall semester.

No. We cannot afford to let the study of Negro literature be absorbed into the commerce of academic life, lost among all the anthologies that are bought in September and sold in January. By maintaining the highest criteria in judging Negro writing, one honors the Negro's culture; by giving the literature of American Negroes the widest possible circulation, in the most authoritative format, scholars justify their profession and permit the humanities and human life to touch, to affect one another. Like the "artist in the city of Kouroo," whose story Thoreau recreates so poignantly in *Walden,* scholar and artist can help to make "a world with full and fair proportions." The material is there; readers wait to know it. How can "the result be other than wonderful?"

The Black View

Problems of
the Negro Writer*

I. THE BREAD AND BUTTER SIDE

by Langston Hughes

THE NEGRO WRITER in America has all the problems any other writer has, plus a few more.

I have been writing books for more than thirty years and have had the good fortune to be published by some of our major houses. During that time it has been my observation that publishers will bring out almost any book they believe is salable regardless of the face of the author. They will frequently even bring out a book they simply consider good. I doubt that a book by Willard Motley or Frank Yerby or James Baldwin would be turned down on account of the author's color. But if James Baldwin wrote six books a year and all six were about the Negro problem, I think perhaps some of them would be rejected [1] on the grounds of subject matter.

Just as a firm with two Japanese novels on their list might not wish to publish another in the same season, so prolific Negro authors who write exclusively about Negroes may find their acceptance limited. Shortly after his wonderful Negro story, "Health Card," in *Harper's* two decades ago, Frank Yerby decided he did not wish to be limited by racial subject matter. He extended his

---

*First published in 1963.

range. Result: a best-selling novel almost every year since then, plus numerous movie sales. However, until recently, novels by and about Negroes had almost no takers in Hollywood — a factor that helped to make publishers chary of such works unless they were sensational or of unusual quality.

Until 1962 there were no major publishers appealing directly to a Negro reading public. The Johnson Publishing Company, owners of *Ebony* and *Jet*, have now set up a branch specializing in books by and about colored people. The titles on their first list are selling well, so that house would not turn down a good Negro book just because it already has a couple in its catalogue this season. Johnson knows how to reach the Negro market; through their widely selling magazines, the company has the necessary publicity and promotional facilities. White publishers, as a rule, do not have the same know-how and have not much cared. But bias is not involved.

Where prejudice operates most blatantly against the Negro author is in the areas peripheral to writing: Hollywood, radio and television, editorial staff positions, and lecturing. Take lecturing, a lucrative field for famous (or even fairly well-known) white writers. Because many women's clubs and forums booking lecturers have teas or receptions following the programs, nine times out of ten, Negro speakers are not invited. Teas are social events: Negroes are not wanted, not even as star names. Many college lyceum programs, too, are booked by not very broad-minded officials. Not only in the South, but in the West and Midwest as well, there are campuses that have never yet had a Negro novelist or poet as a speaker.

For a long time not a single major publishing house in the United States had on its staff any Negroes except occasional clerical workers. It is only in these ever more democratic days since the Second World War that even clerical help has been employed. But now in a few publishing houses in New York there is a handful of Negroes working in capacities above the level of ordinary office routine. In radio and television, however, there are so few Negroes who are not janitors that one hand might have enough fingers to count them. When an author of color sells a novel to Hollywood, if ever he does, he is seldom called to California to work on the script. Almost all well-paying jobs in the mass media are still reserved for whites, no matter how celebrated the Negro author may be.

Everybody knows it is hard to make a living from books alone. Most Negro writers have been teachers. That is as near to a position related to writing as they can get. But a white writer with only an unprofitable first novel to his credit can usually get a fairly high-salaried job in publishing, radio, or TV without half trying. Thus he can make enough money in a little while to compose his next novel. Most Negro writers have to create at night after correcting a hundred student papers.

Added to job difficulties, the Negro writer, of course, suffers from all the other prejudices color is heir to in our USA, depending on what part of the country he lives in or travels. In New York, a Negro going to a downtown cocktail party given for a white fellow-writer may be told by the apartment house doorman, no matter how well dressed the guest may be, "The servants' entrance is around the corner." Such occurrences seem incredible in Manhattan today, but they are not. In the South, on the other hand, nothing boorish is incredible.

Once on a lecture tour I had hardly crossed the Potomac into Virginia when I stopped my car to buy some sandwiches and Coca-Colas. I knew I, a Negro, could not eat sandwiches inside the little roadside lunch stand where I had parked, but I thought I could at least enter and buy some to take out to the car. When I went to open the screen door, a man held it shut. "We have a hole cut for you folks around on the side," he said through the screen. Out of curiosity, I went around to the side of the wooden building. Sure enough; there was a square hole cut there with a sign over it: COLORED. But this is a dissertation on the problems of Negro writers, not of Negroes in general. Writers do have a few little special problems. Negroes however, have a great many more that are too omnipresent to be special.

2. THE LITERARY GHETTO

by JOHN A. WILLIAMS

ALMOST WITHOUT FAIL, a novel written by a Negro is said to be one of anger, hatred, rage, or protest. Sometimes modifiers are used: "beautiful" anger, "black" hatred, "painful" rage, "exquisite" protest. These little tickets deprive that novel of any ability it may have to voice its concern for all humankind, not only Negroes. After the labeling, and sometimes with it, comes the grouping, the lumping together of reviews of books by Negro authors. *Sissie,* my new novel was officially published March 26; it has had four reviews like this already, three with James Baldwin's *The Fire Next Time* and one with John Killens's *And Then We Heard the Thunder.* I was hard pressed to discover who was being reviewed —Baldwin, Killens, or me. I had the same difficulty when I encountered reviews written only about *Sissie,* but whose leads almost invariably began with some reference to Baldwin. [EDITOR'S NOTE: See *SR,* March 30, 1963]

Negro writers are nearly always compared to one another, rather than to white writers. This, like labeling and grouping, tends to limit severely the expansion of the talents of Negro writers and confine them to a literary ghetto from which only one Negro name at a time may emerge. Today it is unmistakably James Baldwin; no Negro writing in America today can escape his shadow. He replaced Richard Wright, who, in turn, may have replaced Langston Hughes.

Editors, too, have been guilty of labeling, comparing, and grouping. "Negro stuff is selling well" I heard an editor say. So publishers have hastened to sign up Negro writers, whose best qualification, often enough, was that they were Negro. Publishing has had its homosexual phase, which dies hard; its gray flannel-advertising phase, its war phase, its Jewish phase. It is now in the Negro phase. To illustrate shifting trends, six years ago an editor whose house is now the hottest because of its Negro talent, said, in essence, in a note to my agent (which was passed on to me — a sign of how grim the business of selling "Negro" books was) that it would be wiser if I were to set aside the obvious personal experiences of being Negro. Financially at least, the change in his point of view has been good for him.

The current trend towards more publishing of books by Negro authors, brought about by national considerations has been beneficial to black writers. Nevertheless, much comparison of their work still exists in the editorial offices. This comes from my files; it is part of a report, dated seven years ago, on a book that I have since published elsewhere: "Mr. Williams is in the vein of Chester Himes, and to my mind achieves a similar power."

Excluding riding the trend, the other attitudes — labeling, grouping, and comparing — provide the biggest block to the expansion by Negro writers of themes and techniques (cared for so little by reviewers today). Perhaps that is the reason for the existence of these attitudes. They are automatic and no one thinks about them much except Negro writers. Either consciously or unconsciously, this kind of bigotry tells more about the reviewer than it does about the book he's reviewing.

A more specific example: In a recent article a writer discussed James Baldwin with me; we were said to be in midstream and about to drown. In our attitudes, I guess. The man did a thorough job, having researched magazines and brought what I had written in some of them to bear upon his subject, my novel *Night Song*. I was impressed. The white woman in the novel, Della, is a social worker who, after her day at the office, comes to the coffee house owned by her lover to help out. But, in view of the crisp way the writer handled his article, I could only conclude that he saw Della merely as a *waitress* because her lover was Negro.

The relationship between mixed couples is always more graciously accepted by the reviewers when related by a white author than by a Negro. Jack Kerouac's one-dimensional Negro girl and her white lover, John Updike's quiet, fleeting references to the same combination, and Robert Gover's hilarious team of Kitten and James Cartwright Holland are a few examples. But would *One Hundred Dollar Misunderstanding* have been quite so well received had Kitten been a Negro social worker instead of a whore, and the inability of man and woman, black and white, to communicate been put on an altogether different symbolic level?

I wish white writers would stop pretending they just can't reach Negroes; I want Philip Roth's little Negro boy in the Newark Public Library to be real, not a symbol of God only knows what, besides guilt. I want Pete Washington in Dennis Lynds's new novel, *Uptown Downtown,* to stop sitting around with his little Italian Catholic girl bemoaning to the point of being a bore the racial situation in America.

For I can smell the *illusion* of concern as quickly as I can smell a phony, and from the same distance. When you do me, do me *right*. Then some of the barriers to the expansion of America's Negro writing talent may fall.

The Negro Writer:
Pitfalls
and
Compensations*

by William Gardner Smith

THIS IS, AS everyone recognizes by now, a world of relativity. We measure the rights of individuals against the rights of the society; the rights of the artist against the rights of his public; the right of free speech against the right of the individual to protection from slander. Degrees of good and evil are measured against other degrees of good and evil.

This apprehension of infinite relativity is, I think, instructive in considering the position of the Negro writer — I speak particularly of the novelist — in American society. For a moment, disregard the mechanical pros and cons, debits and credits — whether it is easier, or more difficult, for a Negro writer to have his work published; consider the purely esthetic question: What handicaps, and what advantages, does the American writer possess by virtue of being a Negro?

Because the handicaps are better known, and perhaps easier to understand, I will consider them first. The Negro writer is, first of all, invariably bitter. There are degrees of this bitterness,

---

*This article, written in 1950, offers both an intriguing insight into the mood of the black writer at mid-century and a perceptive comment on the situation of the committed artist.

ranging from the anger of Richard Wright and the undercurrent of contempt for the white world in Chester Himes to the cruel satire exhibited by George Schuyler in his semi-classic *Black No More*. A writer is a man of sensitivity; otherwise, he would not be a writer. The sensitivities of the Negro writer react, therefore, more strongly against the ignorance, prejudice and discrimination of American society than do those of the average Negro in America.

There are all forms and varieties of this inevitable strain of bitterness in the Negro writer. Sometimes it results in militancy; sometimes in contempt for race and self; sometimes in hatred for the whole of American society, with blindness for the good things contained therein. It is often hard for the Negro writer to resist polemicizing. He is driven often to write a tract, rather than a work of art. So conscious is he of the pervading evil of race prejudice that he feels duty-bound to assault it at every turn, injecting opinion into alleged narration and inserting his philosophy into the mouths of his characters.

Writing of Negroes, the novelist has difficulty with his characterizations. His people usually become walking, talking propaganda, rather than completely rounded individuals. The Negro writer hesitates, perhaps unconsciously, to temper the goodness of his Negro characters with the dialectical "evil." Fearful of re-inforcing stereotypes in the white reader's mind, he often goes to the other extreme, idealizing his characters, making them flat rather than many-sided. Or, conscious of the pitfalls listed above, and anxious to prove that he is not idealizing his Negro characters, the writer goes to the other extreme — in the name of naturalism — and paints the American Negro as an exaggerated Bigger Thomas, with all the stereotyped characteristics emphasized three times over. To strike a compromise — and, incidentally, the truth — is possibly the most difficult feat for a Negro writer. Proof of this is the fact that I have not read one Negro novel which has truthfully represented the many-sided character of the Negro in American society today. Chester Himes, perhaps, has come closer than any other Negro author to such a representation.

It seems that it is difficult for the Negro writer to add to his weighty diatribes the leaven of humor. Writing is an art; the writer works upon the emotions of his reader. Every sentence, every cadence, every description, every scene, produces an emotional response in this reader. Consciously did Shakespeare lead his audiences through one powerful emotion after another to achieve the final, powerful effect of the death of Desdemona at the hands of Othello; consciously did Marlowe lead to the final descent into hell of Faust. In each of these journeys through dramatic experience there were rises and falls; there were moments of stern conflict and moments of relative relaxation; there were moments of tears and moments of relieving laughter.

Too often, however, in Negro novels do we witness the dull procession of crime after crime against the Negro, without relief in humor or otherwise. These monotonous repetitions of offenses against the Negro serve only to bore the reader in time; and in so doing, they defeat the very purpose of the writer, for they become ineffective. One might even say that the chronicles of offenses constitute truth; however, they do not constitute art. And art is the concern of any novelist.

Novels which last through all time are concerned with universal themes. Dostoievski's great Raskolnikov is all of us in the aftermath of great crime; Tolstoi describes the universal ruling class in time of national crisis. The Negro writer is under tremendous pressure to write about the topical and the transient — the plight of the Negro in American society today. It may be that the greatest of such novels will last because of their historical interest. It may even be that one or two will last because the writer has managed to infuse into his work some universal elements — as Dickens did, even when writing about the social conditions in the England of his day. But most Negro writers do not inject the universal element. They write only about the here and the now. Thus, their novels come and they go: in ten years, they are forgotten.

At this point, let me emphasize that the drive of the Negro writer to write about purely topical themes is of fantastic strength, and difficult for the non-Negro to appreciate. Starving and land-hungry Chinese want food and land: they are not much concerned about such abstractions as the rights of free speech, habeas corpus, the ballot, etc. When day to day problems press upon the individual, they become, in his mind, paramount. This sense of the immediate problem confronts the Negro writer. But it is significant to note that we do not today consider highly that literature which arose in protest against, say, the system of Feudalism, or even, in the United States, slavery.

* * *

But there are compensations for these difficulties confronting the Negro writer. They are great compensations.

Writing is concerned with people, with society and with ethics. Great writing is concerned with the individual in the group or tribe; obedience to or deviation from the laws of that tribe, and the consequences. Usually, by the very process of selection, omission and arrangement of his material, the author implies a judgment — approval or rejection of the laws of the society, be they in legal, ethical or religious form. Basic to such writing, obviously, is some understanding of both the society and the people in it.

To grasp social and individual truth, it is my opinion that the novelist must maintain emotional contact with the basic people of his society. At first glance, this appears a simple thing; but, in reality, it is difficult. Consider the material circumstances of the "successful" writer. He becomes a celebrity. He makes money. Usually, he begins to move in the sphere of people like himself — authors, artists, critics, etc. He purchases a home on Long Island. He no longer uses the subway; for now he has an automobile. He lectures; he speaks at luncheons; he autographs books; he attends cocktail parties; he discusses style, form, and problems of psychology with friends in a rather esoteric circle; and he writes. In a word, he moves, to some degree, into an ivory tower; he becomes, in a fashion, detached from the mainstream of American life.

In times of stability this detachment is often not too harmful: for the moral code remains what it was at the moment of the writer's detachment and, despite its rarification in his new environment, still may serve as the wellspring for vital work. In moments of social crisis, however, the established moral code comes into violent conflict with the desires of the people of society. Thus, immediately prior to the French Revolution, the ethics of Feudalism, though still officially recognized, actually were outdated and in conflict with the democratic tendencies of the people; and thus, today, the individualistic and basically selfish ethic of Capitalism, while still officially proclaimed, is in reality contrary to the socialist tendency which has spread over the world, and even made itself felt in America through Roosevelt's New Deal and Truman's election on a Fair Deal program.

The writer who is detached from society does not perceive this contradiction; and thus is missing from his writing some element of social truth. He is behind the times; he is holding onto a shell. Part of the greatness of Tolstoi is that he perceived the ethical, i.e., social, conflict and accurately recorded it.

The Negro writer cannot achieve — at least, not as easily as the white American writer — this social detachment, however much he might desire it. The very national prejudice he so despises compels him to remember his social roots, perceive the social reality; in a word, compels him to keep his feet on the ground. He cannot register at the Mayflower Hotel. He cannot loll on the Miami beach. He cannot ignore disfranchisement, epithets, educational and employment discrimination, mob violence. He is bound by unbreakable cords to the Negro social group. And so his writing, however poor artistically, must almost invariably contain some elements of social truth.

The Negro writer is endowed by his environment with relative emotional depth. What does a writer write about? We have said: people, and their problems, conflicts, etc. But — what problems, what conflicts? Pick up any popular American magazine or book and you will find out — the problem of whether John D., a thoroughly empty individual, should leave his wife Mary C., a thoroughly empty individual to marry Jane B., a thoroughly empty individual. To this problem are devoted hundreds of pages; hundreds of thousands of words. And in the end the reader of intelligence must ask the question: So what?

Emotional depth, perception of real problems and real conflicts, is extremely rare in American literature — as it is in American society generally. Instead of issues of significance, our fiction (our serious fiction) is overladen with such trite themes as that of Tennessee Williams' *The Roman Spring of Mrs. Stone*. America's is a superficial civilization: it is soda-pop land, the civilization of television sets and silk stockings and murder mysteries and contempt for art and poetry. It is difficult, out of such environment, to bring forth works with the emotional force of, say, *Crime and Punishment*.

Here again the Negro writer's social experience is, despite its bitterness, also an artistic boon. To live continually with prejudice based on the accident of skin color is no superficial experience; and neither is the reaction produced by such constant exposure superficial. There is a depth and intensity to the emotions of Negroes — as demonstrated in "Negro music" — which is largely lacking in white Americans. How often has the Negro maid or housecleaner come home to laugh at her white mistress' great concern about the color of a hat, the shape of a shoe, keeping up with the next-door Joneses? How often have Negroes, on the job, laughed in amazement at the inane trivialities which occupy the thoughts of their white fellow workers. And this laughter is logical. The Europeans would understand it. For, what man or woman who has seen a lynching, or been close to the furnaces of Dachau, or been rebuffed and rejected because of his skin color, can really seriously concern himself with the insipid and shallow love affair between Susie Bell and Jerry?

Thus, the Negro writer, if he does not make the tragic error of trying to imitate his white counterparts, has in his possession the priceless "gift" of thematic intuition. Provided he permits his writing to swell truthfully from his deepest emotional reaches, he will treat problems of real significance, which can strike a cord in the heart of basic humanity. He will be able to convey suffering without romanticizing; he will be able to describe happiness which is not merely on the surface; he will be able to search out and concretize the hopes and ambitions which are the basic stuff of human existence. And he will, in Hemingway's words, be able to do this "without cheating." For the basic fact about humanity in our age is that it suffers; and only he who suffers with it can truthfully convey its aches and pains, and thwarted desires. And now, speaking only of this period in which now we live, I should like to point out one last advantage which I feel accrues to the writer by virtue of being a Negro. It concerns the international power struggle.

We live, it appears, in an age of struggle between the American brand of Capitalism and the Russian brand of Communism. This is obvious struggle; and most of the individuals in the world seem to feel that one must choose between one or the other. But is this, really, the root struggle? Or is mankind, the great majority of it, not actually groping for a rational social order, free from the tensions of economic and political crisis, free from war and from dictatorship, in which the individual will be permitted to live according to an ethic all sensible and truly just men can subscribe to?

For a moment, leave the last question. Consider the writer in the American scene, in this day and age. Picture him as being young and filled with ideals; consider him intelligent, sensitive and understanding. Ask the question: Can he approve of Amercan society as it exists today?

I say, on the basis of experience and of individual reaction, no! The young writer will notice many good things, worthy of retention, in the America of today. He will approve of free speech (now being seriously curtailed) ; he will approve the idea of a free press (even though it's becoming a monopoly because of the economics involved) ; he will believe in free artistic expression, realizing that only through freedom can real art survive. But can he approve of the dog-eat-dog existence we glorify by the name of Free Enterprise? — an existence which distorts the personality, turns avarice into virtue and permits the strong to run roughshod over the weak, profiteering on human misery? Can he approve racial and religious prejudice?

The young writer of ideas and ideals, I say, must instantly be repelled by the ugly aspect of American society. The history of our literature will bear this out — at a swift glance, I think of Emily Dickinson, Thoreau, Emerson, Hawthorne, Dos Passos, Faulkner, Henry James, Melville and, recently, Norman Mailer. And, being repelled, the writer seeks a substitute, something which offers hope of cure. Today, at first glance, the only alternative seems to be Russian Communism.

To list the important American writers who have turned from American Capitalism to Communism since the latter part of the nineteenth century would take up more space than this article is permitted. Suffice it to say that nearly every naturalistic writer in America has made this turn. Our young writer of intelligence and ideals, then, makes this turn. He embraces Communism of the Russian brand. And, immediately, he begins to feel uncomfortable.

For he discovers, in the folds of Russian Communism, the evils of dictatorship. He learns about purge trials; and is handed fantastic lies, which insult his intelligence, to justify them. He learns of the stifling of literature, art and music in the Soviet Union. He learns that Hitler is one day evil, the next day (following a pact with the Soviet Union) good, and the next day evil again. He discovers that Roosevelt is today a warmonger, tomorrow a true democrat and peoples' friend, whose "grand design" the Communist Party, U. S. A., seeks only to imitate. He learns that Tito, only yesterday a Communist hero only a little lower than Stalin, has in reality been a spy and a Fascist since 1936. He learns that a book which is "good" today becomes "bad," "bourgeois" and "decadent" tomorrow when the Party Line changes.

In panic does our idealistic and intelligent writer flee from alliance with the Communist Party. And at this point, the advantage of the Negro writer is discovered. For, having become disillusioned with the Soviet dictatorship, where does the white writer turn for political truth? Back to Capitalism, in ninety-nine out of a hundred cases; back to the very decaying system which lately he had left, a system he now calls "Democracy," "Freedom" and "Western Culture." He repeats the performance of John Dos Passos and, more recently and more strikingly (though in another field) Henry Wallace. The things he formerly found unbearable in Capitalism — he now ignores. Prejudice, depressions, imperialism, political chicanery, support of dictators, dog-eat-dog, strong-kill-the-weak philosophy — these things no longer exist. Black becomes white again. And the creative artist is dead! For he is blind.

The Negro writer, too, makes this retreat from Communism — for he, too, is opposed to lies, deceit, dictatorship and the other evils of the Soviet regime. But — and this is the significant point — the Negro writer does not, in most cases, come back to bow at the feet of Capitalism. He cannot, as can the white writer, close his eyes to the evils of the system under which he lives. Seeing the Negro ghetto, feeling the prejudice, his relatives and friends experiencing unemployment, injustice, police brutality, segregation in the South, white supremacy — seeing these things the Negro writer cannot suddenly kiss the hand which slaps him. Looking at China, at Indo China and at Africa, he cannot avoid the realization that these are people of color, struggling, as he is struggling, for dignity. Again, prejudice has forced him to perceive the real, the ticking world.

Denied many freedoms, robbed of many rights, the Negro — and the Negro writer — rejects those aspects of both American Capitalism and Russian Communism which trample on freedoms and rights. Repelled now by both contending systems, the Negro writer of strength and courage stands firmly as a champion of the basic human issues — dignity, relative security, freedom and the end of savagery between one human being and another. And in this stand he is supported by the mass of human beings the world over.

So add it up. The handicaps are great. Many Negro writers — the majority, I should say, so far — have been unable to overcome them. The work of others is impaired by them. But if the handicaps can be overcome, the advantages remain. And, as I said before, they are great advantages. Because I believe that an increasing number of Negro writers will be able to overcome the disadvantages inherent in their social situation, I predict that a disproportionate percentage of the outstanding writers of the next decade will be Negroes.

The Negro
in American Culture

The text represents, with only minor editing, a discussion broadcast early in 1961 over WABI-FM, the invaluable listener-supported radio station of New York. The moderator was Nat Hentoff, former editor of Downbeat; *participants included James Baldwin, author of* Notes of a Native Son (Beacon), Go Tell It on the Mountain (Universal), *and* Nobody Knows my Name (Dial); *Alfred Kazin, author of* On Native Grounds (Anchor), A Walker in the City (Grove), *and* The Inmost Leaf (Noonday); *Lorraine Hansberry, author of* A Raisin in the Sun; *Emile Capouya, an editor at Macmillan & Co.; and Langston Hughes, whose many books include* Simple Stakes a Claim (Rinehart), Selected Poems (Knopf), *and* A Langston Hughes Reader (Braziller).

The relaxed and spontaneous form of the remarks of these distinguished writers provides a candid presentation of attitudes often neglected in the glow of our easy denunciations of southern racists or that cheap statesmanship which calls for "moderation" in regard to elementary human dignity.

Hentoff: To begin the subject, which sounds rather alarmingly vague, I'd like to start with the end of the book review that James Baldwin wrote for *The New York Times* a couple of years ago.

The review was of poems of Langston Hughes, and you concluded by saying that "he is not the first American Negro to find the war between his social and artistic responsibilities all but irreconcilable."

To what extent do you find this true in your own writing in terms of the self-consciousness of being a Negro and a writer, the polarity, if it exists?

BALDWIN: Well, the first difficulty is really so simple that it's usually overlooked: to be a Negro in this country and to be relatively conscious, is to be in a rage almost all the time. So that the first problem is how to control that rage so that it won't destroy you. Part of the rage is this: it isn't only what is happening to you, but it's what's happening all around you all of the time, in the face of the most extraordinary and criminal indifference, the indifference and ignorance of most white people in this country.

Now, since this is so, it's a great temptation to simplify the issues under the illusion that if you simplify them enough, people will recognize them; and this illusion is very dangerous because that isn't the way it works.

You have to decide that you can't spend the rest of your life cursing out everybody that gets in your way. As a writer, you have to decide that what is really important is not that the people you write about are Negroes, but that they are people, and that the suffering of any person is really universal. If you can ever reach this level, if you can create a person and make other people feel what this person feels, then it seems to me that you've gone much further, not only artistically, but socially, than in the ordinary, old-fashioned protest way.

I talked about Langston not being the first poet to find these responsibilities all but irreconcilable. And he won't be the last, because it also demands a great deal of time to write, it demands a great deal of stepping out of a social situation in order to deal with it. And all the time you're out of it you can't help feeling a little guilty that you are not, as it were, on the firing line, tearing down the slums and doing all these obviously needed things, which in fact, other people can do better than you because it is still terribly true that a writer is extremely rare.

HENTOFF: Miss Hansberry, in writing *A Raisin in the Sun*, to what extent did you feel a double role, both as a kind of social actionist "protester," and as a dramatist?

MISS HANSBERRY: Well, given the Negro writer, we are necessarily aware of a special situation in the American setting.

And that probably works two ways. One of them makes us sometimes forget that there is really a very limited expression in literature which is not protest, be it black, white or what have you; I can't imagine a contemporary writer any place in the world today who isn't in conflict with his world. Personally, I can't imagine a time in the world when the artist wasn't in conflict; if he was any kind of an artist, he had to be.

We are doubly aware of conflict, because of the special pressures of being a Negro in America, but I think to destroy the abstraction for the sake of the specific is, in this case, an error. Once we come to that realization, it doesn't get quite as confusing as sometimes we tend to treat it.

In my play I was dealing with a young man who would have, I feel, been a compelling object of conflict as a young American of his class of whatever racial background, with the exception of the incident at the end of the play, and with the exception, of course, of character depth, because a Negro character is a reality; there is no such thing as saying that a Negro could be a white person if you just changed the lines or something like this. This is a very arbitrary and superficial approach to Negro character.

But I am taking a long way around to try to answer your question. There really is no profound problem. I started to write about this family as I knew them in the context of those realities which I remembered as being true for this particular given set of people; and at one point, it was just inevitable that a problem of some magnitude which was racial would intrude itself, because this is one of the realities of Negro life in America. But it was just as inevitable that for a large part of the play, they would be excluded. Because the duality of consciousness is so complete that it is perfectly true to say that Negroes do not sit around 24 hours a day, thinking, "I am a Negro." (LAUGHTER) They really don't. I don't think he does or anybody else. And, on the other hand, if you say the reverse that is almost true. And this is part of the complexity that I think you're talking about, isn't it?

BALDWIN: Yes, I agree completely. I think we are bound to get to this, because white men in this country and American Negroes in this country are really the same people. I only discovered this in Europe; perhaps it was always very obvious, but it never occurred to me before. The only people in the world who understand the American white man are American Negroes — (LAUGHTER) — nobody else.

HENTOFF: Langston Hughes, you have a large continuing body of work, and I wondered if you had felt in the course of your long development as a writer, a change in your feeling of this duality as the conditions around you changed, as the struggle for equality became more militant, and the status, to some extent, of the "Negro writer" began to change.

In other words, to what extent did the society around you change the kind of tension under which you wrote?

HUGHES: I must say that I don't notice any changes as yet. (LAUGHTER)

I happen to be a writer who travels a great deal because I read my poems in public and almost every year I travel over most of the country, south and north. I do, of course, see appreciable changes in some areas of race relations and I trust that my recent work reflects that to some extent, but by and large, it seems to me not really very different from when I was a child. There are still a great many places where you can't get a hamburger or a cup of coffee, or you can't sit on a bench in a railroad station, something of this sort — and not just in the South. Those problems exist in Washington, on the West Coast, and in Maine, you know.

I am, of course, as everyone knows, primarily a — I guess you might even say a propaganda writer; my main material is the race problem — and I have found it most exciting and interesting and intriguing to deal with it in writing, and I haven't found the problem of being a Negro in any sense a hindrance to putting words on paper. It may be a hindrance sometimes to selling them; the material that one uses, the fact that one uses, or that I use, problem material, or material that is often likely to excite discussion or disagreement, in some cases prevents its quick sale. I mean, no doubt it's much easier to sell a story like Frank Yerby writes without the race problem in it, or, yes, like Willard Motley, who also happens to be Negro, but writes without emphasizing the sharpness of our American race problem. Those writers are much more commercial than I or, I think, Miss Hansberry, or James Baldwin, who to me seems one of the most racial of our writers, in spite of his analysis of himself as otherwise on occasion.

BALDWIN: Later for you. (LAUGHTER)

KAZIN: Emil Capouya, from what you've observed in publishing as a whole, do you think that Langston Hughes' point has validity, that the degree of sharpness in which the racial problem is written about, is a deterrent to sales, let's say, in the book field?

I wonder if there isn't a distinction between magazine writing and book writing here.

CAPOUYA: No, I think not. From an editor's point of view, somebody who's professionally interested in buying or selling literary material, an artist and a writer are two different people.

First of all, he's an artist, and as such his claims are absolute. But he's also a commodity, and as a commodity he has no rights at all. He just has a market value.

So to come directly to your question: do I think that the material that a Negro writer may find readiest to hand is questionable from a market point of view, I'd say that each writer is an individual case.

Mr. Hughes suggested that it's been a stumbling block on his road to riches, but that wouldn't be the case obviously for Mr. Baldwin whose business as a novelist is largely with that material. And Miss Hansberry has had a great success, I think partly because of what that great public that went to see that play thought of as exotic material.

HUGHES: May I say that from long experience with publishers, and many of them — I have about six now — it has been my feeling that if a publisher has one Negro writer on his list or two at the most, he is not very likely to take another if the Negro writer is dealing in Negro themes? And it's not prejudice, it's simply — "Well, we have a book, a Chinese novel on our list. We don't want any more Chinese novels."

And the same thing is true in the theater. Once in a blue moon, there's a hit like *Raisin in the Sun*, but the Broadway producers will tell you quite frankly, "No more Negro plays. They're not commercial, we can't sell them. People won't go to the box office."

So if you want to make money out of writing, being a Negro writer, I mean quickly and easily, I would say become a Willard Motley, become a Frank Yerby.

CAPOUYA: I don't think that's the whole truth in relation to the way in which the question was originally posed. Suppose there were two plays about the Jewish East Side —

HUGHES: Yes, it's not a matter really of racial prejudice; it's a matter of the economy we're dealing in.

MISS HANSBERRY: Well, I wouldn't be so quick to decide whether it is or isn't prejudice. There are so many different ways of saying the same thing. It would be more than wishful thinking to me to exclude prejudice regarding Negroes in any area of life. I just don't think that's realistic.

It's prejudice when you can't get an apartment; it's probably prejudice when a skilful writer cannot publish because of some arbitrarily decided notion of what is or is not, as they tell me all the time, parochial material, of narrow interest, and so forth.

In a culture that has any pretensions towards sophistication or interest in human beings, there shouldn't be any designations of kinds of material. A good book should find a publisher.

HUGHES: Since the problem of the writer as a commodity has been brought up, I think it is by and large true to say that for the Negro writer to make a living is doubly hard due to the prejudice that Miss Hansberry has spoken about in other areas related to writing.

For example, I told you that I'm a lecturer and I read my poems. I have been with two or three of the top agencies. Those agencies cannot, as a rule book me at women's clubs. Women's clubs have teas; they do not wish to mingle socially with their speaker apparently, and they do not wish to invite their speaker's friends in whatever town he may be speaking on the program, because it's followed by a social event. Therefore, it's a rare occasion when I read my poems to a women's club.

If you want a job in the publishing industry, try and get it. How many editors of color can anyone name on any of our New York publishing houses? You may find an occasional girl secretary at the switchboard or a typist or a stockroom boy, but for the writer himself to get some sort of work related to his actual writing in publishing is well nigh impossible, I think.

Until very recently, in the last few years, Negroes did not write for Hollywood. Nothing was really sold to Hollywood. That's sort of a new development. I have been writing for 30 years and I've had one Hollywood job in 30 years. Prejudice doesn't keep a writer from writing; if you're colored, you can write all you want to, but you just try and sell it, that's all.

KAZIN: May I go back a moment to the point that Mr. Baldwin began with, this alleged conflict between the social and the artistic in American life?

You know, words like social and artistic are easy to use, and I'm sure that if I had to go through the daily humiliations that certain of my friends go through, I would feel this way.

But let me for a moment, put it on purely theoretical plane, where art may be discussed. America itself has always been a social question. All that's good in American writing, American art, comes out of the profound confrontation of social facts. It was true of *Moby Dick,* of *Leaves of Grass.* It comes out of what I consider to be the driving force behind all things, which is human hunger, human desire. Only it's a question, of course, not of how much you desire or how bad you feel, but how artistically you can realize your desire.

We have to consider two things. One is the current fashion to believe that art is somehow created apart from society, on the basis of purely individual will, as opposed to the marvelous books published in this country between, I would say, 1911 and 1934 or 35, many of which, like Faulkner's and Steinbeck's, Mr. Hughes' and other such books, are based on very real and agonizing social problems. And I must say that in this centenary year of the Civil War, it's hard to forget that the Negro is the central issue in American history, has been the central issue all along, has been the real crux of our history and our aspirations as a people, and that, therefore, the question that comes up is always how deeply, how profoundly, how accurately do we recognize this social kind of drive in our literature right now?

And one thing that's happening right now in middle class writing everywhere is what's happening to Negroes too: people don't have as many beefs as they think they have; they often have no real beefs; they are very often led by purely arbitrary problems, and consequently, a good deal of the tremendous whiplash of hunger, hunger in the widest sense, the deepest sense, has been forgotten here.

I think — to put it very bluntly — that in America there cannot be any conflict between the so-called social and artistic impulse; that one must recognize that what we call art is the most profound realization of some social tendency, and that wherever you don't have this social awareness, social intelligence, then, it seems to me, you don't have art either.

In other words, the Negro has been not merely a writer, he's also been a character, and he's been one of the most profound characters in American literature. I don't mean Uncle Tom, either. I mean a character from Faulkner, a character from many, even, pre-Civil War, novelists, who were always aware of the Negro as a force, a human being, as a problem, as a challenge, as a lover, as many things. And one must not forget that this problem goes to the very essence of our life of civilization.

And that's why I'm so troubled when Mr. Baldwin, for reasons which I can well imagine, but which I want, for once, to pretend I don't understand — opens by bringing up this whole question of the conflict between the social and the artistic.

I think that art is never created when it is too aware of this kind of conflict. I also don't believe in conflicts that are realized. Once there is a conflict, the thing to do is by-pass it and go on to a third force, as such.

I'm thinking, for example, of Mr. Baldwin's *Notes of a Native Son,* which for me in many ways is the most brilliant of Negro books, even though it's a collection of essays, of modern American writing. And I've been struck, in re-reading it, by the power, the brilliance and the vividness of it.

HUGHES: You know what I would say about it? I would say it's the *Uncle Tom's Cabin* of today. (LAUGHTER)

KAZIN: Well, I happen to like this *Uncle Tom's Cabin.* I think it's a masterpiece.

And the reason it's a masterpiece is because the broken glass of the '43 Harlem riot, the miseries of personal friends — all these things have been captured and realized as a piece of art. And the minute one tries to break away from this, tries to get away from this enormous passion, then one is lost.

The other thing is that one must recognize that art is a word that people use, but the ability to create is something which is utterly God-given, accidental, and capricious. And I think, for example, to speak of something I know rather intimately, when the Jewish immigrants, from whom I come, arrived in this country 50, 60 years ago, there was a whole hoard of sweatshop poets and they were miserable people. They worked 18, 19 hours a day; lived horrible lives. None of this poetry that I have seen, in English, in Hebrew, or in Yiddish, is any good at all. And then suddenly in the last 15 years, we've had a group of writers, like Saul Bellow and Norman Mailer and Bernard Malamud and others, who, with enormous surprise to themselves, I think, have suddenly created 5 or 6 really good books, which are as fresh as anything can be.

Now, one reason they've done this is that they've come to recognize their fate as being universal in some sense, and not merely accidental or parochial. I don't mean that they shouldn't write about parochial things, on the contrary, but they've come to recognize the universal in this.

And I ask myself, what is the difference between those lovable, dear people 60 years ago, with their awful sweatshop poetry, and a writer who to my mind is as first-class as Saul Bellow in one or two short things?

I can only say it's a question of the welding together at a certain moment of all these impulses, without for a moment forgetting that intelligence and social passion come into play here. And one mustn't ever try to divide the two. Otherwise, it becomes a problem in the economic history of the writer; it becomes a problem in the social history of the writer; it does not become a problem of art, as such, which is something very different.

BALDWIN: There isn't any conflict between what you said and what I mean. I should clarify my terms some more.

In that particular book review, I was using the conflict between social and artistic responsibility in a very limited and specific way. I know that art comes out of something much deeper than anything that can be named. I know it is always and must be social, because what are you investigating except man and the way in which he lives, and the ways in which he tries to remake his world, and the ways in which he sometimes fails and sometimes succeeds?

Perhaps I was using the wrong word there; perhaps I should have said propagandistic. Because I don't think there's any point really in blinking this fact and I don't think it can ever be used to defend oneself or excuse oneself for failure, which after all has to be personal and private failure.

Now, there's no point in pretending that being a Negro writer in this country doesn't present certain particular hazards which you would not have if you were white. It is perfectly true, as Langston says, that anybody with his comparable reputation and body of work, who was white, would have much more money than Langston does. This is a fact. But the Negro writer is not as interesting a subject to me as the Negro in this country in the minds of other people — the Negro character, as you put it — and the role that he's always played in the American subconscious, which has never really been dealt with. It has always been there, almost like a corpse which no one knows what to do with, floating in the waters of the national life. And really everything in America can almost be defined by the presence of the Negro in it, including the American personality.

To deal with this, I think, is the real challenge one faces. Somehow actually to unify this country — because it never has been united — and to make a wedding for the first time really, between blacks and whites. Because, this is really the history of a very long love affair, and it's this, much more than anything else which Americans are afraid to look at and don't want to believe.

KAZIN: To use a cryptic phrase, the presence of the Negro in America, in the whole imaginative and moral history of this country, is what I call the central fact.

I've been reading Civil War history for the last few months for an article I'm doing, and I'm struck again and again by the enormous effort so many people made in the '30's and '40's of the last century in the North to overlook the Negroes, to make sure that their little Unitarian, Abolitionist hopes would get rid of him. But again and again the fact came up, it could not be by-passed, and it couldn't be by-passed any more by the Abolitionists who looked the other way, than it could be by-passed by the Southern slavemasters. And now, in the midst of this agonizing struggle going on in the South, which the whole world is watching, the fact remains, because of the very nature of American democracy, that never in history has a whole body of former slaves been made the issue of human and civic equality on such a large scale as in this country.

The love affair, which I would say is more a mutual and fascinated awareness of each other, is itself the very incidence of the agony and passion of the Negro's presence in American life. And this is why, when you recognize the social factor, as Faulkner does in his best work — and I'm not thinking here of Joe Christmas — I'm thinking here of the total context he creates — then you recognize the depth of emotion, the depth of commitment out of which art can come.

Now, the economic problem is something else. It is disgusting that a lecturer should have to be banned from a women's tea club because he might have to have tea with them.

But think what a marvelous story this makes, about America: people who think they would like to hear the lecturer, are afraid to have the tea. Note the slightly comic element, not in the sense of being amiable, but in revealing human paradox and hypocrisy.

When I was a professor at a New England college some years ago, there were two Negro boys in the college, a testimony to its

Abolitionist background. And, of course, these boys were miserable and about as lonely as a spar of wood on a Cape Cod beach. But the fact remains that out of this kind of experience would come to an artist, white or Negro, a sense of the extraordinary comedy of social hopes and moral would-be feelings of this country, too — which is, I submit, as close to the life of art as the suffering and anxiety of an individual writer who happens to be a Negro here. And this is why I hope that we will not only remember, as we all must, what is happening to each of us who is a Negro down south, but also of the enormous presence of the Negro as a fact in the American imagination, which again and again has created something which is absolutely inextricable — it cannot be lost, cannot be forgotten, cannot be by-passed, in our minds for a moment.

HUGHES: Speaking of the celebration of the centennial of the Civil War, I have just written yesterday columns for *The Chicago Defender,* for which I write, using my Simple character as a kind of social protest mouthpiece, and I'd like to read you a section because it involves the very thing that you're talking about.

Simple is in the barbershop and this is what he says:

"I sit in that barber chair, thinking about how God must love poor folks he made so many of them in my image. (LAUGHTER)

"You know, as long as I've been poor, I'm not used to it. My papa were poor before me and my grandpa were poorer than that, being a slave which did not even own hisself. So, I was settin in that barberchair thinking, one day the time might come when I will own Old Master's grandson, since him nor none of his white relations won't let me get hold a nothing else."

"What on earth are you talking about," I asked, "reinstating slavery? Are you out of your mind?"

"I was sort of dozin and dreamin whilst he cut my hair," said Simple, "and in snoozin I kep thinkin about how much I been hearin about this here centennial of the Civil War and stuff the white folks has been tellin — intendin to celebrate in honor of the North and South. And they're going to be on parades and meetins and battles and things like they were 100 years ago. One way of making people remember what that Civil War were all about might be to bring back slavery for a month or two, only this time, reverse it. Make the white folks the slaves and me the master.

"I would like to own some of them white Simples on my grandma's side, which were the ones, I understand, tht gave me my name. Oh, I would like to own a few white folks just once."

(LAUGHTER) "Maybe I could work out of them some of the money that they owe my great-grandfolks and never did pay. Else make up for these low wages which I'm gettin right now.

"I would like to own me some rich white slaves, not used to workin like me for hardly enough to pay income tax when April, let alone Harlem rent and balancing your budget."

"Dream on," I said.

"From dawn to long after dark, I would find something for them white folks to do," said Simple, "if I owned them, and come the end of the week, not pay them a cent. That would be a real good way, I figure, to celebrate the centennial. Make it real, not just play-actin, but bring slavery back to its own doorstep. One hundred years, it is time to turn the tables.

"But don't you know, since I was dreaming about all this, the barber cut my hair too short?"

"It looks all right to me," I said, "In fact, I would say, with you, the less hair the better."

"I might have bad hair," said Simple, "But I've got a good-shaped head." (LAUGHTER)

Well now, I very often try to use social material in a humorous form and most of my writing from the very beginning has been aimed largely at a Negro reading public, because when I began to write I had no thought of achieving a wide-public. My early work was always published in *The Crisis* of the NAACP, and then in *The Opportunity* of the Urban League, and then the Negro papers like the *Washington Sentinel* and the *Baltimore American*, and so on. And I contend that since these things, which are Negro, largely for Negro readers, have in subsequent years achieved world-wide publication — my work has come out in South America, Japan, and all over Europe — that a regional Negro character like Simple, a character intended for the people who belong to his own race, if written about warmly enough, humanly enough, can achieve universality.

In fact, I think my Simple character has achieved universality with the very kind of thing that he talks about here in the barber chair, because all around the world poor people have economic problems, all around the world, in almost every country, there is some sort of racial problem. In Japan it's — what do they call them? the Ainu; in India, its the Untouchables; in France, its the *sals Algériens*.

These problems are not limited just to America. But they impose no limitation on the writer one way or another.

Norman Mailer was mentioned — I didn't know he was a Jewish writer until right now — he achieved a universality, in spite of his Jewish background.

And I don't see, as Jimmy Baldwin sometimes seems to imply, any limitations, in artistic terms, in being a Negro. I see none whatsoever. It seems to me that any Negro can write about anything he chooses, even the most narrow problems: if he can write about it forcefully and honestly and truly, it is very possible that that bit of writing will be read and understood, in Iceland or Uruguay.

KAZIN: I agree entirely, Mr. Hughes. I was thinking about the difference between two of Richard Wright's books, one of which moved me enormously when I was younger than I am now, *Native Son,* the other, *The Outsider,* which I don't like at all. I agree with you entirely about the need to be parochial, the need to write out of one's milieu and to one's milieu; in fact, Wright's *The Outsider* is my text to prove it.

When I read about this Negro on a train meeting this hunchback, who made common cause with him because they were both symbols of the outsider, I thought this was weak artistically; I felt it was, as the French say, *voulu,* it was willed, it was not real. What seems to me to be absolutely legitimate, however, were the profoundly touching scenes in which Bigger was involved in *Native Son,* which still is a very powerful and enormously moving book.

We Americans are very symbolic to ourselves as well as to other people. And very often we think of ourselves as being in the forefront of the world. (I think we still are. I still think we're more revolutionary than any other country in the world, at least implicitly, in terms of the kind of society we're trying to build.)

But the point I'm getting at is that the Negro tends very often today to think of himself as being the symbol of man in the outside world, because of the enormous fact of the race problem in all countries of the world, because of the enormous suffering and wars going on right now. The Negro middle class writer in America, may, if he is in Paris, as Wright was, think of himself as being the symbol rather than the fact. And my point is that only when the Negro thinks of himself as a fact can art begin. The minute he thinks of himself as a symbol, then theory creeps in and the whole problem is dis-social, dis-artistic.

When you're writing out of the actual broken glass of the actual confused heats of that race riot in '43 in the Harlem streets, when Jimmy took his father to the grave, then you have the beginning of what you don't understand too well.

There is a certain law for art: not to know as you're writing what everything means. It's being impressed with the fact, not with the significance of the fact. Too often one tends, because of the enormous centrality of the Negro position today in world experience, to say, "Well, we all know what that means," but we don't. It all goes back to one house, one street, one uncle or grandmother, or whatever.

MISS HANSBERRY: I don't think that there should be any over-extended attention to this question of what is or what isn't universal.

I think that Simple, for instance, is as kin to the Shakespearean wise fool as any other character in literature I've ever heard of, but we don't notice the Englishness of a Shakespearean fool while we're being entertained and educated by his wisdom; the experience just happens. It happens because people have rent problems everywhere in the world and because men are opposed everywhere in the world and because men are oppressed everywhere in the world. The point of contact is innate to the piece to the extent that it is true, to the extent that it is art, which is what I think that you were saying.

I have been distressed personally, in connection with something that Mr. Kazin was saying, having to do with the traditional treatment of Negro characters in American literature — let's speak now of non-Negro writers. I was perplexed to find, when I addressed myself to that question in two popular essays, that nobody seemed to know what on earth I was talking about — which, of course, could be a matter of delivery. On one occasion I tried to discuss the character, Walter Lee, the young man in my play, in terms of why, as you said a moment ago, in the so-called white mind, he was still an expression of exoticism, no matter how he had been created. Many people, apparently, recognized his humanity, but he was still exotic to them.

In my opinion, since man is so complex and since I disagree with most of the despairing crowd, if you're going to get ridiculous and talk about man being basically anything, you may as well say he's probably basically good. If that is true, then it is also true that man is trying to accommodate his own guilt always, all of us.

And it seems to me that one of the things that has been done in the American mentality is to create this escape valve of the exotic Negro, wherein it is possible to exalt abandon on all levels, and to imagine that while I am dealing with the perplexities of the universe, look over there, coming down from the trees— (LAUGHTER) — is a Negro who knows none of this, and wouldn't it be marvelous if I could be my naked, brutal, savage self again?

This permeates our literature in every variation: I don't believe that Negro characters as created thus far have overcome that problem. I don't even believe that the Negro artists have overcome it, because we have been affected by it.

For example, the Emperor Jones is not a man in conflict with the world. He is an arch-symbol that never existed on land, sea, or under it; and to the extent that we recognize something about him, we recognize something symbolized in our own minds. I think this would also be true of Porgy.

The discussion of the Negro character has been so primitive in the past, we've been so busy talking about who's a stereotype and who isn't, we have never talked about it as art. I maintain that the problem is that these characters as they've appeared in literature never gained full human stature because the writers who have created them haven't thought about them as men in the first place. It isn't a matter of just wanting to change how they speak. Everytime you say something about *Porgy and Bess,* somebody says, "Well, you know, Negroes did speak dialect 40 years ago." Heavens, they still do. That is not the argument; the argument is that Porgy is not a man.

KAZIN: No, he isn't. I think that American literature written by white people is probably 99.9 per cent full of these stereotypes and that lately we have been treated to the worst stereotype of all, which is what Norman Mailer calls the "White Negro," namely, the noble savage brought back as an example to the bourgeois white American.

BALDWIN: I have some objections to Faulkner's Negro characters. I'll try to tell you what they are. I think the principal one is that not only is there something left out, there is something left out that should be there. Even in the great portrait of Joe Christmas — the only way is to put it as bluntly as possible, then we can go back and modify it — there is something about him which rubs me the wrong way, and it's not his situation and it isn't his dialect, it isn't any of these things at all. What it is is that he's also a kind of apology for an injustice which is really still not being dealt with.

Now Faulkner is a very good example of what I mean. The Southern writers who have written about Negroes and have written about them well have all written about them in more or less the same way, essentially out of a feeling of guilt. What is most mysterious is that it is a guilt to which they cling. It's a guilt without which their identities would be threatened. What is so fascinating about this whole Negro-white relationship in America, is what it means in the American personality to have a Negro around. That is why he's always the noble savage in no matter what guise, from Eisenhower to Norman Mailer, nobody can give this up. Everybody wants to have this sort of walking symbol around to protect something in themselves which they do not want to examine.

But what one deals with in the world every day, really, isn't the world's malice or even the world's indifference, it's the world's ignorance. And it's not ignorance of the Negro or the fact of Negro life as such. It's an ignorance of a certain level of life which no one has ever respected or it's never been real in America. You can almost say — you can say, in fact — that one of the reasons that the Negro is at the bottom of the social heap in America, is because it's the only way everyone in America will know where the bottom is. (LAUGHTER)

KAZIN: Exactly, as you put it, marvelously, to show us where the bottom is, where everything that is fundamental is in our country. But at the bottom, there are people who, understandably because they've been at the bottom so long, will be seen by an imaginative writer like Faulkner in a certain way.

Now, would you want Faulkner to write about the Negro only, so to speak, as he *should* be in our minds, if he were given half a chance, or do you want him out of all these hundreds of years of Southern bondage and Southern slave-owning and Southern prejudice to release that powerful talent and throw it away?

Let me put this in a personal way, if I may — I too come from people who are not altogether unused to prejudice. Now, only 15 years ago a million and a half Jewish children were put into bonfires by the Nazis just because they were Jewish children. It's a terrible fact, part of the incredible oppression of the Second World War. Nevertheless, if I read Shakespeare's *Merchant of Venice*, with its venomous, unbearable portrait of Shylock, though I think it's false, I have to admit it's a great artistic creation. And it seems to me that over the years, one thing that's happened to me as a writer in America, is that I've learned to say that Shylock is a great character and not worry about him so much.

Don't misunderstand me, though. I'm not trying to sermonize on this question. All I'm saying here is that we do have a handful of books that seem to be written out of the bottom, and one mustn't presume too much here too, for this reason: Joe Christmas is not a Negro. No one knows what or who he is. People think he's a Negro, and the point in that great novel — *Light in August* is a very great book, an extraordinary book — is that because people do not know him, but merely see in him what they think he is, not what he really is (he could be anything) — they do everything to him right up to the end. They murder him, they castrate him, and he becomes the dead Christ on the American cross. Again and again, it's made clear, that the fact of Negro suffering has created this figure.

On the other hand, when Faulkner writes a letter to *The New York Times* about segregation in the South, he writes like a damn fool, he writes like any typical, vulgar Mississippian. When he writes a novel which has a Negro character in it, he's a great artist.

HUGHES: Oh, certainly, he's an amazingly good writer. However, it seems to me that he doesn't really and fully understand even the Southern Negro with whom he's lived all his life. Did you see *Requiem for a Nun*, last season?

KAZIN: Yes. It was terrible. I hated *Requiem for a Nun*, both as a book and as a play.

HUGHES: In that play he has his Negro woman who is going to her death for having committed some sort of murder, I believe, which she felt was justified, and the lawyer or the judge is talking to her, and she says she doesn't mind dying, in essence, because she is going to Heaven. And this Southern white lawyer, judge, or whatever he is, says, "What would a woman like you do in Heaven?" And she says, "Ah kin work." Now, that is the most false line in literature regarding the Negro, because no Negro in God's world ever thought of Heaven as a place to work. He just doesn't understand the Negro mind, that's all.

KAZIN: But as a writer, and a very good writer, do you think it's necessary to understand something in order to create a good character? Is understanding, in the deepest human, civic sense, the brotherly sense, is this really necessary for artistic creation?

HUGHES: To create a believable character, you certainly

have to have a certain amount of understanding. And this woman in *Requiem* became so unreal to me.

KAZIN: Yes, I agree with you about that case, but let's consider Dilsey. She was also a Southern Negro, and a character who would cause me the deepest pain and chagrin if I were a Negro; nevertheless, I believe she is a great creation.

HUGHES: Yes, I don't doubt that.

KAZIN: Well, you can't understand Negroes on one page and forget them on another. Because understanding is always the same. It's typical Faulkner, who reveals his limitations in non-artistic areas. But as a writer, once in a while, something is created which comes out of the deepest, most unconscious sense of love.

Let me give you an instance: you may remember that the fourth part of *The Sound and the Fury* opens with Dilsey coming out on the porch. She is portrayed in a typical hand-me-down costume of a woman who has worked for 50 years for this rotting family, the Compsons. The costume itself is demeaning, but the description of Dilsey, everything about her, is of such an extraordinary artistic beauty and intensity that I can never read it without being moved to tears. The thing has been made flesh, and she is there, we know her. This is something very different, I submit, from 101 moralizings that you might get from well-meaning Northern "liberals."

All I'm saying is on this page — and on many pages of that book — he really created a human being, and even when he sees her without understanding in his mind, there was tremendous understanding in his heart.

HUGHES: Yes, and I think another fine Southern white writer, Carson McCullers, is also successful in creating character.

MISS HANSBERRY: I think, Mr. Kazin, that you may be imposing on my earlier remarks a lack of dimension that wasn't there. What I was trying to say is exactly the opposite of what you emphasized. I am not concerned with doing away with the mere traditional paraphernalia of the inexpressive, crude Negro character. That is not the point. I myself, very arbitrarily, after deliberate thought, chose to write about the Negro working class, although I come from the middle class. Eventually, I think more of our writers are going to begin to deal with the Negro middle class, which most white people don't know exists.

But we're not trying to escape from some image of truth. When you spoke a moment ago, you seemed to suggest we would be satisfied if the image were more glossy, more dressed-up. That is not the point. When language is handled truly, and Negro speech used with fidelity — which doesn't have to do with the dropping of g's and misplacing of verbs — when the essence of character is as true and as complicated as — as character should be, whatever character you're dealing with, only then ought we to be satisfied.

There is a comedy line in my play, where the young daughter says to one of her suitors, 'You think this about women because this is what you got from all the novels that men have written." Obviously, novelists have created some memorable women characters. But I am altogether certain that in regard to the inner truths of character, the woman character will always partially elude the male writer. Of course, women, like Negroes, I'm afraid, accept many images of themselves that come from literature, and start to act those roles, but there are other truths, which can be found only by studying people in depth.

You mentioned Carson McCullers. There's a scene in *Member of the Wedding,* when the young Negro nephew of Bernice is being chased by a lynch mob, and she takes the young white boy whom she has nursed all his life — he's about to die, I think, because of some constitutional weakness — and this woman's preoccupation is with that child. I happen to think that it was a lovely play and I believe Bernice's character, but we are now talking about these extra nuances, and my point is that the intimacy of knowledge which the Negro may have of white Americans does not exist in the reverse.

KAZIN: That's absolutely true.

MISS HANSBERRY: William Faulkner has never in his life sat in on a discussion in a Negro home where there were all Negroes. It is physically impossible. He has never heard the nuances of hatred, of total contempt from his most devoted servant and his most beloved friend, although she means every word when she's talking to him, and will tell him profoundly intimate things. But he has never heard the truth of it. For you, this is a fulfilling image, because you haven't either. I can understand that. Obviously Faulkner is a monumental talent, but there are other dimensions of that character, and as I would create her, or Jim, or Langston, there would be a world of difference, and it's this we're trying to get to. I *want* white writers to begin to create Negro characters. We need it desperately.

BALDWIN: Lorraine's point is very important. We have to

look more carefully at the characters created by Faulkner, or by Carson McCullers. Lorraine mentioned that absolutely incredible moment when this woman's nephew is being chased by a lynch mob, and she's worried about this little boy. That scene doesn't reveal anything about the truth of Negro life, but a great deal about the state of mind of the white Southern woman who wrote it.

Regardless of Faulkner's talent, the thing I will not settle for is that this image is maintained. Southerners have an illusion and they cling to it desperately; in fact, the whole American Republic does. These characters come out of a compulsion. Dilsey is Faulkner's proof that the Negro — who, as Langston points out, has been worked and worked and worked and for nothing, who has been lynched and burned and stolen from for generations — has forgiven him. The reason the walls in the South cannot come down, the reason that the panic is too great for the walls to come down, is because when they do, the truth will come out. And it's perfectly true, as Lorraine says, you can't know what I'm talking about, if you haven't been in a home with all Negroes together, if you haven't listened to Dilsey at home — who might be my mother — and heard what she says about the people she works for — and what is more important than that, not only what she says, but what she knows. And she knows much more about them than they will ever know about her, and there's a very good reason for this.

Faulkner has never sat in a Negro kitchen while the Negroes were talking about him, but we have been sitting around for generations, in kitchens and everywhere else, while everybody talks about us, and this creates a very great difference. It also creates — now speaking specifically for the Negro writer — a very great advantage. While I was living abroad in France, somebody said something — its something, I guess, the French say all the time — but this day it was said to me and it rang a bell. He said, "If you want to know what's happening in the house, ask the maid." And it occurred to me that in this extraordinary house, I'm the maid. (LAUGHTER)

MISS HANSBERRY: Which is a different relationship, because the employer doesn't go to the maid's house. You see, people get this confused. They think that the alienation is equal on both sides. It isn't. We have been washing everybody's underwear for 300 years. We know when you're not clean. (LAUGHTER)

KAZIN: I accept everything you say, Miss Hansberry, but I

wonder if you would allow me to try to persuade you that it's still slightly irrelevant to the point I was making.

MISS HANSBERRY: Oh, then I'm sorry.

KAZIN: No, no; as I was irrelevant to your point, you're being irrelevant to mine. This is the way people learn to talk to each other.

My point is this: I don't for a moment mean to say that the truth about Negro life has been accomplished, to use the Biblical phrase, forever. I'm talking about what has actually been done as art.

This is an artistic question, it's not a social question. I know that Negroes have been maids, they have been the drawers of water and the hewers of wood. They have been the slaves and slaves do all the work.

But my point is this: it's something Edward Hopper, the painter, once said, which has stuck in my mind: "Thought is endless, but the picture exists in space and time."

Every Negro walking the streets, every American, is full of the past, the present and the future. No book, either his book or a white man's book, can satisfy him about the truth. Because the truth is not only about what he has and what he is, but what he wants to become, what he wants America to become. Therefore, there is no book that exists right now that in the deepest sense can be satisfying to him.

But a book does exist in space and time. Those distortions of Shylock, or of Dilsey, or of anyone else, horrible as they are to our conscience, nevertheless exist as such. Dostoyevski, Tolstoy, Melville, all the great novelists, have written the most frightfully distorted anti-Negro, anti-Japanese, anti-Semitic, anti-French stereotypes. Do American characters come off much better, in American fiction as a whole? Not always in contemporary American fiction. They are portrayed uniformly as lechers, sadists, masturbators, idiots, bourgeois decadents and the rest. This is a society that is full of self-disgust. It doesn't know what it wants or what it believes, and it's constantly getting rid of its own guilt about its own unsatisfied wantings in that way.

My point is that a book exists in itself, as such, and perhaps — it's hard for a writer to admit — perhaps, all of us who write books are not so busy mirroring life, as we always think we are, as creating life.

For example, Tolstoy created a great book like *War and Peace* and then looked about him and found out something about the actual conditions of serfdom and contemporary Russia: he discovered, what his wife had told him beforehand, that the two things — the thing he had created and the world around him — had nothing to do with each other in any immediate sense.

This is a terrible paradox. But the fact remains that there are no people anywhere like the people in our books or anybody else's book.

Simple is delicious and wise and right because he is a product of Mr. Hughes' imagination. Many people have gone into making him up. He is no one else, he is Simple. This is true of any true character.

It's even true of a good autobiography like Jimmy Baldwin's *Notes of a Native Son,* where we find that the author himself becomes his own myth, as Thoreau said about himself in *Walden.*

I'm not trying to say that Mr. Faulkner is the last word on Negroes in America. God forbid. What I am saying is that something was created, something was not just being talked about, hopeful and wishful, all the time. Something that is true, I think, as such.

BALDWIN: We are talking somewhat at cross purposes, because I cannot disagree with what you say.

KAZIN: But there isn't any argument. We are reflecting on a problem which has many facets. I don't disagree with you about this thing at all. How can I? What is there to disagree about? Do you think I would say that Dilsey is the truth about Negroes in America? That would be a horrible untruth.

BALDWIN: All right, I accept the proposition that perhaps we are not so much reflecting life as trying to create it — but let's talk now not about books but about this country.

I'm talking now about the role of the Negro, and what seems to me to be at stake is that somehow the Negro contains a key to something about America which no one has yet found out about — which no one has yet faced. Contains maybe the key to life. I don't know; I don't want to talk about it in such mythical terms.

My point is that there is a tremendous resistance on the part of the entire public to know whatever it is, to deal with whatever this image means to them.

HENTOFF: I wonder how many doors that key unlocks.

Langston Hughes has mentioned the urge to whiteness among

some Negro writers. This leads, of course, to assimilationist novels, but I wonder if it doesn't also lead, without complete realization on the part of some Negro writers, politicians, and others, to a desire for equality within the white value-structure. Has there been enough questioning of this within Negro writing?

BALDWIN: I feel that there's been far too little.

HENTOFF: In other words, equal for what?

BALDWIN: Equal for what, yes. You know, there's always been a very great question in my mind of why in the world — after all I'm living in this society and I've had a good look at it — what makes you think I want to be accepted?

MISS HANSBERRY: Into this.

BALDWIN: Into this.

MISS HANSBERRY: Maybe something else.

BALDWIN: It's not a matter of acceptance or tolerance. We've got to sit down and rebuild this house.

MISS HANSBERRY: Yes, quickly.

BALDWIN: Very quickly, and we have to do it together. This is to you, Alfred, speaking now, just as a writer. You know, in order to be a writer you have to demand the impossible. And I know I'm demanding the impossible. It has to be — but I also know it has to be done. You see what I mean?

KAZIN: Yes, I see entirely what you mean but let's talk about this presence of the Negro in American history for a moment, because when we really get into the question of the white writers' portraits of Negroes we're talking about this larger question. Maybe that way we can come back to the difficulty we had earlier.

This presence of the Negro in American civilization, I said before, is the central fact about our moral history. And the conflict in the American heart, which exists in Negroes as well as among whites, comes out of a constant tension between what this country is ideally supposed to mean and what it actually has been as such. The problem has become more and more catastrophic and dangerous because of the growing world anxiety about possible world annihilation. Suddenly you begin to realize that people who don't treat their fellow-citizens well are, in a sense, building up a bonfire for everyone else in the same way, as is likely to happen in Africa before our generation is over.

At the same time, this very tension in America between the ideal moral purpose and the reality, also creates two things. One, it creates the fact that we never know quite what we want, as you yourself admitted before. You said you weren't quite sure you wanted equality to disrupt you. And secondly, it creates the white man's constant bewilderment between what he feels abstractly to be his duty, and the actuality of a society in which human beings were held as slaves, and in which, 25 years later, these people were sitting in Washington as senators.

So you have this enormous comedy of American pretension and American actuality, leaving the white man, who is also here, in a constant bewilderment. But whereas you spoke of guilt, I think it's more a sense of an intellectual paradox. Because in order to justify his own presence in this country, the white American has to understand the Negro's place, but to understand it fully, he has to make a gesture of imagination, morally — even religiously, in the deepest sense of the word; yet very often he is debased by his own culture and kept from making this gesture. But this is what happened again and again. This is what happened with the Civil War.

Let's put it this way: who in American history among the white men did make the fullest effort of imagination in your point of view?

It wasn't the Abolitionists; it wasn't Colonel Higginson, leading Negro troops in the Civil War. Who was it? Who would you say it was? I think it's been no one. I think it's a fight which has constantly been in process, constantly going on. But nowhere, in no particular point in space and time can you say this has been understood fully and deeply.

HUGHES: To go back to Jimmy Baldwin's point, at the First Negro Writer's Conference, a year and a half ago, and published in *The American Negro Writer and His Roots,* is a speech by Julian Mayfield, one of our better young Negro novelists. Speaking of the examination of American values by American Negro writers, this is what he says:

"This new approach is suggested by the Negro mother, who having lost one of her sons in the Korean adventures, was heard to remark, 'I don't care if the Army is integrated, next time I want to know what kind of war my boy is being taken into.'

"In the same sense, the Negro writer is being very gently nudged toward a rather vague thing called the mainstream of American literature. This trend would also seem to be based on common sense. But before plunging into it, he owes it to the future of his art to analyze the contents of the American mainstream, to determine the full significance of his commitment to it.

"He may decide that though the music is sweet, he would rather play in another orchestra; or to place himself in the position of the black convict in *The Defiant Ones,* he may decide that he need not necessarily share the fate of his white companion, who after all proffers the hand of friendship a little late. The Negro writer may conclude that his best salvation lies in escaping the narrow national orbit, artistic, cultural and political, and soaring into the space of more universal experience."

HENTOFF: In this regard I'd like to bring up one further thing before we conclude, concerning the future.

In an otherwise rather strange book, *The Negro Novel in America,* by Boone [sic], he has statistics showing that of 62 Negro novelists writing between 1853 and 1952, 40, or two-thirds, published only one novel, 11 more published only 2, and only 11 have published more than two.

Is this largely due to economic discrimination and the like, or is it due to a self-limitation to a single theme, which could only be expressed once?

HUGHES: My guess would be that it was largely due to the limitation of thematic material, and secondarily due to the fact of economics, due to the fact that the Negro people themselves, of whom there are now about 20 million in our country, have not one single publishing house.

We discussed a while ago, you remember, the limitation placed upon the number of Negro novels that can be published in a year.

The same thing is true in the theater. Do we have one serious Negro dramatic theater that belongs to us, that is managed by us, that is directed by us? No. The nearest thing we have to it is Karamu Theatre in Cleveland, which is a part of a settlement house. Formerly it was largely Negro attended, but it does such beautiful productions that now more than two-thirds of its personnel is white, because white people come from all over to work in Karamu. They used to do plays by Negro writers almost entirely, about Negro life, but not anymore. The trend is to integrate everything, so that you kill yourself with an integrated cast.

The trend towards integration in some cases, particularly in the folk field, in my opinion, can go too far, in that it is damaging artistically. For example, I narrated a Gospel song program in Chicago, a winter or two ago, with Mahalia Jackson, and do you know that the people who presented the program integrated the

Gospel singers? Mahalia listened and gathered her fur coat about her at rehearsal, and went home with the parting shot, "Y'all ain't got the beat."

There is a tendency at the moment, in jazz, to integrate every combo, which is wonderful, sociologically speaking. But very often the white players who may come into a combo, will not have that same beat, let us say, that Jonah Jones has, you know what I mean?

MISS HANSBERRY: Are we just skirting abound a larger political question in an effort to avoid it, perhaps? Because, what are we faced with? We are faced with the fact that due to these 300 years of the experience of black people in the Western hemisphere — not only in the United States, though it was least successful in the United States — a possible difference of ultimate cultural attitudes now exists as a reality, so that in Mayfield's statement that you read just now, there are the tones of Negro nationalism, articulated in a far more sophisticated and pointed way than years ago. The question is openly being raised today among all Negro intellectuals, among all politically-conscious Negroes: — is it necessary to integrate oneself into a burning house? And we can't quite get away from it.

There are real and true things existing in the consciences of Negroes today which have to do with why, on two occasions, the American Negro delegate at the United Nations disassociated herself from her government, when we refused to vote for an Algerian Algeria, when we refused to vote for the end of colonialism. When the most compromised element in the Negro population, from which these people are drawn — I mean no offense personally to that lady, I don't even know who she is, but there is only a certain section of Negro life that is allowed to represent us — when they are moved to disassociate themselves in an international hall, and when 10,000 Negroes will come out to greet Fidel Castro in Harlem and wave at him and cheer him everytime he shows his head, this is an indication of what is going on. This dichotomy is going to become more articulate and we are going to see it more and more in Negro literature.

HUGHES: I would like to say that in Lorraine Hansberry's play the thing that comes through is that, in spite of all these differences and difficulties, *this is our house*. That was their Chicago. This is our country. And I for one am intensely concerned and fascinated, by the things that go on here.

Some people have asked me why Richard Wright didn't come

home and why he lived in Europe, and why some of our better Negro artists and writers are living over there. My feeling is that they have a perfect right to live wherever they want to, and to get away from the tensions of the American scene, if they wish. It just happens that it interests me, it doesn't upset me particularly. I like to indulge in these racial arguments and fights and discussions, such as we are having here, about what to do about all this. And I stayed here and I live here because I like it, quite frankly, and I think that we can make out of our country something wonderful and quite beautiful, in which eventually we can even integrate Gospel songs and have them sung well.

CAPOUYA: I'd like to raise a question regarding the sit-in movements in the South. Certainly, a Negro ought to be able to eat where everybody else does; since he's a brother of mine, obviously, that's the first step, before I can be free to eat where I want, too.

But a couple of years ago, when the march on Washington was made, the Negro leaders were saying, "After all, you people are fighting for your lives, you're fighting against the Russians. Why don't you admit us to that status of citizenship where we can help you? Why don't you admit us to the community so we can pull our weight?"

Well, that's a lot of nonsense as far as I'm concerned, and if that's what they're out to get, if they want to get atomized at the same time we do, we'll all be holding hands in Christian brotherly love when the bomb falls. Well, that is stupid.

I would be delighted if the Rev. Martin Luther King would think one step ahead of himself in this sense, and not feel that civil rights for Negroes in the South is the be-all and the end-all. It may be a tactical first step, but if it isn't to move to a higher plane, then I'm not interested.

HUGHES: Well, I heard Rev. Martin Luther King say at a meeting not long ago that perhaps is was the Negro's destiny to save America for itself. And another rather distinguished Negro leader disagreed and said, :"Well, first, certainly, we've got to save it for ourselves."

BALDWIN: I'm delighted that we've got around to this very thorny area. It has always seemed to me that one of the great handicaps of this country in its dealings with the world is that it doesn't know anything about the rest of the world, not in the sense that a Frenchman doesn't know anything about China, but in the sense that it has always avoided knowing those things — I'm afraid you have to call them tragic or black or deep or mysterious or inexorable — which are at the very bottom of life.

One of the reasons that Cuba has been such a disaster is because people in America do not know that just down the road Mexicans and Cubans, and a whole lot of other people in a place called South America, are not only starving, which you can tell by statistics, but are living there. And they don't like to be mistreated. And one of the reasons that we don't know this is our evasion in the world, which is exactly the evasion that we've made in this country for over 100 years, to date it only from the emancipation. Ultimately, it's a moral evasion of oneself, which really menaces — and this cannot be overstated — the very future of this country. That is why there is so little time to save this house; after all, one can always jump, that's not the problem. I don't want to be atomized with you or with anybody, and I don't want anybody else atomized, either.

But the price for American survival is really the most extraordinary and speedy metamorphosis, and I don't know if they're going to make it. But we've got to realize that when people say God, they don't always mean the Protestant God. There are people on the other side of the world, who have been worshipping somebody else for thousands and thousands of years. I do think that anybody who really cares about this must insist on nothing more or less than a moral revolution. Because nothing can be patched up. It's got to be remade.

CAPOUYA: That's so true, but I want to object to something said before, the notion of the white man's guilty secret, and that the Negro has got to be where he is because we have to know where the bottom of the heap is. That's not true: the Negro is where he is because of the long history of slavery, economic rejection, and so on.

HUGHES: At the moment I have a play which I hope will be on Broadway next season. The play was originally entirely about Negroes — about the Gospel churches. However, with the current trend towards integration, some backers said that they would not put money into an entirely Negro-cast play.

Well, the leading lady in my play, who makes a great deal of money out of selling holy water, worked up to having a chauffeur; in my script it never occurred to me that he should be one color or another. I thought of him as a Negro chauffeur because most Negroes who can afford chauffeurs have Negro chauffeurs, but not all. However, when the demand came for integration of my cast, I said, "Well, always in white plays the chauffeurs are Negroes; let's make the chauffeur in my play white, which would not be untrue to life." Adam Powell, I believe, has a white or Japanese chauffeur. Jules Bledsoe, when he was star of 'Showboat" had a white chauffeur, and when people asked him why he had a white chauffeur, he said, "So people can tell the chauffeur from myself." (LAUGHTER)

Well, at any rate, it's not too unusual that some colored people do have white chauffeurs and some have white maids, even in Harlem. And so I thought that would be nice and a little novel to Broadway. Let's have a white chauffeur. Do you know that everybody said, "Oh, the American public wouldn't accept that"? So my play is still not integrated.

MISS HANSBERRY: I gather we are close to conclusion, but, Mr. Kazin, I'd like to pick up something that you said, and to try and bring it up to date for myself.

You said, I thought rather beautifully, that the Negro question tends to go to the heart of various missorted American agonies, beginning with slavery itself. I am profoundly concerned that in these 100 years since the Civil War very few of our countrymen have really believed that their Federal Union and the defeat of the slavocracy and the negation of slavery as an institution is an admirable fact of American life. It is possible today to get enormous books that are coming out on the Civil War and go through to the back of them, and not find the word slavery, let alone Negro.

We've been trying very hard in America to pretend that this greatest conflict didn't even have at its base the only issue that was significant. Person after person will write a book today and insist that slavery was not the issue. They tell you that it was fought for economic reasons, as if that economy were not based on slavery. People spend volumes discussing the battles of the Civil War and which army was crossing the river at five minutes to two and how their swords were hanging, but we have tried to get rid of the slavery issue. Ever since *Gone With the Wind*, it has been an accepted part of our culture to describe the slave system in terms of beautiful ladies in big fat dresses, screaming that their houses have been burned down by the awful Yankees. But when someone asked me to write 90 minutes of television drama on slavery, not a propaganda piece, but, I hope, a serious treatment of family relationships, by a slave-owning family and their slaves, this was considered controversial. This has never been done.

Those millions of Americans who went out only a month or two ago, presumably voted for a Federal president, but our culture does not really respect the fact that if the North had not won, if the Union forces had not triumphed over slavery, this country that we're talking about would exist only in imagination. Americans today are too ashamed and frightened to take a position even on this.

BALDWIN: Yes, this breaks the heart; this is the most sinister thing about it. Not that it happened, not that it's wrong, but that nobody wants to admit that it happened. And until this admission is made, nothing can be done.

KAZIN: How much time do we have?

HENTOFF: Is there anything you want to add?

KAZIN: We should begin the interview.

The Novelist

Testing the Color Line
Dunbar and Chesnutt

by Robert Farnsworth

Paul laurence dunbar and Charles Waddell Chesnutt occupy a unique role in the tradition of Afro-American literature. Both achieved national literary prominence during the post-Reconstruction period. They were the first Afro-Americans to do so. Their prominence in each case rested upon their ability to exploit conventions previously developed by white authors. For Dunbar this seemed a racial cul de sac. Chesnutt exploited his opportunity with greater subtlety. But each found himself frustrated by his audience's indifference, if not hostility, as soon as he tried to step outside the literary conventions which brought him to national prominence.

Both authors also share the mixed blessing of being sponsored to the American reading public by William Dean Howells. In both cases Howells' praise gave them an entrée for which they could not help but be grateful. But also in each case Howells' praise came to establish the restrictive limits under which the reading public was willing to support their writing.

In an introduction to Dunbar's *Lyrics of Lowly Life*, Howells wrote: "What struck me in reading Mr. Dunbar's poetry was what had already struck his friends in Ohio and Indiana, in Kentucky and Illinois. They had felt, as I felt, that however gifted his race had proven itself in music, in oratory, in several of the other arts, here was the first instance of an American Negro who had evinced innate distinction in literature. So far as I could remember, Paul Dunbar was the only man of pure African blood and of American civilization to feel the Negro life aesthetically and express it lyrically. . . . I said that a race which had come to this effect in any member of it, had attained civilization in him, and I permitted myself the imaginative prophecy that the hostilities and the prejudices which had so long constrained his race were destined to vanish in the arts; that these were to be the final proof that God had made of one blood all nations of men. . . .

"Yet it appeared to me then, and it appears to me now, that there is a precious difference of temperament between the races which it would be a great pity ever to lose, and that this is best preserved and most charmingly suggested by Mr. Dunbar in those pieces of his where he studies the moods and traits of his race in its own accent of our English. We call such pieces dialect pieces for want of some closer phrase, but they are really not dialect so much as delightful personal attempts and failures for the written and spoken language. In nothing is his essentially refined and delicate art so well shown as in those pieces, which, as I ventured to say, describe the range between appetite and emotion, with certain lifts far beyond and above it, which is the range of the race."

Howells' position and praise were extremely valuable to Dunbar, but Howells' views became the commonplace critical response to Dunbar's poetry. To Dunbar this was a life-sentence to write a "jingle in a broken tongue." Dunbar's parents were ex-slaves of unmixed African descent. Living when he did he could not help but be influenced by the Horatio Alger myth of success which pervaded American society. For him to compete successfully with white writers on their own terms was to enter the American dream and to strike a giant blow to the restrictive stereotypes of Negro racial inferiority which were swarming up in reaction to emancipation and the Reconstruction effort. He felt that he could best represent his race if he could write with grace and wisdom about any of the conventional subjects of poetry without claiming any special racial perspective. That is how he defined freedom for himself and for his race.

Thus Dunbar saw Howells' praise for his dialect poetry as an albatross around his neck. He wanted to forget the too painfully near past of slavery and look forward to a fully emancipated world where a man would be judged without reference to his race. For this reason he wrote with special urgency to a friend in London: "One critic says a thing and the rest hasten to say the same thing, in many cases using the identical words. I see now very clearly that Mr. Howells has done me irrevocable harm in the dictum he laid down regarding my dialect verse. I am afraid that it will even influence English criticism, although what notices I have here have shown a different trend."

Dunbar's contempt for plantation themes and his impatience with his audience's demand for dialect poetry undoubtedly kept him from exploiting his racial material with power. William Stanley Braithwaite makes a harsh but just summary judgment of Dunbar's poetry: "It is the poetry of the happy peasant and the plaintive minstrel. Occasionally, as in the sonnet to Robert Gould Shaw and the 'Ode to Ethiopia' there broke through Dunbar, as through the crevices of his spirit, a burning and brooding aspiration, an awakening and virile consciousness of race. But for the most part, his dreams were anchored to the minor whimsies; his deepest poetic inspiration was sentiment. He expressed a folk temperament, but not a race soul. Dunbar was the end of a regime, and not the beginning of a tradition, as so many careless critics seem to think."[1]

The limitations of Dunbar's attitude toward his racial material are obvious, but sometimes they seem to have blocked any but the most grudging critical appreciation of his accomplishment. Few critics give Dunbar's fiction any serious consideration. J. Saunders Redding expresses a fairly representative attitude: "Excepting only a few, his short stories depict Negro characters as whimsical, simple, folksy, not-too bright souls, all of whose social problems are little ones, and all of whose emotional cares can be solved by the intellectual or spiritual equivalent of a stick of red peppermint candy. It is of course significant that three of his four novels are not about Negroes at all, and the irony of depicting himself as a white youth in his spiritual autobiography, *The Uncalled*, needs no comment."[2]

Dunbar's novels, besides seeming too frequently to eschew racial material altogether, suffer from a narrative style which often seems old fashioned, even at times quaint. But there are elements in the novels which bear closer scrutiny.

If *The Uncalled* is in some sense Dunbar's spiritual autobiography, the implications of that have never been very carefully examined. Fred Brent, the protagonist of the novel, is an orphan raised by a good hearted but religiously domineering woman who pressures him into the Methodist ministry. He grudgingly accepts the role she lays out for him, although there are numerous indications that his heart is not in it. He rebels against the narrow righteousness of his congregation when the former minister insists upon his making an example of a young girl who has fallen from the straight and narrow path. When he refuses, the minister implies he is doing so to protect himself. He quits his position in defiant relief and accepts the commonly whispered charge that he is the true son of his drunkard father who had abandoned his family before the novel begins. Fred leaves town for the big city in sullen resentment at the pettiness of small town morality. But his first night out he accidentally meets his father who has become a repentant temperance speaker and is on his way home to die. Fred joylessly returns home to reveal himself to his father on his death bed. His duty done he then leaves town free at last to become his own man.

Dunbar apparently was attracted to the ministry and Fred Brent's reservations about small town Methodism probably are Dunbar's own. But there are subtler ties to Dunbar's world than this. The race of the characters is never designated and since there are no racial incidents in the novel and particularly since Fred moves freely through the big city world of Cincinnati, the reader must assume that the characters are white. Yet the novel constantly tempts one to think that the characters are only superficially white. Intrinsically they seem black. The novel is not literally autobiographical, but the controlling figure of Hester Prime echoes so many representative problems of black life, that one is tempted to believe that Dunbar was writing a representative drama of a black young man struggling for freedom and manhood.

Hester is a strong matriarchal figure. She is overzealous in her religiosity. She takes her duty much too seriously and this almost frustrates her realization as a woman, but 'liphalet Hodges who has been too passively patient for too long does win her consent to marriage when he finally forces the issue. Dunbar makes it clear with light irony right from the beginning that there is nothing petty about Hester, that her big heart always masquerades behind her ever present sense of duty:

It is hard to explain just what Miss Hester's position was among the denizens of the poorer quarter. She was liked and disliked, admired and feared. She would descend upon her victims with unasked counsel and undesired tracts. Her voice was a trumpet of scathing invective against their immorality, but her hand was as a horn of plenty in straitened times, and her presence in sickness was a comfort. She made no pretence to being good-hearted; in fact, she resented the term as applied to herself. It was all duty with her.

But Hester is a heroic figure among pygmies. She has a true moral passion compared to the petty gossips and status seeking church people who surround her. In fact Dunbar's view of her community, with the exception of Hester, 'liphalet, and Fred is so bleak that it reminds me of the caustic generalizations Richard Wright made of the barrenness of black life after suffering through his childhood under the domination of an almost maniacally religious grandmother in Jackson, Mississippi:

> After I had outlived the shocks of childhood, after the habit of reflection had been born in me, I used to mull over the strange absence of real kindness in Negroes, how unstable was our tenderness, how lacking in genuine passion we were, how void of great hope, how timid our joy, how bare our traditions, how hollow our memories, how lacking we were in those intangible sentiments that bind man to man, and how shallow was even our despair. . . .

> Whenever I thought of the essential bleakness of black life in America, I knew that Negroes had never been allowed to catch the full spirit of Western civilization, that they had lived somehow in it but not of it.

It is the barrenness of the surrounding world that makes Fred's problem of achieving his own manhood so acute. Hester is an overbearing woman despite her real passion. 'liphalet is a kindly and understanding step-father, but he is relatively impotent. Thus Hester's drive to make Fred a religious leader of his people is extremely difficult for him to resist because he finds no other alternative models. He is vaguely unhappy with his fate, but he only rebels when his community pressures him to act in a manner which violates his sense of human dignity. But in that rebellion he achieves his manhood.

It is tempting to speculate that if Fred Brent is a fictional projection of Dunbar, as Redding and others have suggested, then perhaps Dunbar is describing his own feelings about the barrenness of his position as a Negro writer read primarily for his intimate picture of plantation life in the colorful dialect of his people. Fred leaves town for the larger city and embraces a more cosmopolitan mode of life. Dunbar longed for the freedom of acceptance in the larger national literary world. Writing his story white was perhaps implicitly an effort to make the happy ending of Fred's story come true for Paul Dunbar.

Dunbar published a second white novel in 1901, *The Fanatics*. It centers on the impact of the Civil War on a small Ohio community of mixed allegiances. Families are split and finally rather romantically reconciled. But in the middle of the novel are two chapters dealing with the arrival of a band of slaves in this Ohio town just after General Butler had decreed all slaves contraband of war. The white community's fear of a rapid increase in the black population, the established blacks' fear of the slaves' threat to their precarious social status, and the slaves' hunger for freedom lead to a violently murderous confrontation. The hero of this little story within a story is a young defiant black slave who never backs down either from the bullying bluff of the whites or later from the murderous attack of a white mob. He finally courageously buries his knife in the mob's leader and dies himself. This is no denial of Dunbar's black identity. It is a story filled with the same kind of racial pride and revolt against white racism as inspirits the work of such black literary stalwarts as Wright, Baldwin or Cleaver.

In the same year that *The Fanatics* was published, Dunbar also published his best known novel, *The Sport of the Gods*. This is a novel about a black family who become the scapegoats for a white man's crime. This family begin the novel as devoted servants to a wealthy and aristocratic white family. They are mildly prosperous because they are sober and saving people. When a member of the big house claims a loss of a large amount of money, the Hamiltons are suspected because of their accumulated savings. Berry, the father, is unjustly convicted and sent to prison. The family are scorned by the other blacks for their past uppitiness and success. Joe, Berry's young son, assumes the male leadership role in the family and they move to New York City to escape the stigma of Berry's supposed crime and imprisonment. But the big city life is too fast for this small town family. Joe becomes increasingly dissipated as he tries to become increasingly sophisticated. Kit, his sister, finds a harsh and selfish kind of success on the stage. Mrs. Hamilton, abandoned by her children, sets up housekeeping with a race track gambler. A seedy but shrewd white newspaperman spurred by Joe's drunken protestations of his father's innocence investigates the old crime. Berry's former employer has in the meantime found out the truth but hides it in terrified dread and guilt. Joe hits bottom when his mistress turns him out because she can no longer stomach his weakness. He returns in a quiet mad desperation and strangles her, oblivious to all consequences. The reporter breaks Berry's case and he is freed, but he is a broken man from his harsh prison years. He is brought to New York to find his family disintegrated.

It could have been a powerful story, but it is sketchy and slight. Dunbar depends on melodrama and sentimental clichés rather than thorough going artistic documentation. Yet no black writer prior to this gave such a vivid picture of the cruel exploitation which characterizes the black ghetto. And Dunbar makes it just as clear as does Malcolm X or Claude Brown that the barbarousness of ghetto life is attributable to the poverty of cultural opportunity open to blacks and to their emasculating dependency on white power.

Dunbar's last novel *The Love of Landry* is white and sentimental. It adds nothing to his stature as a black writer. Dunbar's power and position were waning and the novel was a weak effort to achieve a popular gentility.

But some generalizations can be made from this brief review. Dunbar felt little compulsion to speak for black Americans. He often looked upon that role as a limiting and perhaps even demeaning assignment from the white literary world. However, one is tempted to speculate upon the significance of Dunbar's own color in all this. Dunbar was pure black. He often must have assumed in a way for instance that Charles Chesnutt, who could easily have passed for white, would not that there was no need for him deliberately to represent his identity with the black community. He simply was so visibly and well known a member of it. Thus for him to compete on equal terms with white writers was not necessarily to leave his blackness behind him. He assumed that he carried it with him on his fame. But that is the locus of the real problem for Dunbar. For him blackness was too simple. He frequently did not seem to see the value of trying to measure it as a social and racial experience.

Paradoxically Charles Chesnutt, perhaps because he was so close to white in his skin color and because of his close association with whites in his achieved professional and social status, examined the problems of the black man living in a white dominated world with much greater complexity and intricacy. In a sense Charles Chesnutt was to Paul Laurence Dunbar what W. E. B. DuBois was to Booker T. Washington. While Dunbar demonstrated a shrewd ability to exploit the prejudices of his largely white audience and while he served an extraordinarily useful function by simply being black and achieving national literary prominence, yet his work does not look forward. He was not as alive to the currents of literary and social change as was Chesnutt. Dunbar could not discipline himself as well as did Chesnutt to careful realistic documentation. Dunbar seemed wistfully to believe in the near possibility of a truly colorless world. Chesnutt was more pragmatic, believing perhaps in the same ultimate vision, but recognizing more prominently the immediate problems of Southern disfranchisement, Jim Crow legislation, and racial intermarriage.

Like Dunbar, Chesnutt began his literary career by exploiting the sentimental interest of the American reading public in pre-Civil War plantation themes. Chesnutt first began to attract national attention with "The Goophered Grapevine" published in *The Atlantic* in 1887. Unlike Dunbar, literature was for Chesnutt a sideline, since he was also establishing a very successful legal business career in Cleveland. But Chesnutt wrote and published several more stories over the next ten years slowly adding to his national reputation and widening his contacts in publishing and writing circles.

By the late 1890's his reputation and publications warranted bringing his stories together in a book. Houghton, Mifflin and Co. at first discouraged such a publication, but then indicated if Chesnutt had a sufficient number of "conjure" stories they might be interested in publishing a book of them. Chesnutt added six conjure stories to those already published. Houghton, Mifflin eliminated two but agreed to publish Chesnutt's first book, *The Conjure Woman*. It appeared in print in 1898.

When Chesnutt collected his conjure stories he added to the

introduction of "The Goophered Grapevine." This addition plus the repeated pattern of narration of the stories gave emphasis to the narrative frame in which the conjure stories are enfolded. Uncle Julius a shrewd old ex-slave tells his stories to a new employer who has come from the north to begin a grape growing industry and to find a more salubrious climate for his wife's health. The two white northerners who listen to Uncle Julius readily allow Chesnutt to make occasional editorial comment on the horrors of the slave system. But more than that as Uncle Julius learns to distinguish between the intuitive sympathy of his employer's wife and the rather patronizingly indulgent interest of his business-preoccupied employer there emerges a more subtle paradigm of the plight of the Afro-American contemporary to the publication of the stories. Uncle Julius's employer finds it hard to take the stories seriously except as rather cunning but relatively harmless devices to attain or protect some special interest of Julius. He does not respond as deeply to the stories as his wife does, who is not in the least perturbed by the elaborate claims made on her fancy by the conjure elements. Her exclamation at the end of "Po' Sandy," "What a system it was . . . under which such things were possible," is the response Chesnutt through his tales tries to evoke.

The contrast between Uncle Julius and his employer John suggests the contrasts between the black and white experiences. I have summed this up in another discussion:

> Uncle Julius by the end of the book emerges as a shrewd and wise old man. He understands the principles of husbandry and business, but more than that he knows something of the nooks and crannies of the human heart. He knows all about the world John, his employer, likes to pretend does not exist or which he consigns to his women. With this knowledge Julius gains power, not the economic and social power John can take for granted with his whiteness but a power over the more intimate and mysterious secrets of life itself.

> Thus, as John patronizes Julius, he testifies to his own limitations, and it suggests the white world's fumbling inability to appreciate the wisdom, humor, and heart of the black man's experience rooted in the cruelties of the slave experience.[3]

Just as the decision was made to publish *The Conjure Woman,* another story of Chesnutt's in an altogether different mode attracted a great deal of comment. "The Wife of His Youth" appeared in *The Atlantic* in July, 1898. The favorable attention it received plus the initial reception of *The Conjure Woman* caused Chesnutt to suggest a second volume of stories called *The Wife of His Youth and Other Stories of the Color Line.* Houghton, Mifflin readily agreed.

Chesnutt's stories of the color line were for the most part given a contemporary setting. No looking back to the plantation world with its folksy emphasis on customs and language which whites were almost inevitably to find safely distant. Yet these stories also were usually carefully gauged to inform and influence while yet avoiding a direct emotional confrontation. Some of the stories, including the title story, were humorous glimpses into the blue-veined society of Groveland, a fairly obvious cognate for Cleveland. The question of racial identity for those who are predominantly white is a favorite Chesnutt theme. But there are also at least two stories in the collection which can be described as strong protest stories, "The Sheriff's Children" and the closing story "The Web of Circumstance."

"The Sheriff's Children" projects the problem of white responsibility and guilt with bold drama and it clearly touched a sensitive nerve in part of Chesnutt's audience. Nancy Houston Banks wrote in *The Bookman*:

Touching this (the "unapproachable ground of sentimental relations between the black race and the white race") and still more dangerous and darker race problems, Mr. Chesnutt shows a lamentable lack of tact of a kindred sort, an incomprehensible want of good taste and dignified reserve which characterizes his first beautiful story and the greater part of all his work. "The Sheriff's Children" furnishes, perhaps, the most shocking instance of his reckless disregard of matters respected by more experienced writers.

Nevertheless, Chesnutt's touch was deft enough and restrained enough not to alienate a large segment of his reading public. By this time his literary career loked promising enough for him to give up his business career and devote himself full time to writing. He quickly contracted to do a biography of Frederick Douglass and suddenly two publishing houses were willing to publish his first novel *The House Behind the Cedars*.

The House was long Chesnutt's most popular novel, but its concern with the problems of passing now seems historically dated. It is a more sustained story of those who live on the edge of the color line than those collected in *The Wife of His Youth and Other Stories of the Color Line*. Shortly before publication of his novel Chesnutt wrote for the *Boston Transcript*:

> The only thing that ever succeeded in keeping the two races apart when living on the same soil — the only true ground of caste — is religion, and, as has been alluded to in the case of Jews, this is only superficially successful. The colored people are the same as the whites in religion; they have the same standards and methods of culture, the same ideals, and the presence of the successful white race as a constant incentive to their ambition. The ultimate result is not difficult to foresee. The races will be quite as effectively amalgamated by lightening the Negroes as they would be by darkening the whites.

In the 1890s when there was much talk of *The Yellow Peril* and *mongrelization* of the races, this was a daring statement. Now it seems like a wistfully sentimental sell out. Chesnutt, like Dunbar, sometimes presented the road to the promised land as something like our superhighways which pass by the ghettos disdainfully refusing to recognize their existence. But then few people at this time in our nation's history understood the deep-rootedness of racial hostility and prejudice in our national character.

The House Behind the Cedars had been written and rewritten over a period of many years. It was important to Chesnutt to prove that he could handle a lengthy narrative. Its publication along with the generally favorable reception to his two collections of stories gave him confidence to try a bolder story both in literary form and in racial statement—*The Marrow of Tradition*. This novel was stimulated by the brutal attack of a white mob upon blacks in Wilmington in 1898.

The Marrow of Tradition attempts to deal with many segments of a community all at the same time. Several plots are interwoven and not all of them are equally successful. But it clearly underscores the dilemma of the black man living in a Southern community by dramatizing the tension which exists between Dr. Miller, a European trained black surgeon of considerable talent who is dedicated to building a better community for his people, and John Green, a black laborer of imposing physical strength and courage seething with racial indignation which stems from the murder of his father by Ku Kluxers and his mother's pathetic retreat into idiocy.

As the novel builds to its climax of racial riot, John Green attempts to organize the blacks in a crude military self-defense. He asks Miller to lead them. Miller clearly sees the hopelessness of the black's position and refuses the role: "My advice is not heroic, but I think it is wise. In this riot we are placed as we should be in a war: we have no territory, no base of supplies, no organization, no outside sympathy, — we stand in the position of a race, in a case like this, without money and without friends. Our time will come, — the time when we can command respect for our rights; but it is not yet in sight. Give it up boys, and wait. Good may come of this, after all."

John answers this with pointed contempt: "Come along, boys! Dese gentlemen may have somethin' ter live fer; but ez fer my pa't, I'd ruther be a dead nigger any day dan a live dog!"

Chesnutt's mind and conditioning side with the new Negro, Dr. Miller, but John Green exerts a dark compelling power over his imagination.

Chesnutt's ambition caused him to reach beyond his skill in *The Marrow of Tradition*. It has many literary faults, but the reviews it received were little concerned with the literary weaknesses of the book. They were preoccupied with its racial statement. Chesnutt's daughter summarizes some Southern responses: "One paper attacked Chesnutt bitterly for writing a book of lies and slander about the South and condemned Houghton, Mifflin and Company for publishing it. Another characterized the book as utterly repellent to Southern sentiment and one calculated to do infinite harm to the South if widely read. Another called it 'ridiculous silly rot.' A leading Washington paper questioned 'the wisdom of such a book as it arouses bitter resentments in politics and personal relations.'"

But such reactions were not limited to the South. Paul Elmer More, as literary editor of the Boston *Independent*, said that "Chesnutt had done what he could to humiliate the whites." More described the final chapter of the novel as "utterly revolting."

William Dean Howells had previously given Chesnutt's work very welcome praise. This novel, however, severely tested his magnanimity:

> *The Marrow of Tradition,* like everything else he has written, has to do with the relations of blacks and whites, and in that republic of letters where all men are free and equal he stands up for his own people with a courage which has more justice than mercy in it. The book is, in fact, bitter, bitter. There is no reason in history why it should not be so, if wrong is to be repaid with hate, and yet it would be better if it was not so bitter. I am not saying that he is so inartistic as to play the advocate; whatever his minor foibles may be, he is an artist whom his step-brother Americans may well be proud of. . . . No one who reads the book can deny that the case is presented with great power; or fail to recognize in the writer a portent of the sort of Negro equality against which no series of hangings and burnings will finally avail.

Chesnutt had had big hopes for this novel. It was to be the book which assured his literary position by winning him a large audience and critical respect. He was clearly surprised at the reaction it provoked and chagrined at its commercial failure. After such an experience his legal business looked more and more attractive and he returned to it with very little hesitation.

A letter from Chesnutt to his publishers indicates his state of mind:

> I am beginning to suspect that the public as a rule does not care for books in which the principal characters are colored people, or written with a striking sympathy with that race as contrasted with the white race. . . . If a novel which is generally acknowledged to be interesting, dramatic, well constructed, well written — which qualities have been generally ascribed to *The Marrow of Tradition,* of which in addition, both the author and publishers have good hopes — cannot sell 5,000 copies within two months after its publication, there must be something radically wrong somewhere, and I do not know where it is unless it be in the subject. My friend, Mr. Howells, who has said many nice things about my writings — although his review of *The*

Marrow of Tradition in *The North American Review* was not a favorable one as I look at it — has remarked several times that there is no color line in literature. On that point I take issue with him. I am pretty fairly convinced that the color line runs everywhere so far as the United States is concerned.

Chesnutt did not stop writing with this disappointment, but his pride and his confidence had been dealt a severe blow. He published one more novel, *The Colonel's Dream,* in 1905. Like Dunbar's final novel, *The Love of Landry,* it was a white novel. But *The Colonel's Dream* is a better and stronger book. It focusses on the injustices of the convict labor system in the South. Nevertheless it signals even as Dunbars' novel does that its author has no more stomach to confront his predominantly white audience with a racial challenge.

During the post reconstruction period from 1877 to 1901 relations between black and white Americans reached a nadir. Dunbar and Chesnutt bubble out of that period as if in apparent contradiction, but the bubble broke against the racial hostility both authors felt in their audience. On July 3, 1928, Chesnutt was awarded the NAACP's Spingarn medal. His retrospective view of his own career seems sadly sound: "My books were written, from one point of view, a generation too soon. There was no such demand then as there is now for books by and about colored people. And I was writing against the trend of public opinion on the race question at that particular time."

[1]"The Negro in American Literature," *Black Expression,* ed. Addison Gayle, Jr. (New York, 1969), p. 176.
[2]"American Negro Literature," *Black Expression,* pp. 230-231.
[3]Introduction to *The Conjure Woman,* to be published by the University of Michigan Press, Ann Arbor, 1969.

The Lost Potential
of Richard Wright

by Warren French

ONE WOULD LIKE to think that the recent flurry of interest in Richard Wright (I write in the unquiet spring of 1969) is not just a by-product of the fashionable enthusiasm for "Black American Literature," but rather an effort to render at last his due to a man praised too soon for the wrong reasons and too soon dismissed for more wrong reasons. One doubts, however, that this man who so much longed to be recognized as an individual would be freshly honored except as a racial symbol. In death as in life, Wright has been forced to win as a Negro who happened to be a writer the recognition that he desired as a *writer* who happened to be a Negro.

Although much of Wright's best work was done during the 1930s, he was virtually unknown outside the cliquish ranks of the native Communists until 1940 when *Native Son* exploded over the literary landscape, first as a hauntingly controversial novel, then (under the aegis of Orson Welles — another abused genius) as a grimly powerful play. Wright's childhood — the details of which have become internationally known through his own and others' accounts — is a ghastly epitome of the American Negro's experience — abandoned by his father, tossed from one harrassed relative to another, prayed over by ignorant fundamentalists, preyèd upon by Southern bigots and Northern exploiters, traduced by enemies of his skin color who cared nothing for the man beneath and misused by friends of his skin color who cared little more.

Wright wrote some time in the 1930s an excellent novel that has still not received proper attention, but he was persuaded to suppress it by Communist colleagues who thought that it would not serve their cause (It wouldn't have). He listened because only the Communists had granted him any measure of the attention that he needed; but it is doubtful that he could have found either a publisher or an audience for *Lawd Today* in the 30s, because it did not meet the demand of that despairing time for instant remedies for society's aches. The novel does for the experience of the young adult urban Negro what Henry Roth's *Call It Sleep* does for the experience of the urban Jewish child. The long neglect of Roth's sensitive work is indicative of what Wright's fate probably would have been had he published "prematurely."

So he kept grinding out pieces for Communist journals and making time to produce excellent short works like the section on Harlem for the Federal Writers' Project New York City guide and the vivid stories that would be acclaimed when published under the collective title *Uncle Tom's Children* (1938). These stories brought him honor and a contract that would pay his living expenses while he worked on a bigger project but no one has been able to make a reputation solely as a writer of short stories since the pace of American life accelerated in the 1920s. (Even J. D. Sallinger had only a tiny following until the appearance of *The Catcher in the Rye*.) Wright needed to produce a novel. He did.

Hysteria! His Communist friends were chilly (possibly as much because of his personal success as because of his lack of orthodoxy); but when the Literary Establishment raved, Earl Browder held out an olive branch. Wright had had enough, however. His essay, "I Tried to Be a Communist," published in the *Atlantic Monthly* in 1944, is a classic statement of the plight of an intensely perceptive and self-centered man trying to adjust himself to the demands of a group that offers him the helping hand he needs at the price of his personal identity.

Native Son was an extraordinary success not just because it was an exciting novel by a Negro writer, not just because its sensational episodes fed the public appetite for violence, not just because its flights of rhetoric wrung the hearts of the champions of the oppressed, but most of all because it was that rarest of coups — a work that was familiar in form but unfamiliar in content. Wright had managed to produce an innovation within the nearly exhausted framework of the twentieth-century liberal literary tradition. He had written the Negro equivalent of Dreiser's *An American Tragedy*.[1]

Wright consolidated his triumph with his next major work, *Black Boy* (1945), an account of his childhood in Mississippi, which, even with some final chapters deleted, became an emblem of America's shame and a kind of universal history of the genius frustrated by discrimination.

What few noticed in the hubbub over Wright's powerful apologia is that: (1) a great many Negroes and members of other minority groups had suffered as he had without ever being able to find an adequate vehicle for the articulation of their personal grievances; (2) Wright's account had many similarities to other non-Negro portraits of the artist as a young man, including Joyce's famous novel. While the torments that a white man with Wright's sensibility would have suffered would probably have been different —more subtle, more genteel — they would have been none-the-less mortifying because Wright was *doubly* different from his complacent countrymen. Actually his fellow Communists and fellow Negroes probably understood him only slightly better than his white oppressors and not nearly so well as the few of any color or persuasion who possessed his capacity to respond to life.

Wright seemed, nevertheless, firmly established as the most articulate literary spokesman for the oppressed Negro minority in the United States, the first Negro novelist of really major stature. Then about the same time that John Steinbeck left California for New York, Wright left America for France. This parallel is, I think, more than coincidental. Steinbeck is, in many ways, the fellow artist that Wright most nearly resembles. Wright was actually doing in his work for the American Negro what Steinbeck was doing for the little less despised and little more secure white rejects in our society — those who had been left behind in the shift from an agrarian to an urban society.

Steinbeck was able to avoid as open a commitment to Communism as Wright made because the shy Californian distrusted any subordination of the individual to a group and was able to find friends and supporters outside of organized groups. Steinbeck could also write more than Wright during their most productive creative years in the 30s because his talents were not diverted into ephemeral projects. Though he, too, faced privation until his works finally caught on, he was able to produce a novel almost every year during the depression. It is fascinating, though useless, to speculate what a single friend like Ed Ricketts might have done for Richard Wright, whom we tend to forget was only six years younger than Steinbeck and belongs psychologically to the same generation that was shaped by the traumas of the 20s. After World War II, both novelists left the regions that they understood best because they were attracted elsewhere by the promise of greater personal freedom and dignity.

Although some critics have labored to find merits in *The Outsider* and other fictional products of Wright's French period, there seems no reason to deny that his career as a serious creative artist ended with his departure from this country in 1946. Like Steinbeck, he can best be described during these later years as a provocative and increasingly querulous journalist. He became as firmly identified with the Negro struggle for political freedom and self-identification throughout the world as Steinbeck became associated with Adlai Stevenson's sophisticated folksiness as the basis for a democratic society. Steinbeck managed to remain at least a small force in American politics; whereas Wright was scorned by the *Time-Life* empire and other mass-media taste-makers for his tart-tongued pushiness. Both, however, were generally and justifiably considered to have ceased to have any artistic significance.

In an early (1960) issue of *Wisconsin Studies in Contemporary Literature,* Jackson R. Bryer published a list of selected criticism of Wright's work that marked almost the first serious attention the novelist had received from American academicians,[2] except for a separate listing in the *Literary History of the United States* (1948), a work in progress at the peak of Wright's reputation as a creative artist. Ironically, Bryer's compilation appeared as an unintentional memorial just about the time of Wright's death. It indicated that almost all of the writing about Wright in the years before his death had been journalistic reviews of his novels and other writings or discussions of his achievement in accounts of Negro literature. He was still viewed as primarily a popular spokesman for a racial group. Major critics like R. P. Blackmur, Alfred Kazin, and Nathan A. Scott, Jr., had noted his work only in passing. The most noteworthy discussions by younger Negro artists like James Baldwin and Ralph Ellison were not always friendly. Only a few serious critics like Nick Aaron Ford, Richard

Lehan, and Kingsley Widmer had dealt with the relationship of Wright's work to the fashionable existentialist movement in France (which I comment upon elsewhere in a comparison of *Native Son* with Camus' *The Stranger*[3]).

The situation did not improve much during the next decade, although there was extensive discussion of Baldwin's and Ellison's comments on Wright and some brief introduction of Wright to foreign audiences. Most of the comments suggested that Wright's works had been buried with him.

Evidence of a sharp turn in interest was the report in *Dissertation Abstracts* in 1967 of three studies of his works, prepared with an eerie kind of geographical balance on the East and West Coasts and in the Midwest. Then with the dying decade came at last three books about Wright — flood where there had been drought.

Constance Webb's *Richard Wright* is bound to remain the springboard for studies of the author for many years. In the burgeoning tradition of the doorstop biography that began with Mark Schorer's *Sinclair Lewis* and has fattened on accounts of Dreiser, Thomas Wolfe, Fitzgerald and Hemingway, Miss Webb's book provides the student with the data that he needs to begin an analysis of the sometimes joyous but more often tortured life of a misunderstood and exploited man. The book is almost innocent of organization. It is impossible to follow Wright's movements chronologically through the pages, and some important works like *Lawd Today* and "I Tried to Be a Communist" are not mentioned at all. One wishes that the author might have been prevailed upon to group her materials by date as Jay Leyda has done in his extremely useful *The Melville Log.*

Miss Webb is primarily interested, however, in creating a martyrology; and the chaotic structure of her work is compensated for her by her genuine feeling for her subject and by the long excerpts from Wright's own notebooks. Excellently indexed, *Richard Wright* is a book to be consulted rather than read straight through. It is a reference tool that should greatly facilitate the production of critical studies by more orderly if less devoted minds.

Often recently it has been impossible to distinguish between critical books from commercial and university presses, though there should be a difference. The first two long critical studies of Richard Wright, however, serve to exemplify the different purposes the publications of these two establishments can serve.

Dan McCall's *The Example of Richard Wright,* the commercial entry, is quite unabashedly a bellicose, journalistic study designed to try to interest a new generation of readers in Wright's work. The novelist, McCall begins by telling us, "cannot be considered without a sense of uneasy desperation. His voice is a single one, that of a lonely, furious, proud black man from the South, telling us that our culture is crazy."[4]

> "Richard Wright was writing on a wall," McCall continues, "until by the very intenseness and dogged determination of his single vision he sees, shows us the wall on fire; it spurts into incandescence and begins to burn with all the heat of this nation's monstrous capability." (page 17)

"Convinced that 'the Negro is America's metaphor,' " McCall concludes his short, vivid panegyric, "Wright explored the American mind with the equipment America had forced him to bear in his. His work is an example of what Sartre defined as genius — 'not a gift but the way out that one invents in desperate cases' " (page 195). Heady stuff! Designed to make one who fancies himself not a bigoted clod respond to Wright's challenge. *The Example of Richard Wright* exemplifies the stimulating techniques of Madison Avenue made respectable enough to serve the end of "serious culture."

Edward Margolies' *The Art of Richard Wright* (notice the non-committal coolness of this title in contrast to the exhortative quality of McCall's) is a transformation of one of the three pioneering dissertations. It is the fullest and most intelligent account that has so far been published of the meaning and value of Wright's work. Like McCall, Margolies resents the neglect of Wright, but he puts his case into a less urgent language to which those suspicious of mass-media rhetoric may respond:

> ... Wright wove his themes of human fear, alienation, guilt, and dread into the overall texture of his work. Some critics may still today stubbornly cling to the notion that Wright was nothing more than a proletarian writer, but it was to these themes that a postwar generation of French writers responded, and not to Wright's Communism — and it is to these themes that future critics must turn primarily if they wish to re-evaluate Wright's work.[5]

Margolies then leads us quickly through Wright's non-fiction to his short stories and novels, ending abruptly on the downbeat note that "Wright seldom achieved his fullest measure of artistic promise" (p. 167).

Although Margolies' book is the soundest evaluation of Wright so far available, it suffers from one serious shortcoming, possibly as a result of its blossoming from a dissertation and being conceived — under usual academic pressures — as a collection of fragmentary judgments rather than as a unified study that relates the individual analyses to an illumination of a Gestalt in the author's entire production. *The Art of Richard Wright* lacks, in short, a unifying thesis; but since the fragmentary judgments are generally extremely perceptive, no better purpose might be served by a further study at this point than to try to provide the argument that would correlate Margolies' judgments.

The critic's problem is exposed on the final page of his study, where in a discussion of *The Long Dream* he observes that "when Wright removes Fishbelly from the Negro world, and sends him first to jail and then on his way to France to seek his dream, something "untrue" happens to the book. It is difficult to say why." Then Margolies goes on to say, "The most kindly disposed reader is likely to demand that any dream, however long, be related to an authentic environment. And Fishbelly's removal from that environment somehow alloys the dream" (p. 166). The critic fails, however, to bring his two observations together and to pursue their inter-related implications. This failure cannot be condemned very strongly, however, because Margolies is not the first critic to fail to grasp the importance of "authentic environment" to the creation of a major type of fiction.

II

After a conversation with one of his Communist tormentors during the days when Wright was struggling to establish himself in Chicago, the writer recorded this version of part of their exchange:

> "Intellectuals don't fit well into the Party, Wright," [the other] said solemnly.
> "But I'm not intellectual," I protested, "I sweep the streets for a living."[6]

In these days of such stevedore-Schopenhauers as Eric Hoffer Wright's reply may appear to be a disingenuous non-sequitur; but his seeming flippancy provides us with a clue to the understanding of his artistic personality and problems.

Wright's interlocutor was no doubt using the term "intellectual" (as radicals tend to use terms) in a sense nearly as vague as the late President Eisenhower, who apparently considered it simply a synonym for "expert" in any field. If the term *intellectual* is not to degenerate into mere invective, however, in a post-literate world and if it is to serve — as it could! — as a valuable classifying tool, we need to limit its application to those who have the gift of abstracting, who are able to perceive the invisible patterns that permeate the disorder of superficial appearances. This concept does not demand specific educational achievements. A professor with a string of degrees may be merely an untidy filing case full of arcane knowledge, and an unschooled star-gazer may impose a system upon the universe. Thomas Wolfe pinpoints the characteristics of the "intellectual," in his portrait in *Look Homeward, Angel* of Eugene Gant's mother, Eliza:

> Eliza saw Altamont not as so many hills, buildings, people: she saw it in the pattern of a gigantic blueprint. She knew the history of every piece of valuable property — who bought it, who sold it, who owned it in 1893, and what it was now worth. . . . She judged distances critically, saw at once where the beaten route to an important centre was stupidly circuitous, and looking in a straight line through houses and lots, she said:
> "There'll be a street through here some day."
> Her vision of the land and population was clear, crude, focal — there was nothing technical about it; it was extraordinary for its direct intensity.[7]

The understanding of "intellectualism" has been particularly handicapped in the United States by the abusive application of the counter-term, "anti-intellectual" to anyone who happens to disagree with one's ideas. "Anti-intellectualism" does abound in this country, but it is not characterized by a systematic and logical opposition to a set of principles. It is the random reaction against any demand — in the name of anything — that one dispassionately scrutinize the sources and validity of one's feelings. It is the capacity for being so addicted to the "stupidly circuitous" that one cannot look in a straight line.

It is perhaps a measure of our anti-intellectualism that we do not even possess a precise synonym for the type of person who is the opposite of the "intellectual" in the sense that I am using the word — for a person who, for example, is incapable of reducing a tree to a Mondrian-like abstraction of the essence of "treeness," but who is enormously susceptible to the sensory stimulation of each individual phenomenon with which he is thrown in contact.

Hemingway would, I suppose, propose the term "visceralist." Certainly in a famous passage in *A Farewell to Arms,* he has supplied an explanation of the reactions of this type of person:

> I was always embarrassed by the words sacred, glorious, and sacrifice and the expression in vain. . . . There were many words that you could not stand to hear and finally only the names of places had dignity. Certain numbers were the same way and certain dates and these with the names of the places were all you could say and have them mean anything. Abstract words such as glory, honor, courage, or hallow were obscene beside the concrete names of villages, the numbers of roads, the names of rivers, the numbers of regiments and the dates.[8]

Of course, Hemingway is writing about a man who has been betrayed by abstractions; but his betrayal resulted in part from his inability to handle abstractions. Many people have been thus betrayed. Certainly Richard Wright was. Certainly many Negroes have been in the past by white manipulators of racial abstractions, and sadly it seems many Negroes may be in the future by black manipulators. Wright, like Hemingway's Lt. Henry, turned to people for a direct, intense personal response and found he was frustrated by the walls of abstraction that they had erected around them as an invisible shield against the shock of experience.

"Visceralist" seems, however, too limited to a single kind of reaction to counterpoint adequately the multiple implications of the term "intellectual." I would prefer the term "kinesthetist," which might be coined to describe the man who is capable of evoking in others not ideas about how an event or an experience might be categorized, but an actual total physical response to the event — a man who can make the reader "feel" the event by stimulating all the physical senses involved in the experience.

The significance of Wright's comment about being a street-sweeper can now be suggested. It is not the function of the street-sweeper to theorize about the structure of the universe or even the layout of the street system. He may brood over these matters; but if he thinks about them too much during business hours, his efficiency may be impaired. The street-sweeper's function is to perceive and remove each bit of offending litter from public thoroughfares. The job requires a keen eye and muscular coordination. Metaphorically, we can conceive of the writer as street-sweeper as the man who is in immediate physical control of his environment. His talents must be kinesthetic rather than intellectual.

But, one still might argue, a street-sweeper can be a street-sweeper anywhere. Ah, no! It takes as long to possess a complete sense of one's physical environment as to master the details of a celestial system. The old stereotype of the absent-minded professor was in part a folk recognition of the intellectual's lack of kinesthetic skill. The kinesthetist must know his material intimately. If he wields words rather than a broom, he must have mastered their capabilities of producing specific physiological responses. When he moves to a new environment, he must master through every sense its conversations, rituals, and revels. If he is no longer young and flexible in his responses, the task is not easy; if he is already such a public figure that the range of experiences he can acquire in the new environment is circumscribed, the task of mastering this environment may prove impossible. Then he becomes involved in either a nostalgic effort to re-experience a remote past or a preoccupation with intellectual systems that it is not his gift to comprehend.

My theory is that Richard Wright (like John Steinbeck) produced his best imaginative work when he was in immediate, daily contact with the people whose behavior he tried to re-create in his writings — when he wrote about Chicago Negroes as he did in *Lawd Today* and the first two parts of *Native Son*. The further he drifted away from an intimate relationship with his subject, the more contrived and artificial his work became.[9] The fiction that he wrote in France had no relationship to the world of his daily experience. He was able to avoid capitulating to Communism in Chicago and New York because his immediate experience made him aware of the shortcomings of a narrowly ideological response to life, and he sought to write of individual people and their agonies rather than intellectual constructs. In France, however, he succumbed to the enchantment of existentialism, because of his failure to establish the kind of rapport with his total environment that he had in the United States.

These comments should not be construed as condemning Wright. Part of the American infatuation with education rests on the absurd assumption that anyone can be an intellectual if he works hard enough at it and attains the proper degrees. But intellectual capacity cannot be acquired; it can only be trained if the individual already possesses it. Even if it could be acquired it would be of very little value to the creative writer who sought to deal with individual feelings rather than systems of thought. Wright was victimized, I think, not just by a society with a degrading stereotype of the Negro, but by a society whose psuedo-intellectual pretensions (manifested in such cultural patchwork quilts as the *Saturday Review* and *Harpers*) cause it to fail to value adequately those with an extraordinary capacity for a total physical response to an "authentic environment." In the light of these theories, let us examine Margolies' comments on Wright's individual works.

III

Margolies is almost the first to do justice to Wright's early novel *Lawd Today,* which was published posthumously. This depression-time tale of the self-destructive tendencies of a Negro worker in a Chicago post office (where Wright himself had worked) so little attracted the author's doctrinaire-minded associates of the 30s that we cannot even be sure when the novel was written. Even after it was at last published, it was greeted coolly — by militants for doing little to advance the Black cause and by others for appearing to be one of the last outbursts of the "proletarian voices" in which interest had evaporated.

Yet, as Margolies observes, the novel is in some ways more sophisticated than the more famous *Native Son,* which had led critics to suppose that Wright was "ignorant of modern experimental techniques in prose fiction." Had the earlier novel been published "when Wright completed it, such an impression might never have gained acceptance," for it shows the novelist's familiarity with Joyce, Dos Passos, and Gertrude Stein (p. 90).

Margolies goes on to comment that in the novel Wright "wanted to evoke the sights, the sounds, the smells" of Chicago in the 30s. "He wanted to reveal its paucity of spirit, its shallowness of character, its false morality, its sanctimonious pride, and the energy and violence of life that exists below its dreary, placid exterior" (p. 101).

Lawd Today shows that Wright had a talent for objective, critical fiction that he never had a chance to exhibit publicly during his lifetime. In view of the cool reception that greeted the books *Lawd Today* most nearly resembles (like Steinbeck's *In Dubious Battle*, which theoreticians complained misrepresented the programs prescribed for labor organizers), it is unlikely that Wright's novel could have been valued on its own terms. The people of the 30s did not want to see things as they were or to read a work about a Negro which was only in a very limited sense a "Negro novel" (because the principal character's problems would not have been basically different regardless of his race, color, or residence).

Wright did not make the mistake of treating violence and oppression in the "muted form" that Margolies says he did in *Lawd Today* when he wrote the short stories collected under the title *Uncle Tom's Children*. Certainly no one would have suspected that the author of these harrowing stories was much interested in literary experimentation, for they were traditional in structure. As Margolies explains, " in *Uncle Tom's Children*, unlike most modern short stories, the complexities of the narrative line, the twists and turns of the plot, are essential for an understanding of the characters' feelings and the nuances of their emotions." As opposed to the stories of Chekhov and Joyce, which have been the most influential models in the twentieth century, "a good deal 'happens' in Wright's short stories" (p. 59). Wright operated — possibly at the behest of his Communist mentors — in the mode acceptable to the popular magazines and the radical theorists of the day. Although the grim vividness of these stories has caused them to be hailed as outstanding examples of protest literature, they have rarely received attention as examples of the art of the short story.

Native Son was at the time of its publication and has remained such a powerful emotional shock that few people have been able to control their responses well enough to observe that it is a very uneven novel. Margolies produces one of the most carefully balanced judgments of the book yet to appear. After analyzing objectively the important action in the first section of the novel, the critic observes that the latter part of the second section (describing Bigger's flight from his pursuers)

> represents some of Wright's best prose — perhaps for sheer excitement the best narration Wright would ever produce. The sentences — spare of adverbs and adjectives — possess a taut, tense rhythm corresponding in their way to the quickening pace of flight and pursuit as the police inexorably draw in on Bigger (p. 111).

Margolies also observes, however, that "the whole of Book III seems out of key with the first two-thirds of the novel," because whereas the first two books were confined to a realistic account of Bigger's thought and actions, "Book III tries to interpret these in a number of rather dubious symbolic sequences" (p. 113). Margolies quite properly objects to Bigger's attorney's long sociological plea to the jury, which resembles the protracted conversations about the responsibility for Clyde Griffiths' behavior in Dreiser's *An American Tragedy*.

Again Margolies' comments make it apparent that Wright had an extraordinary talent for the reporting of events that allowed the reader to reconstruct them kinesthetically, but that the novelist had little ability to maintain stylistic consistency in his work when he began to present purely intellectual arguments. What Margolies does not point out is that one of Wright's main concerns — that Bigger's crime goes undiscovered as long as it does because as a Negro Bigger is literally "invisible" — is announced, but never effectively dramatized. Ralph Ellison, on the other hand, who is one of the few successful intellectual novelists in recent years, succeeds in communicating this same idea of "invisibility" allegorically in *Invisible Man*. It is an ironic evidence of the inadequacy of much recent criticism that Ellison's involved and intricate allegory is often dismissed as an episodic, picaresque tale, whereas Wright's engrossing picaresque that might have the most powerful impact if the long ideological dialogues were eliminated is regarded as a "novel of ideas."

The uncritical enthusiasm for *Native Son* probably did as much as anything else — except probably the move to France — to doom Wright as a creative artist. His activities during the next decade suggest, in fact, that either he had written himself out or he had no encouragement to produce further work in his most effective vein. He turned from fiction to autobiography and produced what is quite possibly his most valuable work, *Black Boy*, which as Margolies points out succeeds better as a description of the author's "own intellectual and emotional growth" than as an exemplary essay on the demeaning position of the Negro in Southern society: "Insofar as the reader identifies Wright's cause with the cause of Negro freedom, it is because Wright is a Negro — but a careful reading of the book indicates that Wright expressly divorces himself from other Negroes" (p. 19). The most effective parts of the book are the dialogues in which, Margolies argues, Wright "dramatically transports the reader into the situation he is experiencing — and leaves the reader no alternative but to identify with Black Boy" (p. 19). Thus, even in non-fiction (and Margolies points out that it is questionable how much of the book is truly autobiographical), Wright is more effective when he relies on the establishment through kinesthesis of a sub-conscious identification between character and reader than when he attempts consciously to articulate racial positions. *Black Boy* is an outstanding account of a particularly sensitive type of artistic personality striving for identity, but it is as erroneous to read it as an account of the representative Negro experience as it would be to read Winston Churchill's memoirs as an account of the representative British schoolboy's "making his way."

Black Boy probably did, however, have the effect of committing Wright after its publication to maintaining a public stance as a defender of the Negroes' aspirations rather than as an explorer of his own unique situation. Coupled with the move to France that put him out of touch with the physical realities of the Negro situation in America, this attitude meant that until very nearly the end of his life his new works drew upon only a small facet of his vast talent.

Few people have attempted to defend *The Outsider*, Wright's first novel after his move to Paris; but few have pointed out so precisely what is wrong with the novel as has Margolies: "What happens in *The Outsider* is that Wright has created allegorical figures whom he has described in a naturalistic context. The resulting confusion accounts for the failure of the novel" (p. 137). Margolies makes one of his first serious misjudgments, however, when he implies a contrast between *The Outsider* and an earlier story, "The Man Who Lived Underground," which the critic describes as "very nearly a perfect modern allegory" (p. 79).[10] In the original version at least (published in 1942 in *Accent*), "The Man Who Lived Underground" is not an allegory at all, because allegory is an art form in which one thing (character or event) stands for another. The story, however, is an account in the spare style of the second section of *Native Son* of how a man who had been rejected by society might behave given the ideal opportunity to secrete himself from the world. The story is fantastic, but not allegorical, and what Wright succeeds in communicating to the reader is the exultant feeling of the singular individual who has made good his retreat. While Margolies seems more impressed with the second published version of the story — in which the "underground man" comes forth to lead others to his retreat and is shot by a suspicious policeman — than the first, I feel that the second ending is "thought" rather than "felt" and subject to the same objections that Margolies makes to *The Outsider*.

Certainly the penchant for allegory overwhelmed Wright in the ill-conceived *Savage Holiday,* in which he attempted to write of a world with which he had no direct experience. Toward the end of his life he began to recover something of his original strength in *The Long Dream*, in which he returns to the still kinesthetically vivid memories of his childhood; but, as Margolies observes, in the last section of the novel, Wright's feeling for "social detail and concrete physical setting" seems "rather perfunctory." Clearly Wright had not deeply felt nor carefully meditated upon his Paris experiences; or else — once more like Steinbeck — he could not bring himself to discuss his adult experiences like marriage and parenthood with the kinesthetic precision he could his childhood and adult memories of deprivation.

The parallels with Steinbeck that I have several times emphasized deserve to be pressed, because some are remarkable. Wright got off to a later and slower start; there is nothing in his career to compare with the novels from *Cup of Gold* to *Of Mice and Men* that won Steinbeck a hearing and are still responsible for much of his reputation. Beginning with *In Dubious Battle* and *Lawd Today*, however, the parallels are strong. Both novels are remarkable for a cool objectivity in dealing with human tragedy that neither author was able again to achieve. *Uncle Tom's Children* and *The Long Valley,* too, contain analagous accounts of young persons' seeking to free themselves from a repressive environment.

If Steinbeck is only rarely as sensational as Wright (and "Flight" and "Vigilante" do have the same kind of impact as Wright's stories), he did have the opportunity to develop into a far more accomplished artist, as he is in *The Grapes of Wrath*, which, like *Native Son*, deals passionately with an oppressed minority, but which achieves largely through the impact of its carefully calculated form results that Wright could achieve only through the grim details of his narrative.

Both men turned to allegory at almost the same time with *The Moon is Down* and the second version of "The Man Who Lived Underground," but Wright was to give us his last major artistic statement in the form of an ostensibly literal autobiography, *Black Boy*, rather than in the masked form of a cryptic but bitter fictional transformation of observed situations like Steinbeck's *Cannery Row*.

The ill-managed *The Wayward Bus* has parallels to the clumsily allegorical *The Outsider*, as the basically historical *East of Eden* has to the autobiographically inspired *The Long Dream;* but none of these works contributed to their authors' artistic reputations. Both writers also turned principally to journalism in the declining years of their careers. Both wandered about the world. Wright went to the Gold Coast (now Ghana), Spain, Indonesia. Steinbeck visited Russia and Italy and toured the United States with a poodle. Both showed genuine interest in penetrating the masks of the societies they visited and discovering something about the behavior of the common people; but by the time that Wright wrote his last non-fiction book, *The Color Curtain* (1956), and Steinbeck wrote *Travels with Charley*, both were failing to penetrate very deeply beneath the surfaces of things and were living in terms of their private visions rather than serving as hypersensitive media for the transmission of intense personal observations.

When *The Color Curtain* was published I wrote:

> The book . . . is not so much a report of the Bandung Conference as a polemic that uses the conference as a center about which to organize the author's own ideas. As an account of the thoughts of a highly emotional and highly vocal defender of the oppressed, it is stimulating and disturbing reading; but it will not be news to those familiar with Wright's other works that the author's dogmatic conclusions must be regarded with caution.[11]

After a dozen or more years I find that this statement still embodies my basic reaction to all but Wright's early and most distinctly individualistic work. Although his being a Negro made him deeply concerned with the plight of other Negroes, Wright never really understood the problems of a racial group as well as he understood his private reactions as an artist to immediate stimuli. Other Negroes like James Baldwin who have had reservations about Wright's techniques have not been entirely fair, because Wright told us more about what it meant to be an artist in an insensitive world than what it meant to be a Negro. The "rage" that Baldwin objected to in Wright is the outcry not of a racial apologist but of a distressed individual.[12]

Since Wright was a Negro in a culture that denied the Negro individual dignity, he told us harrowing things about what it meant to be both Negro and artist — and thus doubly afflicted in a society that was predominantly white and Philistine; but when he tried to intellectualize his racial position and find personal comfort in moving away from the society with which he could establish a painful sensory rapport, he cut himself off from such a large part of the wide spectrum of stimuli to which he was sensitive that he could function only as a competent, outspoken journalist. As Margolies observes, Wright is "at his best when he is relating something he has just seen, or recording one of his own conversations" (p. 35). He rarely realized his potential; but, as I have emphasized in the parallel that I have kept pushing with another more honored artist, neither did John Steinbeck.

We can scarcely be surprised, therefore, that Wright accomplished no more of artistic merit than he did. We can only be surprised and happy that he achieved what he did and helped to advance as much as he did the dignity of the Negro at the expense ultimately of his own artistic self-realization.

FOOTNOTES

[1]Although in *The Social Novel at the End of an Era* (Carbondale and Edwardsville, Ill.; 1966), I argue that *Native Son* is really more similar to Camus' *The Stranger* than to *An American Tragedy*, the parallel to Dreiser's book was remarked upon by many of the first reviewers of Wright's novel, and the two American books do involve a similar sequence of events.

[2]"Richard Wright: A Selected Check List of Criticism," *Wisconsin Studies in Contemporary Literature,* I, iii, 22-23 (Fall, 1960).

[3]*The Social Novel at the End of an Era,* pp. 174-79.

142

[4]Dan McCall, *The Example of Richard Wright* (New York, 1969), p. 7. (Subsequent page references will be incorporated into the text.)

[5]Edward Margolies, *The Art of Richard Wright* (Carbondale and Edwardsville, Ill.; 1969), p. 3. (Subsequent page references will be incorporated into the text.)

[6]Constance Webb, *Richard Wright: A Biography* (New York, 1968), p. 126.

[7]Thomas Wolfe, *Look Homeward, Angel,* Scribner Library Edition (New York, 1952), p. 104.

[8]Ernest Hemingway, *A Farewell to Arms,* Scribner Library Edition (New York, n.d.), pp. 184-85.

[9]Support for the view that Wright wrote well only about an environment he was intimately familiar with is found in some remarks of Wright's old friend, Saunders Redding, delivered at a symposium in August, 1964, at the Asilomar Conference Center, Monterey Peninsula, California, and transcribed in *Anger, and Beyond: The Negro Writer in the United States,* edited by Herbert Hill (New York, 1966), p. 206: "My feeling is that his abandonment of America did things to him, weakened him emotionally— he no longer had anything to write about. . . . The stories that were written in France after he had left America do not begin to compare with the stories . . . which he wrote here in the States. You can see the difference, the emotional difference; the loss, too, of a kind of skill, particularly a skill in the handling of language. He had forgotten the American idiom. I think France liberated him as a person, and this was good for him, but I don't think France was good for him as an artist."

[10]In fairness, it should be observed that Margolies' comment apparently applies to the second, expanded version of the story, which appeared in *Cross-section,* 1944, edited by Edwin Seaver. My point is, however, that the first version is not an allegory and the second version is far from perfect.

[11]*Lexington* (Kentucky) *Sundary Herald-Leader,* April 15, 1956.

[12]Baldwin's comments on Wright are summarized and analyzed in Maurice Charney's "James Baldwin's Quarrel with Richard Wright," *American Quarterly,* XV:65-75 (Spring, 1963).

Some Examples of Faulknerian Rhetoric in Ellison's *Invisible Man*

by Michael Allen

When he was first working on *Invisible Man* Ralph Ellison felt that naturalistic prose ("perhaps the brightest instrument for recording sociological fact, physical action, the nuance of speech") became "suddenly dull when confronting the Negro."[1] He himself had learned from Richard Wright the naturalist's way of assuring his readers of a measure of sociological accuracy by his tone: we don't need this afterword to guarantee that the Southern ritual of the "Battle Royal" was a pattern "already there in society";[2] or his mention of his "attraction (soon rejected) to Marxist political theory"[3] to authenticate his treatment of "The Brotherhood's" activities in Harlem. But he has said[4] that he could not help learning from Wright; whereas he consciously chose as an artist to be influenced by such writers as Hemingway and Faulkner. His aim was to eliminate dullness from the Negro novel, to restore the ". . . imagination, . . . sense of poetry, . . ."[5] that Wright's books seemed to him to lack.

Hemingway's writing taught him to maintain a vigorous narrative line by means of energetic spare strong sentences. ("I read him to learn his sentence structure and how to organise a story.")[6]

From Faulkner he learned, among other things, to construct out of rhetoric an internal language for his protagonist which deviates more and more from simple narrative lucidity as the deeper rhythms of the personality, its more pronounced preoccupations, emerge. For Darl in *As I Lay Dying* or Quentin in *The Sound and the Fury*, the rhetoric simulates the maintenance by sheer conceptual intensity of a sense of identity which is precarious and schizoid, always on the point of dissolving into flux and fantasy. Ellison's writing is more grounded in naturalism than Faulkner's, more concerned with social, than with psychological identity. But at moments of maximum intensity the clipped sentences lose the tight control which (we assume) the mind of the protagonist-narrator has been maintaining over them. They become sprawled and convoluted to represent his deeper, more unconscious and involuntary response to his experience.

The loose and debased Ciceronian rhetoric which Faulkner used to render consciousness is characteristic of the South. In Ellison's hands it obviously carries social and cultural implications. He makes his protagonist a Southerner rather than an Oklahoman like himself. And the cultural resonance of the style conditions in the reader an intense awareness of how much the speaker shares, at depth, certain characteristic modes of feeling if not a common vision with the Southern whites:

> whom we knew though we didn't know, who were unfamiliar in their familiarity, who trailed their words to us through blood and violence and ridicule and condescension with drawling smiles, and who exhorted and threatened, intimidated with innocent words as they described to us the limitations of our lives and the vast boldness of our aspirations, . . . upon their lips the curdled milk of a million black slave mammies' withered dugs, a treacherous and fluid knowledge of our being, imbibed at our source and now regurgitated foul upon us. This was our world, they said as they described it to us, this our horizon and its earth, its seasons and its climate, its spring and its summer, and its fall and harvest some unknown millennium ahead; and these its floods and cyclones and they themselves our thunder and lightning; and this we must accept and love and accept even if we did not love.[7]

The rhetoric here renders at once the recollected tone of voice of the representative Southern white man and the internal response of the protagonist-narrator to the culture and its tone. It has its own impetus dictated by sound patterns of repetition, antithesis or parallelism. And since, as a style, it assumes the basic pre-existence of certain forms it becomes an appropriate vehicle through which to present the internal quest for identity, which habitually involves tension between tradition and innovation, the half-consciously assumed and the consciously established. The protagonist, a rhetorician himself, described his own early eloquence as "more sound than sense . . . the sound of words that were no words, counterfeit notes singing achievements yet unachieved." And in a parallel way, the half automatic hypnotic rhetoric which displays his thought processes achieves momentary definition and fractures again as it reflects "the uncreated features of his face" (to quote the emendation of Joyce's phrase that the protagonist offers us).[8]

In the passage quoted the antitheses, the patterns of parallelism suggest an apparent formal ordering of experience on the part of Southern society, and the fluctuations of anxiety with which the Negro responds to this order: "whom we knew though we didn't know; who were unfamiliar in their familiarity . . . who exhorted and threatened, intimidated with innocent words. . . ." The very vagueness of some of these oppositions leaves the reader with the urge to achieve greater precision about this ambivalent and complex relationship with culture. And the reader's co-operation in its dramatic realisation is elicited by the very absence of syntactic control. When the whites are described as trailing "their words to us through blood and violence and ridicule and condescension" the reader recognises two pairs of half-synonyms widely separate in association. But this crude momentum of the period, the failure of the syntax to register this separation implies the brutality of the patronising gesture, and on the protagonist's part some kind of numbed acceptance of this brutality.

The importance of effects relying on a combination of formal periodic rhythms and syntactic slackness might be confirmed from a later sequence, in which the protagonist's mind turns from the old workman he is confronting to the social situation he has left:

> You were trained to accept the foolishness of such old men
> as this, even when you thought them clowns and fools; you

were trained to pretend that you respected them and ac-
knowledged in them the same quality and authority and
power in your world as the whites before whom they bowed
and scraped and feared and loved and imitated.[9]

The dignity of the parallel periods simulates something of the
Southern sense of hierarchy and ceremony, the more extended
movement of the second clause suggesting the way the hierarchic
principle extends itself from white into Negro life. But the slightly
ominous note of the repeated "you were trained" together with an
increasing loss of restraint culminating in the flat, undifferentiated
sequence of verbs connected with "and" express the protagonist's
combination of scorn and hysteria, suggest his continued emotional
involvement in the mechanics of the caste-situation. The loss of
control is implied by syntactic omissions: "as in the whites," "and
whom they feared" are the syntactically correct forms, which the
reader has an impulse to restore. Their absence suggests the protagonist's unconscious assumption that the theatrical distance, the
total gap between blacks and whites emphasised by "before whom"
extends to the last three terms also. The reader can only restore
"feared and loved and imitated" to a context which suggests real
relationship with an effort, and in the process the usual implications of the words have been totally undermined.

Sometimes the rhetoric involves conscious irony on the protagonist's part at the expense of Southern civilities and the menacing note beneath: of the view of Negro destiny urged on him
by the Southern white man the protagonist comments wryly "and
this we must accept and love, and accept even if we do not love."
Even here the use of the second "and" rather than "or" demonstrates a too easy acceptance of the sonorous rhythm, and juxtaposes
the two clauses in partial rather than total contradiction. Elsewhere the fluid inclusiveness of the protagonist's attitudes is much
more apparent, so that one sees his attempt to maintain a coherent
and diagnostic attitude to his experience undermined by the tensions and contradictions beneath the surface. Speaking in the fictional present, in his brightly lit cellar he remembers the singing
expected of himself and his fellow students by white visitors and
trustees:

I seem to hear already the voices mechanically raised in the
songs the visitors loved. (Loved? Demanded. Sung? An

ultimatum accepted and ritualised, an allegiance recited for
the peace it imparted, and for that perhaps loved. Loved
as the defeated come to love the symbols of their conquerors.
A gesture of acceptance, of terms laid down and reluctantly
approved.)

Only the word "mechanically" undermines the darkie-song assumptions of the first sentence. In parenthesis one sees the protagonist's
attempt to diagnose and resist the convention although one cannot
at this point know whether "Loved?Demanded" implies a flat
contradiction or simply directs attention to a deeper level. The
sequence of amplifying clauses after "Sung?" seems at first to be
controlled and diagnostic; but its movement increasingly suggests
that the seductive and treacherous assumptions of the familiar role
are no more under control than the rhetoric. In spite of the attempt
at detachment the protagonist's mind is hypnotised by the flow of
its conventionally conditioned memories: the biblical associations
of phrases like "the peace it imparted" imply that the ritualisation
involved both groups, black and white. It was at first the visitors
who "loved" the singing, but "and for that perhaps loved" is
suspended ambiguously, representing the feeling of either group;
it claims to be an amplification, but an unconscious shift of meaning has already taken place, registering the protagonist's lack of
control over the role he has been given. In the next sentence the
involuntary and undictated shift of the word "loved" to the Negro
has taken place: and the reader's attempt to clarify the meaning
defines for him the protagonist's unconscious acquiescence, which
is dramatically emphasised by the more abrupt, over-insistent
reassertion of opposition in the last sentence.

Walter Slatoff[10] has shown how such rhetoric in Faulkner incorporates the opposed and contradictory aspects of a situation in
a state of suspension which cannot be resolved in logical or rational
terms. But as he points out,[11] it is often not only a high tension
between conceptual statements but a powerful dissonance of imagery that confronts the reader, taxing and exercising his urge to find
coherence in what he reads. Slatoff illustrates this second point
from the description of the preacher in *The Sound and the Fury*:

He was like a worn small rock whelmed by the successive
waves of his voice. With his body he seemed to feed the
voice that, succubus like, had fleshed its teeth in him. And

> the congregation seemed to watch with its own eyes while the voice consumed him, ...

The use of similes rather than metaphors, the repetition of "seemed" maintain our sense that it is the power of an extraordinary man that is being described. But there is an extraordinary dislocation between the voice and the man. Imagery of natural process, of Gothic atrocity, of the Roman arena suggests that he is a masochistic victim of his voice. And the voice itself becomes a symbolic voice, the voice of the folk-tradition through which inturned aggression in the face of violent subjugation has been transformed and transmuted in ritual. The point of view throughout the section is that of Dilsey ("They Endured"). But the contradictory suggestions of the imagery, half celebratory, half sardonic can be interpreted in terms of "endurance" only if we keep in mind Faulkner's ironic view of "endurance" as either a moral quality or a biological, almost a vegetable attribute.[12]

Ellison's attempt to "echo a certain kind of southern rhetoric"[13] in the Reverend Barbee's speech to the College involves a similar sense of the ambiguity of the "endurance" of the Negro race: They "sing out their long black songs of blood and bones," cries Barbee,

> "Meaning HOPE!
> "Of hardship and pain:
> "Meaning FAITH!
> "Of humbleness and absurdity:
> "Meaning ENDURANCE!
> "Of ceaseless struggle in darkness, meaning:
> "TRIUMPH . . ."

But Ellison's impulse to parody in this section of *Invisible Man* operates not only at the expense of Rev. Barbee, but at that of the protagonist who was (and is) conscious of "the structure of his (Barbee's) vision within me." That it is not simply gullibility on the protagonist's part that prevents him from rejecting such stoicism is confirmed by the strain of meditation which emerges in *Invisible Man* under the influence of the fourth section of "The Bear" (in which, Ellison has said, Faulkner makes "his most extended effort to define the specific form of the American Negro's humanity and to get at the human values which were lost by both

North and South during the Civil War.")[14] It is of Ike McCaslin's quest for a relationship to his past that we are reminded when Ellison's protagonist says:

> Was it that we of all, we, most of all, had to affirm the principle, the plan in whose name we had been brutalised and sacrificed — not because we would always be weak nor because we were afraid or opportunistic, but because we were older than they, in the sense of what it took to live in the world with others and because they had exhausted in us, some — not much, but some — of the human greed and smallness, yes, and the fear and superstition that had kept them running.[15]

The protagonist here commits himself to a combination of the "endurance" which McCaslin had praised in the Negro, and McCaslin's own kind of obsessive moral responsibility. The choice of the verb, "because they had *exhausted* in us," suggests in the speaker something of the devitalisation produced by obsession which Faulkner inexorably pin-points in McCaslin. The latter suggestion is reinforced by the protagonist's subconscious fear (emerging in his dream in Chapter 25) that he has been emasculated by his experience. It also governs his final mannered presentation of himself as "no hero but short and dark with only a certain eloquence and a bottomless capacity for being a fool to mark me from the rest."[16]

It is our sense of the protagonist as "no hero," as ambiguously poised between a passive role in the world of action and an active role in the world of words that attention to the rhetoric confirms. Our sense that the protagonist is intoxicated by the rhetorical modes of the whites who are both patrons and oppressors is an important component in our response to the book. When his own creative potentialities are suddenly threatened by the Southern Negro-white alliance it is in a girl-singer of his own generation that Ellison's protagonist finds an image of Negro creativity:

> She began softly, as though singing to herself of emotions of utmost privacy, a sound not addressed to the gathering but which they overheard almost against her will. Gradually she increased its volume, until at times the voice seemed to become a disembodied force that sought to enter her,

> to violate her, shaking her, rocking her rhythmically, as
> though it had become the source of her being, rather than
> the fluid web of her own creation.

There is the same dislocation here, the same suggestion of violence
transmuted as in Faulkner's description of the preacher. The
periods are longer and more complex than those in Faulkner,
where the need to maintain Dilsey's point of view inhibited the
rhetorical flow. The girl is singing one of the songs the visitors
either "loved" or "demanded." At first withheld ("almost against
her will"), her surrender to the ceremony ("an ultimatum accepted
and ritualised") is rhythmically enacted by the rhetorical opening
out of the second sentence. Similes like Faulkner's allow the
relationship between voice and singer to assimilate the opposed
possibilities implicit in the racial relationship. Suggestions of rape
('enter her . . . violate her") are poised against suggestions of
infantile security. But the powerful opposition between these two
components of the Negro's "performance" for the white man is
eroded and enervated by the passive constructions in the last two
clauses. These partially mislead the reader, suggesting that he
read the second clause as parallel to the first, instead of opposed
to it, "source of her being" as synonymous with "web of her own
creation." And the need to establish clear opposition between
these two clauses alerts the reader to the perpetual threat that
the protagonist may lapse like the style into drugged and hypnotic acquiescence.

The ring of authenticity about the rhetoric should not be mis-
interpreted. *Invisible Man* was in composition for seven years,
and the protagonist, like Stephen Dedalus, obviously began as an
earlier version of the author. (Richard Wright's quasi-autobio-
graphical naturalism would have a lot to do with this.) And as
with Joyce's novel a rhetoric which the author himself may have
accepted at an early stage in the composition has sometimes been
incorporated into the fictional structure to show how the protagonist's inadequacies are inextricably bound up with his intellectual initiatives. Perhaps Ellison's control over the ironic dis-
tancing of his protagonist is less sure than Joyce's, more like
Faulkner's in, say, the Quentin section of *The Sound and the Fury*.
But the choice of the Southern literary model was a masterstroke
on Ellison's part. By authenticating the Southern cultural conditioning of the central character it detaches the narrative forcibly

from the author, giving the protagonist the same kind of separateness in the North as James's Southern observer in *The Bostonians*, Basil Ransom. And even more important, it allowed Ellison to assimilate to his fictional purpose the central drive of his own literary apprenticeship. Theodore Roethke has suggested in "How to Write like Other People" that "true imitation takes a certain courage. One dares to stand up to a great style, to compete with papa."[17] By using Faulknerian rhetoric to give internal solidity to his protagonist Ellison harnessed all the exploratory energies which could be released by consciously standing up to, competing with, a great white papa.

[1] Ralph Ellison, *Shadow and Act*, London, Secker and Warburg, 1967, p. 26.

[2] *Ibid.*, p. 174

[3] *Ibid.*, p. xxi

[4] *Ibid.*, p. 140

[5] *Ibid.*, p. 16

[6] *Ibid.*, p. 168

[7] *Invisible Man*, Chapter 5. All quotations from the novel occur in Chapter 5 unless it is otherwise indicated.

[8] "Stephen's problem, like ours, was not actually one of creating the uncreated conscience of his race, but of creating the *uncreated features of his face*. Our task is that of making ourselves individuals. . . ." *Invisible Man*, chapter 16.

[9] *Invisible Man*, Chapter 10.

[10] Walter J. Slatoff, "The Edge of Order: the Pattern of Faulkner's Rhetoric," F. J. Hoffman and Olga W. Vickery (eds.), *William Faulkner: Three Decades of Criticism*, Harbinger Books, New York, 1963, pp. 173-198.

[11] *Ibid.*, p. 178.

[12] See Slatoff, *op. cit.*, p. 195.

[13] *Shadow and Act*, p. 178.

[14] Ralph Ellison, "Society, Morality, and the Novel," Granville Hicks (ed.), *The Living Novel*, Collier Books, New York, 1962, p. 94.

[15] *Invisible Man*, Epilogue

[16] *Invisible Man*, Chapter 25

[17] R. J. Mills (ed.), *On the Poet and his Craft: Selected Prose of Theodore Roethke*, University of Washington Press, 1968, p. 70.

An Interview
with Ralph Ellison

by Allen Geller

The interview that follows with the distinguished American novelist Ralph Ellison took place on October 25th, 1963, in Montreal, where Mr. Ellison had gone to deliver a lecture on 'The Novel and the American Experience' at McGill University.

The interviewer was Allen Geller, a twenty-two-year-old Montreal painter who is now in Dublin. Mr. Geller was also the editor of The Montreal Review, *a new magazine that was brought to the verge of publication but that never appeared for economic reasons. The interview with Mr. Ellison was intended for publication in* The Montreal Review. *It subsequently appeared in* The Tamarack Review.

INTERVIEWER: Did you have a difficult time finding a publisher for *Invisible Man?*

Ellison: No, not at all. A publisher gave me a contract while I was serving as a merchant-seaman during the war. He had seen some of the short stories and essays which I was publishing from time to time and called me in and wanted to know if I had other things, and I sent him some of the other things that I had. I had already published a few things but I showed him a number of unpublished things. He called me in, finally, and said, 'Look would you like to do a novel?' I said, 'Yes, that's my ultimate ambition, to write novels.' And he said, 'Well, do you have one in mind?' I said, 'No, I don't have one in mind.' He said, 'Well, we would like to give you a contract.' So he gave me a contract — $1,500 in advance — and then waited about five years before he actually got a book. There was no problem in getting a contract.

Interviewer: You say your book took five years to write. Why so long? Did you find it a hard book to write, or are you a meticulous worker?

Ellison: Well, I write sometimes with great facility, but I question it; and I have a certain distrust of the easy flow of words and I have to put it aside and wait and see if it's really meaningful and if it holds up. It's an inefficient way of working, but it seems to be my way.

Interviewer: Were you influenced at all by Nathanael West?

Ellison: No, not at all. But I was influenced by the comic movies, the Marx Brothers, the Negro comedians. You don't have to go to Nathanael West for tradition. You inherit it.

Interviewer: Well, West, I believe, wrote some scripts for the Marx Brothers in collaboration with his friend S. J. Perelman when they were both in Hollywood.

Ellison: Is that right? Well, this is a long tradition in American life. It's one which is apt to get to you long before you start reading for influence. In fact I hadn't read Nathanael West before I wrote *Invisible Man* and people started telling me about *A Cool Million* and that was the first West that I read and then I went on to the others, *Miss Lonelyhearts, Day of the Locust.* . . .

Interviewer: I notice that you're an admirer of Malraux who visited us recently in his role as Minister of Culture of France. In the States you don't have anything like a ministry to promote art, but what effect do you think Kennedy is having on the literary scene?

Ellison: He's certainly paid more attention to writers than any other president in a long time, that is in a social way — except for President Roosevelt, who was the architect of the writers' projects (at least it was during his administration) and that gave me a chance to be a writer. I first started writing under WPA — that is, I was able to give time to writing because I could do work for them and learn to do my own. . . . I think it will be a little while before we can get a clear idea of the effect of the New Frontier upon literature.

Interviewer: You also studied sculpture and painting for a while, I believe?

Ellison: I studied sculpture for about a year, a year and a half, and found out that I had a certain knack of doing naturalistic sculpture, but after a year I gave that up. . . . I thought of myself as a musician in those days.

Interviewer: To get back to *Invisible Man,* you said last night that you do not concentrate on theory or form when writing; you said that 'the content will dictate the form' —

Ellison: No, I meant this last night. When you are influenced by a body of literature or art from an earlier period, it is usually the form of it that is available to you; the content changes so rapidly. By that I meant that the work of literature is at its best when it has processed the content into the form itself.

Interviewer: There are many scenes in *Invisible Man* which are surrealistic. Does that mean that your vision of some aspects of American life is surrealistic?

Ellison: You see, that's from the outside. I mean, it's looking at what is done in a book and assuming that it comes from a theory and I know the theories. Let's put it this way — I'm a highly conscious writer. I know what has been done and just about who did it because I've read the books, I've studied them. Now having said that, you don't want to confuse the theory of surrealism with the eye that sees the chaos which exists within a given society.

Interviewer: No, I realize that you do not use theory to interpret what you see or mechanically change reportage into a certain style. What I meant is, in a descriptive sense is your vision of life directly surrealistic?

Ellison: I try to see life as it is. I try to see it in terms of its contradictions, in terms of its values, in terms of its pace, in terms of its nervous quality. Now what is called surrealism in one place might be seen as mundane reality in another. In highly formalized sections of society (and this is true of the United States), in the decorous areas of society, you don't always see the individual in his naked state, but if you go to Sixth Avenue in the Broadway section of New York, it takes on a kind of surface atmosphere — people standing on the street talking to themselves, winos walking along. . . .

Interviewer: You said that you are a highly conscious writer aware of what other writers had already done. Doesn't this inhibit you, inhibit your writing in any way once you know this has been done, and this has been done. . . ?

Ellison: No, there's no reason for not doing it again in your own way. You're not going to make a completely new novel. Fiction is by now a traditional form, the techniques are known, but you have the advantage of bending the techniques to your own uses, and the more guns you have in the arsenal the better you can fight the battle. I know that certain very sublime pieces of fiction have been done and there would be no point in trying to imitate them, but you do have the obligation to know what has been done and how it was done so as to give your own imagination the freest range.

Interviewer: What problems have you had as a writer?

Ellison: Problems of understanding what's happening around . . . problems of self-discipline, problems of making my fiction do what I think it should do, problems of distraction, problems of wanting to go off and hunt instead of sitting at the typewriter. The usual problems which writers have.

Interviewer: At the end of *Invisible Man* the hero is waiting in his cubicle, waiting for the right moment for action. What exactly does this mean? He is still left in a dilemma. After all his many experiences, after finding out that the concepts he started out with were superficial, after getting a more realistic view of the world, abandoning religion, his academic aims, his cultural background, the Communist Party, all his political and social theories—

Ellison: It wasn't the Communist Party.

Interviewer: It wasn't the Communist Party?

Ellison: No, it wasn't called the Communist Party. It was like that, but —

Interviewer: Well, he eventually comes to a personal view of life which is more realistic and mature. But where does he go from there? What is the action he waits for? You have your hero say, 'All sickness is *not* unto death,' a reference to Kierkegaard's work, implying that he had already freed himself from the 'sickness' through his experiences. Kierkegaard discusses a similar development in *Stages on Life's Road* and he reaches the conclusion that you have to have a religious or mystical experience to continue or complete you life. But your hero seems to have *had* this experience by the end of the novel — yet he still does nothing.

Ellison: Yes, he had a mystical, prophetic dream of war toward the end of the book. But you mustn't miss the fact that it's *his* book, not mine, and the writing and publication of his experience is an act of self-definition and also an act of some social significance. The moment had occurred.

Interviewer: Yes. Well, I asked you this question yesterday. If one is not able to recreate his experience in art, where would that same hero be? Yesterday you said you wouldn't have the slightest idea. But a person could have very similar experiences, go through this process and end up in the state of hibernation that your hero is in at the end of the novel. What would he do then. . . ?

Ellison: Well, he certainly would learn to deal with himself. Whatever he did when he returns, so to speak, should be based on the knowledge gained before he went underground. This is a question of self-knowledge and ability to identify the processes of the world. Beyond that he has his freedom of choice. I wouldn't want to impose that upon anyone. I certainly would not suggest that he follow some plan which I thought would be good for me as an individual.

Interviewer: Agreed, it's not a plan or moral system that I ask about, but the psychological point at which your hero escapes the den. It is a large step from the underground den to creating the memoir. What springs him, releases him, and allows him to continue. Define the type of action he needs. He is obviously not going to go out and find a job, blend into society and be satisfied. He is now too aware an individual to —

Ellison: To want a job?

Interviewer: No, not to want a job but to dismiss the experiences he has gone through, to forget them.

Ellison: Well, he doesn't dismiss them. One of the things he recognizes is that he is responsible himself for so much of what he went through. He recognizes that had he not been so willing to do what other people wanted him to do he would have been saved so much of the agony of his experience. So it implies that when he gets back, doing whatever he's going to do, he will be more himself. He will not be so willing to be a good boy and he will have a better idea of how the individual functions creatively in society.

Interviewer: But he can't start off with an idea of what he is. All his experiences made him something. When he dismisses his early influences and ideals, does he get all his standards from himself?

Ellison: No, he does not get all his standards from himself. He gets them from a lot of people within the action. He even gets some things from the fellows who burn the apartment — Dupré and that crowd; he gets something from Mary, some knowledge of who he is and how he should live in the world and how to square his ambitions with his background. He's learning all the time.

Interviewer: There's never an emphasis on religion or the religious in *Invisible Man*?

Ellison: No, he isn't a religious individual.

Interviewer: Does the hero believe in God?

Ellison: I suppose he did at the beginning. There are religious moments in the book, but he was committed to a materialistic solution finally — during his political activities.

Interviewer: But not finally; not at the very end while he's waiting in his underground den.

Ellison: While he's in his underground den he's trying to recreate the world as he discovered it.

Interviewer: Last night you stated that the main theme of American literature was the search for values, the individual's search for identity; and, of course, this is also the main theme of *Invisible Man*. Do you intend to continue this theme in your writing, in the new novel you're working on . . . ?

Ellison: Well, you don't choose the theme, the theme chooses you. But yes, that theme does come into it along with the theme of memory or the suppression of memory in the United States. One of the techniques which seems to have worked out for taking advantage of the high mobility which is possible in the States is forgetting what the past was, in the larger historical sense, but also in terms of the individual's immediate background. He is apt to make light of it. The immigrant will become ashamed of the language of the parents, the ways of the forefathers; and you have this, what I call 'passing for white', which refers to a form of rejecting one's own background in order to become that of some prestige group or to try to imitate the group which has prestige at a particular moment.

Interviewer: Well, isn't this the existentialist dilemma, the necessity to dismiss the past, to live in the present. What Mailer calls hipsterism?

Ellison: The hipster, although Mailer doesn't quite understand it, is not simply living in the present, he is living a very stylized life which implies a background because it takes a good while, a lot of living to stylize a pattern of conduct and an attitude. This goes back very deeply into certain levels of Negro life. That's why it has nuances and overtones which Mailer could never grasp. He is appropriating it to make an existentialist point which doesn't seem to me to be worth making.

Interviewer: Am I wrong to assume that Rinehart in *Invisible Man* is a hipster?

Ellison: He's not a hipster in Mailer's sense. He is a kind of opportunist who has learned to live in a world which is swiftly changing and in which the society no longer has ways of bringing pressure . . . or even identifying him. Thus he can act out many roles. He's a descendant of Melville's 'Confidence Man' to that extent.

Interviewer: In today's society, would this be an aim — to divorce oneself from society in that way? This is what the grandfather of your hero seems to be saying in the anarchic advice he gives in the first chapter — to go along with the society on the surface only, but actually to subtly undermine it, to act without it.

Ellison: Not to act without it but act against it, to collaborate with its destruction of its own values. That's the way that a weak man, that weak old grandfather — physically weak, that is — found for dealing with a circumstance, but his grandson actually writes his memoirs. *Invisible Man* is a memoir of a man who has gone through that experience and now comes back and brings his message to the world. It's a social act; it is not a resignation from society but an attempt to come back and to be useful. There is an implied change of role from that of a would-be politician and rabble-rouser and orator to that of writer. No, there's no reason for him to lose his sense of a social role. But I think the memoir, which is titled *Invisible Man,* his memoir, is an attempt to describe reality as it really exists rather than in terms of what he had assumed it to be. Because it was the clash between his assumptions, his illusions about reality, and its actual shape which made for his agony.

Interviewer: In this sense would you consider yourself an existentialist writer — since you dismiss all these myths as well? I know the term has been abused. . . .

Ellison: Yes, the term has been so abused. Let's say that if I were to identify myself as an existentialist writer, then it would be existentialism in the terms of André Malraux rather than Sartre.

It would be in terms of Unamuno, let's say, without the religious framework, rather than Camus's emphasis.

Interviewer: Last night you expressed respect for Melville. Now in *Moby Dick,* in Ahab, you not only have an example of a social rebel such as you have in *Invisible Man,* but you also have what Camus calls a metaphysical rebel.

Ellison: Yes, you do have a metaphysical rebel.

Interviewer: In *Invisible Man?*

Ellison: No, not so much, because he doesn't have that level of conscious revolt. Ahab is a highly articulate individual and individualist who has gone through a conscious consideration of his philosophical position, who has broken through certain boundaries by having gone through them — even love of the family and so on. As he says, tell Starbuck, I guess, 'I do have my humanities.' Well, this is on a higher level than my character in *Invisible Man.*

Interviewer: What type of characters appear in your new novel? Do you examine the theme of rebellion to the extent that it becomes metaphysical, or are you dealing with people who have been integrated into the rhythm of society?

Ellison: Well, it's about a number of people. One man learns how to operate in society to the extent that he loses a great part of his capacity for, shall we say, poetry or for really dealing with life. And another man who seems caught at a very humble stage of society seems to have achieved quite a high level of humanity. But you see when I'm writing fiction I'm not thinking philosophy. These are tags which come later. I'll leave that to the critics. I won't try to classify my characters that way. You write to discover what you can, to make what you can of your intuitions, your themes, your talent, and so on. But if the great novels are novels which depict metaphysical rebels, then one hopes that these people will be metaphysical rebels. If you mean, however, characters who press the extremes of their situation, who try to make as much of what they will to do and what happens to them, the circumstances which they find themselves in — if you mean metaphysical to that extent, yes, these will be characters who move in that direction, to the extent of their given condition.

Interviewer: What I meant by metaphysical was extending the moral condemnations to the universe. A paradox, because man is the moral force and the universe amoral. For example, Ahab's anger at Moby Dick (a symbol for amoral force in the universe).

Yet he wants to destroy the whale. Here Ahab is imposing a moral condemnation, condemning the world for what it is.

Ellison: Yes, he does. I guess we can approach this a little more specifically by pointing out that Melville was attempting to create a tragic hero. Certain things had happened to this man; for instance the whale had bitten off his leg. He had been a very successful captain — that is, financially successful. He was then pressed beyond the concern with simply slaughtering whales for their food and oil value and it became a matter of seeing in the whale the inscrutable nature of existence, of man's relationship to the total scheme. Well, is this moral or immoral? It's moral, it seems to me, as it embodies and expresses the individual's obligation to discover the extreme limits of his own possibilities, because through this, then, he discovers his true relationship to nature and society and so on — in this case to society and to nature, the society of the ship. He did everything he could to lead them into this reckless chase and to instill them with some of his own passion. He then goes on and threatens them; he uses the harpoon which is the symbol, shall we say, for technological development and skill, threatens them to make them follow Moby Dick and then discovers that he could not impose his will upon nature. Now you can call Moby Dick evil, you can call him a number of things. Melville has a lot to say about it (or Ishmael does) in the chapter called 'The Whiteness of the Whale'. Ahab as a tragic hero is sure to be destroyed because he has gone beyond the point where the individual can impose his will upon the chaos of the world.

Interviewer: Well, he has taken over the position of God in assuming the responsibility for the moral state of the world.

Ellison: I don't think he's taken over the position of God. I think he's acting as a god-like man, a man who would assume that it is possible to pierce through the mask and to discover ultimates. But that in itself is carrying out a very profound moral mission in terms of the obligation of human beings to learn as much as they can about the nature of life. The human being has the obligation to learn as much as he can about where he is and what he is for several reasons. The species can only continue to survive and to develop to the extent that this is done — in a disciplined way, one hopes, but if not it must be done anyway. Now that's one thing — a man's relationship to the universe, to the chaos of nature and so on which he tries to understand, tries to glean the laws. Secondly there is the obligation of man as a member of society and there is inevitably a clash between these two roles. Society sets up its own ethics, its own moral system in order to make it possible to survive and to render justice and to reduce chaos to a minimum. This is not a God-constructed world. I don't think God constructed society. I think it's man-made, and man plays it by ear far too often. And it becomes quite a moral problem, an ethical problem as to how man operates within that structure and what he does to himself and to his fellow man, what he does to the resources of society.

Interviewer: Must the individual persist even though it will destroy him?

Ellison: Well, he has to decide what does destroy. Good and evil, destruction and creation, are so closely linked that you don't always know what's going to happen. We know that up until the discovery of the bomb and even as a result of that we have come upon many life-saving techniques in many, many fields — techniques of peacefully using and creatively using resources of this world. We know that the industrial revolution was tied up with warfare, chaotic disruptions of the existing social systems, and so on.

Interviewer: Well, to take a smaller segment of society, you say that society is more or less an abstraction agreed upon to have a large amount of people function as efficiently as possible —

Ellison: Let's not call it an abstraction because this is real life. It's an arrangement. For all of the continuity of civilization, each society is a sort of improvisation, especially when it's changing so rapidly as most societies are now. There was a time, I guess the Middle Ages, or even during the Renaissance, when there was a slower degree of change and you could say that you had real stability, but now that is impossible. Most societies are strictly improvisations hoping to move towards a point of maximum stability. In the United States the change has been so abiding throughout our history that we more or less accept it as given now, and you hear fewer complaints about the change except when they start tearing down a fine old building, or an especially attractive model of a car goes out of production — you get complaints on that, but not about change itself.

Interviewer: What about another type of change? You say society is an arrangement. The arrangement in the U. S. supposedly says that the Negroes have had equality for a hundred years.

Ellison: No Negroes have had any illusions that we've had

equality. In fact I don't think anyone has because we've been fighting in the courts for a long time, in the state and county courts and so on, for an increase in our participation as citizens. There's been no illusion about that in the States, but a very conscious fight between groups of men who say that we shouldn't have it and have the political power to frustrate our achieving full citizenship and a group of other men who have played ball with them from time to time, and another group of men who have not yet found ways of overlooking their own interests to work out this problem for the nation itself. That's not a system where a lot of people are pretending that something exists when it doesn't.

Interviewer: Well, I wasn't referring to the people, I was referring to the laws. The laws say yes, while reality says no.

Ellison: It's an interpretation of the laws. You can't deal with it in such bulk terms.

Interviewer: Granted that society is an arrangement. What means can a group within that society use to change the arrangement when they interpret a law in a certain way and see their right to certain civil liberties? What means should they employ to attain their ends? Up to now, as you say, they've been using the law courts. Here in Quebec, a separatist group has resorted to violence to gain what they deem their rights. Why hasn't the Negro used more aggressive means to gain his ends? Why hasn't he used violence, which is a traditional means of revolt? Why hasn't there been a riot similar to the one that ends *Invisible Man*?

Ellison: There were two riots like that in New York. I reported the riot on which that one is based for the *New York Post* in 1943. It was during the war and there was a lot of tension and after some altercation between a policeman and a Negro soldier and his mother and wife in a bar, Harlem just exploded and they rioted for a day and a night and destroyed many of the white businesses in Harlem from about 110th Street up until 145th Street. Most of the business area in Harlem, the neighbourhood grocers and so on, was shattered, looted, burned. . . .

Interviewer: And that is where you gained the material for the riot scene in the novel?

Ellison: Well, some of it, but that's an imaginative construction which is based upon pattern, but the reality behind it was that a riot did occur, just as another similar riot occurred in 1935 when I was still living in Alabama. I hadn't been to New York yet. But violence as a means of achieving freedom in the United

States has not been practical for Negroes — certainly not in the South where we are outnumbered and where the major instruments of destruction are in the hands of Whites. It would be foolish to have tried it that way. But there have been individual revolts and showdowns all along. These things are not publicized. But it seems to me far more effective, and there's no doubt but it has been effective, to work upon the basis of what is there and that is the Constitution of the United States. As long as the Supreme Court interpreted the 'separate but equal' clause as being the law of the land, then people who are citizens of that land, especially those who have very little power, had nothing to do but obey it. But that didn't stop them. They agitated to change the interpretation of the law, and in 1954 it was done. It takes far more courage for some of the children to walk on the streets of Birmingham, Alabama, with police dogs after them and with threats of tear gas and shootings — it takes far more courage to do that than to put a plastic bomb into a mailbox.

Interviewer: Isn't it also a matter of time? Many Negro leaders have said that the Negro wants his rights now, not in another fifty or seventy-five years.

Ellison: We do want our rights now. But you don't get rights by destroying them. No, when violence occurs, violence will be answered in some way, but if you are playing the long game — if you've learned the necessity of discipline. . . . What's happening in the United States is something far more complex than just a group of people and their allies challenging an existing horror. What you see happening, I think, is that the best of the American tradition is now finding its expression through these Negroes. That is what's important. That the moral and physical courage that has been typical of Americans, of America at its best, has now found roots among my own people. This is a matter of time. This is a matter of knowing the nature of your opposition. And you should recognize this: most Negroes have never desired separation. Separation isn't the question. Their goal was always to be a functioning part of the governing apparatus with equal participation. This is our goal. If the goal were to achieve separation or to seize control of the government, then violence would be something to think about. But intimidation can be imposed by marching barehanded before police dogs and cattle prods and it requires physical and moral courage. That intimidates, and it's a more subtle form of fighting and a more effective one than I think you recognize.

Interviewer: James Baldwin has shifted his position from novelist to spokesman for the Negro Revolt at present. Do you find that you are being asked to play the role of spokesman?

Ellison: Well, you're asking me to play it right now, but it's a role that I refuse because I recognize what Baldwin doesn't recognize — that is, when you deal with political power you should have some structure behind you and he doesn't. He has no way of imposing his will. There's no apparatus, really, which is not to say that he is not doing some good, but it's a limited good and he speaks with a kind of freedom which is politically unrealistic.

Interviewer: Do you think he does a better job as spokesman than as novelist?

Ellison: I'm not so sure. I prefer his essays to his novels as well as to his pronouncements about the situation, but that isn't for me to decide. If there are people who are moved and who are moved toward changing their view of themselves and the world, I think this is all to the good. The one thing I do know is that this is no role for me. I'm not that kind of a speaker and I think I can best serve my people and my nation by trying to write as well as I can.

Interviewer: Baldwin lately seems to have laid emphasis on his being a Negro; you seem to consider yourself an American in —

Ellison: I consider myself both and I don't see a dichotomy. I'm not an American because I arbitrarily decide so. I write in the American tradition of fiction. My people have always been Americans. Any way you cut it, if you want to think in racist terms, the blood lines were here before the Africans came over and blended with them, as they were here before the Whites came over and blended. So racially, in terms of blood lines and so on, American Negroes are apt to be just as much something else as they are Africans. Now that's one thing. Culturally speaking, I inherited the language of Twain, Melville, and Emerson, after whom I'm named. No, it makes a very dramatic statement when you say, 'I look at Mr. Baldwin's prose you see that he is not writing in the Negro idiom, even, not as much as I do. He's writing a mandarin prose, a Jamesian prose, which tips you off to where he really comes from.

I believe any novel becomes effective to the extent that it deals quite eloquently with its own material — that is, you move from the specific to the universal — and that there's no reason why any novel about a Negro background, about Negro characters, could not be effective as literature and in its effectiveness transcend its immediate background and speak eloquently for other people. I think that's the obligation, to try to write so truthfully and so well and eloquently about a specific background and about a specific form of humanity that it amplifies itself, becomes resonant and will speak to other people and speak *for* other people. This is an obligation. I feel that just as I feel this. It isn't a question of where I want to stand. When I decided to write fiction in the U. S., I committed myself to the obligation of all American novelists — which in no way contradicts my role as Negro. I am responsible to the extent that any individual can be responsible for at least continuing the best traditions of the American novel. I think Baldwin is faced with that too. . . . Now I might write a bad novel. Maybe this novel I am working on is a bad novel. If it fails it won't be because I decided that I was not an American but only a Negro or because I decided that I was not a Negro but only an American. There's no way of doing it. It would just be an instance of a failure. But the obligation is there. I think that certainly as an essayist Baldwin is speaking in an old American tradition and speaking very eloquently; which, again, contradicts in no way his role as Negro although his role as Negro does not really account, absolutely, for the quality of the essays.

Interviewer: You're saying that Baldwin is using an imposed style.

Ellison: I'm not saying that it's an imposed style. I'm saying the emphasis upon the Negroness is an imposition, that he can't help being a Negro any more than he can help being an American writer. He was born here, he has been nourished on the forms of American literature. To the extent that we can use these forms and techniques and draw from the uniqueness of Negro speech and from the uniqueness of our experience as Americans, we have something to add to the general quality of American fiction, American literature, and so on. But beyond that it isn't a matter of making a choice: you're just stuck with it. I could never be a French writer, for instance. I could have gone to Paris and become involved in existentialist politics as Richard Wright did, but it didn't improve his fiction; in fact it helped encourage some very bad tendencies in his writing.

Interviewer: *The Outsider* is an example of this existentialist influence.

Ellison: Well, I think he was writing better existentialist fiction when he was writing *Uncle Tom's Children*.

Interviewer: There is a large amount of theory in *The Outsider*, a large amount of undisguised philosophy.

Ellison: Well, he talked ideas instead of dramatizing them. But there *is* an existentialist tradition within American Negro life and, of course, that comes out of the blues and spirituals.

Interviewer: Yes. One would think that the existentialist novel would not be a novel of ideas, not the novel of Sartre, but a more dramatic novel like *Invisible Man* which never mentions philosophy yet presents the exact dilemma of existentialist man.

Ellison: Well, it's a matter of getting at the condition through the resources of fiction rather than boot-legging in philosophy, in that sense. That is, philosophy in art should be dramatized, it should be part of the given situation, part of the motivations of the characters, a part of their way of confronting life. This is dramatized. Thus, from that point of view you might say that much of the great literature has been existentialist. Just as *Job* is an existentialist fable. *Oedipus Rex* is existentialist, the "How Long Blues' is existentialist.

Interviewer: Now, what position do you take in the Negro Revolt?

Ellison: Let's put it this way. I've always tried to express or to create characters who were pretty forthright in stating what they felt the society should be. And I've tried to present that. I've tried to present the moods of my people as I know them to be and I tried to present the potentialities within that situation as I could discover them through fiction. Ten years ago *Invisible Man* was published and people thought — well they always thought it was an interesting book. Now people are reading it and they think that I invented Malcolm X. What I'm trying to say is that each of us has his role to play and fiction is not a meringue; it is a serious and responsible form of social action itself.

Interviewer: What role are you playing politically?

Ellison: What do I do? I belong to the Committee of One Hundred which is an arm of the legal defence committee of the NAACP. I vote. I try to vote responsibly. I contribute whenever I can to efforts to improve things. Right now one of the things I'm trying to do is to point out that it's a more complex problem than that of simply thrusting out your chin and saying 'I'm defiant'. That's all right, but defiance has to have some real role. One of the big problems facing the country, facing my people specifically, is to prepare to take advantage of the breakdown in the old segregated system. One of the great failures of Negro education, education for Negroes in the U.S., is its failure to prepare the Negro student to understand the functioning of the larger American society. This was more or less planned right from the Reconstruction when the colleges were built. For one way of dealing with the Negro problem was to prepare Negroes to accept the status quo. This has changed, of course, over the years, but it's possible for a Negro student to grow up in the U. S. without having a real feeling of how the society outside of the Negro community operates. He might know how it operates politically, he might know how it operates in terms of social welfare and so on, but then there are other areas, and one of the obligations of the American writer who is Negro is not to simply say that this is no good, but to say why it isn't good, to give his Negro readers at least some insight into the processes of society as they actually exist. This is very important.

Interviewer: Even with this help there are few who will be able to escape this forced provincial system.

Ellison: I don't think it's forced. That's another distortion that you are apt to get from reading some people. Negroes *like* being Negroes.

Interviewer: But if they did want to take advantage of the larger culture it would be a difficult process because the barriers still remain. Now there may be one or two in a few thousand who—

Ellison: No, no, that isn't true. You have many, many, many who are doing it, but the process is as the barriers go down to step up the number of people who will find their way. . . .

Interviewer: Why shouldn't the barriers go down quicker?

Ellison: Why shouldn't they go down quicker? I want them to go down quicker but it isn't that simple. Simply to take down a barrier doesn't make a man free. He can only free himself and as he learns how to operate within the broader society, he learns how to detect the unwritten rules of the game, and so on. But that is what any provincial does; this is what any white provincial has to learn. It's just been easier for him to learn, that's all. Why shouldn't it be easier for the Negro? The reason is because it's political, because there's economic power involved, because there's a great deal of fear involved, and so on. Should it be changed? Yes. When? Today. The question is how.

James Baldwin
Caliban to Prospero

by Brian Lee

To be constantly praised as one of America's greatest essayists must in some ways be very galling for a man who obviously wants, more than anything else, to be recognised first as a novelist. The particular social condition Baldwin diagnoses in his essays is the same one that makes the creation of a fictional world virtually impossible for a Negro novelist. His essays subtly explore the ambiguities and ironies of a life lived on two levels — that of the Negro, and that of the man — and they have spoken eloquently to and for a whole generation. But Baldwin's feelings about the condition — alternating moods of sadness and bitterness — are best expressed in the paradoxes confronting the haunted heroes of his novels and stories. The black singer in 'This Morning, This Evening, So Soon' muses wryly over his luck in being able at last to enter his own life: ". . . everyone's life begins on a level where races, armies, and churches stop. And yet everyone's life is always shaped by races, churches, and armies." The moment of liberation from the prison of a society which has hitherto denied him his humanity, comes for this man when he falls in love:

> Never, in all my life, until that moment, had I been alone with anyone. The world had always been with us, between

us, defeating the quarrel we could not achieve, and making
love impossible. During all the years of my life, until that
moment, I had carried the menacing, the hostile, killing
world with me everywhere. No matter what I was doing or
saying or feeling, one eye had always been on the world —
that world which I had learned to distrust almost as soon
as I learned my name, that world on which I knew one
could never turn one's back, the white man's world.

Eventually he is impelled to return to the world he briefly escaped
from, and the rest of the story tells of his last days in Paris as he
prepares himself emotionally for his encounter with America. This
story is easily recognisable as the fictional counterpart of an essay
called 'The Discovery of What It Means to Be an American' and
was, in fact, published eighteen months after it. In the essay
Baldwin writes about his own attempt to get away from the
dehumanizing society of New York, and about his recognition in
Europe of his common Americanness: "I left America because I
doubted my ability to survive the fury of the colour problem here.
. . . I wanted to prevent myself from becoming *merely* a Negro;
or, even, merely a Negro writer. I wanted to find out in what way
the specialness of my experience could be made to connect me
with other people instead of dividing me from them." It is of
course the same complex fate against which other Americans have
had to struggle, complicated in Baldwin's case, by the fact of his
colour. And in the fight to hold on to his threatened identity,
he has had to make compromises analogous to those effected by
his predecessors: Henry James, for example, who wanted to write
in such a way that Americans would take him for a European,
and Europeans for an American, but who only succeeded in
eliminating from his fiction the traces of any external world; or
T. S. Eliot, who sacrificed his American identity to become, not an
Englishman or a Frenchman, but a European — a citizen of no
recognisable country. So Baldwin too has retreated from his natural
arena, that American society where the wider, public life is shaped,
and gives shape to, the inner experiences of human beings, into
an underworld which, if it is treated realistically, exists only at the
periphery of the wider society, or if it is not, comes to represent
a private refuge from the world at large. Occasionally he does
emerge, of course, to evoke momentarily, but powerfully, that
world he has lost in exchange for another country, and to give

the lie to Eldridge Cleaver who says of Baldwin's characters that they all "seem to be fucking and sucking in a vacuum." In this short scene from 'Sonny's Blues', awareness of the environmental pressures, social and economic, is never relaxed for a moment. On the other hand, it is not allowed to control the scene and stifle its life, as sometimes happens in Dreiser's novels, and in Richard Wright's:

> On the sidewalk across from me, near the entrance to a barbecue joint, some people were holding an old-fashioned revival meeting. The barbecue cook, wearing a dirty white apron, his conked hair reddish and metallic in the pale sun, and a cigarette between his lips, stood in the doorway, watching them. Kids and older people paused in their errands and stood there, along with some older men and a couple of very tough-looking women who watched everything that happened on the avenue, as though they owned it, or were maybe owned by it. Well, they were watching this, too. The revival was being carried on by three sisters in black and a brother. All they had were their voices and their Bibles and a tambourine. The brother was testifying and while he testified two of the sisters stood together, seeming to say, amen, and the third sister walked around with the tambourine outstretched and a couple of people dropped coins into it. Then the brother's testimony ended and the sister who had been taking up the collection dumped the coins into her palm and transferred them to the pocket of her long black robe. Then she raised both hands, striking the tambourine against the air, and then against one hand, and she started to sing. And the two other sisters and the brother joined in.
>
> It was strange, suddenly, to watch, though I had been seeing these street meetings all my life. So, of course, had everybody else down there. Yet, they paused and watched and listened and I stood still at the window. '*Tis the old ship of Zion,*' they sang, and the sister with the tambourine kept a steady, jangling beat, '*it has rescued many a thousand!*' Not a soul under the sound of their voices was hearing this song for the first time, not one of them had been rescued. Nor had they seen much in the way of rescue work being done around them. Neither did they especially be-

lieve in the holiness of the three sisters and the brother, they knew too much about them, knew where they lived, and how. The woman with the tambourine, whose voice dominated the air, whose face was bright with joy, was divided by very little from the woman who stood watching her, a cigarette between her heavy, chapped lips, her hair a cuckoo's nest, her face scarred and swollen from many beatings, and her black eyes glittering like coal.

Such scenes were exceptional, though, and if Cleaver is wrong in saying that Baldwin flounders when he looks beyond the skin, he is right, at least, to emphasize the fact that he really excels when he gets inside his characters.

The possible modes of existence for anyone seeking refuge from a society which refuses to acknowledge one's humanity are necessarily limited, and Baldwin has explored with some thoroughness the various emotional and spiritual alternatives available to his retreating protagonists.

His first novel, *Go Tell it On the Mountain,* explores the psychology of religious experience. Harvey Breit has likened it to Joyce's *Portrait of the Artist as a Young Man,* but it seems to me, both in its strengths and weaknesses, to be much closer to another great autobiographical novel, *Sons and Lovers.* Baldwin is perhaps not Lawrence's equal in his ability to realise the physical presence of the world of objects — there is too much of Dickens in his descriptions — but John Grimes' response to the suffocating world of his childhood reminds one very strongly of Paul Morel:

The room was narrow and dirty; nothing could alter its dimensions, no labor could ever make it clean. Dirt was in the walls and the floorboards, and triumphed beneath the sink where roaches spawned; was in the fine ridges of the pots and pans, scoured daily, burnt black on the bottom, hanging above the stove; was in the wall against which they hung, and revealed itself where the paint had cracked and leaned outward in stiff squares and fragments, the paper-thin underside webbed with black. Dirt was in every corner, angle, crevice of the monstrous stove, and lived behind it in delirious communion with the corrupted wall. Dirt was in the baseboard that John scrubbed every Saturday, and roughened the cupboard shelves that held the cracked and gleaming dishes. Under this dark weight the walls leaned, under it the ceiling, with a great crack like lightning in its center, sagged. The windows gleamed like beaten gold or silver, but now John saw, in the yellow light, how fine dust veiled their doubtful glory. Dirt crawled in the gray mop hung out of the windows to dry. John thought with shame and horror, yet in angry hardness of heart: *He who is filthy, let him be filthy still.*

John, like Paul Morel, turns away from the pain and pressure of his immediate environment in search of "unimaginable glories," and the last section of the novel, 'The Threshing Floor', dramatises the battle that is waged in his soul between God and the Devil, the flesh and the spirit, the temple and the world. Like Lawrence, Baldwin falters before the mystical experience he tries to describe and we are left at the end with only words; words which are used repetitively, rhythmically, symbolically, and sensuously, but not successfully, to convey the transcendental experience. It is difficult not to read *Go Tell it On the Mountain* in the light of Baldwin's own brief but intense experience of salvation and worship, as he tells of it in *The Fire Next Time.* But within the created world of the novel the resolution lacks conviction, having been artistically undermined by the long, central section in which the past lives of John's father, mother and aunt are presented naturalistically with a wealth of social and psychological detail. In the novel, spiritual and social facts do not have the same ineluctable connection that they assume in the essay.

If the love of man for his fellows proves to be an illusion, and the love of God for his creatures proves to be another, it is still possible to maintain a viable existence in either the microcosmic world of sexual love or in the imaginative world of art. Baldwin's attempt to substitute Eros for Caritas, first in *Giovanni's Room* and then in *Another Country,* is a failure, not because he makes the mistake that Lawrence did, of trying to hypostatize the physical in the metaphysical, but because he drains the sexual act of reality by using it as the vehicle for a variety of metaphors. First, there is the fight waged by the Negro characters against the whites in which the chief weapon is the myth of Negro sexuality. So that when Rufus Scott in *Another Country* seduces the Southern girl, Leona:

. . . he cursed the milk-white bitch and groaned and rode his weapon between her thighs. She began to cry. *I told you, he moaned, I'd give you something to cry about,* and, at once, he felt himself strangling, about to explode or die. A moan and a curse tore through him while he beat her with all the strength he had and felt the venom shoot out of him, enough for a hundred black-white babies.

Or there is Rufus' sister, Ida, who turns herself into a black, white man's whore:

And I thought about what I could do to them. How I hated them, the way they looked, and the things they'd say, all dressed up in their damn white skin, and their clothes just so, and their little weak, white pricks jumping in their drawers. You could do any damn thing with them if you just led them along, because they wanted to do something dirty and they knew that you knew how.

Rufus eventually succumbs to the myth completely, and in his failure to break through to another human being destroys both Leona and himself. Ida, on the other hand, painfully forces her white lover, Vivaldo, to meet her on a level beyond myth where they can achieve a genuine human relationship.

That Baldwin is infinitely more perceptive than those who criticise his handling of sexual relationships, hardly needs demonstrating here. Eldridge Cleaver's description of Rufus epitomizes the distortions of vision to which men are subjected by their prejudice:

Rufus Scott, a pathetic wretch who indulged in the white man's pastime of committing suicide, who let a white bisexual fuck him in the ass, and who took a Southern Jezebel for his woman, with all that these tortured relationships imply, was the epitome of the black eunuch who has completely submitted to the white man.

Nevertheless, Baldwin's own metonymical distortions of complex social relationships do constitute an artistic failure.

Next, there is some attempt made in the novel to explore the mutually exclusive worlds of the Bohemian and the Bourgeois in the story of Richard and Cass Silenski. Cass, in an effort to escape the meaninglessness of the middle class life into which she was born, marries Richard, who, to her chagrin, sells out his talent and is content to settle for the life of a successful but mediocre writer. The history of their marriage, and its collapse, is seen almost exclusively in terms of sexual domination, emasculation, and finally, isolation. Again Baldwin seems guilty of oversimplifying the intricacies of social and psychological interconnections.

Finally there is the central role played in the novel by the Southern white homosexual, Eric. It would be misleading to say that he is used merely in a metaphorical way; Baldwin's imaginative sympathy gives to the character a particularity which precludes one from making such easy judgements. But there is, both in the given elements of his character, and in his relation to all the other characters of the novel, a representative quality nonetheless. When Baldwin describes Eric's childhood in Alabama, with the boy's baffled sense of guilty alienation, he is obviously drawing heavily upon his own experience as a Negro youth in a white man's world:

> Long before the Negro child perceives this difference, and even longer before he has begun to react to it, he has begun to be controlled by it. Every effort made by the child's elders to protect him causes him secretly, in terror, to begin to wait, without knowing that he is doing so, his mysterious and inexorable punishment.

Moreover, Eric's role, acted out in this affair with Cass and his brief sexual encounter with Vivaldo, is to bring them through love to a sense of their own identities. And this too, is exactly the part Baldwin envisages the Negro playing in American society:

> You must accept them (white people) and accept them with love. For these innocent people have no other hope. . . .
> In this case, the danger, in the minds of most white Americans, is the loss of their identity.

Eric, in fact, has the characteristics of the White Negro as Norman Mailer describes him in his essay on the subject. Baldwin, in the course of saying why he finds Mailer's ideas "downright impenetrable," himself describes the existential plight of the Negro in terms that are used again in *Another Country* to define the homosexual, who, like the Negro, has to create his standards and make up his definitions as he goes along.

What Baldwin seems to have arrived at in his first three novels, is the painful discovery that there is no other country. Mountains and tiny, cluttered rooms are both, in their different ways, uninhabitable. So too is the refuge that Sonny seeks in the long short story, 'Sonny's Blues'. Sonny is the self that Baldwin only escaped from by rushing into the Church. Having had his head "bumped against the low ceiling of (his) actual possibilities," Sonny sets out on a headlong, futile flight which only ends in the "deep and funky hole" of drug addiction. Brought back to Harlem by his brother he takes up his broken career as a jazz pianist, and in the final scene of the story transmutes his sufferings, and those of his people, into the language of art. Perhaps because he does not demand so much from jazz as he does from religious or sexual experience, Baldwin conveys here his sense of how the unavoidable agonies of life can become the means to — not salvation, not rejection — but creative living:

It was very beautiful because it wasn't hurried and it was no longer a lament. I seemed to hear with what burning he had made it his, with what burning we had yet to make it ours, how we would cease lamenting. Freedom lurked around us and I understood, at last, that he could help us to be free if we would listen, that he would never be free until we did. Yet, there was no battle in his face now. I heard what he had gone through, and would continue to go through until he came to rest in earth. He had made it his: that long line, of which we knew only Mama and Daddy. And he was giving it back, as everything must be given back, so that, passing through death, it can live for ever. I saw my mother's face again, and felt, for the first time, how the stones of the road she had walked on must have bruised her feet. I saw the moonlit road where my father's brother died. And it brought something else back to me, and carried me past it, I saw my little girl again and felt Isabel's tears again, and I felt my own tears begin to rise. And I was yet aware that this was only a moment, that the world waited outside, as hungry as a tiger, and that trouble stretched above us, longer than the sky.

The hero of his latest novel, *Tell Me How Long the Train's Been Gone,* is also an artist who, like Sonny, uses his art to transform his sorrows into life. Leo Proudhammer is a Negro actor recovering from a near fatal heart attack, who spends his time in hospital brooding over the central events of his life, and interpreting its general meaning. Those metaphors, which in the earlier novels and stories, concealed as much or more reality as they revealed, are here examined afresh. Or rather they are recognised at last for what they are, and as such rejected. And whilst the novel sometimes seems to have been written out of a weary cynicism, lacking the intensity and power of some of his earlier fiction, it also has compensating virtues. What they are can only be demonstrated by more extensive commentary.

Leo's first major flashback, to his childhood in Harlem, invites comparison with *Go Tell it On the Mountain.* The two worlds are from the same recognisable source, but the angle of vision is different. The evil world of cops, crime, squalor, and poverty, from which John Grimes escapes into the Church, is the only reality here. For Leo's father, and for his brother, Caleb, God is a sick joke, the object of their most bitter irony: " 'Thanks, good Jesus Christ. Thanks for letting us go home. I mean, I know you didn't have to do it. You *could* have let us just get our brains beat out. Remind me, oh Lord, to put an extra large nickel on the plate next Sunday.' " This is Caleb, as a boy, after he and Leo have been stopped and searched by the police. Yet it is also Caleb who later becomes a pastor at *The New Dispensation House of God*, and who recounts to Leo, in one of the most moving and compelling scenes of the novel, the story of his conversion. Baldwin does full justice to his character here, and Leo faces the reality of his brother's experience too: "I did not know, when Caleb walked into The Island on that far-off night, how many ways there were to die, and how few to live." He faces this reality but recognises that it can never be a reality for him, and after brutally rejecting his brother's God, resigns himself sadly to living henceforth without either brother or God.

Leo also has to learn to dispense with what Baldwin calls the "all-white-men-to-the-sword-and-all-white-women-to-my-bed bull-shit." The story of his relationship with Barbara King has all the elements in it of that earlier one between Rufus and Leona in *Another Country.* Barbara is a beautiful, white, Kentucky heiress, making her way in the theatre. Leo, like Rufus, could easily allow himself to become trapped within the racist myth which denies the possibility of love between two such people. Baldwin does, indeed, describe the pressures they have to live with: the entrenched prejudices of her parents and his; the constant, lascivious questionings of the reporters about their private lives after they have become celebrities; the physical menace they have to endure from enraged thugs when they are young and unprotected by the respectability of fame. This is the world from which there can be no permanent escape; a trap, not of their own making, within which they must learn to live without bitterness. In order to have a life together at all they must sacrifice most of the things that people take for granted: marriage, children, a home. And even so, their best moments come when they can momentarily turn their backs upon the world, as in their brief, romantic idyll on the mountainside. It is instructive to compare their lovemaking in this scene with that between Rufus and Leona:

Barbara began to moan. It was a black moan, and it was as though, trapped within the flesh I held, there was a black woman moaning, struggling to be free. Perhaps it was be - cause we were beneath the starlight, naked. I had unzipped the sleeping bag, and the August night travelled over my body, as I trembled over Barbara. It was as though we were not only joined to each other, but to the night, the stars, the moon, the sleeping valley, the trees, the earth beneath the stone which was our bed, and the water beneath the earth. With every touch, movement, caress, with every thrust, with every moan and gasp, I came closer to Barbara and closer to myself and closer to something unnameable. And her thighs locked around me, sweeter than water. She held me, held me, held me. And I was very slow. I was very sure. I held it, held it, held it, held it because I knew it could not be held. All this had nothing to do with time. The moment of our liberation gathered, gathered, crouched, ready to spring, and Barbara sobbed; the wind burned my body, and I felt the unmistakable, the unanswerable retreat, contraction, concentration, the long, poised moment before the long fall. I murmured, *Barbara,* and seemed to hear her name echoed in the valley for a long time. Then the stars began to grow pale. I zipped the sleeping bag over us. We curled into each other, and slept. We had not spoken.

If this is still Lawrentian, it is at least true to the best examples of Lawrence, and not the worst.

A more difficult, because more pervasive, myth that has to be dealt with, is that concerning the role Negroes are forced to play in American society. At the time of his heart attack Leo is booked to play a part in a movie. It is a part which does not specifically require a Negro actor, and is seen as a breakthrough by those who have always thought the summit of a Negro actor's ambition should be to play Emperor Jones or Othello. With bitter and telling irony Baldwin calls this movie *Big Deal*. That a man should have come so far as Leo does, only to achieve the status on the stage of a human being is a bitter irony indeed. But the history of Leo's acting career is the history of the American Negro in miniature; he graduates from one stereotyped role to the next, discovering no viable connection between the image he must project and his sense of his own life. When he does eventually play white parts, though, he finds to his surprise that these too bear little relation to any discoverable reality, and he concludes that "the people who destroyed by history had also destroyed their own." Moreover, Leo's problems do not diminish with his growing fame. The Negro who makes it is as remote from the rest of humanity as those who don't, and Baldwin creates a frightening picture in the novel of the making of Public Man — a man not unlike James Baldwin.

The autobiographical elements in *Tell Me How Long The Train's Been Gone* are not very well concealed. Baldwin, like Leo, is a "fat cat" now, and this novel is, in a sense, his *Big Deal*. It is not a great novel. In some ways it is not as good as those he wrote previously — certainly it lacks the intensity of much of his earlier writing. What has been gained, though, is ultimately more important. One of Baldwin's constant complaints has been that the Negro has been deprived of his language, and he has written, therefore, like a man trying to invent his own; sacrificing, in the attempt, truth to rhetoric. Now he seems to have realised the futility of this, and has decided to come to terms with the only language he can have. Consequently he has written a novel with the truth in it: the work of "an honest man and a good writer."

Another Country:
Baldwin's New York Novel

by Mike Thelwell

"... To become a Negro man, let alone a Negro
Artist, one has *to make oneself up* as one goes along.
This had to be done in the not-at-all metaphorical
teeth, of the world's intention to destroy you. This
is not the way this truth presents itself to white men,
who believe the world is theirs, and who, albeit,
unconsciously, expect the world to help them in the
achievement of their identity."
                         "*—Black Boy Looks at white Boy.*"

LATE in 1960 James Baldwin came back to America after a protracted period of European exile. He said on arrival that he didn't
know if he was glad to be back, but that he needed to be, and that
he had never really *seen* the country before. He said that he had
two books in process, a collection of essays called *Nobody Knows My
Name* and a novel called *Another Country.* What was the novel
about, he was asked. He shrugged, impatiently, looked a little
exasperated and said, "Look, its over five hundred pages long . . .
what's a novel usually about anyway, its about five people in New
York . . . now."

Naturally someone asked how New York got to be "another

country" and he answered logically enough, "Well, that depends on where you are, does it not?"

The book appeared in 1962 to what is euphemistically called "mixed notices," but what actually happened is that the New York literary establishment, with only three notable exceptions, greeted it with some of the most fatuous, inept, and at times downright dishonest criticism that I had ever seen. A number of reviewers, for whatever reason, became so incensed at the book that, completely losing whatever tenuous grip they commanded of the tenets of their craft, they gave vent to some of the most parochial, ill-tempered, irrelevant, and distasteful attacks on Baldwin's personal life and character. I remember reading these notices and becoming increasingly angry and perplexed at what I saw as either a near complete failure of vision, or displays of personal malice. Certainly, I could recognize little of the book I had read in these notices. So, when I was sent a copy for review, I spent much space reviewing the reviewers, because as I wrote then,

> Sometimes it chances that the critical response to a work of fiction will reveal as much about the society that produced that work, as the work of fiction itself. *Another Country* has proved to be such a work: too important to ignore and too cruelly honest and threatening to deal with objectively. At least this seems to have been the experience of some of our most prestigious critics.

I then proceeded to praise the book's strengths extravagantly, while ignoring its weaknesses. About this time I happened to see the author and asked how the book was doing.

"Very well," he said unhappily, "very well indeed . . . *outside of New York*. The notices *here* have been terrible, vindictive . . . I really don't understand it."

I suspect that if he ever was really confused by the critical reaction in New York, he is no longer. But at the time he seemed very hurt. Despite the fact that this was his fifth book, it was his third novel, and he was, in terms of his career under a kind of "second novel" pressure for a number of reasons. That is, his real second novel had been written in France, set in France, and had been widely conceded to be "delicately crafted, skillfully written, sensitively observed," but a *tour de force,* a kind of minor aberration. The second "serious" work was still to come, and this was of course *Another Country*.

In fact it appeared that the critical response did, at one point, succeed in shaking his confidence in the work. A T.V. interviewer asked him whether he agreed with the critical judgement that *Go Tell It On The Mountain* was his finest novel.

"I know some people are saying that," he replied, "and I am glad they like that book so much. But it *was* written ten years ago. No writer likes to feel that he is getting worse. This is a book I *had* to write. Now I can go on. I had to write this book."

The fact is, of course, that in terms of a purely formal and sterile graduate school kind of aesthetics, *Mountain* and *Giovianni's Room*, may be better examples of a certain example of the *form*, but neither have the range, the power, the relevance nor the passionate vitality and vision, of the later novel. And, significantly, neither early book speaks as explicitly of the relationship between white people and black people.

It must be said that by the term "New York establishment" I do not mean simply the magazines published in the geographic area of the city, but that area on the eastern seaboard that has as the focus of its literary activities New York, the area that would be within what Walter Lippman would call "The New York sphere of influence."

The response was not of course at all of a piece in terms of what was said of the book. But whatever the conclusions, the *method* of approach showed remarkable consistency. The cleverer critics chose simply to discuss abstractions to do with the "form of the novel" the "concept" of the novel, the "structuring" of the novel, ignoring the comment that the novel makes on the contemporary New York experience. Most adopted tones of unctuous regret, "the fine gifts of Baldwin the essayist seem unfortunately to conflict with the novelistic sensitivity," which being interpreted implies that the one way of ordering experience and perceptions is at irreconcilable odds with the other, which is nonsense. What it really *means* is "Stick with the essay boy, and leave the 'higher form' to us."

Most, as Norman Podhoretz pointed out, left sufficient space for "An earnest tribute to Mr. Baldwin's talents, calling him one of our very best writers, and voicing a pious confidence in his ability to do better in the future."

Different ones "of these critics of style" objected to all kinds of peripheral trivia, making sure that whatever element they chose to focus their indignation on was all but irrelevant in terms of the real vision and judgment of experience inherent in the book. For the most part that seemed to me to be the ploy, an escape into trivia or the aesthetic formalism that has the advantage, especially in a form as diffuse as the novel, of being arbitrary, and capable of serving any cause.

Another very common characteristic of this group was an ill-disguised tone of patronage, subtle but unmistakably present. The second group of critics, less clever and devious, made the error of doing battle with the vision of experience expressed. What came out there — mainly in the daily newspaper notices, joined on this occasion by the weekly *Village Voice* which surprised with the strident middle-class chauvinism and moral rigidity of its review — was a hysterical, threatened, shrill howl of heterosexual outrage and indignation. To anyone reading these notices, the urbane and sophisticated New York had in fact become "another country," one of repressive, white, middle-class babbittry which saw the book as the spearhead of some insidious homosexual conspiracy to subvert the sexual sensibilities and responses of the reading public, an attack on marriage, on the virility of the white male and the sexuality of the white female, and just about all of their accepted assumptions about human relationships. And, as has been pointed out, this was not generally true of the reviews which came out of the West, Midwest, and even parts of the South. Why?

An example of the first group is Paul Goodman, who defines his own relationship to society in terms of a personalized and esoteric radicalism, and who saw the characters as being without "social consciousness," and complained about the city of the novel not being the city he knew, complaints which even if true would hardly be important. The second, is, incidentally, less of a comment on where Goodman imagines he lives, because Goodman's "Empire City" notwithstanding, this is *the* novel of contemporary New York. I am convinced that this fact is part of the explanation of the New York response, but more of that later.

Another critic saw the characters as "paper thin," an apparent protest against the absence of convoluted Faulknerian family trees and psychiatric case histories. The best example of the hysteria of the second group of reviewers appeared in the *Village Voice*, usually so self-consciously hip. This man, the writer of the most tendentious and obtuse piece on the book, had his sensibilities outraged because some homosexual relationships are rendered as being no more destructive than heterosexual ones, because the only sexual relationship between a white couple "which is graced by matrimonial vows" is presented as being empty, and because the comments of a Negro woman character on white society, "is marked by a non-feminine crudity." What this character (Ida) did say to her white lover (Vivaldo) simply was "You is a fucked up bunch of people." A remark worth two paragraphs to this reviewer.

In the middle of all this, Granville Hicks' intelligent and sensitive review stood out as evidence that everyone was not rendered incapable of honest and compassionate criticism by the book. Thank the Lord for that old gentleman. If one believes that the book is flawed, but that its faults become very insignificant beside its formidable accomplishments — the illuminating energy and passionate interpretation of experience and social and emotional reality — the question becomes what happened to these critics? Part, but only a very small part, of the answer, is the sheep-like unacknowledged borrowing of insights that this group is prone to. This results in a situation where a few widely-read early reviews tend to influence the attitudes and vision of the writers who grind out subsequent commentary, so an escalation of opinion takes place. For some reason, it is infinitely more *chic* to have panned a book that your friends liked than to have praised a book in print, when everyone else is disparaging it.

However, unless the state of book reviewing is even worse than its most trenchant critic admits, this does not approach an explanation of the critical reaction to *Another Country*. There must be other more significant answers.

Norman Podhoretz outlines the general dynamic of what I also suspect must have happened. In an article called "In Defense of a Maltreated Best Seller" published in *Show* magazine, he writes:

> But in spite of all this (the scattering of good notices and the enormous sales) I stand by the word maltreated. With few exceptions, (*Newsweek* among them) the major reviewing media were very hard on *Another Country*. It was patronized by Paul Goodman of the *New York Times Book Review*, ridiculed by Stanley Edgar Hyman in the *New Leader*, worried over (with it must be said, genuine distress) by Elizabeth Hardwick in *Harpers*, summarily dismissed by the *Times'* anonymous critic, loftily pitied by Whitney

Balliett in *The New Yorker*, and indignantly attacked by Saul Maloff in the *Nation*.

Podhoretz finds "it hard to believe that these wrong-headed appraisals of *Another Country* can be ascribed to a simple lapse of literary judgment," especially in the cases of Goodman, Hardwick and Hyman, whom he calls "first-rate critics." He is eloquently silent about the competence of the other three.

After fretting about certain explicit misjudgments on the parts of these "first-rate critics," Podhoretz guesses that,

> all these critics disliked the book, not because it suffers from this or that literary failing, but because they were repelled by the militancy and cruelty of its vision of life. Granville Hicks was right when he called the book "an act of violence" and since it is the reader upon whom this violence is being committed perhaps one ought to have expected that many reviewers would respond with something less than gratitude.

This judgment is, I believe, accurate; the question that must be answered has to do with the *nature* of this violence, and the values that the reviewers felt to be threatened by Baldwin's version of our experience. Rather than risk doing violence to Mr. Podhoretz's explication of the impact of the book (those elements that the critics found dangerous), I shall repeat it in some detail.

> Whites coupled with Negroes, heterosexual men coupled with homosexuals, homosexuals coupled with women, none of it involving casual lust or the suggestion of perversity, and all of it accompanied by the most serious emotions and resulting in the most intense attachments — it is easy enough to see even from so crude a summary that Baldwin's intention is to deny any moral significance whatever to the categories white and Negro, heterosexual and homosexual. He is saying that the terms white and Negro refer to two different conditions under which individuals live, but they are still individuals and their lives are still governed by the same fundamental laws of being. And he is saying, similarly, that the terms homosexuality and heterosexuality refer to two different conditions under which individuals pursue

love, but they are still individuals and their pursuit of love is still governed by the same fundamental laws of being.

Putting the two propositions together, he is saying, finally, that the only significant realities are individuals and love, and that anything which is permitted to interfere with the free operation of this fact is evil and should be done away with.

Now, one might suppose that there is nothing particularly startling in this view of the world; it is, after all only a form of the standard liberal attitude toward life.

. . . But that is not the way James Baldwin holds it, and it is not the way he states. He holds these attitudes with puritanical ferocity, and he spells them out in such brutal and naked detail that one scarcely recognizes them any longer — and one is frightened by them, almost as though they implied a totally new, *totally revolutionary conception of the universe*. And in a sense, of course, they do. For by taking these liberal pieties literally and by translating them into simple English, he puts the voltage back into them and they burn to the touch.

. . . *Another Country*, then, is informed by a remorseless insistence *on a truth* which however partial we may finally judge it to be, is nevertheless compelling as a perspective on the way we live now.

. . . But in the end, the failures of *Another Country*, however serious, seem unimportant beside the many impressive things Baldwin has accomplished here.

. . . I believe that *Another Country* will come to be seen as the book in which for the first time the superb intelligence of Baldwin the essayist became fully available to Baldwin the novelist, in which for the first time he attempted to speak his mind with complete candor and with a minimum of polite rhetorical elegance, and in which for the the first time he dared to reveal himself as someone to be feared for how deeply he sees, how much he demands of the world and how powerfully he can hate.

It would be difficult to dispute Mr. Podhoretz's observation of that quirk of the liberal personality, expressed by an unreasoning terror of any thought implementation of their platitudes. And it is almost certain that much of the confusion surrounding the reception of the book is merely further evidence of this old truth, operating in precisely the manner that he describes. But the critical paranoia must have its roots in other equally significant reactions.

In terms of the literary culture the book takes on monumental proportions as it represents a direct assault, not only on a few sterile sexual and social taboos, but on the cultural hegemony, the dictatorship of perception and definition, of the Anglo-Saxon vision as it operates through the literature onto the society. It presents a self-consciously and even arrogantly *black* consciousness refuting and demolishing certain cherished notions about the "quality of life" in society, presenting an unapologetic and relentless vision of white society and white characters as they are registered in a black consciousness. Here the critics are confronted by white characters, in roughly similar social positions and backgrounds, to themselves, and they do not like the image in which they are cast. This is a real-world example of precisely the kind of inversion that is accomplished in the "class conscious" drama of Jean Genet, where masks are adopted, class roles reversed, and social relationships are viewed from the perceptions of the previously mute and oppressed. Baldwin's book represents a similar clash of sensibility and experience, and I am convinced that the reviewers were just not prepared to have their class prerogative of defining and interpreting the dynamics of their own social experience assumed by this black man from Harlem. They were not prepared to accept the Negro characters' comments on the white characters, simply because the identity between themselves and some of the whites in the book is too close. It is one thing for a precocious black boy to paint lyrical and moving pictures of life in Harlem, but it is, as the Southern lady remarked, a "nigger of a different color" when this analytic vision is directed into their living rooms and bedrooms. It is one thing, in novels written by blacks, to have stock white characters carry the burden of white society's guilt re the Negro, the acceptance of which has become a perfunctory obligation of the liberal soul anyway, so it constitutes no real threat. It is entirely different to have them on terms of social and sexual equality with tough and commanding *Negroes* who expose gaping human and emotional inadequacies in these white characters, and openly attribute these inadequacies to cultural human backruptcies within the white establishment. This irony is unacceptable precisely because it reverses the tradition coming from the very beginning of American literature, in which white perceptions and sensibilities, and a white consciousness interprets, defines, and gives form — hence a kind of reality — to all relationships of all characters within the society. It is because no previous novel by a Negro has ever appropriated this function so completely, probingly, and relentlessly that the white reviewers were constrained to ignore or disparage this vision. In this respect the significance of *Another Country*'s being a *regional* novel cannot be over-emphasized. The experience it describes is in many respects peculiarly New York, the conditions which operate are not to be found in quite the same way anywhere else in the country. This is the anxiety-ridden, abrasive, neurotic and merciless world of the artistic underground. What the characters seek is not simply love, and an end to loneliness, but to "make it." They are seeking to force the society to come to terms with their own existence, that is to say, seeking their public identity. So the natural insecurity of the modern human situation is for them heightened by the competitive and spiritually destructive hustle of New York's talent jungle. There are among the major characters, two writers, one actor, a singer and a T.V. producer. And as Truman Capote put it, "a boy's got to hustle." Their common enemy and the source of much of their neurosis, is anonymity and obscurity. They are all past the first flush of youth and some have begun to establish the basis of their fame and success. It is significant that the one character that seems to have established working terms on which to confront his own identity is Eric, the actor, who is "making it" on pretty much his own terms and without having done visible violence to his creative integrity. That he is also unrepentantly bi-sexual and appears to have made his personal peace with that reality also, is undoubtedly the cause of much of the heterosexual indignation that greeted the book.

The other successful characters are Ellis, the meritricious and exploitative T.V. executive, and Richard Silenski, who is a prototype of the typically middle-class white American male. He is presented as a well-meaning but limited man, hampered by the restricted vision and sensitivity of the white establishment consciousness, who is well on his way to being a successful writer for T.V.. He is the prototype of the objects of Baldwin's severest criticism. "The writers . . . who are not to my mind really writers. They are respected as articulate responsible spokesmen for society, yet the image they have of the society is nothing more than the popular image and their role is merely to recreate and keep alive that image." These are the only two characters who stand in the mainstream of contemporary success, so to say, and they emerge as the least sympathetic figures in the book. They also happen to be the people in the book with whom most reviewers would tend to identify themselves.

The other major characters, five in number, constantly struggle with more or less success, to avoid the stereo-typing of identity and response, that the society demands, and the self-willed and deceptive "innocence" that Baldwin has said is the burden and insulation of white folks.

These must be the "five people in New York." They are Rufus Scott, a priapic and charismatic jazz drummer, his sister Ida, an aspiring singer who becomes the lover of Vivaldo Moore, an unsuccessful writer, Eric Jones, a white southern actor who is returning from France, and Cass Silenski, the wife of the writer Richard, who has a brief affair with Eric.

At the time the novel opens, this group, with the exception of Ida, is scattered after what was a period of great closeness and affection. Rufus is starving on the Bowery, Eric is in France, Cass is at home being a wife and mother, and Vivaldo, lonely and frustrated, is frequenting their old village haunts in the company of a bitchy and destructive woman painter. We learn that despite a deep mutual affection in the group, they were basically united, for reasons that are never made clear, by a deep, almost worshipful admiration for Rufus. They are also united by a number of factors including ambition, youth, and an optimistic and idealistic commitment to their various crafts.

They are reunited at the end of the first section by the death of Rufus who commits suicide after a painful and violent affair with a white southern girl. The dispersal and reunion is essential to Baldwin's central purpose which is the revelation of each character's, if not growth, then at least progression, toward insights, perceptions and the recognition and acceptance of truths about themselves, a process which can be called the loss of innocence. So the difference between what the characters imagined themselves to be, and what they discover that they are, is revealed in conspicuous relief by the juxtaposition of then and now.

These five characters who find themselves in New York from Harlem, New England, The South, and Brooklyn are further united by having rejected their roots, and the identity imposed by those connections. They now face the responsibility of a dual and perhaps conflicting definition of themselves. The first responsibility is to shatter their social anonymity by achieving a "name," a public identity, by coming to terms, in a public sense, with the society. This pressure seems to be most insistent and demanding in New York. The complementary responsibility is to achieve coexistence with their emotional needs, which entails constructing an emotional identity which can only be done in intimate relationship with other people. Both of these urges are simply a response to the fact that human beings have no identity except in these terms, and are reactions against existential nothingness.

These five characters share this situation, but they do not start from the same place. Eric, for example, is aware of his isolation and the hostile posture of the general society towards him because he is an outcast and a refuge from the society of his youth. Thus, by demarking and defining the nature of his alienation, his bi-sexuality has done him a service, and he *knows* he must accept full responsibility for self-definition.

Similarly, the Scotts, being Negro, recognize that they must wrestle with the white-defined society for the right to self-definition — to be what you can be, to someday read your rightful name — in the teeth of a society that is quite ready with a gratuitous and shameful set of definitions for them. In this sense they are never as "innocent" as Vivaldo, Cass and Richard who begin with the assumption described here

> This is not the way this truth presents itself to white men, who believe the world is theirs, and who, albeit, unconsciously, expect the world to help them in the achievement of their identity.

Rufus and Ida are presented as being beyond this *naïveté*. They are too familiar with the excesses of violence, the possibility of exploitation both sexual and spiritual, the gratuitious humiliation and denial of *lebensraum,* and the varieties of potential rape with which the society has surrounded them, to ever believe in society's myths in quite the same way as Cass, the New England aristocrat. But this knowledge is not, in practical terms, a liberating force, and is not even wisdom since it cannot easily be communicated or applied. For it has been gathered not merely at the price of "innocence," but at the cost of a bitterness and distrust which is so massive as to be insupportable. This knowledge, neither cerebral nor intellectual, but which as a function of experience, is almost pathological, renders the possibility of communication between the Scotts and their *"innocent"* white lovers difficult or impossible on any deeply significant level. Elsewhere, Baldwin has written that "people who strive to preserve their innocence after the justifiable time for that innocence has passed become monsters." Another and equally grim application of this aphorism must go, "people who are prematurely deprived of hope, illusion, and innocence become ruthless."

As this operates in the novel, both Rufus and Ida Scott have fewer discoveries to make, and fewer illusions to lose, than their white lovers. No less vulnerable, they are, because of their slum kid's gutter knowledge, somehow less surprisable. They both have white lovers who are committed to the attempt to create relationships grounded in respect, decency, and genuine and enduring love. This goal, (though obsession may be more descriptive, since these characters seem to be motivated by a desperate and obsessive faith in the liberating possibility of love) ensnares Rufus and Ida too. They both at first resist and reject any possibility of that kind of a commitment, but are gradually led by their own needs to suspend this protective armour of earned cynicism, and to commit themselves to the attempt. Once they are "reached" by their relationships they become victims of a new kind of vulnerability. Precisely because they do not have the "innocence" of a Cass, or the comfortable blindness of her husband, they must *will* themselves to participate, despite their dearly bought vision of the reality of pain, and hatred, of anguish and love as inseparable entertwine in the act of living, despite their knowledge that simply to live is a terribly dangerous thing, and that we "all must pay our dues." Instead of "innocent" victims, they are informed victims, because despite their "alienation" and their very hip knowledge of the protean shape of destruction within the society, they cannot escape it, and their choices and responses are defined by this fact.

Because many of his responses are conditioned by the process by which he received his knowledge, Rufus cannot control his increasing paranoia or the violence that is evoked in him. He looks at the body of his white lover and asks himself, "If she were Negro would I want her." He finds that her body (the possession of which is allegedly the ultimate phallic triumph of the Negro man, and the ultimate insult to the white man, but this is a formulation of the white male mind made into a kind of social reality) her love, a physical and spiritual commitment which is so total as to be almost a capitulation, is not enough. But since he can neither accept and forget, nor completely reject her the relationship moves from violence to violence, abuse to abuse, and ultimately to destruction and madness. He is unable to escape his emotional conditioning, received at the hands of society.

His younger sister Ida, comes out of Harlem to do battle with the forces that she is convinced destroyed her brother. She *knows* the enemy and is not about to be seduced into lowering her protective isolation. She resists any but the most superficial relationship to Vivaldo, is not about to expose herself in the same way Rufus did, and will not be deluded into recognizing even a possibility of tenderness and compassion. When you run with the wolves, you howl like a wolf. So by maintaining her non-involvement she is able, by prostituting herself to Ellis's lust, to manipulate his attempt at exploitation to the advantage of her career. In so doing, she is acting out of her experience, that of the black woman in Harlem. But the burden is too great, for her to sustain, and she ends up responding with compassion and tenderness to Vivaldo's earnest, if bumbling, faith in the possibility of communion. At the end of the book, she is going against the evidence of her experience, and is making a desperate commitment to the relationship. One gets the impression that she knows better, but must force herself to try.

One critic perceives all the characters as being "self-centered," and so they are, as who isn't? But their isolation, or alienation if you will, does not admit of so pat a dismissal, as I have been at pains to point out. They are — those that indicate any hope of positive development — involved in "making themselves up as they go along." They are isolated — but in the most existential and agonizing sense of the word. In their necessary rejection of the glib and ready-made they are forced to construct a new reality, to impose their own order and definition on the chaos in which they move, if they can. This is the challenge which they accept, and their only resources are in their own tangled emotions, their own desires and needs (which they are forced to take issue with in their totality and there is, apparently, nothing as shattering as the encounter with our true image) and the depths of their own spirit. Baldwin writes of Eric, and it is true in large degree of them all, that

He could not accept the hideously mechanical jargon of his age, saw no one around him worth his envy, did not believe in the cures, panaceas and slogans, did not believe in the vast grey sleep called security — and he had to make his own standards and slogans as he went along. It was up to him to find out who he was, and it was his necessity to do this, so far as the witchdoctors of his time were concerned, alone.

It is this character, Eric, who aroused most of the male chauvinist objections to the book. He is less tormented and uncertain than the other characters, and consequently strangely attractive to them. Many critics resented that this bi-sexual actor is presented as having attained a measure of peace in the acceptance of his own reality (as opposed to the identity that dominant conventions would impose), and that Cass Silenski is able to find with him a dimension of emotional integrity, that is not possible with her all-American writer-husband.

What this character represents is more subtle than simply an attack on the virility of the conventional American he-man. His ability to discover what and who he is, to accept this, and to be honest to his emotional impulses, however socially unacceptable they may be, is an expression of one of Baldwin's major insights. Perhaps more debatable and more interesting, however, are the emotional implications of bi-sexuality.

The tone of the writing is, as Podhoretz says, meant to deny any moral significance to the categories homo and hetero sexual, since these are social rather than natural distinctions. The point is not simply that these is a sexual dualism of greater or lesser strength in each individual, and that physical expressions of this are not *necessarily* perverse. The point is that emotional responses between and across the sexes are determined by puritan society's rigid (and arbitrary) separation of social functions and roles into categories of male and female, and the attendant pressures on the individual to repress and suppress natural responses which do exist. This leads to an unnatural fragmentation not only of experience but of emotional sensibilities, and a rapidly approaching point at which the gap between the "feminine sensibility, the feminine mystique" and the male perspective will be unbreachable. Notice too, that while, thanks to the feminist revolt, women are gaining access to experiences — not necessarily overtly sexual —

situations, roles, and styles of life which had been reserved to men, there is no indication of a similar reciprocal broadening of male possibilities. I once heard a young writer confounded by the question, "How on earth do you ever hope to become a writer when you begin by arbitrarily excluding yourself from a whole area of human emotional experience?" This question may be meritricious, but it expresses something of the Tiresian quality that has been written into the character of Eric, in that out of his own sexual ambiguity — a fairer word might be flexibility — he is able to relate to vastly different needs in Cass and Vivaldo.

This is mentioned because I feel it has some relevance to the perceptions of the author, who is able to illuminate and probe into areas of experience and emotion convincingly and passionately, largely because of his awareness of emotional attitudes which are generally characterized as exclusively male or female. But I do not wish to belabor this.

Finally, although the book has its faults, and the most distracting of these have to do with an uncharacteristic note of sentimentality and too much of a self-consciously aphoristic and apocalyptic rhetoric, its accomplishments and its importance far outweigh these. Whether or not one agrees with the vision of the *meaning* of contemporary experience presented, no one denies that the book is an accurate, perceptive and truthful expression of the texture, feel and consistency of that experience. That is the first and major responsibility of the novelist. My own feeling and that of everyone I talked to when the book first came out was, despite anything else, "He is telling it like it is." I can not remember anyone, white or Negro, who did not feel that the book spoke directly and fiercely to many aspects of their own particular experience.

Equally important in evaluating this book, is a consideration of the place it represents in the body of Baldwin's work, and what that work represents in the flux of the American literary culture. Returning to New York with his perceptions sharpened, and with a vision that combined the freshness of the stranger with the knowledge of a native, he was able to excavate and display patterns, relationships, insights which had never been presented in quite the same way, with courage and candor. And this book, the book he was *compelled* to write more for truth and relevance than for "Art," is the one in which he confronts most fully the anguished issues peculiar to our age.

As Robert Sayre says "certainly one mark of his achievement, whether as a novelist, essayist, or propagandist, is that whatever deeper comprehension of the race issue Americans [presumably white Americans] now possess has been in some way shaped by him. And this is to have shaped their comprehension of themselves as well."

This revolution of consciousness that he has engendered is a social reality as much as a literary one. It is scarcely possible to write today on this issue without, consciously or not, making use of assumptions and relationships which first emerged as startling insights in Baldwin's work. He has single-handedly broken through a dead-end of platitudes, sociological clichés, complacent white assumptions, and a monopoly of consciousness which had, since the thirties, just about lost their usefulness. How was this possible?

Mostly one only speculates, but certain things can be pointed up. Intellectual techniques and practices have a natural tendency to atrophy and stagnate, to *reinforce* themselves endlessly to the point where once useful truths became meaningless platitude. With this atrophy of language and concept, goes a limiting of vision and imagination. Generally, this had happened in America. One has only to read the Negro writers of the fifties to see how enclosed they were in the respectable terminology and analysis of the thirties, but it is hardly necessary to outline this vast canon of accepted American assumptions on the race question at this time.

Suffice it to say that these assumptions were based on a few meager studies by some Negro scholars and a Swiss sociologist, and heavily on the fact that whole areas of the real history of the country had been rewritten by whites, in service to the necessities of white political, economic and cultural objectives. The basic cultural power-relationship, which decreed that the interpretation of the race question was to reflect only the whites' definition of themselves and the Negro, has persisted since the very beginning of literature in this Country. A one way mirror.

The social ferment of the thirties did produce Richard Wright's and Ralph Ellison's magnificent efforts to balance this, but the very nature of the intellectual focus of that period — fervently political, predominantly one of class politics and economics — while establishing necessary and important horizons, could not incorporate other significant perceptions. When Baldwin left the country during the cultural and political depression which followed the economic depression, there was a need to go beyond the revelations and discoveries of the thirties. But how and to what?

I think the sojourn in France helped provide Baldwin with necessary analytical tools, and a new way of seeing. Specifically, he was affected by the French existentialist sensibility, particularly that of Sartre, who while exploring the nature of the emotional warfare between one consciousness and "the other," concepts of alienation and emotional annihilation of the individual, never lost sight of certain Marxist concepts of class power and class influence. Genet's work, filled with revelatory insights into class perceptions and class subjectivity, and demonstrations of the transformation of relationships and situations that are caused by a simple shift in point of view, his work with the function of the "Mask" and the "Role" in determining social behavior (readily applicable to the American racial situation), affected the consciousness of the French intellectual generally.

The most meaningful of these insights in Sartre, Genet, and the French absurdists is their sophisticated understanding of the role of *power*, between individuals and between classes, the power to control language, and through language, expression and perception and thus even historical interpretation.

Baldwin's use of this insight is pervasive, beginning with the simple disclosure that the American Negro as the object of this kind of white power, had been defined in the public and indeed, his own consciousness, by white *needs*. This being so, the possibilities are overwhelming. First, an examination of the elements of the "image" of the Negro in the culture, literature, and public consciousness could reveal, albeit sometimes in disguised and inverted form, useful truths about the psychological needs of the white image maker and his culture.

From this it followed that if the image and identity of the Negro was in such large measure a product of *white cultural power*, then this condition could only be completely understood and changed by close and probing scrutiny of white society. "One can not understand where Negroes are today, without understanding twice as much about where white people are. . . . There is no Negro problem, there is a white folks problem. . . . The form and content of oppression are reflections of the fears and needs of the oppressor. To survive the oppressed must understand and use these. Why did the white need to create the 'Nigger'?"

If these are not new insights, at least the probing and sweeping application that Baldwin made of them resulted in vast break-throughs, most important of which is the willingness, at least of some whites, to accept that those perceptions coming out of the peculiar history, experience and vantage point of the Negro do have a validity and a dimension in describing contemporary social realities, which is not possible for the consciousness operating from "white" assumptions and perceptions.

Like the white rulers in Genet's *The Blacks* who were not pre-pared to be examined and discussed by the blacks, or the mistress in *The Maids*, also by Genet, who could not recognize herself as reflected in her maid's perceptions, America's dominant culture group was ill-prepared to cope with a Negro analysis of the culture. If he had done nothing else, Baldwin's determined insistence on interpreting events and attitudes affecting Negroes, both historical and contemporary, in terms of what they indicated about the initiators would be a major contribution.

Baldwin's *Another Country* is the first example of these sensi-bilities in operation *qua* "pure" literature. However the specifics are phrased, it is this fact that is at the base of much of the critical virulence that greeted the novel. But it is this fact also that will ensure its lasting significance. Its existence breaks the ground for the others that, one hopes, will follow.

Disturber of the Peace: James Baldwin

An Interview conducted by

Eve Auchincloss and Nancy Lynch

Iᴛ ᴡᴀs ʀᴇᴘᴏʀᴛᴇᴅ *somewhere recently that your friend Norman Mailer said to you, in anger: "You're little, you're ugly, and you're as black as the ace of spades." But your comeback was not recorded.*

Oh, I just laughed. After all, it's true. But the point is, why, after all these years, did he have to say it? I mean, it's his problem, really, and I think it has to do with the fact that like most white liberals — though I'm not accusing him of being one exactly — he has always lied to himself about the way he really feels about Negroes.

Most people would say liberals have done more for the Negro than anybody else. Why are you so hard on them?

This has been on my mind for a long time, but it was triggered when I went on the Barry Gray show to protest the fact that the Anti-Defamation League had given a medal to Kennedy for his record on civil rights and to protest the fact that William Worthy was being indicted by the Justice Department for having re-entered his own country illegally, which as far as I know is an impossibility for an American citizen. And Barry Gray was very angry at me. What he finally said was that I should be picketing Governor Ross

Barnett; I shouldn't be picketing my friends. And that made me mad, and I said that one of the hardest things anyone has to survive in this country is his friends. That made him madder. When it was over I began to feel there was involved in all this — in the case of a great many people who think they are on our side of the fence — a will to power that has nothing whatever to do with the principles they think they are upholding. They are operating in this part of the forest because this is where they find themselves, and it is easy for them — but it has nothing whatever to do with love or justice or any of the things they think it has to do with. And when the chips are down, it comes out. Their status in their own eyes is much more important than any real change. If there were no Negro problem, I don't know what in the world they would do. Their pronouncements have nothing to do with reality, that's what I object to. Reality is involved with their relationship to themselves, their wives, their children; but this they have abdicated entirely, and use, then, me, the Negro, as an opportunity to live safely.

Does this apply to people who work for CORE and such things?

Those people, in my book, are not exactly liberals. I'm not talking about them. You can't say they're accomplishing nothing, really, because they're indispensable on a certain level. But their work has no resonance. It's all sort of meaningless, you see, like that group of anarchists in *The Secret Agent.* They're in the back room and that's where they stay.

And when the revolution comes, it doesn't come from them?

It doesn't come from them. It comes from some place you never thought it was coming from. And this is what they don't seem to know. I don't know — between the kind of sad incompetence of most workers for the Lord and the rigid egotism of the self-styled leading liberals it's very difficult to choose. Some of these liberal columnists, the professional bleeding hearts, have the public ear, but what they do with it is simply to reassure it. They sound as though they're being daring, but they're not. If reality broke into one of those columns, God knows what would happen! And when it threatens to, they get up on their hind legs and say, "Don't attack your friends!" I watched one of them in Paris one night trying to pick up the toughest, most evil, black blues singer in the world. He was drunk and weeping and she was calming him as though he were five years old. A cat who doesn't know when he's facing one of the world's top bitches! He doesn't even know it? What else doesn't he know? If you don't know that, then what *do* you know? And what good can you possibly do me? They make no connection between what they do in nightclubs and what they say in print, no connection between the ruin of their children and their public pronouncements.

Well, what's this hypocrisy covering up? You've seen Norman Podhoretz's article in Commentary, *telling how he grew up in a poor neighborhood alongside a large Negro population. And all through his childhood the Negro was someone who bullied you and beat you up on the one hand and on the other who enjoyed freedom of license no Jewish boy was allowed. And he says this animosity and envy is still buried in him.*

What Norman does in that piece is exactly what I'm asking all these high-minded white liberals to do: to tell the truth, what he really feels about Negroes — which is, as well, a confession about himself. But he is not lying about it. I'm sure that all the liberals I'm scoring off have stories very much like him, and they lie about it. But he says he hated and feared Negroes and that the little boy in him still does. The little boy in *them* still does, too, only they pretend he isn't there.

But what's the source of the bad feeling, basically?

It's very complicated, and a terrible, vicious circle, but there's no point lying about it. In any case, we all grew up with a great gulf fixed between whites and Negroes, and it makes Negroes per se exotic, strange, different, other. And whatever is "other" is frightening. The entire society reinforces this difference so that you have to be afraid of them; you aren't given much choice. And if you're afraid of them you've got to hate them. If it is so that no one really ever gets over his beginnings, then liberals are all liars, because this is true of them, too, and they pretend it isn't. And this is shown whenever you get to the personal level with them.

The sense of otherness is a fact we all recognize, anyway. But what can we do to overcome it?

In order for a person to cease to be other, you've got somehow to break through that thing which divides you and get into each other's lives. And this almost never happens. It doesn't never happen, but it almost never happens, and never at all within the liberal context, because the whole rhetoric is designed to prevent that from happening.

For instance?

Well, you certainly cannot talk to anybody in terms of great monolithic abstractions. You can't talk about The Negro Problem. What the hell are you talking about? Either we're talking about you and me, or we're not talking.

Do you ever worry that some of the things you say may only serve to reinforce feelings of guilt and fear in white people?

I think that what I feel about guilt is that it is like a festering sore that must be worked upon until it's opened and the pus can run out.

But in criticizing Native Son, *you said you felt Richard Wright had made a mistake in presenting a character who would make people feel frightened and guilty. Yet you yourself have expressed a certain amount of pleasure in the way Black Muslims frighten white people.*

I know what you mean, but as a matter of fact the Muslims frighten me very much. I consider them really irresponsible in the most serious way — irresponsible in terms of what I consider to be their obligations to the Negro community, as all racists are irresponsible. They batten on the despair of black men.

You think they have nothing to offer, really?

No. If they were organizing rent strikes among the people who live in those ghettos in Harlem right now, organizing just one block not to pay the rent until the landlords did something about the rats and the houses; if they were spotlighting concrete things, proving to Negroes that there were certain things they could do for themselves . . .

But is there anything?

There is nothing they can do for themselves so long as they don't think there is. That's part of the price of being a Negro: you're demoralized so soon. If the Muslims were operating on that level I would have no quarrel with them, perhaps, but they're doing something else. It's just another inflated store-front church. It has that emotional value and that practical uselessness, only it's more dangerous. And another thing bothers me. I suppose it is the effect they can have on the country itself. Not so much the Muslim movement, but a whole area they represent—all the anguish that Negroes endure in this country, which no one wants to face. And the Muslims are the only people who articulate it for white people—and also for Negroes, I must say. And they frighten white people half to death. When you consider the ignorance that reigns in this country from top to bottom, it seems clear to me that the

Muslim movement could act as a catalyst to turn the place into a concentration camp in no time at all.

How could that really happen?

If we'd been mad enough to go to war with Cuba, how many Negroes do you think you could mobilize out of Harlem? "Why should I go shoot Cubans? The government cannot protect me in Mississippi, but is willing to mount a whole invasion to bring freedom to the Cubans"—you really have to be an idiot not to ask that question. And God knows, if that does come about, the Muslims will not fail to ask it. You can put Elijah Muhammad and Malcolm X in jail, and maybe a couple of hundred thousand others. But if you've done *that*, then you might as well forget the war, because you've lost it.

Do you think the Negro can use the international situation as a power lever?

It depends on a great many other things, because you can use it as a power lever only to a very limited extent. The Negro situation here has not changed because of the cold war and the international situation, but the Government is aware of some things, and it is attempting to meet them by putting Negroes in the window, not to change things, but to create good propaganda. Of course, this doesn't help. What one needs is something that kids in the South are terribly aware of—some way of using such limited power as one has really to force the Government to investigate murders in Mississippi, and to bring pressure to bear on the cities to begin to deal with the Negro population.

How can it ever be done?

One's got to assume that it can be done, but how can it be done? Well, for example, in the South—which is clearer than the North—when a white man murders a black man, nothing can be done about it. But recently I went along with a field secretary of the N.A.A.C.P. in Mississippi to investigate a murder that had been hushed up. We rode around through those back roads for hours talking to people who had known the dead man, trying to find out what had happened. And the Negroes talked to us as the German Jews must have talked when Hitler came to power. It was a matter of turning the car around so that the license plate couldn't be seen from the road. And talking to people with their lights out. We had hoped to discover that the sheriff, who had forced the man to be buried without an inquest, had also murdered him. If he had, then *in principle* the

Justice Department could have been forced to act. But it turned out it was not the sheriff but simply the storekeeper, who was a friend of his. And there was almost no way for the Justice Department to act, because the law-enforcement interests in the South have very strong ties with Washington, and the whole political structure in Washington is partly designed to protect the Southern oligarchy. And Bobby Kennedy's much more interested in politics than he is in any of these things, and so, for that matter, is his brother. And furthermore, even if Bobby Kennedy were a different person, or his brother, they are also ignorant, as most white Americans are, of what the problem really is, of how Negroes really live. The speech Kennedy made to Mississippi the night Meredith was carried there was one of the most shameful performances in our history.

Why?

Because he talked to Mississippi as if there were no Negroes there. And this had a terrible, demoralizing, disaffecting effect on all Negroes everywhere. One is weary of being told that desegregation is legal. One would like to hear for a change that it is *right*! Now, how one begins to use this power we were talking about earlier is a very grave question, because first of all you have to get Eastland out of Congress and get rid of the power that he wields there. You've got to get rid of J. Edgar Hoover and the power that he wields. If one could get rid of just those two men, or modify their power, there would be a great deal more hope. How in the world are you going to get Mississippi Negroes to go to the polls if you remember that most of them are extremely poor, most of them almost illiterate, and that they live under the most intolerable conditions? They are used to it, which is worse, and they have no sense that they can do anything for themselves. If six Negroes go to the polls and get beaten half to death, and one or two die, and nothing happens from Washington, how are you going to manage even to get the ballot?

It seems very hopeless.

One cannot agree that it is hopeless. But that's the way it is. And the only hope we have is somehow to get in Washington, or *somewhere*, enough weight to begin to change the climate.

What happens to people like Meredith who put themselves in the front lines?

Aha. You can hold yourself together during all the action, but inevitably there's a great reaction somewhere. Some of them go to mental institutions. It's very hard to take. I got a taste of this only once. When I went to Tallahassee for you [MLLE, August, 1960] I was living in a motel on the highway and there were trees along the road, and my room was the very last one. I would come back around midnight. Since I was the only Northern Negro in town, I was terribly visible, and my light was the only light on late at night, because I was typing my notes. I couldn't avoid thinking about the highway and those trees. I couldn't get over it by saying, "Don't be silly, Jimmy." And I was scared half to death. But I got through it and finally went to Paris. I was having lunch with a friend the day I arrived and suddenly I began to shake. And I stayed at his house for two days. I was afraid to be alone. And that taught me something about how much greater the pressure must be for those kids now. The reaction has to come, it has to come. Lately I talked to the only Negro boy in an integrated school in New Orleans. He stood and moved like a little soldier, and it was very impressive and very frightening. Because no boy his age can possibly be that controlled and not pay for it later on somehow.

Do you think school desegregation was a good place to begin? Putting all the onus of this on the children?

At this point there would be no good place to begin, really. But in another way those beautiful children are the only people who could have done it.

Movies and beaches, all that, seem like effort lost.

Well, it isn't entirely, though. What one's trying to do is simply make white people get used to seeing you around without a broom in your hand! I think it's just as important as the schools, because the wall has been built on every single level and has got to come down on every level. The Government, for reasons of its own, prefers that Negroes in the South work on voting registration rather than try to desegregate buses or bus stations or coffee counters or stores, and, God knows, not to have any boycotts. Well, of course, the Government's being very clever about that. It will take years to get the vote, in any case, and if you're doing that and nothing else, then the vote's safe another fifty years.

What do you think of the idea that Negroes can't get anywhere until they begin to mobilize as a real group?

I don't know on what principle it would mobilize itself, that's the trouble.

But whether you like it or not, you are thrust into a sort of

*role as spokesman for The Negro — a group that ought not to be
a group. How do you feel about that role? Maybe you didn't
elect it, and yet . . .*

And yet it's true.

Can you speak for those millions?

I can't. I don't try to.

*The neo-Africans don't seem to think you speak for them.
What about them?*

They are romantic American Negroes who think they can
identify with the African struggle, without having the least idea
what it's about. They want to see black men in power, simply,
and it's more interesting to see a black statesman in his robes at the
U.N. than to consider what kind of a statesman he is.

Do they actually want to live in Africa?

They think they do, but they don't stay. The Africans don't
want them. They can't *use* them. You can't deal with anybody
who pretends that he doesn't come from where he comes from;
you can't respect him and you can't trust him. Maybe I can go
to Africa and think that I'm an African looking for my tribe — and
where is it? But they hear the way I talk and see the way I walk,
and they don't like me any better for pretending I don't come from
Harlem. And Africans remember, though neo-Africans do not,
when American Negroes would not speak to Africans. But I do
feel very involved with the students in the South. I don't consider
myself a spokesman for them either, but I do think that they trust
me and I can't afford to fail them. That controls me more than
anything else in this context, because no one else seems to be doing
it, really. And kids need somebody who will talk to them, listen
to them. They want you to respect their questions.

What do they ask you?

Well, they ask real questions. "What would you do if your
teacher told you that instead of picketing and engaging in sit-ins,
you should get an education first?" one boy asked me. And I
said, "I would tell my teacher that it's impossible to get an education in this country until you change the country." And the boy
said, "Thank you." And that does something for me.

*To go back to our fear of the Negro, haven't you also suggested
that sex is at the bottom of it?*

Yes, I think it has something to do with the whole Puritan
ethic, the whole idea that the flesh is something to be ashamed of.
The burden that is placed on you because you're a Negro male is

terrifying, and it says something about the poverty of the white cat's bed or the white chick's bed, which today is very hard to believe.

But we love to talk about sex!

That's right, and that's where the Negro comes in. If a Negro is present in a room, there's a great silence then. Sex is on everybody's mind, but nobody's going to say anything. You can see people, almost in the middle of sentences, shifting gears and making wild right turns. They wanted to talk about sex, but now they're not going to, because here sex *is*, right in the middle of the room drinking a dry martini. And it all becomes extremely polite and antiseptic. But on the other hand, at four o'clock in the morning, when everybody's drunk enough, then extraordinary things can happen. It's very hard to describe. It's something I want to do in a novel.

Why this poverty of the white cat's bed?

I have some hunches. It has something to do with Puritanism again. It has something to do with the whole role of women in this country since the country got here. Something to do with the scarcity of women and the roughness of the country. I don't mean just physical roughness, I mean the loneliness, the physical loneliness of it. When you were crossing it, it must have been terrifying. And it has something to do with the Indians. White men married Indians and slept with them and killed them, too.

Do you think history operates this way in people's unconscious?

I think it operates this way *actually*. This has to be so. Because when the chips are down in any crisis, what you have to draw on finally is not what happened in the time that you yourself have been on earth, but what came before you. This is what gets you through your crisis finally. And somewhere in yourself you carry all of that. You have to be in great trouble to turn to it and use it, or to suspect that you have to; but when you are in trouble, that's what you turn to, which means it must be there.

In your writing you've always been hard on everyone, white and black, but lately you seem to be getting harder and harder on white people.

What I want to do in the play I'm working on now is somehow bring that whole thing together — what white people have done and also what black people are doing. And I don't know how to put that.

Well, everything you've said about white people has been

negative; yet you say that blacks have something to give us without which we'll perish.

I think that's true. If the Negro doesn't save this country, then nobody else can. And if I can find another word than Negro it might be closer to what I mean. I don't mean the Negro as a person; I mean the Negro as an experience — a level of experience Americans always deny.

One of the most puzzling things you've said is that your darkness reminds white men of their death.

I meant what I said: if you are a Negro dealing with people all day long, all year long, all life long, who never look at you, then you have to figure out one day what they *are* looking at. Obviously it isn't you. When I was seventeen, working for the Army, I could not have been a threat to any white man alive. So it wasn't me, it was something he didn't want to see. And you know what that was? It was ultimately, yes, his own death. Or call it trouble. Trouble is an excellent metaphor for death. The white man knew he would not like to be me. People who certainly are not monsters on any other level will do monstrous things to you, semi-deliberately or deliberately, designed to protect their wives and children. This is what is meant by keeping you in your place. If you move out of your place everything is changed. If I'm not what that white man thinks I am, then he has to find out what *he* is.

Do we use status to make up for identity?

Exactly. And therefore I'm the only cat that has any identity, because it's in my skin. I've got a built-in identity for other people, which is more than they have for me, more than they have for themselves, too. And they fear and despise one for it.

How about when you look at us? Are we just blobs?

No. You never could be for me, because you all have too much power. I can be a blob for you, but you I have to study in order to survive. And this can kill you, but if it doesn't kill you it gives you a certain beat. It isn't a business of what people say. Listen to what they're not saying. A lot of Negro style — the style of a man like Miles Davis or Ray Charles or the style of a man like myself — is based on a knowledge of what people are really saying and on our refusal to hear it. You pick up on the beat, which is much more truthful than words.

They say that people deprived of the full use of their intellects make up for it with unusual powers of intuition. This would be true of the Negro, surely?

You live almost entirely by your intuition. It has to be highly developed. And the intellect, anyway, is one more way of avoiding yourself. One must find a way to get through to life or to experience, but that can't be done intellectually.

You must get a real sense of who you are, anyway. How would you define identity?

I don't know. It's some respect for the self, which has something to do — as my good friend Sidney Poitier says — with knowing whence you came. And really knowing that. And in some way, if you know that, you know something else, too. I can't tell precisely what it is you know then, but if you know where you were, you have some sense of where you are.

Evidently "whence you came" once stood between you and a sense of who you are.

It inevitably does, I think, for everybody. It has to. You have to accept it. You can't run. I know, because I've tried. And I think who you are has something to do with responsibility, too.

To whom and what?

The kind of responsibility that means that you haven't got time to weep, because you have too much to do, the pressures are too great. It's learning very soon that there are no excuses, that if you fail, it's because *you* failed. And of course it doesn't mean you won't — one way or another everybody does. Everybody has to deal with this question of who and what he is. I have to deal with it because of the kids, the students, and I have to deal with it because I'm a writer. Writers have to make use of it all, every bit of it. That's all you've got. You take it or you die.

But in a way wasn't it easier for you to find out who you were because you were a Negro and had to face your suffering?

Yes. But there's something else, too. Hannah Arendt told me that the virtues I described in *The New Yorker* piece — the sensuality I was talking about, and the warmth, and the fish fries, and all that — are typical of all oppressed people. And they don't, unluckily, she said — and I think she's entirely right — survive even five minutes the end of their oppression.

And what we think of as the Negro's innate qualities are just desperate stratagems that people who have nothing else use to stay alive?

And you make do with nothing, and you get, if you survive, a kind of authority from that. You really have to know yourself to find resources to make do with the minimum. But you wouldn't do it if you weren't forced to do it. And the moment you're not forced to do it any more, you stop doing it.

And Negro millionaires are as far removed from reality as anybody else?

Insofar as they are pretending to be white.

You said you yourself once felt that you didn't know whether you were black or white. What did you mean?

Well, I meant I didn't know who I was at all. They used to say to me, "Don't act like a nigger." Acting like a nigger meant eating with your hands or scratching yourself or cursing or fighting or getting drunk or having nappy hair — all those things. And for a long time I spent a lot of effort trying not to act like a nigger. I slicked my hair down, never raised my voice, had perfect table manners, and of course it didn't help at all.

You were just being a cultured Negro!

I was being a cultured Negro. I was always wearing a sort of iron corset. And it didn't make me white. And it didn't make me a man either. And it means I couldn't talk to white people, because I was talking in a certain kind of way, and I couldn't talk to black people either, because I was too busy not being one of them. And I hated white people from the bottom of my heart. And I hated black people for being so common! I realized, too, that if a white man were doing any of those things I was told not to do, no one would say he was acting like a nigger. It was only me who was acting like a nigger, because I *was* a nigger. No matter what I did, I was acting like a nigger. So I decided to act like a nigger, or at least act like *me*.

What did you mean when you said that a black person should cultivate the nigger within?

Well, I mean this. If I want to beat up a doorman, maybe I don't beat him up, but I have to know that that's what I really want to do. That I'm not being the poised, controlled, civilized cat that I dream of myself as being at all. That if a policeman hits me. I'm very probably going to try to kill him. And if I don't do it, it won't be because I don't want to. It will be because something else is operating and I know that I have to do something else. But I know it is *there*. That's my only protection against it.

And it's not a matter of black or white at all?

It's a matter of not telling any more lies than you can help. And some black people know that and some white people know that; and for the rest . . . well, there are very, very few.

Is there any hope for the body politic?

No, not now. We'd be very lucky if we had a great man in the White House right now, *if* we had a great man. We do not, but *if* we did . . .

Have you ever known anyone who seemed to you great?

James Meredith. He's a very tough and loving little man.

Still loving? Has he repressed his hatred?

On certain questions I don't think that hatred any longer operates. I don't think I hate anybody any more. It's too expensive. I stopped trying to be white. It's a law that if I hate white people I have to hate black people.

Any other people you think great?

A man named Jerome Smith. He's one of the student leaders in New Orleans and one of the veterans of Jackson, Mississippi — beaten with brass knuckles until he was entirely numb; not simply out, but numb. He's still being treated for it. He's very young. He was a longshoreman. And he is a tremendous man.

Why is he tremendous? Because he survived?

No, he's tremendous because he knows what happened. If anyone has a right to hate white people, Jerome certainly does. But he doesn't hate. He does not.

You said you used to hate yourself. How did you get over it?

Well, I think it has everything to do with my brothers and sisters. You can't be involved with that many people so young without doing one of two things: either you reject it all, or sooner or later you begin to realize that it is part of you. And I loved them very much. I didn't always. At the very beginning I did. I did — and I do. In a way you take your worth from other people's eyes. And a friend in Switzerland did something, too. In a way he saved my life by refusing to allow me to be paranoid about my color. He did it by not being sorry for me. And my mother had something to do with it, too. I think she saved us all. She was the only person in the world we could turn to, yet she couldn't protect us.

She doesn't sound like that consoling black-mammy figure that we whites are so enamored of. The maids we know, for instance.

Yes, who's all wise, all patient, and all enduring. But it's emotionally too easy, because in fact those maids have sons who may by this time have turned into junkies because their mothers can get jobs and they can't. I'm sure all the people my mother worked for thought of her that way, but she wasn't like that at all.

She was a very tough little woman, and she must have been scared to death all the years she was raising us.

Scared of what?

Of those streets! There it is at the door, *at the door!* Whores, pimps, racketeers. It hasn't changed either, by the way. That's what it means to be raised in a ghetto. I think of what a woman like my mother knows, instinctively has to know, has had to know from the very beginning: that there is no safety, that no one is safe, none of her children would ever be safe. The nature of the ghetto is somehow ultimately to make those skills which are immoral the only skills worth having. You haven't got to be sweet to survive in a ghetto; you've got to be cunning. You've got to make up the rules as you go along; there aren't any others. You can't call the cops.

What about your father?

He was righteous in the pulpit and a monster in the house. Maybe he saved all kinds of souls, but he lost all his children, every single one of them. And it wasn't so much a matter of punishment with him: he was trying to kill us. I've hated a few people, but actually I've hated only one person, and that was my father.

Did he hate you?

In a way, yes. He didn't like me. But he'd had a terrible time, too. And of course, I was not his son. I was a bastard. What he wanted for his children was what in fact I became. I was the brightest boy in the house because I was the eldest, and because I loved my mother and I really loved those kids. And I was necessary: I changed all the diapers and I knew where the kids were, and I could take some of the pressures off my mother and in a way stand between him and her — which is a strange role to play. I had to learn to stand up to my father, and, in learning that, I became precisely what he wanted his other children to become, and he couldn't take that, and I couldn't either maybe.

Did he affect your ideas of what you could do in the world?

My father did one thing for me. He said, "You can't do it." And I said, "Listen, m———— don't tell me what I can't do. I can't do it? Don't tell me I can't do it. You'll see."

Why couldn't you do it, according to him? Because you were black?

Because I was black, because I was little, because I was ugly. He made me ugly. I used to put pennies on my eyes to make them go back.

But out of that an identity emerged.

Yes, all those strangers called Jimmy Baldwin.

Who are some of them?

There's the older brother with all the egotism and rigidity that implies. That tone will always be there, and there's nothing I can do about it except know it's there and laugh at it. I grew up telling people what to do and spanking them, so that in some ways I always will be doing that. Then there's the self-pitying little boy. You know: "I can't do it, because I'm so ugly." He's still there some place.

Who else?

Lots of people. Some of them are unmentionable. There's a man. There's a woman, too. There are lots of people here.

It's been said of you that you have two obsessions: color and homosexuality.

I'm not absolutely sure I have two obsessions. They're more than that.

Whatever they are, are they interrelated?

Let's go back to where we were talking about the Negro man and sex, and let's go back again to the American white man's lack of sexual security, and then let's try to imagine what it would be like to be a Negro adolescent dealing with those people to whom you are a phallic symbol. American males are the only people I've ever encountered in the world who are willing to go on the needle before they'll go to bed with each other. Because they're afraid of this, they don't know how to go to bed with women either. I've known people who literally died out of this panic. I don't know what homosexual means any more, and Americans don't either.

You don't think it's a disease?

This is one of the American myths. What always occurs to me is that people in other parts of the world have never had this peculiar kind of conflict. If you fall in love with a boy, you fall in love with a boy. The fact that Americans consider it a disease says more about them than it says about homosexuality.

What about societies where homosexuality becomes very open, as it has here or did in Germany during the Twenties?

When it becomes open as it has here, it becomes a disease. These people are not involved in anything resembling love-making: they're involved in some kind of exhibition of their disaster. It has nothing to do with contact or involvement between two people —which means that the person may change you. That's what people are afraid of. It's impossible to go through life assuming that you know who you're going to fall in love with. You don't. And everything depends on the fashion in which you live, on the things to which you will not say no, the risks you are prepared to take.

What's going to keep black people from becoming just like white people once they've broken down the barriers?

That's what frightens me when we talk about what we call The Negro Problem. I realize that most white people don't realize that the Negro is like anybody else, just like everybody else. And that when this situation ends, assuming we live to see that, something else will begin, which may be just as terrible as what we're going through now. And what some of the students in the South know is that it's not a matter of being accepted into this society at all. It is a matter of demolishing it in some way, which has nothing to do with the Kremlin. It's a matter of transforming it; it's a matter of not making your peace with it; it's a matter really of building Jerusalem again, no matter how corny that may sound.

Wouldn't most people rather escape it than transform it?

You can't escape. You have *not* walked out of the industrial society because you say you have or because you're wearing a beard. You're still right here where you were; you haven't moved an inch.

How about your years in Europe? Was that an escape?

I'll say this: I know very well I survived as a writer by living abroad so long, because if I had not been living abroad, I would have been compelled to make more money.

Are you ever tempted to go back?

All I can do is work out the terms on which I can work, and for me that means being a transatlantic commuter. What's most difficult is that you are penalized for trying to remain in touch with yourself. I have a public life — and I know that, O.K. I have a private life, something which I know a good deal less. And the temptation is to avoid the private life because you can hide in the public one. And I've got excellent reasons for doing it, because what I'm doing is very admirable — you know, all this jazz. Except that that is not the most important thing! The most important thing is somewhere else. It always is — somewhere else. But it's not my life, and if I pretend it is, I'll die. I am *not* a public speaker. I *am* an artist.

You are stealing from the artist to pay for the Negro?

Yes. It's one of the prices of my success. And let's face it, I am a *Negro* writer. Sidney Poitier, you know, is not simply an actor; he's a *Negro* actor. He's not simply a movie star; he's the *only* Negro movie star. And because he is in the position that he is in, he has obligations that Tony Curtis will never have. And it has made Sidney a remarkable man.

Can a Negro ever talk about anything but being a Negro?

I get so tired of black and white, you know, so tired of talking about it, especially when you can't get anything across. What you have to do, I suppose, is invest the vocabulary with something it doesn't contain yet. Don't you see what I'm trying to do? I'm trying to find another word besides Negro to say what I mean, and I can't use tragedy.

Why not?

Because I haven't figured out the terms on which I can use it yet. All I know . . . I suddenly thought of all the Negroes who don't know anything either.

As we've talked now, you have translated Negro into terms which . . .

Which have nothing to do with *that*.

Which have nothing to do with that. And which is what we've really been talking about.

Which is the only thing *to* talk about. I don't know. Nothing will happen to change all that before we die — that vocabulary.

And we have to go on talking about black and white, and that's not it at all.

That is not enough, and it isn't interesting. I don't think much will happen, except disaster, to change things.

The fire next time?

Yes. People don't give things up; things are taken away from them. I'm not frightened of another war really. I'm just frightened of chaos, apathy, indifference — which is the road people took to Auschwitz.

The Negro Writer
and the
Communist Party

by Wilson Record

Rᴇʟᴀᴛɪᴏɴsʜɪᴘs ʙᴇᴛᴡᴇᴇɴ ɴᴇɢʀᴏ writers and the Communist Party in the United States today are quite blurred and tenuous. Only to a very limited degree have Negro authors been responsive to the program, ideology and organizations of the Communists during the past two decades. There are no immediate prospects that the Party will attain an influence among this rapidly growing group such as it had during the 1930s and 1940s. Negro writers are not now likely, as were such men as Richard Wright in another era, to turn to the Party as a source of help, guidance and discipline. The fact that some of them, such as John Killens, today use loosely certain Marxist phrases and labels should not be taken as any serious indication of their Party affiliation or even sympathy. While they are critical of American society, that posture develops primarily from a discontent with its racial system rather than its economic institutions as such. And the Negro writers project solutions primarily through drastic change of the racial order rather than of the capitalist or mixed economic system. The pseudo-Marxism, vague and contradictory, of such militants as James Forman, has little intellectual or artistic attraction for serious Negro literary men.

Why has the Party lost its influence among the Negro writers and why has it failed during a period of radical racial upheaval, in which writers have been highly influential, to command the attention and support it once did? The answers to such questions are complex, and they cannot be explored in detail in this brief essay. However, one can identify certain major forces at play and offer a rough assessment of some of their consequences. Perhaps the most obvious thing about the Communist Party today, and a major reason for its rejection by Negro writers, is its age. It is an old organization and linked with other old organizations that are thought to have failed notably in dealing with race relations issues after having had ample opportunity to do so. Negro writers tend to be young. They belong to a generation that is highly critical of organizations carrying over from past decades. They tend to reject not only the old "moderate" organizations, such as the National Association for the Advancement of Colored People (NAACP) and the National Urban League (NUL) but the old "radical" ones as well. At the same time Negro writers have participated frequently in the organization of new militant agencies, both cultural and political, with a strong emphasis on racial pride, identity and separatism. A good example of this is found in the recent organization of the Negro Ensemble Company, a theatre troupe in New York City which encourages the production of plays about Negroes and proposes to use only Negro actors in its offerings.

The Communists are looked upon as old-fashioned and blinded by age to the moods and needs of Negroes in a racially segregated urban world. Party members themselves tend to be in their middle or late years and have had quite different formative experiences. Their validity is strongly questioned by most of the Negro writers who, although they may differ sharply on specific issues, are unified in their rejection of the older racial ideas and leaders. In various ways, as artists and frequently as activists, the new Negro authors are calling for new men to seek new goals. In this process they ignore the crucial efforts of older race men who in many ways made present militancy feasible. In their novels, essays, and short stories contemporary Negro writers are likely to depict their elders as inept, conforming, and ashamed of their color. And, of course, they repudiate the examples of most earlier Negro poets, novelists and essayists such as Paul Laurence Dunbar, Sutton Griggs, and Charles Chesnutt whose works are seen as denying the basic values of Negro life and culture and disdaining identity with the common Negro.

It is significant in this connection that the Communist Party has not been able to attract the active participation of a first-rate young Negro writer during the past decade. Its most recent book on race conflict, *Ghetto Rebellion and Black Liberation,* was written by Claude Lightfoot, a fifty-nine year old Negro who joined the Party back in the 1930s. And it does not appear to have significantly penetrated any of the new cultural groups emerging from the Negro ghettos and providing young Negroes as writers, actors, and singers indigenous settings in which to cultivate their talents. Negro writers on occasion may pay some tribute to the Negro Communists of an earlier day. However, it is usually made quite clear that the latter played a good but limited role in time and place and are no longer "relevant."

A great many charges have been made, usually by white conservatives disposed to see "conspiracies" in most organized Negro protest and revolutionary action groups, that young Negro militants, particularly intellectuals and writers, are followers of the Communist Party and are taking their cues from Party leaders in the United States and the Soviet Union. These same conservatives seem to have developed a remarkable appreciation of older Negro leaders and writers such as Roy Wilkins, Langston Hughes and A. Philip Randolph. The evidence for the conspiracy view is far from convincing and alternate explanations are more plausible. The age of present Party members and their leaders, while no guarantee that Party influence among Negro writers will remain negligible, is nevertheless a chronic handicap which the Party is not likely to soon overcome. In failing to appeal to young Negroes the Party has cut itself off from a group out of which has come the most militant and forceful of today's Negro writers.

Essayists such as Eldridge Cleaver and autobiographers such as Claude Brown, and the late Malcolm X, not to mention articulate activists like Rap Brown and Stokely Carmichael, are relatively young men and the audiences that have been most responsive to them have been young Negroes, those who have come of age during the past decade and for whom the future is long and problematic. LeRoi Jones, perhaps the most effective and out-spoken critic of the white dominated society, is still in his mid thirties. The writers from the Watts area in Los Angeles, whose plays, poems, essays and short stories appeared last year in *From the Ashes: Voices of Watts,* are in their 20s and 30s. Their varied writings evidence only the most cursory of Marxist influences and one searches in vain for convincing evidence of Communist Party guidance.

The personal and artistic sensibilities of the young Negro writers have been shaped largely by their experiences of the 1950s and 1960s. They not only witnessed but also felt keenly, in emotional depth and despair, the destruction of hope that a viable and equalitarian society might emerge from removal of the legal props of racial segregation. Their disillusionment is deep, and little is occurring now which will reduce it. They are frequently disgusted with the older generations of Negroes who retain some hope that they can "make it" in the white world. While a few older Negro communist sympathizers may be accorded a certain honor by the new generation of Negro writers, they are not likely to be thought of as sources of political aspiration. The late W. E. B. DuBois, who joined the Party when he was in his 90s, and the ailing Paul Robeson are honored primarily for their defiance of white society and not for the political mode of its expression. The Party's invocation of the memories of these two men with such frequency is another indication of its failure to reach and influence young Negro artists and intellectuals today.

Some of the Negro militants are, no doubt, influenced by Fidel Castro and Ché Guevara. Among them are Negro writers such as LeRoi Jones and Eldridge Cleaver who advocate violence and urban guerilla warfare as strategies in the racial struggle. But this response does not signal an acceptance of either official Party organization or ideology. Castro and Guevara are viewed heroically, as young men who openly defied a system of white American control and personified a violent challenge to it. Negro authors are by no means immune to the romantic aura which surrounds "Che" and "Fidel." One cannot help being curiously impressed by even radical Negro writers today who evidence no great knowledge of or sympathy with the system which Castro has established in Cuba. They do not see Cuban communism with its rigid economic organization and centralized political control as meeting the Negro's need in the United States. It is likely that as Castro's system becomes fixed and as the men who command it age, it will appear even less attractive.

Negro writers seeking to establish their own autonomy and those minimal freedoms which their own cultural and artistic growth requires are also put off by the continued prominence of whites in the Party. The desire on the part of Negroes generally and of the Negro writers particularly to be free of white domination does not bode well for the Communists. The Negro writers of today are not extensively acquainted with the dominant roles in the Party's Negro program played by whites in the 1930s and 1940s. However, they do know that the Party was not really exceptional in its paternalistic and patronizing response to Negro writers during the period of its greatest influence. And they know, too, that the Party did try hard to influence such writers of the 1950's and 1960's as the late Lorraine Hansberry and Ossie Davis. They have also the tortured testimony of their predecessors, particularly Richard Wright, Ralph Ellison, and Chester Himes, who witnessed beyond the point of endurance attempts of white Communists two and three decades ago to force Negro needs and aspirations into a rigid Party mold.

In a recent book, *The Crisis of the Negro Intellectual,* Harold Cruse, in anger and indignation, traces the efforts of white communists to divert Negro writers away from racial and cultural themes and toward class and political concerns. He charges earlier and some recent Negro writers themselves with willing submission to Party dictates in exchange for small help and slight favors. This influence, Cruse argues, much too heatedly in my view, stultified the creative Negro writers, although some of them were successful in spite of it.

It must be said also that a disproportionately large number of white influentials in the Party have been Jews and that the organization's decline among Negro intellectuals is due partly to an increasing Negro anti-Semitism. Not limited to Negro ghetto dwellers, it finds concrete expression in the writings of dramatists such as LeRoi Jones and Negro autobiographers with extensive ghetto backgrounds. Jews are not likely to be portrayed as heroic or even sympathetic people, perhaps at best as weak liberals. The key roles played by Jews in the Negro struggles of the 1950s and 1960s is no longer interpreted sympathetically by many of the Negro intellectuals. This may be seen as a part of a larger pattern of the Negro's casting off his white dependency. But it takes a peculiar form when Negro writers insist on their exclusive capacities for interpreting Negro life, a job heretofore in which Jewish writers have been quite prominent.

Nor are Negro writers very much persuaded by the efforts of the Party to place Negroes in fairly prominent official positions.

There persists the conviction that the Negro Communist is really white-sponsored and is not his own man, that his range of discretion is quite narrow and that his judgment is poor to accept such a role. Also, the Negro writer is likely to regard the public display of the Negro in the Party as another instance of "tokenism." Party practice is not regarded as significantly different from that of other white-dominated organizations seeking to ease its conscience or to curry favor with Negroes. White influence in the Party means that it can neither be taken over by Negroes or significantly influenced by them. While the Russians may not have retained a Stalinist grip on the Party in the United States, their influence is still dominant and they are operating through leaders who are white and cut from the older cloth.

The growth of Negro race consciousness and race pride expresses itself in many ways. Demands are made both for a greater Negro influence in existing organizations, which would be transformed in the process, and for separate Negro organizations. Religious, professional, educational, political and economic groups have all experienced challenges, from "black" caucases within and "black" pressure groups from without, to accord Negroes special recognition and to right historic wrongs. Negro writers have been prominent as advocates and participants in such organizations. And they have been among those who have benefitted by the results. However, they are not likely to find it very profitable to challenge white control of the Communist Party. They can be expected to concentrate on more influential organizations with greater resources and located at the center of action. The Party's emphasis on class and economy is thought to harbor continued white dominance and to perpetuate Negro dependency on white funds and white leadership.

A third handicap of the Party in attracting Negro writers is the failure of the Soviet Union to symbolize a system in which racial and ethnic differences are no longer a basis for prejudice and discrimination. While some Negro writers and artists in the past applauded Soviet treatment of its minorities, most of them remained quite skeptical about the Party's widely proclaimed affiliation with a nation and a movement that had "abolished racial prejudice by abolishing its capitalist roots." More than one Negro writer has observed pointedly that there are no Negroes in the Soviet Union and that the Communists have never had to deal with a minority within its borders as different as Negroes are

from whites. The Russians are still thought to have little under-·
standing of Negroes in Africa or America and to be unaware of the
deeply-rooted racial antipathies growing out of a distinctive racial
past and violently imposed forms of Negro subordination.

There is also the suspicion that Negroes would not fare very
well in the Soviet Union. Negro intellectuals in the United States
have become keenly sensitive to Africa during the past two decades
and have been angered and distressed by evidence that casts
serious doubts on the capacity of the Communists to deal fairly
with African Negroes. The widely publicized experience of
Africans who have gone to the Soviet Union for further education
is not encouraging for the Party. The treatment these visitors
have received has frequently been discriminatory and hostile.
Another handicap has been the marked tendency of Soviet advisors
and technicians in Africa to remain isolated and to limit associations with citizens of the host nations. While this might be a
standard practice of Soviet citizens abroad, it is interpreted by
American Negro intellectuals as in part the result of strong feelings
of racial antipathy among the Communists; it suggests that col-
lectivist forms of economic and political organization are no guarantee that racial prejudices can thereby be removed. Few Negro
writers today are pointing to the Soviet Union as a model which
could be or ought to be followed in the United States. Rather
they emphasize the distinctiveness of the Negro and the inability of
formal ideologies and planned political orders to recognize unique
historical and psychological experience and incorporate it in suit-
able institutional arrangements.

Still another reason for the Negro writers' strong reservations
about race relations under communism is the experience of various
ethnic and national groups in the Soviet Union during the past
half century. They see no convincing evidence that communism
has led to greater freedom for the pursuit of distinctive national,
ethnic, and cultural group goals. On the contrary, they have been
impressed by the suppressive character of Soviet communism and
have speculated on what a similar system in the United States
would mean for the development of a distinctive and culturally
unique way of life for Negroes. What, some have asked, would be
the implications for Negro music, art, literature and political and
social organization? The Negro writers are concerned with the
experience of the Jews in the Soviet Union and are not unmindful
of the anti-Semitic programs and postures of past and present

Soviet leaders. The anti-Zionist position of the U.S.S.R. and the periodic intensification of pressures on Jewish scholars, artists, writers and teachers within its borders make a strong impression on the Negro writers who can more readily identify with these fellow intellectuals.

Nor does the Soviet Union appear to be moving toward a more liberal policy with respect to its internal minorities. At an earlier time the Party in the United States attempted to convince Negroes that suppression of "reactionary" minorities was essential to establishment of a new order and the achievement of a society free of racial and ethnic prejudice. This interpretation gained some acceptance in Negro intellectual circles in the 1930s and 1940s when the Soviet experiment was in its first quarter century. But it is not nearly so convincing now that stale middle-age is being reached. Indeed, the Negro writers seem to have concluded that Soviet communism, as it has handled minorities during the past half-century, provides no blue-print for ordering the future of the Negro in the United States. Had the Soviets been more successful in this regard, there undoubtedly would have been much greater involvement of the Negro intellectuals, particularly the writers, in the Party during the past quarter-century.

A fourth cause of the Negro writers' reluctance to identify with the Communist Party is their intensified race consciousness leading to an emphasis on nationalism and separatism and a condemnation of integrationist movements and organizations. By no means would this generalization apply to all Negro writers. However, one cannot help but be impressed by the efforts of these young men and women to articulate what is distinct about the American Negro experience and to see in it a source of pride and inspiration. Being Negro is thought to be essential not only for knowing the meaning of white prejudice but also for achieving a certain feeling of joy, freedom, and "soul," experiences unavailable to whites or to those Negroes who have accepted white values, goals, and life styles. In this view organizations such as the Communist Party, with a current emphasis on integration and on class rather than race as a basis of differentiation, are seen as threats to the Negro's identity and a barrier to his further achievement of political as well as cultural autonomy.

The heavy demand for "Black Studies" programs in the colleges and universities, articulated primarily by young Negro intellectuals, and the glorification of the Negro's African and American past are both a partial repudiation of things white and European. Marxism and the ideologies and organizations developed from it during the past half-century are looked upon as being white and western in character and therefore alien to the Negro's basic traditions and psychology. The Negro writers today are among those who most forcefully insist that abstract interpretations of the human past and the human condition, which Marxism offers, invariably ignore the historic distinctiveness of Africa and of the Negro's experience in America. Such abstractions, which force and bend events to fit a preconceived mold, preclude the Negro writer's independent and open search for meaningful association of art and experience in the lives of people with whom he has an undeniable identity and to whom he feels a growing obligation.

Of course, there is much over-reaction in the Negro writers' denigration of things white and their glorification of things black. Further, the specific political and economic changes implicit in their critiques would be extremely difficult to realize in practice. The Negro writers remain quite vague about means and time-tables for righting social wrongs and advancing the race. And it is far from clear just what ought to follow rage. Some of them seem to feel that once they have laid bare the suffering of fellow Negroes and called the white man to account, and exhorted the outcasts to assert themselves their responsibilties are at an end. Others take the position that the Negro writer has a larger racial responsibility and can refuse to become actively engaged only by the false pursuit of art-for-art's-sake or by perhaps inadvertently becoming a collaborator of the white oppressor. Most Negro writers are agreed, however, that it is extremely difficult for them, at this stage of race conflict and of their own development, to go beyond race "themes." Both personality and art are thought to be so racially bound that escape, even if wanted, is impossible. If that is the case, then it becomes a matter of first importance that they look intensively and artistically at the Negro experience itself through Negro eyes, without the distortions inherent in nineteenth century European social theories. In these circumstances Communist ideologies and organizations tend to be classed with other such ideas and systems which have never really been applicable to Negroes in the United States or Africa. The Negro writer's adherence to them can but reduce his vision of his fellow Negroes and limit him as a man and as an artist.

If the Party could provide some substantial and specific forms of help to Negro writers today, it would have a much better chance of influencing them as artists and social activists. In the 1930s and 1940s it was able to give some aid and comfort to struggling Negro writers such as Richard Wright. The Party had publications of its own and it had some influence in magazines and publishing houses. It could therefore provide outlets for novels, plays, poetry, and essays which the conventional publishers were likely to reject. It sought, of course, to exert an organizational and ideological influence on the content of the Negro writers' work and was to some degree successful, as is clearly indicated in Richard Wright's *Native Son*.

There was, in addition, a substantial Communist and Communist-influenced audience for the Party publications. This meant that the Negro writers who chose or accepted Party help could find prepared readers and thereby get wider attention than was likely through the regular commercial channels. However, the great bulk of whatever audiences they reached was white, primarily white intellectuals. Politically these audiences were radical or liberal. They had a certain awareness of the Negro without much idea of the depth or complexity of race conflict or of their own basic feelings and antipathies. Party sponsored writers, even if they were able to do so, only rarely dealt with the psychological complexities of race in personality and society.

During this time Negro writers were not supported by Negro readers and it is doubtful if more than a half dozen of the former could have lived on incomes from sales in Negro communities. Some kind of white "sponsorship" was essential to at least getting started. And the Party, eager to secure a following among Negroes, did not hesitate to provide money, outlets, and guidance. Wright dealt with all of this in his tortured essay in *The God That Failed*. Ralph Ellison explored the same development in thinly-veiled form in his great novel *Invisible Man*. Ellison, one critic has observed, "felt the Party's branding iron," but survived the experience and "mastered it artistically." The same observation might be made of Chester Himes whose attacks on the Party in his novels were direct and by no means subtle.

The Negro writer today is not in a position of dependency comparable to that of two or three decades ago. Indeed, the demand for his output is likely to be greater than he can possibly meet. And the pressure on Negro writers to write more and to write quickly has resulted in poor writing by men of limited talents and mediocre performances by competent men. In addition, there has developed during the past decade a heavy demand for Negro literary men among colleges and universities so that many of them now have, if they wish, a substantial and steady source of income, not to mention audiences of thousands of college students. The personal and creative implications of these developments for the Negro writer are complex and characterized by no little ambiguity. Their exploration would require, however, a quite separate and extensive essay. The main point to be made here is that the Party's help is no longer needed and might well be rejected if offered. The success of two recent plays by Lonnie Elder III and Charles Gordone may be a good measure of the growing ability of Negro dramatists to find producers for their works which allow them full freedom to say what they will about the seamier as well as the more inspiring side of Negro life.

There is, in addition, a growing general audience of Negroes for the works of Negro writers. The growth of race awareness, race pride, and literacy and higher education among Negroes makes for an ever expanding group that will buy and read books and articles about themselves. There have always been vast Negro audiences for Negro artistic products. However, their audiences were most responsive to the musical and dramatic forms of expression which were consistent with their own experiences and creative impulses. Now there is developing an effective Negro demand for the novel, the short story, the poem, and the literary essay which will make for greater autonomy for the Negro writers. Under these conditions the Party will find it exceedingly difficult to provide help that can not be readily obtained by the Negro writer on his own without the accompanying political and ideological pressures. It needs to be emphasized, too, that the radical white students in colleges and universities, both in and outside such organizations as Students for a Democratic Society, have come to constitute significant audiences for writers such as LeRoi Jones, James Baldwin, Eldridge Cleaver, Ossie Davis, and the late Malcolm X. Their various postures of injury and defiance and fighting back, appeal, curiously, to those who are white, middle-class, well-educated and assured of "making it" in the present society.

However, there are emerging certain new threats to the autonomy of the Negro writer which may in fact be much stronger than those posed by the Communists at an earlier period. These come from militant Negro groups who can claim some credit for the changes under which Negro writers have been able to gain opportunities and recognition. Such groups, concerned primarily with racial power and not with civil liberties, are quite capable of trying to impose a political and doctrinal conformity of their own. Directly or indirectly they may seek to force a black rather than a red party line on the Negro writers. The threatening and frightening of moderate Negroes by militant groups such as the Black Panthers is not an uncommon part of the contemporary racial scene. This carries into the cultural realm when such men as James Baldwin are accused of being "white writers" and when the charge of "racist" is hurled at Negro authors who do not take simplistic, extremist postures on current issues.

Negro writers are already anticipating that they may well have to choose between their own personal and artistic integrity and a new kind of political and racial conformity. Some of them seem to have made their choice already and are not altogether subtle in their use of racial yardsticks in measuring their own and others' work. This is most clearly seen in a recent series of essays by a dozen or so Negro writers condemning collectively the best-selling novel, *The Confessions of Nat Turner*, by William Styron, a white southerner with well-established literary credentials. It has always been difficult to make a clear distinction between art and propaganda in works dealing with race in American society. And only rarely have historians, novelists, dramatists, and essayists been able to transcend their biases in a sustained way. In the circumstances it is perhaps too much to hope that Negro writers can somehow be exceptional. But it may be possible to anticipate that Negro writers a decade from now will be able to get sufficiently beyond race and politics to give a universal significance to what now carries the strong stamp of topicality, provincialism, and special pleading.

In this brief essay I have tried to gauge the more important forces affecting the interplay of Negro writers and the Communist Party in the United States. The Communists have been unable to effectively channel, either politically or culturally, those moods and aspirations of Negroes which have been forcefully articulated by a wide range of Negro creative people. Negro writers in particular have not found Party organization and ideology significant or useful in their work. It is likely to remain the case as the vast and increasingly violent Negro-white conflicts unfold in the decade ahead.

Contemporary
Negro Fiction*

by Hoyt W. Fuller

JUST PRIOR TO the United States' entry into World War II, the
late Winston Churchill appeared before the joint houses of Congress in Washington, and at the conclusion of his address quoted
the following lines:

> If we must die, O let us nobly die,
> So that our precious blood may not be shed
> In vain; then even the monsters we defy
> Shall be constrained to honor us, though dead!
>
> .   .   .   .
>
> Like men we'll face the murderous, cowardly pack,
> Pressed to the wall, dying, but fighting back!

Most of the senators and representatives who heard those lines
heard them for the first time, and though unquestionably moved,
had no idea that the eloquent words issuing from the lips of the
British Prime Minister were written by an American. And many
of them, had they known the identity of the poet, would have been
grossly affronted; for the lines recited by Mr. Churchill were taken

---

*This article first appeared in 1965 and is reprinted by per-
mission of the author.

from the poem, "If We Must Die," written by the Jamaican-born Negro, Claude McKay, a leader of the Harlem School of the Black Renaissance.

There was, of course, a sort of delicious irony in Mr. Churchill's borrowing a Negro poet's words to persuade the American Congress to join Britain in a war again Nazi racism. Mr. McKay, a defiant and uncompromising foe of bigotry, was what in polite circles these days would be called "a militant Negro," and he had written his poem as a sort of a poetical call-to-arms to Negro Americans to resist the assaults of white terrorists with all the counterviolence of which they were capable. The poem had been written in the early years of the twentieth century, during the period when southern whites, with the particular aid of the rampaging Ku Klux Klan, were reimposing their mastership over Negroes, stripping them of every right and privilege accorded them by the Thirteenth, Fourteenth, and Fifteenth Amendments. The rest of the country, through inaction, had condoned the rape of Negro rights in the South. And even in the North a series of riots had served to warn Negroes against taking too seriously their rights and status as free American citizens.

Such a poem as Mr. McKay's, then, would scarcely have been looked upon with favor by congressmen even twenty years after it was written. However, in the context in which Mr. Churchill chose to use it, the poem could hardly have been considered more appropriate. It was, evidently, a favorite Churchill poem, for he also had read it before Parliament.

In any consideration of Negro literature it is well to keep in mind that, inevitably, the racial realities being what they are, a large portion of the American reading public must find itself out of sympathy with the content of much of that literature. In *After The Lost Generation,* critic John W. Aldridge's well-regarded evaluation of the post World War II crop of young writers, he begins by stating, "One cannot speak of fiction without sooner or later speaking of values." Mr. Aldridge also says that "ideally, the writer and the reader should share the same values, so that the material which the writer selects as valuable enough to write about will automatically be valuable to the reader. . . ." But in practice, if not in principle, the two major races in America often have different values, or at least different ways of interpreting the same values. And since, in Mr. Aldridge's opinion, "the writing of novels is basically a process of assigning value to human experience," the line of conflict is drawn.

"The novel," Mr. Aldridge says,

> so long as we require of it a narrative form and function, must always have to do with the actions of men within the framework of a particular society; and it must also, so long as we require of it the validity of serious art, endow these actions with meaning. To satisfy these requirements, the novelist begins always with the meaning which he, as a unique sensibility, brings to the experience which he has chosen as his material. This amounts to no less than everything that he is or has become up to the moment of writing, and that part of everything he is which he is able to communicate in language to the reader.

In other words, the reading public, which primarily is white, must be cognizant first of the nature and purpose of literature in general before taking the further step toward the appreciation of that literature produced by Negroes. The failure or refusal of both critics and the public to do this in the past has resulted in the attachment of stigma to the designation, "Negro literature," making it easy, when desirable, to dismiss much of this literature as inconsequential. It is common, for example, to hear Negro novels referred to as "protest literature," the clear implication being that "protest" in this context is equated with mere propaganda. But an objective examination of much of the literature which the public considers "great" will reveal this literature to have overtones of "protest." Mr. Aldridge classifies the early work of Ernest Hemingway, John Dos Passos, Theodore Dreiser, and Sinclair Lewis as "protest" literature, and these writers produced the most impressive body of work of any literary generation in the country's history.

Mr. Aldridge also classifies as "indignant" much of the work of the post World War II generation of writers — Gore Vidal, Norman Mailer, Merle Miller, Irwin Shaw, and Vance Bourjaily among them — saying that their novels "have buried in them a surgical, despairing hatred." The eminent poet and critic Mark Van Doren said in *The Private Reader* that "all literature propagates ideas," and Ernest Hemingway has observed that "writers are forged in injustice as a sword is forged. . . ."

Why, then, the persistent branding of the serious writing of Negroes as "protest literature"? In an interview with writers from the *Paris Review,* Ralph Ellison struck through to the heart of the reason. Asked if he considered his novel, *Invisible Man,* "as a purely literary work, as opposed to one in the tradition of social protest," Ellison replied that he recognized

> no dichotomy between art and protest. Dostoievsky's *Notes from the Underground* is, among other things, a protest against the limitations of 19th century rationalism. *Don Quixote, Man's Fate, Oedipus Rex, The Trial* — all of these embody protest even against the limitation of human life itself. If social protest is antithetical to art, what then shall we make of Goya, Dickens, and Twain? One hears a lot of complaint about the so-called "protest novel," especially when written by Negroes. . . .

"Perhaps, though," Ellison also said,

> this thing cuts both ways: the Negro novelist draws his blackness too tightly around him when he sits down to write —that's what the anti-protest critics believe — but perhaps the white reader draws his whiteness around him when he sits down to read. He doesn't want to identify himself with Negro characters in terms of our immediate social and racial situation. . . . The white reader doesn't want to get too close, not even in an imaginary re-creation of society. Negro writers have felt this and it has lead to much of our failure.

The point was made with even more directness by critic Carl Milton Hughes, who is not a Negro. "Paradoxically enough," he wrote in *The Negro Novelist,*

> knowledge that the dominant group may or may not have a national guilt feeling about the situation but has a vested interest which prevents alleviation of it makes the novel with Negro authors an instrument of criticism. Thus, the Negro novelist as critic of American society is in keeping with Freud's thesis that "we may expect in the course of time changes will be carried out in our civilization so that it becomes more satisfying to our needs and no longer open to reproaches we have made against it."

Or to put it more bluntly still, Negro literature is dismissed as "protest literature" because, if it deals honestly with Negro life, it will be accusatory toward white people, and nobody likes to be accused, especially of crimes against the human spirit. The reading public must realize, then, that while it is the duty of any serious writer to look critically and truthfully at the society of which he is a part, and to reveal that society to itself, the Negro writer, by virtue of his identification with a group deliberately held on the outer edges of that society, will, if he is honest, call attention to that special aspect of the society's failure.

On the other hand, if the Negro writer is concerned with creating a work of art, he will do much more than that. And most Negro writers are deeply concerned with art. "Negroes do not answer to rules other than writers of other races," writes Rosey Pool, English editor of the anthology *Beyond the Blues.* "It is just that their experience is different." And Robert A. Bone, author of *The Negro Novel in America,* goes farther:

> Like any other artist, the Negro novelist must achieve universality through a sensitive interpretation of his own culture. The American Negro, however, has not one but two cultures to interpret. He bears a double burden, corresponding to the double environment in which he lives. He must be conversant with Western culture as a whole, and especially with the traditions of English literature of which he is a part, and at the same time be prepared to affirm a Negro quality in his experience, exploiting his Negro heritage as a legitimate contribution to the larger culture.

Poet-playwright LeRoi Jones, speaking as a Negro artist, describes his responsibilities in these words:

> High art must reflect the experience, the emotional predicament of the man, as he exists, in the defined world of his being. It must be produced from the legitimate emotional resources of the soul in the world. It can *never* be produced by evading these resources or pretending they do not exist. It can never be produced by appropriating the withered emotional responses of some strictly social ideas of humanity. . . .

The contemporary Negro writer, more often than not, marches to the music heard by LeRoi Jones. This does not mean that most Negroes writing today are investing their work with the searing fire and anger so evident in Mr. Jones's three produced plays, *Dutchman, The Slave,* and *The Toilet.* Just as each writer's experiences will vary in quality and in intensity, so will his sensibilities. Nevertheless, with one or two exceptions, Negro writers of today have ceased apologizing for their material, "the legitimate emotional resources of the soul in the world." They are saying, in effect, that they will no longer be victims. They are determined finally to destroy the power of white-perpetrated myths over their lives. Professor Bone failed to understand this when he wrote:

> The Negro must still structure his life in terms of a culture to which he is denied full access. He is at once a part of and apart from the wider community in which he lives. His adjustment to the dominant culture is marked by a conflicting pattern of identification and rejection. His deepest psychological impulses alternate between the magnetic poles of assimilationism and Negro nationalism.

Professor Bone was looking back over the period of the Black Renaissance and the years leading up to World War II and, in so far as he was evaluating that generation of writers, his statement has much substance. It is true that some of the writers in the twenties and thirties, Walter White and Jessie Fauset among them, sought in their novels to illustrate how little difference there was between Negroes and whites, even going to the extent of presenting heroes and heroines white enough to pass. After all, it is natural for man to want to belong, really belong, to the society which nurtured him. And it is also true that writers like Claude McKay and Wallace Thurman, members of the so-called Harlem School, sought to emphasize the nobility and the humanity of the ordinary Negro. But, while what Professor Bone calls "assimilationism" has been embraced by Negro writers of each generation, hope springing eternal, the Negro nationalism of the twenties and thirties simply had no place to go. The Negro audience for books reflecting such an outlook was small indeed, and even it was under continuing pressure to adjust its appetite to the white image. And with no audience, and with little hope of one, it is difficult for a writer to go on striving.

But something of surpassing importance happened in the world in the years following 1940, and this singular event had — and will continue to have for some time to come — a profound effect on the Negro writer. The old edifices of power, quietly crumbling for decades, finally collapsed in the great convulsion of World War II; and, in the resulting disarray, the white masters of the West discovered that their grip had been forced loose from nonwhite peoples everywhere. Suddenly it became clear that, in time, not being white would not automatically doom a man to a subordinate status in the world, not even in America.

The more independent, or defiant, mood of the contemporary Negro writer in his work then should not be narrowly construed as "nationalism." It is indicative of much more than a passing spasm of chauvinism. Many critics — some of them Negro — have listened to the militant voices of the James Baldwins, the LeRoi Joneses and the John O. Killenses and have declared, with exaggerated boredom, that they have heard it all before. But they are in magnificent error. *Another Country,* flawed as it certainly is, is no conventional novel crying out against white oppression and begging for the mercy of tolerance and equality. That white critics have chosen to see it in such a context may be symptomatic of their own status orientation: it is part of the traditional attitude toward Negro writing to expect it to plead for tolerance. However, to read the novel in this light is to miss its point altogether. In a very real sense, *Another Country* is not even about Negroes at all. Rufus and Ida Scott, the only two Negroes in the novel, are symbols and catalysts, representing the dark abyss of the human soul for which Americans have so strong a fascination and from which they are eternally in flight. The book deals with the absence — or the failure — of love in the great American metropolis and in the lives of some of the people who inhabit it. In an essay published in *The Contemporary American Novel,* critic Robert Sayre writes that "Love and death are the real subjects of *Another Country,* neither of them 'in the infantile American sense,' to use one of Baldwin's phrases, but in the profound ways that they are also the subjects of a poem like 'The Waste Land.'" *Another Country* is in fact an incredibly misunderstood book, certainly maligned for the wrong reasons — those reasons being its blunt treatment of interracial and homosexual relationships — and probably, with its all but phenomenal sales, also read for the wrong reasons.

Mr. Baldwin is aiming at much more than sex and race, those twin bugaboos of the American psyche. His target is as big as the nation. "We should note that the title, *Another Country,* is lively with irony," Mr. Sayre observed,

> for the novel presents a world as we know it but as it has not before been put in fiction to be seen, "other" by its ominous distance from what it ought to be and from real human needs, and then "other" as some private land where a handful of people have honored and renewed themselves. This tension epitomizes the book's role in Baldwin's vision.

What some of the critics perceive as "nationalism" in the work of Mr. Baldwin, then, is something else again. Mr. Baldwin, like many other Negroes, writers and nonwriters, feels that Americans have disowned the fundamental principles of humanity, justice, and love, and that in doing so they have profoundly scarred the nation's soul. He feels that the Negro masses, by virtue of their long and forced exclusion from the so-called "mainstream of American life," alone have retained a vision of a society constructed on the principles of justice and equality. Writing of the post World War II crop of young white writers, John W. Aldridge made the following comments on the land in which they live and work:

> America is more than ever a machine-dominated, gadget-minded country. There are more Babbitts now than when Sinclair Lewis invented the term and the expatriates shouted it in their battle cry for freedom, art and exile. But who cares today to take up that cry, to denounce again with the same fury, or to escape forever into artistic exile?

Well, the young Negro writer cares, and he cares because he has caught a vision of a possible new America, a renewed America, and he would like to see it saved. But, he is saying to all who would listen, it *must* be a new America. In the words of the late playwright, Lorraine Hansberry, a growing number of Negroes "are not so sure that they want to be integrated into a burning house."

The contemporary Negro writer, unlike so many of his white fellow writers, looks toward the future with hope, but hope with a difference. He does not visualize the lifting of racial barriers as merely a facilitation of the Negro's move into the so-called "mainstream of American life." He sees the ending of racial restrictions as one of many moves — albeit a crucial one — that the American people as a whole must make, in order to reaffirm the nation's basic principles and to give the nation the moral and spiritual strength necessary to survive in the world which is rapidly evolving. And if, in the past, it seemed that the Negro writer was appealing to the moral conscience of the nation, it appears now that he is *warning* the nation that the old empty promises and gestures will no longer suffice. This is the essence of the bitter, stabbing plays of LeRoi Jones. In *Dutchman,* the first and perhaps the best of the trio of produced plays, the Negro protagonist, having made every conceivable concession to the white image to which the society demands that he conform, finally turns on his teasing, tormenting white adversary and spews out a rain of hate. In *The Toilet,* a work intended to shock in its every aspect — from the setting in a boys' latrine to the scatological language used by the young characters — unleashed hate is omnipresent and oppressive. In *The Slave,* a play all but drowned in both hate and symbolism, the Negro and white characters perform their charade of malice and murder while the world outside the room is at war. While the Negro man and his white ex-wife play their terrible game of love and loathing, their daughters, the fruit of their convoluted relationship, are destroyed by an exploding shell in the room above. Hate has begotten hate, and death is everywhere. Unless the nation chooses to see, then this can be its legacy.

There are, of course, gentler voices speaking in softer cadences. In *Many Thousands Gone,* a "fable" published in January, 1965, by a Chicagoan, Ronald L. Fair, the grim pageant of rural Mississippi is transformed into a rollicking laugh-fest, edged with the ice of sobering truth. But in the end, as the comedy gathers to its close, the reader realizes that all those poor, innocent, lovable old darkies from the cotton fields have murder on their minds. A few seasons back, young William Melvin Kelley in *A Different Drummer* also used fantasy to make his chilling point: perhaps it is not the oppressed Negro, after all, who stands so desperately in need; at least the Negro has endured and grown strong under deprivation — but what of all those defenseless southern psyches, encrusted now with a patina of evil and guilt that no power on earth can remove? And Robert Boles, just twenty-one, in his first novel, *The People One Knows,* draws a portrait of a sensitive, well-bred, even *aristocratic* young Negro, struggling valiantly and alone against the racism that nothing in his background has prepared him to confront, and almost losing, but not quite, not quite. At least, he does not lose to the impulse to self-destruction, as Rufus Scott did in *Another Country*. No, he makes another choice. He turns his back on his best friend and the girl who loves him, both white, and turns instead to a deaf-mute companion, an Outsider like himself. Nationalism? Nothing of the sort. William Faulkner saw his black Mississippians as forever enduring, but James Meredith at Ole Miss and James Chaney from his martyr's grave shattered that dream forever.

In spirit, more than a conscious approximation, the contemporary Negro novelist and playwright is the heir of Richard Wright, one of the century's most powerful literary craftmen, and it is appropriate to go back to 1940, the date of the publication of his *Native Son*, in considering contemporary Negro fiction. The late Mr. Wright wrote that both Negroes and whites "possess deep-seated resistance against 'the Negro problem' being presented, even verbally, in all its hideous fullness, in all the totality of its meaning," and he created Bigger Thomas for their discomfort. Bigger was thoroughly unattractive, with no single redeeming characteristic. He flew in the face of the tradition of presenting a Negro hero who, though abused by a prejudiced society, remained upright and steadfast to the end. Bigger was a bum. Negroes disliked him for this reason, and also because Bigger's behavior revealed what Negroes would have preferred that white people not know — that Negroes are fully capable of hating white people, and of murdering them. White people were either baffled by Bigger or else, if they were liberals, made uneasy in the speculation that, just possibly, they had been right about Negroes all along. Certainly it was not possible to wrap him in pity and wail at his fate. This brutal, rapist, murdering bum of a man is — as Lerone Bennett, Jr. has observed — the most memorable Negro character in the annals of fiction. But Bigger was a breakthrough. After him, despite the disapproval of the Negro critics, Negro authors would frequently, and in a variety of dramatic contexts, present Negro protagonists who were less than lovable. Rufus Scott, the ill-fated jazz musician of *Another Country*, was a direct descendant of Bigger.

If *Native Son* arrived on the literary scene with unprecedented impact, Richard Wright's two later novels failed to arouse similar attention. This is not surprising. Neither *The Outsider*, published in 1953, nor *The Long Dream*, published five years afterward, possessed the shock of revelation that had characterized the first novel, though the author's relentless, driving prose lifted both novels above the average. Most of the criticism of both *The Outsider* and *The Long Dream* was centered in the proposition that, since Richard Wright had been in exile in Paris for so many years, he was out of touch with the new American realities. Life in America, the critics claimed, could not possibly be as frustrating and difficult for Cross Damon of *The Outsider* and Fishbelly of *The Long Dream* as it had been for Bigger Thomas. But while it is true that there have been, in the years since 1940, certain dramatic changes in the status of certain Negro Americans, these changes have affected only a special segment of the Negro population, and these primarily in the metropolitan centers of the North and West. As news stories out of Mississippi and Alabama illustrate, conditions are little improved in the native region of all Richard Wright's leading characters. And fictionally, as late as 1963, the talented Junius Edwards produced a novel called, like McKay's poem, *If We Must Die,* which suffered at the hands of the critics, precisely because, in mood, technique, and situation, it too closely resembled the Wright books.

The appearance of *Native Son* and its astonishing success persuaded publishers to release the novels of other Negro writers and, in the inevitable rush into print, some superior books were made available to the public. Perhaps the most promising novelist to follow in the wake of Richard Wright was Ann Petry, a superb but uneven literary craftsman. *The Street*, her first novel, deals with the struggle for dignity of a Jamaican migrant in Connecticut. Lutie Johnson's story proved, if proof was needed, that an attractive, intelligent, and industrious Negro woman in enlightened Connecticut remained very much at the mercy of the same forces that hounded her counterpart in darkest Mississippi. Another good novel to follow *Native Son* was William Attaway's *Blood on the Forge,* the story of three brothers from the backwoods of Kentucky who flee to the steel mills of Pennsylvania after a fight with their white overseer on the farm. The trials and disintegration of these men in the unfamiliar urban ghetto is the theme of the novel.

Toward the end of the forties and in the early fifties, when the interest in Negro literature dropped to one of its periodical low ebbs, a group of exceptional novels appeared. One of the best and least known was Owen Dodson's *Boy at the Window,* published in 1951. A sensitive book written with gentle effectiveness, it dealt with the coming of age of a Negro boy in a middle-class area of Brooklyn, not yet gripped by the fever of segregation. The year before, William Demby's *Beetle Creek* appeared, describing the destructive influence of a mean, poverty-ridden town on the lives of its inhabitants. And in 1952 came Ralph Ellison's highly praised *Invisible Man,* a technically brilliant, complex, highly controlled work. *Invisible Man* describes the adventures of a young Negro from the South making his wild, bumbling way through the maze of life in New York City. But it deals finally with the essence of the two political poles — capitalism and communism — and the essential fraudulence of both of them. It is a difficult, elusive, subtle, ironical, mischievous, satirical novel, but one which leaves the reader, ultimately, with little sense of its life. The book is full of memorable scenes and incidents both dramatic and surreal, but it has no memorable characters.

The novels of Chester Himes, perhaps more than those of any other Negro writer, reveal the strong influence of *Native Son.* The first of these novels, *If He Hollers, Let Him Go,* moves with much of the swift-plowing pace of Richard Wright's style but without his astonishing power. The hero, Bob Jones, is an intelligent, literate defense worker in California, eventually trapped in a sex-and-race situation with a provocative southern belle employed in the same plant. Himes's second novel, *Lonely Crusade,* is an advancement of a similar theme, this time with emphasis on labor union politics, communism, and the frustrations of the Negro trying to make his way in a hostile and treacherous white world.

It did not take long for the already limited audience of the novels of Negro life to grow weary of work like Himes's. Agents, publishers, editors, and even high-school and university instructors, sold on the postwar liberal idea of brotherhood, or else simply unwilling to consider fiction dealing with Negro life, persuaded many Negro writers to abandon the Negro as the subject of their novels. Or, at least in some cases, Negro writers succeeded in persuading themselves.

In an article published in 1950, Saunders Redding placed the blame on Negroes. "Season it as you will," he wrote, "the thought that the Negro American is different from other Americans is still unpalatable to most Negroes." Whatever the excuse, then, Negro writers in droves deserted Negro subjects. Himes wrote a book called *Cast the First Stone;* Ann Petry's entry was *Country Place;* Zora Neale Hurston, a writer out of the thirties who had achieved success with the artful handling of Negro folklore, turned to poor southern white characters in *Seraph on the Suwanee;* Frank Yerby began with *The Foxes of Harrow* in 1946 and has produced a similar best-selling novel almost yearly since; the late Willard Motley published three novels, all with white protagonists; and even William Gardner Smith, whose *Last of the Conquerors* was the first novel in what was to become the new national orientation of young Negro writers, found it expedient in his second novel, *Anger at Innocence, t*o take a stab at just being a writer, not a Negro writer.

For that, plainly, is the argument behind the Negro writer's temporary abandonment of Negro themes. What Professor Bone has termed "assimilationism" had strongly influenced the writers of the forties, fed as they were on the slogans of the war years, the military victory over the Fascists, and the illusion that a new era of freedom and equality had been ushered in. It was during this period that James Baldwin, whose moving autobiographical novel of life in a storefront Harlem church, *Go Tell It on the Mountain*, had given notice of the emergence of a major new talent, wrote his famous essay attack on Richard Wright, "Everybody's Protest Novel." And Richard Gibson, like Baldwin an expatriate in Paris, working on *A Mirror for Magistrates,* a novel that was published in England and not in this country, scolded those who advised Negroes to write about what they know. Railing sarcastically, Mr. Gibson wrote: "You are not free, he [the Negro writer] is told. Write about what you know, he is told, and the Professional Liberal will not fail to remind him that he can not possibly know anything else but Jim Crow, sharecropping, slum ghettos, Georgia crackers, and the sting of his humiliation, his unending ordeal, his blackness."

Well, as Mr. Baldwin's subsequent collection of rather extraordinary essays has shown, to say nothing of his controversial third novel, there is plenty to protest about. And Mr. Gibson, who returned home for a time, only to be driven by bitterness to leave again for North Africa, devoted his talents for a while to writing pure antiracist tracts. As for the others, only Miss Petry chose not to flee the American scene, and she has not been heard from in a novel since. Motley died in Mexico; Frank Yerby lives in a luxurious villa in Spain; and both Mr. Smith and Mr. Himes are residents of Paris. In any case, their fling at being just writers, not Negro writers, over, Mr. Smith and Mr. Himes have returned to Negro themes.

Several of the newer of the young writers continue to write about white people as well as Negroes, but they write about the people or the kind of people with whom they have been intimately associated and indeed, in this sense, they are "just writers, not Negro writers." They have emerged from a social milieu in which, for the first time in America, differences in status and privileges are minimal. In *All the Rest Have Died,* a sensitive novel which barely escapes being precious, actor-playwright Bill Gun writes about a young Negro actor very much like himself, in the middle-Bohemia of the art and theater world in New York. In *The People One Knows,* Robert Boles, the son of a wealthy white architect and a Negro mother, brought up in the capitals of Europe and on Cape Cod, writes of life among American whites in the U. S. Army and of the Europeans who have been his friends and lovers. James Baldwin's *Another Country* is populated by the kind of people he is likely to meet around New York and Paris. And LeRoi Jones, apart from living and working intimately with whites in his capacity as instructor at the New School for Social Research and at the Totem Press, happens to be married to a lady who is white. Because these are all talented and serious writers, what their novels reveal concerning the people they write about is worth knowing and pondering.

Finally, there are at least three Negro novelists who have been all but ignored in the clamor over the more colorful writers. They are literary craftsmen of a high order, and they are growing in power and art with each new work. Julian Mayfield, author of *The Hit, The Long Night,* and *The Grand Parade,* received little encouragement from the critics, despite his good work. He lives now in Ghana, where he writes political columns for local newspapers. A new place of exile. John A. Williams, the talented novelist who won the unhappy distinction of being the first nominee for the Prix de Rome to be refused by the Academy (and they never gave him a reason), supplements the royalties from the award-winning *Night Song* and the more recent *Sissie* with fees from magazine pieces. And Ernest J. Gaines, whose fine novel, *Catherine Carmier,* received almost no attention in 1964, one suspects because of the simplicity of its style and theme, is one of the most promising of the contemporary crop. His "The Sky is Grey," a long short story published in *Negro Digest,* tells us as much about the rock-hard, soul-deep dignity of the ordinary Negro as any work ever has. And *Catherine Carmier,* like the shorter story a sadly loving look at the author's southern homeland, gathers together in a finely woven pattern all the subtle, heartbreaking relationships native to the region. *Catherine Carmier, Sissie,* and Mr. Mayfield's first two novels, *The Hit* and *The Long Night,* succeeded through the writers' instinct and craft. Their authors hear the siren call of the critics urging them to enter "the mainstream of American literature," but they remain unswayed. LeRoi Jones has said, "Just by being black, the Negro is a committed non-conformist. . . . You don't have to be weird. . . . If you are black and in America, man that's weird." While these writers might use less colorful language, they know with Jones that by virtue of being black they are outside the American mainstream, and the price they would pay for straining towards it would be the destruction of their integrity as men and as artists. Critic Cynthia Ozick has written:

> It is a commonplace but curious law of the Outsider that the more he strives to fashion himself emotionally after the Insider, the more he proves himself Outside — and without benefiting his real condition. The Negro is not yet inside America — which is what the shouting is all about. Until he is, his good manners will be bad manners, his decency will be an indecency, and his sense of the proprieties will be the most shocking impropriety it is possible for him to commit against himself and against the idea of a human being.

And the best of today's Negro writers believe this to be so.

The Negro Writer
as Spokesman

by James W. Tuttleton

It is quite possible that much potential fiction by Negro
Americans fails precisely at this point: through the writers'
refusal (often through provincialism or lack of courage or
opportunism) to achieve a vision of life and a resource-
fulness of craft commensurate with the complexity of their
actual situation. Too often they fear to leave the uneasy
sanctuary of race to take their chances in the world of art.
—Ralph Ellison

From crispus attucks to Malcolm X and Martin Luther King,
Jr., the American Negro, speaking for himself, has rarely been
heard above the din and babble of white voices speaking for him.
Some of the white voices have spoken not so much for the Negro
as for a reactionary social order in which the Negro would find
himself subordinated through race, caste, and color. The apologists
of reaction — from Calhoun, Tilman, Vardaman and Bilbo to
Ross Barnett, Leander Perez and George Wallace — have assumed
an arbitrary right, throughout the agonizing racial history of the
United States, to speak for the Negro, down to him, at him, and
about him. Few large-minded students of the American social
order have accorded any merit to the dogmas of reactionary racism.
But such has been the power of conservatism in the United States
that for most of our history, reactionary racism has been institu-

tionalized, through law and custom, in most features of our public life.

But equally obnoxious to the American Negro, particularly today, is the voice of white liberalism speaking in his behalf. Before the advent of black power militancy, white liberals were necessary to the emancipation and progress of the American Negro. Without the army of lawyers, politicians, professors, social workers, clergymen, editors, and like public forces for change, the Negro would doubtless be more socially and institutionally enslaved than he now is. And to a great extent, white liberals are still necessary. But white liberals, like their conservative counterparts, often speak not so much for the Negro as for their own version of an ideal American social order. And in frequently looking at the Negro as merely a white man with a black face, and in surrendering to the self-complacency of their own radical rhetoric, white liberals have often permitted distinctively Negro interests, aims, and aspirations to get warped or lost. The treatment of the Negro by the American Communist Party is a conspicuous case in point.

In 1965, disturbed by the fact that most midcentury voices speaking for the Negro seemed to be white voices, Robert Penn Warren published *Who Speaks for the Negro?* In a series of taped interviews Warren sought to put on record the voice of the Negro speaking for himself. *Who Speaks for the Negro?* was an attempt "to find out something, first hand, about the people, some of them anyway, who are making the Negro Revolution what it is — one of the dramatic events of the American story."[1] What Warren found out — in talking to simple share-croppers, yard-boys, manual laborers, black editors, union leaders, college presidents, and others —was that beyond the non-negotiable demand (in unison) for respect and recognition no single voice spoke for the Negro. Individual Negroes spoke for themselves and articulated many similar and dissimilar, harmonious and contradictory views with respect to major issues that concerned them: the nature of integration, the relationship between black power and political power, the role of the Negro as "redeemer" of American society, non-violence vs. militancy as a strategy of black progress, the "specialness" of the Negro "personality" and "culture," the debt or reparations owed the Negro by white society, the relationship between Negro art and propaganda, the rate of historical process vs. Freedom Now urgencies, and so on.

The dilemma of the black man — that there is no concensus

as to what should be done, in what order of priorities, or by what means — is uniquely the dilemma of the black writer. For he, preeminently, is expected to be, in some sense or other, a "spokesman" for his race. He experiences, perhaps more sensitively than his brothers, that psychological doubleness which W. E. B. DuBois described, a "double consciousness," that "sense of always looking at one's self through the eyes of others, of measuring one's soul by the tape of a world that looks on in amused contempt and pity. One ever feels the two-ness — an American, a Negro; two souls, two thoughts, two unreconciled strivings, two warring ideals in one dark body, whose dogged strength alone keeps it from being torn asunder."[2] If the black writer suffers a cultural schizophrenia, he also experiences the daily humiliation that is the lot of his black brethren. He shares the sense of rage and outrage that burns in the heart of every sensitive black man. He is constrained, like them, to protest against the conditions in which he finds himself, to give vent in action to the pressures of rebellion within him. But to throw himself into the life of politics, direct action, agitation-confrontation, is to surrender his role as spectator, mediator and artist, to manipulate his imaginative energies, to dissipate and perhaps to damage his literary gifts. And if, in his role as writer, he is seduced by the overtures of the militant sociologist, he sacrifices the autonomy of his imagination to the services of a social cause: he becomes the racial apologist, the polemicist, the black propagandist — and forfeits thereby the "permanence," "artistry," and "universality" which are the presumed aim of every writer. What is he to do?

I

For every black writer the example of Richard Wright bears on his dilemma. Mississippi-born, ghetto-educated, Richard Wright was appalled by the harsh realities of Negro life in America, organized and expressed his rage in *Native Son* (1940), *12 Million Black Voices* (1941) and *Black Boy* (1945), despaired of seeing any changes in the conditions of that life, and left the United States for Paris in sorrow, anger, and deep anguish. The example Wright offers to other black writers is the literature of social protest. In the portrait of Bigger Thomas and his family in their filthy, one-room, rat-infested tenement; in the vision of Bigger's hatred and fear; in the dramatization of his mindless impulses to violence against the whites who oppress him; in the narrative of the murder of Mary Dalton and Bigger's trial, Wright sought in *Native Son* to protest, through the mode of naturalism, the sociological conditions determining the lives of urban Negroes and to put on record precise notations of the inner though inarticulate psychology and intense emotionalism of the black man in America. Though *Native Son* is marred by overt courtroom Marxist propagandizing, the novel was a black bombshell in white America: it exposed to unconscious whites everywhere the barely suppressed wrath and rage of what had seemed merely docile, servile, shuffling, psalm-singing darkies. But "no American Negro exists," as James Baldwin has written, "who does not have his private Bigger Thomas living in the skull. . . ."[3]

Native Son, for the would-be writer, for the black intending fabulist, was a dead end. Or so it seemed, at any rate, to Baldwin. In "Everybody's Protest Novel," "Many Thousands Gone" (reprinted in *Notes of a Native Son*) and in "Alas, Poor Richard" (reprinted in *Nobody Knows My Name*), Baldwin took Richard Wright to task for his naturalistic reduction of the complex Negro experience to that of racial victim. Where was Bigger's "discernible relationship to himself, to his own life, to his own people, . . . to any other people"?[4] Where was the sense of shared experience among Negroes? Wright did not provide it. He eliminated several layers of Negro experience in order to create a stereotype of Negro martyrdom, a stereotype no more revealing of rich Negro humanity than Uncle Tom or Aunt Jemima. Such falsifications of complex experience are the mark of the social protest novel. Baldwin urged upon black writers a fuller, more complex approach to characterization in which, whatever the quantum of racial agony, the whole vision would be rounded, balanced, and purified in the alembic of the artist's imagination and, therefore, successful in aesthetic terms.

This is not the place to rehearse the quarrel between Wright and Baldwin over what Wright called "all that art for art's sake crap."[5] The argument is self-evident in Baldwin's essays and has been adequately described in Maurice Charney's "James Baldwin's Quarrel with Richard Wright."[6] Nor is it germane to the point to observe, with Irving Howe, that Baldwin has not yet succeeded in composing the kind of novel he counterposed to the work of Richard Wright.[7] It is not even relevant that Baldwin, after Wright's death, performed a *volte-face* and began to write essays and novels of social protest — although it may make it appear that

Wright was right all along and that Baldwin eventually came to his senses. Baldwin's change of mind is not relevant because the issue of the danger to the writer who is urged to become a spokes-man for social protest is still a live issue. The risks for the writer as artist are still very real. His talents, his imaginative vision, the sources of his artistic energy — all may be perverted or dissipated if his writing does not spring instinctively and intuitively from that well of inspiration that is personal and unique to him. What could be clearer than the waste of great imaginative talents conspicuous in propagandistic works like Hemingway's *To Have and Have Not,* Faulkner's *Intruder in the Dust,* even Baldwin's *Another Country?*

II

If Baldwin, whose talent is flagging — judging from *Tell Me How Long the Train's Been Gone* (1969), never wrote the kind of novel he counterposed to *Native Son,* perhaps Ralph Ellison has in *Invisible Man* (1952). (The aspiration to high art is a particularly taxing one for the black writer with any kind of artistic conscience: Ellison has not yet been able to complete a second novel.) *Invisible Man* is still the best American novel written by a Negro because of Ellison's great imaginative gifts and his well-nigh religious devotion to craft. In its way it is a more powerful articulation of Negro protest than *Native Son* (and all of Baldwin's work) because of the richness of Ellison's language, the extravagant inventiveness of his imagination, the fullness of scene, episode and character, the careful control of structure and symbolism, and the depth and complexity of his racial, social and political reference. All of these put *Invisible Man* virtually in a class by itself. But it is a vexing work for the radical militant critic because it does not make an explicit protest like the work of Richard Wright.

Invisible Man has of course been bitterly attacked for aban-doning Wright's "black anger" and "clenched militancy," for Ellison's refusal, as Robert Bone has put it, "to enlist his image-making powers in the service of the cause."[8] But while Ellison and every other black writer seems condemned to play off the Negro experience against the white world, or the Negro's interpretation of it, the postures of despair, alienation, and feverish militancy need not be, and probably should not be, the only stance or strategy for the black writer to take. Yet these are the postures black critics are now insistently urging upon black writers. Baldwin and Ellison are now called passé because they are too keyed on the white world, on Western cultural values.

III

The understandable impulses to black political separatism in this country have given rise to a mystique of black aesthetic separatism. A new racial psychology is currently developing in the United States and according to black critics, a new literature is called for to accurately reflect and express the new Negro sensibility. Warning black writers from trying to enter the "mainstream" of American letters, black critics have begun to assert a new "black aesthetic." Based on Frantz Fanon's view that "in the time of revolutionary struggle, the traditional Western liberal ideals are not merely irrelevant but they must be assiduously opposed," young separatist Negro authors "have set out in search of a black aesthetic, a system of isolating and evaluating the artistic works of black people which reflect the special character and imperatives of black experience."[9]

The July 1968 issue of *Negro Digest*, of which Mr. Fuller is Managing Editor, was given over to exploring the opinions of thirty-eight black writers on issues like the "black aesthetic." While no unanimity in the poll was evident, some of the views expressed throw light on the literary separatism now fashionable. Larry Neal, for example, argued:

There is no need to establish a black aesthetic. Rather, it is important to understand that one already exists. The question is: where does it exist? . . . To explore the black experience means that we do not deny the reality and the power of the slave culture; the culture that produced the blues, spirituals, folk songs, work songs, and 'jazz.' It means that Afro-American life and its myriad of styles are expressed and examined in the fullest, most truthful manner possible. The models for what Black literature should be are found primarily in our folk culture, especially in the blues and jazz. . . .

Strictly speaking it is not a matter of whether we write protest literature or not. I have written 'love' poems that act to liberate the soul as much as any 'war' poem I have written. No, it can't simply be about protest as such. Protest literature assumes that the people we are talking to do not understand the nature of their condition. In this narrow context, protest literature is finally a plea to white America for our human dignity. We cannot get it that way. We must address each other. We must touch each other's beauty, wonder, and pain.[10]

Central to this rejection of the white world as audience, central to this rejection of Western liberal ideals, has been the repudiation of the test of a work of art in terms of its *universal* applications. This rejection strikes to the heart of aesthetics, as it is conventionally subsumed under the category of metaphysics dealing with the definition, creation, and experience of beauty in the world. Universality as a norm of values has been rejected by the militant critic because it is the test by which a good deal of black literature has been dismissed as inferior. As a substitute for norms of value based on the conventional canons of aesthetics, the Organization of Black American Culture has tried to formulate a definition of this "black aesthetic" that is expressive of the mystique of Negritude currently fashionable. The substance of this aesthetic is apparently (and I say "apparently" because none of the definitions is adequately precise) the extent to which and the accuracy with which black writing incorporates and expresses the uniquely black elements of American life — the folklore, the music (spirituals, blues, work songs, and jazz), the distinctive idiom of black cats, the special cuisine (soul food), the dance, dramaturgy and religion of the American Negro. These elements are viewed as materials to be organized with the purpose not merely of protesting the Negro's degradation, but of asserting his virtue and beauty and condemning the white race. As LeRoi Jones has put it: "The Black Artist's role in America is to aid in the destruction of America as he knows it. His role is to report and reflect so precisely the nature of the society, and of himself in that society, that other men will be moved by the exactness of his rendering and, if they are black men, grow strong through this moving, having seen their own strength, and weakness; and if they are white men, tremble, curse, and go mad, because they will be drenched with the filth of their evil."[11] There is more than an echo of black magic in all of this: Jones is reaching back for the strongest racial power his heritage affords him. In this way, the role of the black writer is to ritualize the race's fundamental myths, ideals, and values. As Larry Neal has put it: "The oldest, most important arts, have always made their practitioners stronger. Here I refer to the Black Arts, ju-ju, voodoo, and the Holy Ghost of the Black Church. . . . We are Black writers (priests), the bearers of the ancient tribal tradition. . . . As writers, one of our sacred functions is to reconstruct our ancient tradition and to give that tradition meaning in light of the manner in which history has moved."[12]

IV

On a less mystical, more political level, this revolutionary aesthetic of destruction has been succinctly defined by Ron Karenga: "Black art must expose the enemy, praise the people, and support the revolution."[13] In *The New Black Poetry* (Karenga's statement is its epigraph and manifesto), Clarence Major, the editor, observes in his introduction that many of the poets chosen are "full-time militant activists" because "droopy concepts of western ideology are already obsolete": "The capitalist imperialist, Euro-American cultural sensibility has proven itself to be essentially anti-human and is being rejected not only by black poets — black people — but also by the white radical activist."[14] An example of this aesthetic of destruction is offered by Harry Edwards' poem "How to Change the U.S.A.":

> For openers, the Federal Government
>   the honkies, the pigs in blue
> must go down South
>   and take those crackers out of bed,
> the crackers who blew up
>   those four little girls
> in that Birmingham church
>   those crackers who murdered
> Medgar Evars [sic] and killed
>   the three civil rights workers —
> they must pull them out of bed
>   and kill them with axes
> in the middle of the street.
>   Chop them up with dull axes.
>   Slowly.
> At high noon.

With everybody watching
on television.
Just as a gesture
of good faith.[15]

Well-structured and well-paced in its parallelism, tightly organized
and carefully controlled, vigorous in diction and rich in ironic
emotional effects, this poem expresses an attitude as vicious, blood-
lustful for revenge, and as anti-human as any expression of the
"Euro-American cultural sensibility" I am familiar with.

Like nearly all racial protest works by Negroes, it is obsessed
by race victimization, though here the general fate of black bru-
talization is given precise concretization in the catalogue of the
black martyrs. (Two of the unnamed civil rights workers were of
course whites.) What is suggestive, from the point of view of the
psychic genesis of these hate emotions, is that the poet or narrator
would make other whites the instrumentalities of black revenge.
This kind of poem is distressing to contemplate because calls for
revenge-assassinations as "gestures of good faith" do not seem likely
to effect that revolution of consciousness, to create that trans-
cendent "new man," that "new humanism," which the poet S. E.
Anderson has called the purpose of the black aesthetic revolution.[16]
One is hesitant to say this because it exposes one to the counter-
claim of white racism, and because apologists for the new black
aesthetics have condemned in advance whatever negative responses
to it the white critic may experience: "The movement," Hoyt
Fuller has claimed in "Towards a Black Aesthetic," "will be
reviled as 'racism in-reverse,' and its writers labled as 'racists,' op-
probrious terms which are flung lightly at black people now that
the piper is being paid for all the long years of rejection and
abuse which black people have experienced at the hands of white
people. . . ."[17] 'Buked and scorned blacks have been at the hands
of whites, but this kind of writing — I do not fling the term lightly—
is patently racist.

It seems to me that black critics and writers would do well
to contemplate the quality and humanity of their protests against
the social order that has degraded them. Apologists of black revolutionary aesthetics may complain about "the effrontery of white
critics in presuming to sit in judgment on the quality of black life
and on the character of the literary expression which grows organ-
ically out of that life experience."[18] But the white critic *must* judge

the moral and aesthetic character of black writing as well as that of every other kind of writing that falls within his purview. It is his function and duty to do so — both as a man concerned about the quality of human life reflected in his culture, and as a critic, aware that literature has consequences and concerned about the quality of writing that bears upon the literary traditions he cherishes and wishes to preserve. For it is the critic who is able to bring to bear upon a literary work the full range of aesthetic, moral, social, historical and psychological implications that illuminate the literary work.

Thus the critic, black or white, must not only understand the poet Larry Neal when he says, "Culturally and artistically, the West is dead. We must understand that we are what's happening."[19] But he must also qualify and correct the statement by defining the extraliterary purposes of this kind of rhetorical exaggeration, by setting the poems of writers like Neal, Claude McKay, Langston Hughes, and Gwendolyn Brooks into a context of works including those of Eliot, Auden, Pound, Yeats, and Lowell. Understanding is also demanded of the critic who ponders the views of the black poet Etheridge Knight: "The Caucasian has separated the aesthetic dimension from all others, in order that undesirable conclusions might be avoided. The artist is encouraged to speak only of the beautiful . . . his task is to edify the listener, to make him see the *beauty* of the world. And this is the trick bag that Black Artists must avoid, because the red of this aesthetic rose got its color from the blood of black slaves, exterminated Indians, napalmed Vietnamese children, etc., ad nauseum. . . . When the white aesthetic does permit the artist to speak of ugliness and evil — and this is the biggest trick in the whole bag — the ugliness and evil must be a 'universal human condition,' a flimflam justification for the continuous enslavement of the world's colored peoples. The white aesthetic would tell the Black Artist that *all* men have the same problems, that they all try to find their dignity and identity."[20] When the critic contemplates such indictments, while acknowledging the dismal and bloody history of white colonial exploitation, he must insist that there *is* a fundamental ground of humanity on which men *do* experience the same problems. And he must balance the view of Fuller and Knight with the counter-claim of writers like Saunders Redding and Robert Hayden that there can be no such thing as a black aesthetic. As Redding has observed, "aesthetics has no racial, national or geographic boundaries."[21] The struggle of the individual with an oppressive society is only one angle of a triad — the others being the individual's struggle with himself and his struggle with nature. Arriving at a full measure of one's identity and dignity is a colorblind, universal problem — at all times and in all places. It is an optimistic, groupthink Negro who can reduce the ubiquity of human evil to the forms of white racism. And it is a cynical black writer who can exploit the agony of the Negro by reducing the tragic conditions of human life to the manipulations of sociology and politics: "what an easy con-game for ambitious, publicity-hungry Negroes this stance of 'militancy' has become," Ralph Ellison has lamented.[22]

Yet this kind of reduction is precisely what underlies the militancy of some of our black critics. Thus in the "Introduction" to his anthology *Black Expression*, Addison Gayle, Jr., dismisses, as inappropriate material for black artists, age-old metaphysical quests. "Who am I? What is my identity? What is my relationship to the universe, to God, to the existential other? is of no value to a Negro community daily confronted by the horrors of the urban ghetto, the threat to sanity and life in the rural areas of the South, and the continual hostility of the overwhelming majority of its fellow citizens."[23]

The vision of Negro American life implied in this dismissal of psychological, theological, and existential questions is shuddering to contemplate. It reduces the Negro to the role of merely victim of white brutality. It conceives of all Negroes as Bigger Thomases — mindless, inarticulate, totally determined, sub-human creatures incapable of experiencing creative freedom, intellectual curiosity, or liberating self-consciousness. The spectacle of the black critic thus circumscribing the range of black writing is full of pathos indeed, for it lulls the black writer into believing that any kind of careless, undisciplined craftsmanship is acceptable — as long as it voices the outraged Negro sensibility. Thus the hysterical emotionalism of much of LeRoi Jones' recent work, or the anarchic rant of Yusuf Rahman in "Transcendental Blues," recently published in an anthology called *Black Fire*, edited by LeRoi Jones and Larry Neal:

> White maggots will not military your
> babies down dead
> again

White maggots will not mercenary
    your fertile Nile to ache with pus
        again
My spears shall rain
I-can't-give-them-anything-but-drops-of-hate
erasing them
exterminating them
so humanity can have a clear slate
Just keep me constant
    ebony lady
LOVE ME EBONY LADY
LOVE ME EBONY LADY.[24]

IV

The truth is, of course, that as appalling as the conditions of
Negro life in America generally are, the Negro writer may be a
spokesman for joy, not rage. There is no necessary reason why
this should be so, but his Negroness may be the very force within
him making for his acceptance of the world, his affirmation of it
in spite of all the pain it affords him, in his struggle with nature,
society, and himself, in his effort to achieve a sense of his own
dignity and identity. Thus, after reciting the material deprivations
of her tenement childhood in relation to the warmth and love
among her family, Nikki Giovanni concludes in "Nikki-Roasa":

". . . I really hope no white person ever has cause to write
about me because they never understand Black love is Black
wealth and they'll probably talk about my hard childhood
and never understand that all the while I was quite
happy."[25]

It is precisely possible to understand in a general way the childhood
of this young woman because of the way in which she has dramatized the transcendence of poverty and pain through the redemptive power of love.

To the avenues of transcendence I wish to return in a moment.
But in the meantime, I believe that it is worth pointing out that
the sensitive white can understand the way in which family love,
soul-brotherly love, and erotic love can constitute "Black wealth."
For beyond the accident of race, such manifestations of love are

common to all men and are expressions of a "universal" kind of experience. The judgments of white critics are no doubt irritating to black militants: the novelist John O. Killens has asserted that "White critics are totally — and I mean totally — incapable of criticizing the black writer. . . . They don't understand Afro-Americanese."[26] But whatever the subtleties and nuances of the black idiom, it is merely a variant of our mother tongue. And the view that the white critic cannot dig it — cannot experience, enter into, understand, criticize and judge the work of blacks — is a gross exaggeration intended to humble white critics, minister to black fraternity and solidarity, and focus the efforts of young writers like Neal, Rahman, and Lawrence Benford toward the revolutionary social goals of the so-called black aesthetic.

If the Negro writer aspires to be a spokesman for his race, even to be a militant-activist dedicated to the emancipation of his people, he must learn the strategy by which moral and aesthetic purpose may be fused in the transformation of private experience into the public ritual of art, a ritual that affirms and celebrates the mystery of human life. That strategy Hemingway described in *Death in the Afternoon*. Paraphrasing it, Ralph Ellison has written: "For I found the greatest difficulty for a Negro writer was the problem of revealing what he truly felt, rather than serving up what Negroes were supposed to feel, and were encouraged to feel. And likened to this was the difficulty, based upon our long habit of deception and evasion, of depicting what really happened within our areas of American life, and putting down with honesty and without bowing to ideological expediencies the attitudes and values which give Negro American life its sense of wholeness and which renders it bearable and human and, when measured by our own terms, desirable."[27]

A moment ago I spoke of how Nikki Giovanni's little poem asserted the possibility, on the day-to-day level, of transcending pain through the redemptive power of love. For the black writer, another way of transcendence is open. It lies in his recognition that the conditions of one's fate may be transformed and transcended not only by the power of love but also through the power of the artist's imagination. Literature has power — the word serving both to liberate and to destroy. But to liberate, the word must be an expression of the writer's creative freedom and must be brought somehow into relation with the literary traditions it can extend and express. Whatever may be the vestiges of an African tradition available in the United States, Negroes here are, willy-nilly, Americans and share in as well as contribute to the "Western" cultural tradition. This may be galling to some Negro militants, but it can be a source of enrichment to the Negro artist who can establish himself in relation to it. Addison Gayle, Jr., has asserted that "the Negro critic must demand that the Negro writer articulate the grievances of the Negro,"[28] but grief is not the only emotion the Negro experiences and must not be the only luxury permitted him. Negro humanity is fuller in its range than this inadequate term of self-definition. I am not arguing here an art for art's sake attitude. But I am arguing for a creative use of the freedom and of the tradition available to whoever would write works men would not willingly let die.

To get into relation with this tradition, to discover this way of transcedence, is to be released from the extrinsically imposed obligation to be merely a propagandist, merely a protester, merely a voicer of black fire, black rage. It frees him, the writer, from the illusion, commonest among whites, that race has a positive value. It frees him to explore, appropriate and transform the Western cultural and literary tradition which is his birthright, as well as the birthright of white writers. To engage with this tradition is not to ignore the viability of sociological realities as the material of Negro art. Once again, the insights of Ralph Ellison provide a valuable touchstone for the Negro writer: "I've never pretended for one minute that the injustices and limitations of Negro life do not exist. On the other hand, I think it's important to recognize that Negroes have achieved a very rich humanity despite these restrictive conditions. I wish to be free not so that I can be less Negro American but so that I can make the term mean something even richer. Now, if I can't recognize this or if recognizing this makes me an Uncle Tom, then heaven help us all."[29]

FOOTNOTES

[1]Robert Penn Warren, *Who Speaks for the Negro?* (New York 1965), "Foreword," n.p.

[2]W. E. B. DuBois, *The Souls of Black Folk* (New York, 1961), pp. 16-17.

[3]James Baldwin, "Many Thousands Gone," *Notes of a Native Son* (New York, 1968), p. 33.

[4]*Ibid.*, p. 27.

[5]James Baldwin, "Alas, Poor Richard," *Nobody Knows My Name* (New York, 1961), p. 157.

[6]*American Quarterly*, XV (1963), 67-75.

⁷Irving Howe, "Black Boys and Native Sons," *A World More Attractive* (New York, 1963), p. 112.

⁸Robert Bone, "Ralph Ellison and the Uses of the Imagination," *Anger, and Beyond: The Negro Writer in the United States,* ed. Herbert Hill (New York, 1966), p. 102.

⁹Hoyt W. Fuller, "Towards a Black Aesthetic," *Black Expression: Essays By and About Black Americans in the Creative Arts,* ed. Addison Gayle, Jr. (New York, 1969), p. 268.

¹⁰Quoted in Abraham Chapman, "Introduction," *Black Voices: An Anthology of Afro-American Literature,* ed. Abraham Chapman (New York, 1968), p. 48.

¹¹LeRoi Jones, "State/Meant," *Home: Social Essays* (New York, 1966), p. 251.

¹²"Statements on Poetics," *The New Black Poetry,* ed. Clarence Major (New York, 1969), p. 141.

¹³*Ibid.,* p. [5].

¹⁴*Ibid.,* p. 15.

¹⁵*Ibid.,* pp. 48-49.

¹⁶*Ibid.,* p. 140.

¹⁷Fuller, p. 264.

¹⁸Hoyt W. Fuller, Review of Dan McCall's *The Example of Richard Wright, New York Times Book Review,* May 18, 1969, p. 8.

¹⁹Larry Neal, "Statements on Poetics," *The New Black Poetry,* p. 141.

²⁰*Ibid.,* pp. 141-142.

²¹Quoted in Chapman, pp. 48-49.

²²Ralph Ellison, "The World and the Jug," *Shadow and Act* (New York, 1966), p. 130.

²³Gayle, "Introduction," *Black Expression,* pp. xi-xii.

²⁴*Black Fire,* eds. LeRoi Jones and Larry Neal (New York, 1968). Of such poems Mr. Jack Richardson has observed, in "The Black Arts" (*New York Review of Books,* [December 19, 1968]), that an insidious madness is infecting "Negro literature and . . . the criticism surrounding it. Dragged out into America's social chaos, the new literature, instead of analyzing the lunacy behind the slogans of racial struggle, has begun to embody it. The *Black Fire* view of art may be extreme, but the madness filters into much better writers than those in this anthology, and it is a madness far from divine: deadening, awkward, simplistic, strident — in every way inimical to the antic, the unique, the odd and personal. It is the madness in monuments and behind lapidary epigrams, and it settles like a stylish uniform on those who let themselves be drafted into its service." (p. 11)

²⁵*The New Black Poetry,* p. 54.

²⁶"Seminar on Black Culture Begins at Columbia," *New York Times,* March 2, 1969, p. 49.

²⁷*Shadow and Act,* p. xviii.

²⁸Gayle, "Introduction," *Black Expression,* p. xv.

²⁹"Robert Penn Warren and Ralph Ellison: A Dialogue," *The Reporter* XXXII (March 25, 1965), 48.

About the Contributors

MICHAEL ALLEN is a lecturer in English at Queen's University, Belfast and has visited Yale as an ACLS Fellow and taught at Smith College. He is the author of articles on various American writers and has published a study of *Poe and the British Magazine tradition* (O. U. P., New York, 1969).

JAMES BALDWIN was born in New York City in 1924 and is the author of four novels: *Go Tell it on the Mountain, Giovanni's Room, Another Country* and *Tell Me How Long the Train's Been Gone*. He has also published two plays, *The Amen Corner* and *Blues for Mr. Charlie,* and three volumes of essays, *Notes of a Native Son, Nobody Knows My Name* and *The Fire Next Time.*

PAUL BREMAN is an antiquarian bookseller born in Holland in 1931, whose hobby is publishing the work of afro-American poets. His privately printed series, 'Heritage', started in 1962 with Robert Hayden's book, *A Ballad of Remembrance* (which won the Grand Prix de la Poésie at the Dakar Festival of Negro Arts in 1966). Breman is also the author of a book on *Blues and Other Secular Folk Songs* (1961) and editor of several anthologies including *Sixes and Sevens* (1962), the first anthology of the 'new black poets', and the forthcoming *You Better Believe It: The Penguin Book of Black Verse.*

WAYNE COOPER At the time of writing this essay Cooper was a graduate student in American History at Tulane University, New Orleans, Louisiana.

HAROLD CRUSE was born in Virginia but raised in New York. He has worked as a free-lance magazine writer and social critic and was for a time a community organiser in Harlem collaborating with LeRoi Jones in the Black Arts Theatre. He is presently the director of the black studies programme at the University of Michigan. He is the author of *The Crisis of the Negro Intellectual* and *Rebellion or Revolution*.

LONNE ELDER spent his youth in Jersey City and then moved to Harlem where he made his living for a time in various after-hours joints. He wrote poems and short stories and, after meeting Douglas Turner Ward, turned to the theatre. His first play, *Ceremonies in Dark Old Men* was eventually produced by the Negro Ensemble Company, of which he is now an active member.

RALPH ELLISON was born in Oklahoma in 1914 and studied at Tuskegee Institute. In 1936 he went to New York where he met Richard Wright and thereafter began to write. Since 1939 his work has appeared in national magazines and anthologies. His first novel, *Invisible Man,* published in 1952, received the National Book Award and the Russwurm Award. From 1955 to 1957 he was a fellow of the American Academy in Rome. He has served as Visiting Professor of Writing at Rutgers University. Much of his work has been collected in *Shadow and Act*.

ROBERT FARNSWORTH is a professor of English at the University of Missouri at Kansas City. He is a founder member of the local chapter of CORE and in addition to publishing numerous articles in academic journals has prepared an edition of Charles Chesnutt's *The Marrow of Tradition* and written an introduction to the same author's *The Conjure Woman*.

WARREN FRENCH is presently chairman of the English Department at the University of Missouri at Kansas City. He has also taught at the universities of Mississippi and Kentucky as well as Stetson and Kansas State. Professor French is the author of *The Social Novel at the end of an Era* as well as books on Frank Norris, John Steinbeck and J. D. Salinger. He is also the editor of a series of books on American literature and is a regular reviewer for the *Kansas City Star*. A collection of his reviews was recently published by the University of Missouri Press.

HOYT FULLER is Managing Editor of *Negro Digest*, has taught writing at several universities, and has contributed widely to important journals and magazines. He has been published often in anthologies and is a frequent contributor to *Collier's Encyclopedia*.

RICHARD GILMAN was formerly the drama editor of *Newsweek* magazine and literary editor of *The New Republic*. He lectures at Columbia University and has been on the faculty of the Salzburg Seminar.

THEODORE GROSS is Associate Professor of English at City College. He has published in the *Yale Review, The South Atlantic Quarterly, Georgia Review, Colorado Quarterly, Bucknell Review* and *Critique*. He is the co-editor of *Dark Symphony*: *Negro Literature in America* and author of studies of Albion W. Tourgée and Thomas Nelson Page. He is presently Visiting Professor of American literature at the University of Nancy.

LORRAINE HANSBERRY was born in Chicago in 1930. Her first play, *A Raisin in the Sun* was produced on Broadway in 1959. It was awarded the New York Drama Critics Circle Award. Her second play *The Sign in Sidney Brustein's Window,* was staged in 1964 and closed with the author's death in January, 1965. She left behind a third play, *Les Blancs*, which in some degree was intended as a response to Genet's *Les Noires*.

GERALD HASLAM was born in 1937 and is an assistant professor at Sonoma State College. He has published many articles on American literature in academic journals. He has two books pending: *The Forgotten Pages of American Literature* and *Black and Beautiful*: *The Literature of Afro-Americans from Slavery to the Present*.

LANGSTON HUGHES, who died in 1967, was the author of many volumes of poetry from *The Weary Blues* (1926) to a collection published in the year of his death. Hughes wrote a number of plays, including the highly successful *Mulatto* (1935) and was justly famous for his stories and novels about Jesse B. Simple. He also wrote two autobiographical works; *The Big Sea* and *I Wonder as I Wander*.

DAN JAFFE is a professor of English at the University of Missouri at Kansas City where he teaches creative writing. He is a recipient of a Hopwood Award for poetry and is the author of *Dan Freeman* (1967). His poems and reviews have appeared in many national publications. He has also collaborated with Herb Six on the production of an opera, *Without Memorial Banners*.

BRIAN LEE is presently tutor in American studies at the University of Nottingham. He has taught at Kings College, London, and at Antioch and was an ACLS fellow at Harvard. He has published articles in academic journals, specialising in Henry James and D. H. Lawrence. He has published an edition of Byron and is currently working on a book on Henry James.

WALTER MESERVE is presently Professor of Speech and Drama at Indiana University. He is associate editor of *Modern Drama* and has published a number of articles in academic journals. His edition of *The Complete Plays of W. D. Howells* appeared in 1960. He has also edited and contributed to *Discussions of Modern Drama* and is the author of *An Outline History of American Drama*.

JORDAN MILLER is chairman of the department of English at the University of Rhode Island. In addition to articles published in academic journals he is the author of *American Dramatic Literature, Eugene O'Neill and the American Critic* and *Playwright's Progress: O'Neill and the Critics*. He is also the author of a forthcoming biography of Elmer Rice and the editor of a collection of essays on *A Streetcar Named Desire*.

LOFTEN MITCHELL is a native of Harlem and a well-known playwright. He performed with the Rose McClendon Players and studied at Talledega College and Columbia University. His plays include *A Land Beyond the River, Ballad of the Winter Soldiers* and *Star of the Morning*. He held a Guggenheim fellowship grant in 1958-9 for playwriting. He is also the author of *Black Drama: The Story of the American Negro in the Theatre*.

GERALD MOORE was born in London in 1924 and educated at Cambridge University. In 1953 he went to Nigeria to work as an extra-mural lecturer and subsequently directed the extra-mural department at Makerere College in Uganda. He is a member of the Committee of *Black Orpheus*, the Journal of African and Afro-Asian Literature. Together with Ulli Beier he has edited a collection of *Modern Poetry from Africa* and is the author of *Seven African Writers*. He is a lecturer in African literature at the University of Sussex.

LARRY NEAL is a poet and essayist. He has been associated with LeRoi Jones and the Black Arts movement for several years, publishing in *Soulbook, Black Dialogue, Negro Digest* and *Liberator*. With Jones he is the editor of an anthology of black writing called *Black Fire*.

LOUIS PHILLIPS is a young poet, critic, and photographer who lives in New York City and teaches English at the U. S. Maritime Academy. He has been widely published in journals and magazines and has published several volumes of poetry.

ALLEN PROWLE is a graduate of Sheffield University and is presently teaching French in Lincolnshire. He is editor of *Lincolnshire Writers* and his poems are to be published in a forthcoming book. He is the recipient of several awards for poetry.

WILSON RECORD received his Ph.D. in sociology from the University of California at Berkeley. He has published in excess of seventy-five articles and has written four books on Negro-white relations in the United States, the latest being *Race and Radicalism*. He is also the author of the definitive study *The Negro and the Communist Party*. Wilson Record is white and has been concerned with the applied as well as the academic aspects of race relations.

JEAN-PAUL SARTRE, the French writer and philosopher, is the author of several novels, including *La Nausée* and the trilogy, *L'Age de Raison*, *Le Sursis* and *La Mort dans L'Ame*. His plays, which frequently embody his philosophical ideas, include *Les Mouches*, *Huis Clos* and *Les Mains Sales*. As well as a series of literary and political essays he has published a number of complex and important philosophical studies, the most important being *L'Etre et le Néant* and *L'Existentialisme est un Humanisme*.

WILLIAM GARDNER SMITH published his first book, *Last of the Conquerors*, at the age of 20 and followed this three years later with *Anger at Innocence*. He went to Paris in 1951 and wrote his third novel, *South Street*. He subsequently married a French *lycée* teacher and decided to stay in France. He has two children, one born in Paris and the other in Africa. A fourth book, *The Stone Face*, was published in 1963.

MIKE THELWELL is a native of the West Indies. He was educated at Howard University and the University of Massachusetts. At present he is assistant professor of English at that institution and is in charge of establishing a department of Afro-American Studies there. An activist in the black liberation struggle in the United States and the Third World, Thelwell has worked in Mississippi and the Deep South for the Student Nonviolent Coordinating Committee and the Mississippi Freedom Democratic Party. He has served as a consultant to the National Endowment for the Humanities, is a Fellow of the Society for the Humanities of Cornell University and has recently been awarded a writing fellowship from the Rockefeller Foundation. His work has appeared in *Negro Digest*, *Freedomways*, *The Partisan Review*, *The Massachusetts Review*, *Presence Africaine*, *Short Story International*, *Ramparts Magazine* and such anthologies as *The American Literary Anthology 1968*, *Story Magazine Prize Stories 1968* (First Prize) and William Styron's *Nat Turner*: *Ten Black Writers Respond*, Beacon Press 1968. Thelwell is presently working on two novels, one of which concerns the slave rebellion led by Nat Turner in 1830.

DARWIN TURNER is Dean of the Graduate School at North Carolina Agricultural and Technical State University. He has published a book of poems and numerous articles and reviews on literature by Negroes.

JAMES TUTTLETON received his Ph.D. from the University of North Carolina and taught for a while at the University of Wisconsin. He is presently assistant professor at New York University. He has published many articles in learned journals and is the editor of Washington Irving's *Voyages and Discoveries of the Companions of Columbus* and the author of forthcoming books on Edith Wharton and *The Novel of Manners in America*.

JOHN A. WILLIAMS is a Negro novelist. His books include *Journey Out of Anger* and *The Men Who Cried I Am*.

Index

*Some other books published by Penguin
are described on the following pages.*

MODERN POETRY FROM AFRICA

Edited by Gerald Moore and Ulli Beier

This modern poetical geography of Africa is unique. It draws on sixteen countries to present the work of black poets writing in English, French, and Portuguese, although all the poems, many of which appear for the first time here, are presented in English. As a sample of contemporary African writing they reveal an interesting blend of public and personal statements.

Poetry composed in African languages has been left out, because no two editors could possibly have covered the enormous field. This omission, however, does not impair the clear picture of emotional, social, and political pressures (fashionably termed 'Négritude') as they are reflected by Africa's imaginative or committed poets today.

RETURN TO MY NATIVE LAND

Aimé Césaire

Cahier d' un retour au pays natal (translated in this volume by John Berger and Anna Bostock) was written thirty years ago but seems to belong very much to our own time. Its theme is the future of the Negro race, expressed in the spirit of Frantz Fanon or Malcolm X or the Olympic athletes who raised black-gloved hands in Mexico. Nevertheless this is no political tract, but a poem of remarkable lyricism and probably the most sustained to have been inspired by the French Surrealist movement.

Césaire's life and work is discussed at length in an introduction which has been written for this edition by the South African poet, Mazisi Kunene.

AFRICA IN PROSE

Edited by O. R. Dathorne and Willfried Feuser

This original Penguin collection covers writing in European and native languages from the whole African continent in the last hundred years. It adds depth and perspective to our understanding of Africa's current literary revolution. This, as the editors make clear, is not a spontaneous creation but was produced over a period of time by minds grappling with the changing realities of emergent Africa, and adapting to their own use the received linguistic tools to express them. This anthology reveals the beginnings of the African novel written in French and English, the recent attempt to write prose in vernacular languages, and the experimental writing which is now taking place. Many of the translations have never before appeared in English.